"Every once in a while a book comes along with the 'wow' factor. This book totally met all of my criteria for that. From the opening page, I was struck by the sheer beauty of the writing.... This is a definite book for anyone. I guarantee that there's a character you can identify with. Hopefully, it'll help you learn a little something about yourself as well. Join Vic on her journey towards self-discovery and allow yourself to be swept up."
— Minding Spot

"*No Story to Tell* tells a terrific story of a survivor finally taking a risk that will shake her world."
— Midwest Book Review

"This was a 'no holds barred' kind of read with a delicate touch that I definitely recommend!"
— Bookin' It Up

"*No Story to Tell* is about re-creating one's world—something to tell one's self more than other dreamers and idlers! Fascinating read, Ms. Steele!"
— Crystal Book Reviews

"This intriguing story of self-discovery should be on every readers' to-be-read list. It will have you questioning how you are living your life."
— Jersey Girl Book Reviews

"*No Story to Tell* by KJ Steele is intense and thought-provoking. In many ways it defies description. It has to be experienced and it is an experience not to be missed."
— Single Titles

No Story to Tell

No Story to Tell

KJ Steele

Studio Digital CT, LLC
P.O. Box 4331
Stamford, CT 06907

Jacket design by Barbara Aronica Buck
Author photo © 2011 by Michael Steele

Story Plant paperback ISBN-13: 978-1-61188-206-3
Fiction Studio Books e-book ISBN-13: 978-1-936558-60-5

Visit our website at www.TheStoryPlant.com

For information, address Studio Digital CT.

First Fiction Studio Printing: October 2011
First Story Plant printing: May 2015

Printed in the United States of America
0 9 8 7 6 5 4 3 2 1

This novel is dedicated to all those who have traveled this path
with dignity and grace.
You are our teachers.
Thank you.

~ Acknowledgments ~

They say it takes a village to raise a child. Well, the same could be said for creating a book. It is, at times, a solitary act, but one greatly influenced by a multitude of people. This novel exists because of many people's inspiration, encouragement, patience, and knowledge.

I would like to thank Dona Sturmanis, my first writing teacher, who saw "veins of gold" in my early work and encouraged me forward. The Humber College Creative Writing program which was invaluable for me as a place to safely incubate and grow my fledgling endeavors. A heart-felt thank you goes to my mentor, Don Thomas, who woke me up to all the possibilities within.

This novel, however, would not exist were it not for Peter Murphy, who so charmingly shoved me out of my comfort zone, and Lou Aronica who so graciously caught me.

I am indebted to Fiction Studio Books for the opportunity to bring this amazing story to life.

And, a special thank you to Victor, Carrie, Chantelle, and Cara, who have always supported me in my "writerly ways." You have been the wings of my belief.

~ Chapter 1 ~

Won't last the night. Be the lucky one to see the dawn," the doctor had decreed, lowering his old owl head.

But she had lived to see the dawn and thirty-seven more years full of dawns not experienced by the good doctor himself. Life is a cruel joker and her birth was the cruelest joke of all. She had been a slimy, baby-bird embarrassment that had slipped out unexpectedly after the main show. The doctor was appalled to have the pathetic thing slide into his hands and quickly passed it off to his nurse, who dutifully bandaged it up in mountainous folds of blankets. Not quite knowing what to do with the unfortunate mass, she'd plopped it into a bassinet and pushed it aside, while the doctor assured himself and the bewildered parents that mercifully the tiny thing was too weak to survive and would soon die.

She did not die, however, but rather stubbornly held that gossamer thread of life until six days later fate, refusing to be outwitted, had delivered the other twin up in exchange. Her father had been livid, railing at the doctor to explain the actions of that bastard, fate, and his bitch dog, death. He insisted on a reversing of the facts, something . . . anything, to make life fair. But the doctor, the wisest man in their little town, could offer no more than a mute apology. The child had simply quit breathing and died in its sleep. The doctor sat like a great sagging Buddha; her father demanding a blessing, he offered up empty hands grasping for meaning they could not find.

When it became clear that she would not die, they grudgingly took her home and gave her a name. The name was not hers really, but rather borrowed from her dead twin who now lay anonymously under six feet of earth and a cross dismissing him blankly as "Baby Stone." For the few days of his life, his name had been Victor— victorious one. But he'd failed to live up to his namesake, life cutting him down before he'd even lived a week. The name was simply transferred to her, the booby prize. And so, at seven days old she became Victoria and, thus christened, continued to tremble on into life despite the predictions against her. And perhaps, she mused now looking at the black-and-white photos, just perhaps, in spite of them.

The baby picture had not been taken of her but of her twin brother and was as close as she'd ever get to seeing herself as a newborn. She'd not been expected to live and therefore, in her parents' minds, hadn't really existed. Practical to a fault, they had been hardworking, hard-minded farm folks. No sense in wasting time on things that didn't pay. Photographs chronicling her life hadn't begun until she was just about a year old. By that time her parents had gotten past the disappointment of their loss and accepted the fact that she was there to stay.

She'd never seen the pictures of her brother until after her parents' deaths, and she'd inherited the job of rooting through the cobwebs of their lives. Her mother had buried the photos deep in the attic, away from Victoria's prying eyes so there'd be no occasion for prying questions. It was dead and gone and done with. No sense dragging up things you couldn't change. It was her mother's signature phrase, one Victoria heard over and over again. Sooner or later it referred to almost all the things in her mother's life.

She looks closely now at the photograph which is tucked inside the frame of her dresser mirror. Off to the left side she can just see a fraction of another bassinet holding a bundle of blankets that she assumes must contain herself, inadvertently caught by the span of the camera. Or it could have just been another baby in the nursery. She tells herself it doesn't matter. But it does.

The mirror is a collage of pictures, so full of photographs one can hardly see themselves in the small circle of glass that still reflects outwardly. Several times over the years she had started to take them down, but she could never complete the job, the thought of condemning her family memories to the bottom of some drawer filling her with guilt. Beside the baby picture are her mother and father staring out from the last photo taken of them together. One can hardly describe them as together. Her father spreads out across his recliner, his leather face crumpled into a tight-lipped scowl, as if life were causing him great pain. Beside him rises his cane, hard and unyielding, a constant companion in his later years. Across from him cowers his wife, perched lightly on the sofa's edge gazing foggily into the camera with skilled confusion.

He died three weeks later, her mother waking to find him cold and stiff in the bed beside her. The doctor said he'd been dead for quite some time, and her mother had needed a sedative after realizing she'd slept soundly against his corpse for most of the night. She'd been almost giddy for the first few months after his death, but gradually a dull disillusionment settled over her as she realized that even in death he refused to leave her. It was a massive disappointment. She still felt his presence and heard his tyranny of criticisms roll through her head. Finding her few aspirations could not be extricated from under his dead disapproval, she'd finally relented and followed him to the grave.

Below the photograph of her parents, Victoria's own head emerges from her father's feet. Glistening brown hair tugged into a severe bun crowns what others called an attractive face. She was young when the picture was taken by her dance teacher. One could scarcely trace her to the feeble root she'd sprouted from. At seventeen, she smiled into life. Defied fate to hold her down. Bitterness touches her lips now as she looks into her own naive face so full of expectation. She looks at her young body, lithe willow wrapped in a green dress that fit like life itself. She envies her youth. Envies the luxurious optimism that only the uninitiated can possess.

Auntie May's words come clear to her. As a child they had made no sense, hopelessly twisted and wrong. But they speak truth to her now.

"They said you'd be the lucky one iffin' ya lived to see the dawn, Victoria, but I'm tellin' ya the other one . . . now he is the lucky one, God's truth. Gone straight home to the arms of Jesus. Oh yes, you'll see you will. He's the lucky one sure enough."

She had no picture of her Auntie May. An odd duck. That was how her mother had described her own sister. Two bricks short of a load. Victoria could only recall snatches of their moments spent together, and the rest she made up to suit herself, creating an aunt a little less bizarre and a lot more brazen, with a laugh free and clear as a mountain stream. But the truth was she'd been the town's crazy lady, and before Victoria's seventh birthday she'd been conveniently swept away.

Overlapping her father's recliner is a picture of her husband, Bobby, victorious hunter, resting one foot on the carcass of a deer, its frozen marble eyes fixed infinitely into a future they would not see. He was young then and still exuded all the charm and vitality of youth. She studies the smile frozen on his face, but it is not a smile. Even at such a young age he was pitted against an invisible enemy, and his kill, this conquest, was merely practice in annihilating his tormentor.

Bobby's rifle nuzzles against his slim hip like a lover, its metallic glint running harsh and unforgiving at the edge of the photo. Its echo runs parallel in her father's cane. She shifts the photos, covering Bobby. Scarcely able to deal with one of their images, she has no strength for two.

It's ironic, she thinks, how she never wore the green dance dress again after the photo was taken. Never worn for the purpose it was created. Never really worn at all, it still hung somewhere in the back of her closet, brand new yet old, carefully hidden behind layers of cast-offs. Her father hadn't exactly been opposed to the idea of her taking dance lessons. He simply did not care one way or the other. His only concern in the whole matter had been about the cost. He had refused outright to forward one cent toward it, and so Victoria had worked out an arrangement with her dance teacher, sacrificing three days after school and part of her weekends to look after her teacher's four children in exchange for lessons. Her mother had enlisted her help with getting the dress. Or rather, she'd persuaded her to tell her father that it was a hand-me-down from her dance teacher.

It wasn't lying, her mother had explained. It was the only way they could get a new dress for the dance competition that was coming up in the city. And her mother had saved the money herself a bit at a time over the last nine months, pilfering it from her grocery allowance. It was an important competition. The biggest one of Victoria's life, and if she danced well, really well, she had a chance at being offered an opportunity to dance in the city. She was a brilliant dancer. She knew it. Her teacher knew it. The whole damn town knew it. If anyone bore the chance of slogging free from the suctioning mud of Hinckly, it was she.

For some inane reason her mother had assumed she would be allowed to accompany her daughter for the weekend and watch her compete. When she began making noises in that direction, however, her husband had glowered her into silence.

"Whadda ya mean you're going along? Whadda ya 'spect me to do? Ya think I'm gonna work all day an' then come home an start fixin' my own bloody supper? Bloody hell, woman . . . that what you bin thinkin'? Huh? Ya thinking I'd be fixin' my own supper? Well, ya never was much bloody good at thinkin', was ya? Was ya? Was ya?"

And he kept roaring at her until she began to shrink, shaking her curlered head vigorously and pleading with him to lower his voice. "No dear . . . course not. Don't yell, dear. Please don't yell, someone might hear. I'm sorry, don't know what I was thinking. I wasn't thinking. I just plain wasn't thinking." And on and on it went, her pouring out slop and him devouring it to fuel his rage.

Later that night a fight broke out. Victoria knew it would. They always started over anything and nothing. Potatoes mashed instead of boiled. Something said or not said. It didn't matter what it was, it was as inevitable as the thunder after the lightning. But all that mattered to Victoria that June night when she was seventeen was that she'd had enough of his voice pounding into the floor of her upstairs room. The scene still ran across her mind's eye in vivid colors and staccato, slow-motion images; the scent of lilacs floating preposterously through the air as her father lurched through the kitchen dragging her mother by his black belt looped tight around her throat.

Victoria stood transfixed between time as the figures again performed before her, and again she wondered at the gleeful snarl on her father's face, glittering excitement in his dark, green eyes. Her mother's hair tumbled askew from blue and pink curlers as he hauled her, bawling like a bull into the living room. Strangled squawks emanated from the peach satin nightie that bumped along behind him, and Victoria remembered with disgust what had so repulsed her that night. The nightie had fallen down over one shoulder, and her mother's breast had slipped out, saggy as a deflated pink balloon.

She had been startled to hear her own voice, shrill and foreign shouting at them to stop.

"I hate you! I hate you! I hate you both!"

The bellowing abuse had abruptly ceased, her father fixing her with a genuinely shocked stare.

"No, Poppy, I'm sorry," she'd cried out remorsefully. "I don't hate you. I don't. I love you, Poppy. You know I do."

She had not returned the look of her mother who lay on the floor hacking up phlegm.

A stranger's eyes lock with her own in the mirror, fixing her with a cold, critical stare. She is disturbed to see how time has altered her face. Shallow lines, dry riverbeds, travel to obscure destinations, each uninvited one making itself more and more at home. Though not deeply set, they offer an unwanted glimpse into the future. Hair whispered with silver falls forward around her face, and she peers out like a child from under a blanket.

Turning away abruptly, she flows through the trailer into the living room in search of her car keys. Stepping over the dieffenbachia spread prostrate across the rust carpet, she adjusts the rabbit ears on top of the television in a futile attempt to clear the reception. She despises living in the trailer. Despises living on a farm that provides an abundance of nothing except dust. Some days the wind churned so furiously that the trailer simply disappeared, swallowed in it. And when the wind finally stopped, the dust settled back over everything like a dirty white death shroud.

Bobby got really frustrated with her efforts to have houseplants. Said it was a plain waste of money trying to keep them alive in the sunless trailer. She knew that. She'd been trying for almost twenty years. But something in her couldn't quit. Each time the space under the window sat empty, a raw unsettledness gnawed away at her until she filled its void with another glossy green offering.

He used to laugh at her. Laugh at her and call her crazy. But over the years he'd quit laughing and now he didn't say much of anything to her at all. Just looked past and mumbled how he didn't understand her. He was right about that. He didn't understand her. She couldn't hold it against him though. How could she expect him to understand her when she didn't even understand herself? She picked the limp plant up and sat down on the sofa. She could offer it no miraculous cure or healing touch, and when it fell back to the floor she didn't try to stop it. Her attention was diverted by a pile of record albums stacked against the wall. Pushing the plant aside, she pulled the albums into her lap. Slowly she slid the top record free and traced the shiny circles with her finger. A thin scratch ran raggedly across its black face. *Giselle*. The collection had been a Christmas gift from her dance teacher, and this had been her favorite. The rest of the cases were empty. Bobby and his friends had decided one drunken night that they would make good discs for skeet shooting and had taken the whole collection outside where one of them had spun the records into the sky while the others opened fire with their shotguns. Even drunk, they were

not bad shots and several of the albums were blown to smither-
eens. The few that landed *safely* were scratched beyond use on the
gravel driveway. Somehow, this one had suffered only slight damage, and Bobby, feeling remorseful, had offered it back to her like
a peace offering the next day, along with assurances that he would
replace the others. But he never did replace them, and the incident
was never spoken of again.

She put the albums down and walked through the trailer
searching for her keys, flutters beginning in her chest as her keys
were nowhere to be found.

"Damn you," she exhaled quietly. Had he taken them again?
Hid them from her as punishment for some supposed injustice?
It wasn't beyond him, although she used to believe his wide-eyed
innocence as he claimed he hadn't realized he'd thrown his coat
over top of them or had them in his pocket. The sun had come out
fighting that morning, and his plaid jacket hung unneeded in the
porch. Her hand dove into the pocket, recoiling quickly as it collided with cold metal. Nerves jolted, she swore silently. How many
times had she asked him to keep that thing in the case with the rest
of his collection? He was proud of the gun, cherished it like a family heirloom, even though his father had picked it up at a yard sale
for ten bucks and a pack of cigarettes.

She reached in again, carefully, withdrew Bobby's old Enfield
revolver, dug out her keys and his Swiss Army knife. Replacing the
gun, she walked back into the kitchen, opened the middle drawer
and deposited the knife underneath the stack of dishtowels.

The telephone rang sharply behind her and without thinking
she grabbed it, then cursed herself for doing so as Bobby's mother's
voice grated like grit through the line.

"Is Bobby there, dear?"

"Oh, hello . . . mother," she tacked the word on awkwardly; it
still felt false coming from her lips. She would have much preferred
to call her mother-in-law by her first name, Helen, but Bobby
wouldn't hear of it. He felt it sounded offensive. That his mother
might be hurt.

"Bobby's not in right now. He went out early this morning. Can I take a message for you?"

Victoria recited the words without intent as she glanced at the wall clock. Both women knew that after spending the better part of her life on the farm herself, Bobby's mother was more than aware her son wouldn't be found in the trailer at mid-morning. It was loneliness alone that drove her to call her daughter-in-law for a small bit of company, although her staunch pride prevented her from admitting even to herself that this was so.

"Oh, no dear. That's not necessary. I'll just tell him myself when he next comes for a visit. I don't suppose he'll be by yet this week?"

"Umm. Not sure. He's pretty busy with the farm right now." Victoria ground her teeth. She loathed getting trapped in these nonconversations between Bobby and his mother.

"Well," the older woman sighed. "That's okay. So busy that boy. Always helping somebody with fixing something. Not that they ever help him back, mind you. Tsk. You really should try to get him to slow down. You don't want him to end up having an accident like the one that took his father, do you?"

"No. Of course not," Victoria replied, offended, but having learned early on that silence was her best defense.

"Well," another sigh, just slightly more pronounced. "Maybe you could find time to come by for a visit then."

"Uh-huh. Maybe, I'll try to get in next week, okay? I could set your hair for you again, if you'd like." Victoria didn't particularly enjoy doing her mother-in-law's hair, but she knew the older woman liked having someone make a bit of a fuss over her. Every couple of weeks Victoria tried to take the time to visit her, curling her stick-straight hair into gentle waves and painting her brittle yellow nails a soft pink.

"All right. But just remember that Tuesdays I like to watch my shows and Wednesday mornings are no good either because we have crafts to do. Maybe come on Thursday. But not after two because I like to rest then. And if you come in the morning, remember I won't be in my room. I like to go down to the activity center then and sit by the window. I've got to go early now because that Babs Johansen keeps trying to steal my spot. No one likes her much around here except Jake Woods, but everyone knows he's crazy as a crackerjack. She's always stirring up trouble like that, Babs is, but Sara Friesen and me don't reckon she's gonna last too long anyhow. Skinny as a runt pig you know and always sick with one thing or the other. Just like that Mr. Hall's wife, and she didn't last long neither once they put her in here, just six months. I thought she'd go sooner, but Sara guessed it just about right on the button. She's got a way with these things, Sara does—"

"Umm. Look, I'm running a little late. Maybe I could phone you back later."

"Oh, yes, well of course. Don't let me be keeping you. Got plenty to do myself today."

"Hmm. Okay. Maybe I'll try to call back later on."

"Well, not around dinner. Dinner's at five and if I don't get down there by ten to, that Babs Johansen sneaks into line and gets herself into first place. I suppose you heard about Joe Dempsey then?"

"Who?"

"Joe Dempsey."

"No, I didn't hear about Joe Dempsey," Victoria replied, biting her lip in aggravation. Not only did she not have time to hear about Joe Dempsey's problems, she had no idea who Joe Dempsey even was.

"Yes, well, it was awful. Just an awful, awful thing. And it should have never happened in the first place. Tsk."

"Mmm."

"And now he's dead. Poor Joe."

"Well, I'm sorry to hear that."

"Yes. Well, so was I. Always such a shock these things. Tsk. And such an awful way to go too. Just awful."

"Yes, that's too bad," Victoria agreed, inching her purse toward herself and searching out her lipstick.

"It was supposed to be locked you know."

"What was?" she asked, carefully tracing a perfect pink M onto her top lip.

"Well, the door of course," she was answered peevishly.

"Ahh."

The old woman's voice croaked off to a scrappy whisper. "The night nurse left it open. There was a sign right on it, too, clear as day it was. Said, make sure to keep that door locked. But she left it open, that nurse did. Doesn't make you feel very safe that kind of stuff happening. Sara Friesen and me think she should lose her job. Well? Don't you think she should?"

"Uh-huh," Victoria agreed as she took a tissue from her purse and smacked it with a bright pink butterfly kiss.

"Sara Friesen started a petition and I signed it too. Most everyone did. Even Berty 'cept he didn't know what it was cause he still ain't right in the head. You remember Berty don't you? He had that gibbled up boy remember? Or was that a girl? Tsk, such bad luck that family—"

"Mother, I really do have to get going. I'll—"

"Oh. Well, of course dear. I just thought you'd like to know about poor old Mr. Dempsey."

"Mm-huh. Well, thank you. I'll be sure to tell Bobby."

"Yes, please do. He'll want to know about that. He drank it you know."

"Drank what?"

"Why, the cleaning fluid."

"Who drank cleaning fluid?"

"Well, Mr. Dempsey, dear. I told you that already."

"He drank cleaning fluid?"

"Yes, he sure did. Drank the whole jar straight up."

"Why would he have done that? Why would anyone do that?"

"Well, I suppose because he was thirsty."

"But to drink cleaning fluid? That's awful."

"Tsk. Well, of course he didn't know it was cleaning fluid. Probably thought it was alcohol. Sara Friesen said he had quite a problem that way and she would know because he was her cousin. Sara said if that nurse doesn't lose her job she's gonna raise some Cain and believe me when Sara raises Cain, God himself stands up and listens."

"Hmm," Victoria murmured, grabbing a pen out of a drawer and making a note to check on things at the home. "Well, I really am sorry to hear about Mr. Dempsey, Mother. I've never heard you mention him before; did he just come in?"

"Oh my, no. Joe had been in the home for quite some time before it happened."

"Really? I don't think I ever met him. Did you know him well?"

"Oh, no no. Goodness me dear, I didn't know him at all. He lived out on the prairies somewhere. Anyhow, Sara told me all about it when we signed the petition. She's gonna send it off to the home where it happened. Now, darn my silly head, why can't I think of the name of that place?"

Victoria held the phone at arm's length to ensure the thoughts going through her head did not find their way into her mother-in-law's ear. The incident, which she vaguely recalled reading about two years earlier, was beginning to resurface in her mind.

"Did this not happen a long time ago?"

"Well, yes. It's a bit ago now, I suppose."

"Quite a bit ago, actually. Like two years ago."

"Two years already? Tsk, tsk. Isn't it just a marvel how time flies?"

"Just a marvel." She looked at the clock and ticked off how late she was already going to be. "Well, I really must run." A weighted silence hung on the line followed by a tiny, pained breath.

"Yes, well I really should be running along myself. Babs's daughter comes by to read this morning and they usually don't mind too much if I listen as well. Berty sometimes comes too but half the time he just falls asleep and snores so then I can't hear. Sara thinks —"

Failing a peaceful end to an impossible situation, Victoria set the babbling telephone onto the table and pulled open a drawer.

Pulling a wire whisk and a grate out she proceeded to rub them together loudly right in front of the receiver then picked the telephone back up.

"Good heavens, dear. What on earth was that racket?"

"Oh, it's just this phone. We've been having some trouble with it. Sometimes it just cuts right out."

"Oh. Well, you'd better get it fixed. I thought my hearing aid plumb exploded in my ear. Babs said that happened to her once and I've been a little nervous to wear mine ever since. You never can be too sure with Babs, though. Sometimes she lies. And a minister's wife, too. Ain't that just a dandy? Sara Friesen says we should —"

With one fluid, agitated motion Victoria grated the whisk hard, yanked loose the cord and silenced the telephone. Feeling a bit like a fugitive, she grabbed up her purse and bolted through the door.

~ Chapter 2 ~

Shielding her eyes from the stabbing sun, she descended the rickety board stairs to the derelict Ford Galaxie that was her car. An archaic heap, it struggled through the same protest of noises each time she tried to start it. She'd inherited it from her father, her mother having no use for it as she'd never learned to drive. The few times her mother had gone anywhere she couldn't walk to, her husband had taken her, and of course he was in the driver's seat then.

Victoria had always been ashamed of the car. Even when her father had first bought it, it had looked worn out and tired, somebody else having already consumed its best years. In the years since, Bobby had managed to resuscitate the car more times than she cared to remember. It still embarrassed her to drive the car through town, but Bobby wouldn't let her take his truck and leave him stranded without a vehicle. So it boiled down to either swallowing her pride or staying home; that's how Bobby saw it. She'd long ago decided it would be far easier to swallow what little was left of her pride than to be dependent on Bobby like her mother had been on her father. Although, with Bobby being adamant that no wife of his was going to work, she'd pretty much ended up that way, anyhow.

Thanks to her mother-in-law she was now hopelessly late. She felt grateful when the car finally settled into an agitated cadence as she steered it down the long, washboard driveway that connected them to the main road. As the car rattled along, Victoria looked out to where Bobby's tractor rose like a metal monument from the partially mown field. Her heart softened. Poor Bobby. It must have broken down again. He tried hard to make the farm pay. She had to give him that much. But at times it seemed God himself was against it. Or maybe the land was just tired of giving. Maybe it had nothing left to give. Bobby's family had worked it for three generations, and while he had experienced some good years, they all paled in comparison to his father's. Or at least that's the way Bobby remembered them, his own success remaining a distant falling star far beyond his reach.

The weather seemed intent on frustrating his efforts. If spring rains didn't drown his chances of a good crop, then he could be sure the heavens would split loose just after cutting time. There had been summers when the land had burst into a luxurious green carpet, and Bobby had spent jubilant hours stamping the field into thousands of perfect rectangular bales. "My old man never had a crop like this. Ain't never bin so much hay on this here land," he'd boast, giving himself a verbal pat on the back. With the arrival of fall sales, however, prices had invariably plummeted as everyone flooded the market with their unexpected bounty.

The soil itself was a sickly gray, an unproductive pallor, but Bobby didn't seem to notice. Year after year he'd joggled around and around on his tractor, forcing the field to yield up its meager blessing. Around and around. Year after year after year. Always going but never getting anywhere. It struck Victoria as absurd, almost humorous in a tragic sort of way. But the futility was lost on him. He was driven by an inner compulsion to succeed, to do well and gain his dead father's approval. Desperate to leave the world with a bigger shadow than when he'd entered, he coveted something tangible to testify to his existence.

She turned her signal light on then quickly flipped it back off. An old habit it refused to die, but it was uncalled for. She'd easily have detected a vehicle coming even if it were a mile in the distance. And of course there was no one coming. She knew there wouldn't be; there never was. As she stepped on the gas, the car stumbled forward, dragging a tail of blue smoke behind it. The valley ran forever, flanked by fortress walls of rocks and trees. She suspected most people felt secure living in the lap of the valley's walls, but she resented their constant presence, the way they loomed over her like an overpowering gatekeeper. Drifting along in a bored stupor for ten or fifteen minutes, she was rudely awakened by a violent jolt that seized the wheel from her hands. The car staggered like a drunk, bouncing angrily through deep ruts. She wrestled with the wheel, but the car ignored her frantic maneuvering until she slammed both feet onto the brake, causing it to stop, then stall.

"You stupid damn son-of-a-bitch. You stupid, useless piece of crap. Shit!"

She pressed her head against the seat and closed her eyes. Maybe this time, if luck was with her, the crippled heap would die beyond even Bobby's capabilities, and she could at long last relieve herself of it. But, as much as she relished the thought, she knew better. It had stranded her many times on this road, and nothing would prevent it from doing so again. She stared out the window. A menagerie of cracks, collected over too many years of driving down gravel roads, spread out in every direction like dozens of streets in a bustling city.

The summer sun had dried the spring mud into cement, and the road still held a perfect record of the lives that had passed by there four months earlier, bearing silent witness to all that happened in the valley. She was struck by the sameness of it all. The field on the left side reflected back in the field on the right, the road carefully dividing them like a dutiful sentry. She strained into the distance to see farther, but the gray and the green slipped into one another, merging into a tight fist that obliterated any glimpse beyond it.

Frustrated, she pounded the steering wheel, seized the worn silver blinker control and yanked at it until it yielded to her rage and was dismembered. Falling back into the seat with white-knuckled, trembling hands, she held up the mortally wounded piece of chrome, its impotent wires dangling loosely. A triumphant grin marched across her face as adrenaline fired through her body.

Feeling exalted, she closed her eyes and savored the moment. Experiencing each nerve that stood screaming for recognition, she felt totally alive. Happy.

She didn't know how long she had sat there, but when she opened her eyes again, the trail of dust that had followed her was gone. Settled back to the ground to await her return trip when, like some demented dog, it would insanely leap up again and chase her back home. A sound floated to her, barely discernible. Sitting up, she searched her rearview mirror. Far off she could just make out a plume of gray rising like a feather into the blue sky. She kept her eyes riveted to it, curious to see who would be her savior today.

A little kick of nerves darted through her as the vehicle steadfastly made its way closer, closing the gap between them. A white truck charged forward before a wall of dust. A white truck. Only one person in all of Hinckly dared to own a white truck and, of all the people in the valley, he was one of the few she barely knew.

Elliot Spencer wasn't a local. He'd moved into the valley about a year earlier, buying a rundown farm on Johnson Road and, local gossip had it, paid cash. It had surprised her to hear someone had actually chosen to move to Hinckly but apparently that's what Elliot had done. He was an artist. Successful as well, the town said; and they watched his life, fascinated.

The white truck pulled up right behind her, filling her rearview mirror with its chrome bumper as she stiffened against the impact that she was sure would come. Elliot Spencer was definitely a city boy. People who grew up in the country didn't crowd each other the way city people did. Used to having lots of space around them, they appreciated people who kept that in mind. She leapt quickly from her car and started back toward him, not wanting him any closer than he already was to her disheveled wreck.

"Hi there. Looks like you're having a little car trouble," he said, leaning out his partially opened door.

"Yeah, I am." She squinted into the sun, trying to make out his face. "Guess it's about time I bury this relic and buy a new one."

She laughed lightly, as if it would be nothing for her to toss the car away and replace it, a worn pair of slippers.

"Hey, funny you should say that. My neighbor was just saying yesterday he might sell his Impala. Maybe you should give him a call. You must know Benson Ferguson, hey?"

"Oh, yeah. Of course. Went to school with his son. And his wife is Bobby's cousin." She stopped, embarrassed by the brush she was painting herself with. "Sort of like that here. Pretty much tangled up with everyone in a small town."

"Yeah, I've noticed. Must be nice, though. Growing up where everyone knows your name."

Victoria smiled ambiguously. Outsiders always saw it that way.

"I suppose it wouldn't be so bad if that's all they knew."

He eyed her a question.

"People around here like to make it their business to know everyone else's business. And not just your own business, but the business of your family for generations back. So you're always kind of judged on the reputation of your forefathers, so to speak."

"Hmm. Doesn't sound like such a bad thing."

"Depends on your forefathers," she quipped and they shared a laugh.

"Yeah, guess that's true enough. Benson was telling me about this one old character they found strung up in the kitchen wearing nothing but his wife's knickerbockers round his neck. Story like that has to be pretty hard for a family to live down."

"I'd imagine," Victoria agreed as she looked out over the field. She wondered if Benson Ferguson had bothered to tell him that the 'old character' had also been reputed to be a good, honest man his whole life, the loving pastor of a small congregation which had abruptly fired him over some long-forgotten misunderstanding. She wondered if he had mentioned that the 'old character' had been Bobby's own great-grandfather.

"Come on. Jump in and I'll give you a ride to town. I'd offer to fix your car but I'm a lousy mechanic."

He laughed at himself and she laughed as well, but the remark sounded odd to her, strange coming from the mouth of a man. Hinckly's men, the men who had formed her molds and impressions of masculinity, would not have laughed at such a deficiency, much less admit it. To do so would have been a slight against himself, a cause for ridicule. In the valley where farming and logging were the primary sources of income and most men did a little of each in order to survive, a pair of hands skilled enough to revive an engine or repair a break often meant the difference between the black line and the red.

"Did you have a purse?"

"Oh. Yes. Thank you," she said, turning back to the abandoned car, unlocked and with the keys still in the ignition. There were no Samaritans good enough to steal it. Walking back to the truck, she was very aware that he was intently watching her. No, not watching. Studying. Her body felt disconnected, each limb disjointed and out of sync with the rest. Terrified that she might trip and fall, she willed each foot not to betray her. Seizing the handle, she took a deep breath, clambered up into the impossibly clean cab and closed the door behind her with a muffled oomph.

"I'm lucky you came along," she said. "There's not much traffic on this road."

"Not many hitchhikers either," he winked. "Especially not pretty ones."

"Oh. Well—" she mumbled, searching in her purse distractedly.

Elliot maneuvered carefully around her car, which sat crookedly on the side of the road. Passing it by, Victoria was appalled to see how bad it really had become: like she had gone to the junkyard and helped herself to the rusted bones and broken spines and pieced together some sort of automotive Frankenstein. Watching in the mirror she was relieved when the dust rose up and blotted it out.

"You have a great walk by the way. You a dancer?"

"Yes! Well, no. Not anymore. But I used to be when I was younger."

"Yeah. I could see it in your walk."

"Really?"

"Really. I used to go out with a dancer."

A rogue wave of emotion crashed over her, and she looked away quickly. It had been a long time since she had thought of herself as a dancer, a dream she thought she'd buried long ago. Now, the thin ache rising inside her was so raw, so tender and tremulous that it was obvious that although she may have buried her dream, it had been buried alive. Taking a deep breath, she marched her mother's words out before her and paraded them through her mind: *No use dragging up things you can't change.*

"Well, I'm not a dancer anymore. It was just something I did for a while as a kid."

"What do you mean you're not a dancer anymore? Of course you are."

Victoria frowned as she looked over at him. "Well, not really. I haven't danced for years."

"Oh. So what you mean then is that you don't dance anymore."

"Right. That's what I said."

"No. You said you weren't a dancer."

"Oh. Well, same thing."

"Uh-uhh. Not at all. You'll always be a dancer whether you dance or not. The same as a poet is still a poet whether or not he writes down his thoughts, and a painter is no less a painter even without his canvas. You'll always be a dancer because that's how you interpret the world. To dance is just your outward expression of that interpretation. Right? So, do you teach?"

"No."

"Really? That's a shame. Never thought of opening your own studio?"

The suggestion surprised her and she quickly denied it. But the accuracy of it left her private thoughts feeling naked and exposed. Opening her own studio had long ago been her most consuming passion. But Bobby would hear nothing of it, her plans vaporizing like soap bubbles as they met his irritated resistance.

Elliot's words confused her. She no longer felt like a dancer, and yet she'd thrilled to hear he'd seen signs of those qualities still evident in her. That he so readily believed her capable of having her own studio. For a brief moment she almost allowed herself to believe it. But, as she let her mind drift deeper, she couldn't find even the shadow of a dancer. Really, she couldn't find anyone at all.

Questions began to flood through her mind about this man who with one look was able to identify a part of her she had long ago forgotten about herself. She cast a casual glance his way. He was better looking than she'd first thought, his bright face enhanced by strong, prominent cheekbones and lively blue eyes that sparkled with an unruly freedom that seemed swept into being by the sun, surf and waves. He was a transplant in Hinckly, there was no mistaking that, as conspicuous as a seashell on the forest floor.

She made a split-second survey around the interior of the truck. You could tell a lot about people by the way they kept the inside of their vehicles. Bobby's truck was a catastrophe of overdue bills, lost invoices, empty cigarette packages, greasy paper towels and a myriad of used automotive parts. In a perpetual state of disarray, he forbade her from cleaning it up—said he liked it that way. It irritated her that he wouldn't at least try to keep some order, but it was useless to nag him. The contents of her car on the other hand, decrepit as it was, were in perfect order. Tight little piles of bills and receipts lay on the seat in an orderly line, like school children waiting for the bus. Each month was laid out separately; it gave her a sense of comfort to be able to scan the events that had combined to form her year to date. The trailer was far too crowded to find any more space in which to file the completed years: she'd taken to snugly binding everything together each January and placing it in the trunk.

Elliot's truck was empty of any papers whatsoever. As a matter of fact, the emptiness is what struck Victoria the most about it. The dash was empty, as was the seat, the floor, even the little plastic garbage bag swinging lazily from the ashtray was empty. It was not the sort of display she would have expected from an artist, and her curiosity was piqued. For the first time she felt glad for the fifteen miles they still had to travel together before they reached town.

"It's a beautiful valley, hey?" he said in an energetic, upbeat way that suggested he expected her to agree.

"Hmm. Yeah, I guess so. Sometimes I wonder what it would be like to live somewhere else though."

"Oh yeah? Like where?"

"I don't know. Anywhere."

"Why don't you move then? If you're not happy here?"

He'd caught her short and she looked up quickly, wondering if this too was something he could read from her body.

"I am happy," she said defensively. "I never said I wasn't happy. I just wonder about what it would be like somewhere else. Sometimes you wonder—"

"Not me. I don't waste too much time wondering. If I want to know about something, I just do it. Life's too short to spend it wondering. That's how I ended up here. Thought it would be interesting to live in the country, stuck a pin in the map and here I am."

"You stuck a pin in the map?"

"Yeah. Didn't matter to me where I went so long as it was in the country somewhere. That's how I've always decided where to go."

"By sticking a pin in a map?"

"Yeah. Simplifies the whole process."

Victoria laughed. She'd never heard of anything so bizarre. "Well, so much for planning."

"Aw, planning. Planning kills half the adventure."

"And so, when you get bored with it here you just what? Stick another pin in the map and off you go? That easy?"

"Yep, that easy. Gone."

Victoria rested her head against the seat, a slow smile creeping across her face as she shook her head. "Can't even imagine."

"Why not? Why spend your whole life somewhere you're not happy . . . ? Oh yeah, forgot. You are happy. But in a hypothetical situation it wouldn't make much sense, would it?"

"No. I suppose not. But things just aren't that simple for most people. Sometimes people's lives just get too complicated."

"Maybe. Maybe not. Maybe people just think it's too complicated . . . or want to think it's too complicated." He looked at her fully. "So, you've always lived here, then?"

She looked out at the blurred fields as they blew past. "Pretty much."

"Never had any thoughts as a young girl to run off to the city?"

"Ya. For a while I did."

"And?"

"I don't know. Got married. Things changed."

"Hmm. So, you live a long ways out this road?"

"Pretty far. About another fifteen miles back."

"I must have gone right past your place then. What side of the road are you on?"

"The left." She whispered the words dryly.

"In the trailer?"

She cringed. What must he have thought as he drove past the filthy trailer, surrounded by the dilapidated sheds strewn haphazardly around with a complete disregard to order?

"Ya. In the trailer." The words drained out of her, revealing at once all that she wasn't and never would be.

"Oh yeah. I know your place. You have the most amazing rock bluff behind your field. I'd love to climb it sometime and do some sketching. If that would be okay with you and your husband. What's his name again?"

"Bobby."

"Oh yes, Bobby. Seen him a couple of times around town. Sounds like he's quite the mechanic. Benson said there's not a guy around who can re-build a faster engine. That true?"

Victoria shrugged. "That's what they say."

"He grow up here as well?"

"Yeah, more or less." She felt agitated as the conversation turned to Bobby. Elliot had casually mentioned meeting him, but

Victoria could only guess about what sort of performance her husband may have delivered.

"So, what about you? Where did you grow up?" She watched him, alert to see if he was aware he'd been played, but the telltale muscles of his face revealed nothing.

"Well, I sort of grew up all over. My dad's job was better suited to a single guy, so we were always moving." He shifted in his seat, the words seeming to stir something in him. Wondering what private pain had intruded upon them, she barely resisted an urge to reach across and touch his face.

"Anyhow, we got to be expert packers. My brothers and I could have a house boxed, loaded and ready to go within two days." He pulled himself up straight and laughed lightly, looking across at her. "I miss the adventure if I get grounded for too long now, though. After high school a buddy and I spent a couple of years backpacking around Europe."

"Really? I'd love to go there. What a great experience that must have been."

He laughed suddenly, loudly, startling her. "Well, if you can call sleeping in the rain and half-starving great experiences, then I guess it was! No. Really, it was. I wouldn't trade those memories for anything."

Victoria searched her own mind for memories she wouldn't trade for anything but found none. Her whole life, thirty-seven years, without one cherished memory. She could erase her whole existence and be just as far ahead. Maybe farther.

"Tell me about Europe. I'll probably never get there myself."

"Of course you will. Just go. Nothing is stopping you. Except maybe yourself."

"You make it sound so easy."

"That's because it is."

"Maybe for some people." She shot him a wry look.

"Okay. Look, I'll tell you just enough so you'll have to go see it for yourself. And seeing it's only a small part anyhow. You can do that with a good book. The real magic lies in the smells and the sounds and the tastes. The colors. Know what I mean?"

Victoria nodded a smile, relaxing against the door as he fell into a rambling discourse about his years in Europe. She studied his handsome, almost beautiful face as he glided through his memories with ease, pausing from time to time to remember details that didn't matter.

They'd bumped into each other only briefly in the short time that Elliot had lived in the valley. The usual meeting places where the inhabitants of a small town eventually meet up—auction sales, town meetings, weddings, funerals—but she'd never spent any time really talking to him. Watching him now, she couldn't understand why. Who else would she have moved on to talk to? And who else could have had anything worth talking about?

Elliot's stories continued on, tumbling freely as each experience called up another faded memory from the trenches of his mind. His face became a cast of characters. His eyes played out each bit player's part, changing from sad and compassionate to eloquent and debonair, depending on the accompaniment given by his wide, expressive mouth. She watched his hands as they occasionally let go of the wheel and joined the storytelling with graceful, almost feminine swirls. It made no difference whether he controlled the wheel or not, the truck roared straight ahead, chewing up the road in front of them and belching out a storm of gray in their wake.

Cloudy shapes began to swim in the distance, and she was more than a little disappointed to see town emerging from them. She watched him, desperate to imprint his features on her mind. She traced the outline of his face, her eyes running across his incredible white teeth, feeling their smoothness, pausing to taste the lusciousness of his edible lips. Her fingers strained under their skin as if bound in a tight glove, restricting their urgent desire to reach out unhindered and glide deep inside the careless blond ringlets that caressed his neck. And she knew that, if she could hold on to it, she'd found a memory she could keep forever.

~ Chapter 3 ~

The Eldorado. The name, in keeping with the opulent structure, had been a presumptuous step toward the future. But the future, as it is wont to do, took a vicious little side step and watched without compassion as the lofty building fell into a long downward spiral of decay, its proud namesake reduced to a preposterous illusion. Built with an optimistic eye on the horizon, the hotel, at its conception, had been the epitome of luxury. Its creator had been a man of vision who years before, had envisioned a railroad slicing through the valley with a prosperous city emerging along its spine. Unfortunately for himself, his marriage and several business partners, his vision had been cloudy: the tracks wound through Fort George, two hundred miles to the south instead, bypassing Hinckly altogether.

Bud and Pearl Bentley acquired the hotel eventually, the bank all but giving it to them, in its desperation to be rid of it after a decade with no takers. Hinckly had never been overburdened with progressive thinkers, but when the hope for a railroad disappeared, the few that did exist vanished along with it. Bud had busied himself right away with dismantling the massive letters of the sign, stripping off their brass overlay and selling it for salvage. If you knew what to look for, you could still make out the hotel's former name, imprinted like a shadow on the faded wood of the towering facade. Tacked across three of the letters hung Pearl's hand-lettered sign: PEARLS CAFE − GOOD EATS − CHEEP ROOMS. Bud had hammered it into place, Pearl directing him from the street below. But as neither of them were real sticklers for details, the sign had never hung any too straight, and after the first winter the weather had more or less destroyed it. Over the years, the rooms upstairs had gradually been stripped of their embellishments and filled with rotting men and rancorous mice, each learning to tolerate the presence of the other. Pearl ruled over all of them with a snarly temper and the ever-present threat of eviction. One time, in an uncharacteristic burst of Christmas bravado, Bud had clambered up the ladder and strung blue lights across most of the roof, and every year since, Pearl would plug them in the first of December and leave them on twenty-four hours a day until the month was over. A few of them still worked.

The cumbersome entrance door had twisted in its frame, and Victoria wrestled with it for some time before she managed to wrench it open. Thick leaded-glass panes decorated the top half of it, and when the door jarred open suddenly they gave an ominous shudder. One of them had been smashed out and was covered with cardboard like a patched eye.

The lobby of the hotel had been dressed for success and even now still retained a glimmer of its faded flamboyance. A curved staircase swept down from the upper floor and delivered itself into the lobby with all the flourish of an elegant lady joining in a ballroom dance. A legion of oak soldiers ran up its length, a smooth brass railing balanced with perfection on their finely turned heads. Here and there a comrade had fallen victim to various vandals, and dark gaps stood in their stead.

Victoria started as a coarse murmuring rose from the gloom then ceased. She strained to see who else was with her in the cavernous room, but the crystal chandelier with its thick garnish of lacy gray cobwebs offered out only a meager light. It came to her again, louder this time, and followed by the appearance of a face in a hole in the railing near the top of the stairs. The face, brown and sunken as a bruised apple, peered down on her, its lifeless eyes taking her in.

"Hey. Hey, 'toria. Up here. You got a smoke? Hey. Hey, ya 'member me?" And then, hoping she did, "Hey, you got a smoke I could bum, 'toria?"

Victoria stiffened as if splintered nails were scraping down her spine. She refused the impulse to look up at him, acknowledge him. She moved quickly across the lobby toward the café entrance, his voice growing louder behind her.

"What'sa madder, baby? You don' 'member me? Hey, I betcha do. Ya, I sure do betcha do." And he laughed a bit, as if it were too difficult to talk and a laugh would suffice just as well.

She ignored his words as if they hadn't a hope of penetrating her ears and entering her mind. Ignored him as if he did not exist. And why not? Billy Bassman was a pig. Handed his welfare check over to Pearl each month in exchange for her squalid room and cheap whiskey, pretty much taking over where his older brother left off. His brother had lived for seven years in the hotel and died there as well, three days short of his twenty-fourth birthday.

A black stain on the burgundy carpet still marked the spot where he'd lain bleeding to death, passersby just assuming he was out cold again. No one was ever quite sure why he'd been stabbed, and no one was fool enough to venture who'd done it, but the town had its theories. Seemed most likely it'd been the result of a misunderstanding.

She'd have never guessed back in high school that Billy Bassman would follow in the infamous, staggering footsteps of his brother. He was a couple of years older than her, but they'd been in the same class at school, he having failed grade three twice. Good-looking, with an almost comical over confidence, she'd thought he was the type who'd really go places. And he had gone places. Spent a few years traveling with a circus and a couple in jail then returned back to Hinckly, his desire for adventure apparently satiated while his desire for whiskey was not. Her stomach twisted to think he'd ever touched her.

The restaurant's solid wood tables still reflected some of their original charm, but the cloth booths were either stained or split,

and Bud Bentley had dutifully solved both problems with a lib-
eral application of silver duct tape. Rose sat alone in the corner
by the window. She stood apart in Hinckly, a rose planted among
thistles, some things in common but not at all the same. Hers was
an exotically attractive face, and over the years she'd developed a
penchant for wrapping herself in layers of brightly colored, flowing garments. Victoria had watched Rose's face with the curiosity
of a child, trying to discern which features she possessed that so
elevated her in the ranks of beauty. But it wasn't as simple as any
one feature—like say, beautiful eyes or a brilliant smile against
swarthy skin, although she boasted these and more. It was perhaps
the intensity of the life lived through them. A smile from Rose lit
the day and erased storm clouds from the skies, whereas her fury
could erupt unforgiving as lava, raging black eyes smiting her foe
from the earth. But it was a rare thing to see Rose mad. Chronically
cheerful, she made the best of what came her way, although by all
accounts much of that had been hard.

"There you are. I was starting to worry."

"I'm sorry, Rose. My stupid car again. Quit completely this
time. Just after Patterson's place. Have you been waiting long?"

"I was a little early."

Of course you were, Victoria thought but kept the comment to
herself. Rose was always early. Irritatingly so. Still, Victoria had
never felt particularly close to anyone before she'd met Rose, with
the exception perhaps of a childish bond with Auntie May. Dance
had been her devoted partner until she'd married, and if it had
been friendship she desired then, she certainly didn't find much
of it with Bobby.

"Have you ordered?"

"No. Pearl came by once with coffee and I haven't seen her
since. Do you want me to get you one?"

"Sure. If you don't mind."

"Not at all."

Nobody was allowed behind Pearl's counter, including Bud,
unless there was something that needed patching up. Rose was the

first one audacious enough to even try it, and for some incomprehensible reason Pearl would grudgingly allow her. But any other nitwit guileless enough to attempt it got hollered back into his seat with a velocity that threatened the windows.

Although Rose definitely had her detractors, the general feeling held around town was that anyone who could move beyond the wall of suspicion grating out from Pearl Bentley must be a bit of an enigma. Rose's ability to do so had magnified her in some of their eyes almost to sainthood.

Pearl came in from the kitchen just as Rose set the coffee on the table and sat down. She scurried over, her ratty head bobbing tightly, her manner prickly.

"I could have gut ya that. Ya could'a just hollered, ya know."

"Yes, I know, Pearl. But you seemed awfully busy today and I thought I'd save you the bother."

"Ain't no bother. Jus' holler next time, eh?" Pearl stood fidgeting like a moose tormented with black flies, scratching first one arm then the other, twitching her shoulders and flinging her head to the side as she talked. Clearly she would have liked to unleash a tirade that would fly to hell and back, but she bit her lip, literally, narrow yellow rodent teeth all askew.

"You gonna wanna eat, too?" She eyed them thinly.

"Give us a few minutes, okay?" Rose said.

Pearl shrugged, grumbled and left.

They spent a few seconds in silence as they attempted to decipher the deletions and additions scribbled across the menu, prices adjusted with a strip of masking tape and a red pen. But Victoria couldn't focus on the words, her mind dissolving into fragmentary images of Elliot's face, his free-flowing voice and voluptuous hands. Yearning filled her, contractions of discontentment gripping her like hunger pangs, and yet the menu in front of her held nothing that even remotely interested her. She wanted to sit, quiet and alone, and walk back through every moment they had shared. She wanted to remember each word that had slid from his tongue and roll it gently through her mind, savoring it like the tenderest of morsels.

"Know what you're having yet?" Rose's voice broke in.

"No. I'm not really that hungry. Maybe I'll just have some soup."

"Soup! Vic, you have to have more than that. You don't start taking care of yourself you'll end up sick. Look at you . . . a good strong wind comes up and it'll blow you right out of here."

"I wish." Victoria smiled quietly. She had to admit she enjoyed the fuss Rose made over her, clucking at her with concerned admonishments about her sporadic eating habits and diminishing weight. "Maybe if I was lucky it'd blow me all the way to Europe."

"Europe?" Rose offered her a questioning glance. It was not like Victoria to dream beyond her expectations.

"Yeah. This morning when my car broke down I got—"

"I thought Bobby was going to fix that car for you," Rose said, concern clouding her face.

"He is."

"Hmm."

"He is, Rose. He's just really busy right now and—"

"Well, I'm sure he is busy, Vic," Rose said softly. "But I'm also pretty sure I saw him over at JJ's this morning, tinkering on that old car they're always playing with."

"He was?" She hated it when the conversation turned on her like this. She'd stood embarrassed in front of the town many times over the years when Bobby had gotten busy helping his friends, leaving her waiting to be picked up after grocery shopping or various appointments. But, for reasons she couldn't explain even to herself, whenever Bobby's irresponsibility came up, she was the first and only one to rise to his defense.

"Oh ya. Well, that makes sense 'cause I saw the tractor was broke down and he probably had to come in and get some parts to fix it."

"Okay, Vic. Whatever. I just wish he'd take a few minutes to spend some time on your car for once and make sure you're safe—"

"Rose, that's a bit much. I was just fine. It was broad daylight, for crying out loud." Irritation burst out through her words like starlings from a thicket.

"Hah!" Rose slapped long manicured hands together. "Broad daylight. So what? I guess I don't have to remind you that perverts have no problem performing in the full light of day. Yuck, forget it. I don't even want to think about it. I'll wreck my lunch. Just be careful, Vic. I worry about you. You have no idea . . . no idea." And with that she closed her eyes and gave her head and hands a dainty little shake as if she was trying to fling off bad memories. And in all likelihood she probably was.

The whole town had been amazed when Rose had started dating Steve six months after she arrived, but no one more so than Steve himself. A spindly, bookish bachelor, he was an amazingly nice and proper guy. Which of course proved an ongoing detriment to his love life. But Rose had obviously found in him assets no one else had bothered to uncover and, much to the dismay of the town's male population, she married him. When it became apparent that a baby was growing long before the sanctified date, the boys had spent many melancholy nights at the bar discussing their poor luck, slack jawed and feeling cheated.

They were delighted then, six years later when the truth finally came out, and they embraced it open-armed, their wounded prides redeemed. Details slipped out slowly at first. Rose later admitted that, so devastated and shocked herself by the extent of Steve's betrayal, she was hesitant to expose him lest no one else would believe such vile things about such a seemingly sweet and innocent man. She needn't have worried. The town had always thought Steve a bit odd, and now they had the facts to prove it. Finding a receptive audience, Rose broke the dam and spilled a torrent of horrible, descriptive stories of Steve's demented abuse, complete with graphic details that would stick in the mind, causing a person to look at everyone through fearful, suspicious eyes. After all, if such a pit of deviant decay could secretly possess such a kind and, to all observances, peaceful man like Steve, how could anyone really know what prowled unseen in the banished thoughts of those around them? Sadistic fantasies might well be waiting to be unleashed on some unsuspecting, trustful soul.

The town had gone ballistic. Ignited by hatred and inspired by fear, it would not rest until he was punished. Some even talked of putting an anonymous bullet through his head. Some had refused to believe it without proof of course—his pastor, his kindergarten teacher, a few others—but after the phone calls began, even they had had to concede. The calls came during the day when dads and husbands were sure to be at work and, although the line was bad and his voice muffled in a vain attempt to disguise it, he had given so many obvious clues as to his identity that people thought he must have been drunk or insane or probably both.

One day he was just gone. Left Rose with three kids, house, car and bills. Fortunately he'd also left a bit of money, and she managed okay with the town's help and the added bit she brought in from her job as a seamstress. And the town did help her, felt protective over her and perhaps a little guilty for what had happened; after all Steve had grown up out of their loins. Where he had gone no one knew, no one cared. They were just glad to be rid of him and prayed he wouldn't come back. Some prayed he was dead.

Victoria felt a little annoyed that their lunch conversation had got off to such a bad start. She felt like she had a special delicacy to offer Rose, but all the negativity was souring it.

"Well, I guess I got lucky today." She tried to start again. "I got a ride right away with—"

A bustle of wrinkled cotton invaded their space.

"More coffee," announced Pearl, already spilling it into their cups, not waiting for an answer.

"What can I git'cha to eat?" Her guarded brown eyes slid toward Rose.

"I'll have the tossed salad with a turkey sandwich."

"It ain't tossed, it's jus' salad . . . dressing?"

"Italian, please."

"Ain't got none."

"French?"

Pearl shook her head defiantly.

"Ranch?"

"Nope."

"Well . . . what do you have?" Rose countered, raising her eyebrows and rolling her eyes surreptitiously at Victoria.

"Thousan' islands."

"That's all?"

"Yep. You want it or not?" Pearl was known to have the patience of a gnat.

"Okay, sure. That would be lovely." Rose smiled.

"You?" Pearl dropped her head in Victoria's direction. Victoria had no idea what she wanted, hadn't even seen the menu, but Pearl's tapping pencil gave the feeling expediency was crucial.

"Same. I'll just have the same, if that's okay," she blurted, although she disliked turkey sandwiches.

"Okay with me. I don't give a damn what'cha eat," Pearl grumbled as she walked back to the kitchen.

Victoria blotted up the coffee that had spilled over the edge of her cup and filled her saucer. Messiness annoyed her. She rearranged the cutlery into a precise row: bottoms even, a finger's-width space separating the knife and spoon. She felt heavy hands pressing her shoulders down toward the seat, and she let her head fall with a silent sigh, too weary to sit tall. Rose had no idea of the effort it took for her to try and retain some dignity in this town with Bobby's actions constantly driving her down. Sometimes she wished she could just open up and let the truth of it all fall free. Release all the lies and half-truths and closeted secrets that had slowly woven themselves into the fabric of her life. But there were some things not talked about even in a small town. And Hinckly was a small town in every conceivable way.

"I got a ride with someone interesting today."

"Oh. Who's that? Someone get lost?" They both laughed, but she could see she had Rose's attention.

"Elliot Spencer." To her alarm his name came out singsong, an infatuated schoolgirl grin skipping across her face. She blushed, dropping her eyes to avoid Rose's curious and somewhat startled stare.

"Oh my. Tell me more."

"Nothing to tell, Rose. He gave me a ride, that's all."

"Must have been quite the ride." Rose fluttered her lashes teasingly.

"Rose. It was nothing like that. It was just a ride."

"Hmm. Bet once Bobby dear knows who's giving you rides to town he'll find time to fix your car, hey?"

"Rose—"

"Maybe you should just let him know if he doesn't take care of you maybe someone else will."

"Bobby doesn't do well with stuff like that, Rose. You know that. Just leave it alone, okay? Elliot was just nice to talk to, that's all."

"Oh, I know. I'm sorry. I know I shouldn't harp on it all the time, but it worries me, you being stranded like that. So, what'll happen when he does find out who gave you a ride into town?"

Victoria's eyes flashed Rose's mouth shut. Their eyes locked.

"He'll be mad."

"How mad?"

"Rose, look. Bobby's got his things, I know that. But he works hard, he comes home most nights . . . I'm not unhappy." The words came out thin, tinny as she searched for more to bolster them up.

"You're not unhappy?" Rose looked at Victoria. Victoria looked out the window. A spider, black and agile, labored in the corner creating a meticulous invisible web.

"But can you say that you're happy? Honestly? Can you, Vic?"

"Rose, what the hell's the difference? It's the same bloody thing!"

"No it's not, Vic. It's not at all the same."

"Okay, then. All right! I'm happy, okay? I'm fine. See?" Victoria gave Rose a comical, fake smile and Rose smiled back quietly.

Dishes clattered onto the table between them, and Victoria was glad for the distraction even though the racket jolted her nerves like an unpleasant encounter with the electric fence.

"What this gunk is supposed to be is anyone's guess," Rose said, and Victoria looked up to see her push her salad aside—it was drowned under a mutated concoction of unrecognizable brown dressing. Victoria followed suit, took a bite of her sandwich and chewed it dryly. Lunch at Pearl's could sometimes be a bit of an ordeal, but Hinckly only offered two other options and in comparison Pearl's was the boast of the town.

"Okay, so you're happy."

"Well, of course there's room for improvement," Victoria conceded. "But really things aren't so bad. Just different maybe than what I'd thought."

Pearl appeared beside them, splashed more coffee at their cups.

"What's the madder wit' yer salad? It's what ya ordered," she accused.

Victoria looked at Rose. Pearl was cantankerous at the best of times and having someone reject her food was definitely not the best of times. Ice set across her sour face, shiny pebble eyes fixed straight ahead, her receding chin quivered slightly in its effort to contain a mouthful of words. She drew her stooped 5' 2" up full and put a hand on each hip, scrawny elbows sticking outward like weapons. Given a helmet and gun, she would have looked ready to march into war. Victoria ducked her head and shuffled her napkins. One thing about Pearl's place you could count on: no matter how slow the service, how mixed up the order, or how lousy the food, the customer was always wrong.

But not Rose. For a time, Pearl and Rose had almost become close, but eventually and perhaps inevitably, a misunderstanding had come between them. Now, they lived in a troubled truce,

Pearl being her disagreeable self while Rose slowly wound her way through the maze of insecurities and pride.

"It's a lovely salad, Pearl. But we'd ordered Thousand Islands dressing and I'm not sure that's what we got." Rose crooned the words, watching Pearl's belligerent face.

"Is so."

"Well, you must have a different brand than I do then because this definitely doesn't look like any Thousand Islands I've ever seen. Is it a new brand, Pearl?"

"Naw, not really. I just added some other stuff to it 'cause there wasn't much left."

"Kind of created your own dressing then, hey?"

"Yeah. Sometimes ya git little bits left over in the bottles. I just mixed the ones you ordered though . . . mostly. There ain't no sense throwing it out. Ya gotta be careful in the res'rant business. You wouldn't know 'bout that, but ya do. Least ways iffin ya want to be successful. Everyone does it. Ya don't know it . . . but they does." Pearl struggled to hang on to her anger, but she withered as she talked, Rose not interrupting but just letting her talk herself empty.

"Well, that was very kind of you to make that dressing up for us Pearl, but we'd prefer just Thousand Islands all by itself."

"But I only got one bottle left."

"Well, good. It shouldn't be a problem then should it?"

"But . . . it ain't opened yet. I gotta keep my costs down, ya know. Ya don't know nothin' 'bout runnin' a res'rant. I gotta keep my costs down." Pearl's eyes were running a little wild as she felt herself being pushed beyond her will.

"Pearl," Rose said, her voice rising as she began to lose patience. "We'd like our salads the way we ordered, please."

"But, I'd have to make new ones!" Pearl's eyes stretched wide, her mouth gaping in protest.

"That's right. Listen, Pearl, you remember what we talked about, right? You remember what you told me?"

Pearl's head gave an imperceptible nod, a flickering of fear shadowing her eyes.

"Well, okay then. We don't want to get back into all that now, do we?"

Pearl shook her head, her gray face slumping as she scooped the salads up and shuffled off toward the kitchen. Halfway there something caught her eye, and Victoria noticed her mood seemed to brighten considerably. Following her gaze out the window Victoria could see a flashy Buick depositing a rather disoriented-looking couple out onto the sidewalk. Both were impeccably dressed. The man wore a crisp navy sports jacket, a glowing white shirt and gray slacks. His wife was a study in black. Calf-length black skirt and chin-height black turtleneck set off by a somber pair of black pumps. The only ingredient saving her from complete dowdiness was an expensive-looking pearl necklace, which entwined itself around her elongated, erect neck. These she played with anxiously while perusing the outside of the hotel, rubbing the pearls like an impromptu rosary. Pearl stood stock-still as she watched them edge closer to the café, her eyes slit in careful concentration.

"Can I help ya?" she called out cheerfully as soon as they had scraped open the door and took a couple of tentative steps inside.

"Uh," the woman uttered then stopped, apparently tongue-tied by such a ludicrous suggestion. Her quick, pinched eyes made an indiscreet, unfavorable judgment against the room and its occupants.

"I'm not sure," droned her husband. He spoke as if something sticky had lodged itself in the roof of his mouth.

"You folks from around here?" Pearl asked as she slithered around behind them to discourage any thoughts of leaving.

"Ow! No," the woman retorted brusquely. "We're not from anywhere around here. We're from Montreal. And before that, London, England."

"Hmm. Well, that explains the funny way yous speak," Pearl replied. "`Spose you come up for the funeral today, then?" she said with a slight indication toward the woman's black attire.

Victoria smiled over at Rose as a few of the regulars cast smirks and glances around the café, everyone knowing there was no funeral in Hinckly that day.

"Uh, no," the man said, hesitatingly taking a step backward as Pearl inched toward him. "We're not here for the funeral. We're not here at all, actually. We were just passing through on our way up to Alaska and thought we might stop for something to eat."

"Well, you's lickety-split right in time," Pearl said, smiling grittily. She shuffled a few steps closer to him and again he stepped backward, Pearl slowly but surely edging him toward a booth with all the skill of a well-seasoned herd dog. "Ain't it jus` a stroke of luck? I was jus` gittin` this here table all set up with this here house salad." She waved her hands forcibly toward him, and he sat down abruptly to avoid being pummeled by a salad bowl.

Moving quickly, Pearl positioned herself in front of his booth, sealing off his escape. Seeing her husband ensnared, the woman had little choice but to follow suit. Which she did, all the while slicing daggers at him as she attempted to seat herself in the booth without actually coming into contact with it.

"Ow. No, thank you," she said, recoiling slightly as Pearl plunked a wilted salad down in front of her. She peered disdainfully down her pinched nose as if the bowl contained boiled rat entrails.

"Not optional. It's house salad. Everyone gits one."

With a pronounced, indignant sniff, the woman glared. First at Pearl, and then, finding that unproductive, at her poor entrapped husband, who responded by fiddling with the top button of his shirt.

"Uh. Oh. Perhaps you mean, it's on the house?" he interceded gently.

"Mean nuttin' of the sort," Pearl shot back. "So, yous from jolly ole England, is ya? Me own roots comes from over there. Descended from one of the Kings, I am."

She paused and was promptly rewarded by an unbelieving eyeroll from the wife.

"What? Yous don't believe I is a direct descendant of a King?"

"Well!" the woman huffed, shooting her husband a vicious look.

"Uh. A King from where, may I ask?" the husband responded carefully.

"He were an English King. Me maw's paw's great-great-grand-auntie were married to him."

"Married to a King?" the woman spurted dubiously.

"Yep."

"Which King?"

"Henry."

"One of your ancestors was married to King Henry?"

"Naw. Not King Henry. Henry King. Henry George King, to be exact," Pearl guffawed, exploding into a wild hyena laugh, snorting at intervals to catch her breath.

Appalled, the wife drew her shiny coiffed head out of range of the errant bits of spit escaping Pearl's mouth. Suddenly becoming aware of a trickle of laughter around them, the husband realized too late that they had been the hapless victims of a well-worn local joke. Not sure if he should be outraged or relieved, he settled on the latter when he realized Pearl still blocked the exit to his seat. His wife, thin nerves frayed, fingered her pearl necklace frantically, as if praying for protection.

"Nice beads," Pearl said as she started to walk away. "I'll git ya some coffee while yous decide what yous want to eat."

Rose and Victoria shook their heads. It was a wonder Pearl had any customers at all. Over the years she had kicked so many people out of her place that had it not been for her tendency to forget what was inconvenient to remember she'd have run herself out of customers entirely. The tyrant of necessity, however, dictated that she let them back in.

"So, what was it you were saying?" Rose asked, attempting to pick up the thread of their interrupted conversation. "Something about life not being as good as it seems?"

Victoria's mind scrambled. Was that what she'd said? She couldn't pull the words back to her. "Is that what I said?"

"Something like that. Look Vic, I'm not trying to be unkind; it's just that you haven't seemed happy for a long, long time. It bothers me to see you this way. Maybe you should just be honest with yourself, okay?"

Victoria looked away. Picked at her sandwich. Time hung paralyzed above her, awaiting an answer.

"Okay. All right. I guess you're probably right. I suppose there're some things I'd change if I could. But I can't, Rose. You know how Bobby is. So, what's the point of talking about it?"

"Hmm. I know. Life can disappoint a bit, can't it?" Rose said, her hand reaching across to give Victoria's arm a small squeeze.

Pearl's return temporarily deflected Rose's attention, and they watched in silence as two crisp salads, comprised almost exclusively of iceberg lettuce, were placed on the table accompanied by a virgin bottle of Thousand Islands.

"Thank you, Pearl. Those look just lovely."

Pearl grunted, dropped the bill on the table and was gone.

Rose picked it up, looked it over and shook her head. Sneaking a quick peek to make sure Pearl wasn't watching, she took a pen from her purse and adjusted the total.

"Rose!" Victoria hissed quietly. "What are you doing?"

"I'm not paying that much for those crappy salads. Don't worry about it, Vic. She'll never notice."

Victoria sat upright, nervously watching Pearl's movements behind the counter until she felt sure Rose's audacious move had gone unseen.

"So. A little. Or a lot?" quizzed Rose, scarcely missing a beat from their previous conversation.

"A little or a lot what?" Victoria feigned a confusion that, although worked very well with others, was usually swept quickly aside by Rose.

"You know what, Vic. Disappointed. Are you just a little disappointed with your life or are you really disappointed with it? Come on now, be truthful." Rose leaned toward her, elbows on the table, her cold coffee swirling moodily in her cup as a velvet shawl of dark curls fell around her bright blue shoulders.

"Okay. Okay, I guess you're right, Rose. Sometimes I wish things had turned out differently. Sometimes maybe I wish I had gotten out when I had the chance."

She glanced quickly at Rose to see if this confession had shocked her, but Rose had already picked it up, packaged it away and moved on. It was one of the traits that made it so easy to share things with her. She never offered judgment or advice, just listened. Victoria shifted in her seat, not able to find a comfortable position. She felt unclean, as if she'd confessed her bowel of iniquity and then regretted her repentance. She began to tidy the table. Dishes were stacked into matching sets. Cutlery and serviettes found matching pairs. Rose had used five creamers and Victoria gathered them, annoyed at the imposition on her symmetry.

"So, tell me about your ride in."

"Oh. Not much to tell, really. He told me about some of the places he's traveled to. He seems really nice." Victoria grabbed a handful of napkins and began to snap them into tight, defensive little origami figures. She didn't want to talk about Elliot. She felt selfish and wanted to cradle his memory close to herself, not taint it with the opinion of others.

"Hmm. I'm sure he is very nice. Seems like it anyhow." A touch of quiet. "So, is he rich?"

"Rose!" Victoria attempted to admonish her with a frown. "How would I know if he's rich? I just got a lift to town with him, I didn't check his bank account."

"Too bad. I would have." And they laughed, happy to relieve the tension between them. But it was true. She'd never have come straight out and asked, but they both knew if Rose had spent twenty minutes in Elliot's company she'd have gained most of his past, his future and a good deal in between, including his financial position and marriageability.

A glimpse of white ticked across Victoria's eye, and she literally leapt from her seat. "Oh! There he is already, I've got to go." She flustered her purse open and began digging.

"You're getting a ride home with him, too?" Even Rose could not contain her surprise, and it pleased Victoria to see it.

"Yeah. He said he was going back that way anyhow. He wants to take some pictures off McCully Hill or something. It's not a special trip or anything," she jabbered as she threw too much money beside the origami flower that the bill had blossomed into. "Bye, Rose. It was fun."

"But, what about . . . ? Never mind, I'll phone you later."

Victoria hurried across the street as the white truck pulled in and parked. She worked to slow her pace as a tall figure, graced with the lean muscles of a runner, hopped from the truck and walked toward her, his faded denims and black T-shirt casually doing him justice as his curls flirted in the breeze. Flipping her hair back, she greeted him with a sunny smile.

~ Chapter 4 ~

Hinckly sported a few paved roads, but the one that ran out past Elliot's farm was not one of them. It was pockmarked with frost heaves and potholes, and the truck more jostled than drove along it. Victoria hadn't realized Elliot's offer of a ride home had included a stop by his house to pick up camera equipment, but the prospect of seeing his life up close, as well as spending even more time in his company, was not an unpleasant one. What was unpleasant was the knowledge that Bobby was sure to find out what she'd been up to, and his reaction was bound to be less than pleasurable. She pushed the thought aside and took a deep breath, determined to enjoy the moment.

Elliot had picked up groceries in town, the three bags reclining on the floor between them emblazoned with *Lucky Dollar* in a stark, black-and-white lie. There were only three grocery stores within a two-hour drive of Hinckly, and Mr. Graves owned them all. The largest of these was the Lucky Dollar, a tight-fisted business that offered a hodgepodge of sundry items, everything eternally on sale and everything infernally overpriced. The only dollars to be considered lucky were the many that filled the cash register of Mr. Graves, who daily practiced his swindling techniques and, by all accounts, had become quite skilled.

As the truck rumbled along, the plastic bags shimmied down like loose knee socks, revealing a cosmopolitan mix of packages. Some contained standard household staples, but others she recognized only vaguely from cookbook pictures. Still others she could only guess at: bok choy, capers, cherrystone clams, tapioca, some mutated form of mushrooms, a tiny bag of dried leaves. Victoria picked up the bag of leaves and turned it over to read the label. Tarragon. She looked at Elliot then quickly back to the groceries, as if trying to connect the two. Elliot, catching her glance, misread the question in her eyes.

"You like tarragon? I have the best recipe for tarragon chicken. Practically had to beg it from a friend of mine back East. Would you like to try it? I can give it to you if you want."

Victoria nodded and smiled at his enthusiasm. "Sure, sounds good." She'd never met a man before who cooked anything that didn't start with a can opener and end in a pot.

"Remind me when we get out to the house, okay? You have to be open to trying new things, though. There's a few unusual combinations, but it tastes great. I promise. You like trying new recipes?"

"Uh-huh. I try making a lot of different things. I'd get bored just making the same stuff over and over like some people do." She smiled her lie at him convincingly. She'd get the recipe, but she knew already she'd never make it. Bobby liked his talk easy, his life simple, his food plain, and he bore a cast-iron resistance to change that was as impervious as the granite cliffs that formed the valley.

"You'll have to plan ahead when you want to make it, though. Some of the ingredients have to be ordered in special, and Mr. Graves likes at least two weeks' notice."

"Oh. I was wondering about that. I don't think I've seen half this stuff in the store before."

Elliot rolled an easy laugh through the truck, running his hair back from his face with long fingers.

"No, I wouldn't think so. Most people around here seem to be pretty much meat-and-potato types, but that's okay. Mr. Graves is more than happy to order things in for me. Makes sure it's worth his while, though, I'll tell you that! I don't know how people afford to buy groceries for whole families here. I find it way more expensive than in the city."

"Well, I guess maybe that's why they just stick to meat and potatoes. Doesn't it make you mad?"

Elliot looked at her with the trace of a frown. "Well, yes actually it does. I personally think it should be against the law to have such a boring diet as that."

"Oh. Well, that's not what I—" Too late she saw the sparkle playing in his eyes and realized he'd been teasing her. "Very funny. What I meant was, doesn't it make you mad that he rips you off like that? I hate shopping there. He jacks his prices up so high I always get this bizarre urge to steal half my groceries just so I can break even!"

"Well, I wouldn't recommend doing that." Elliot grinned at her over-wrought frustration as he rummaged in the bag closest to him and pulled out two sunset-orange nectarines. "Want one?"

"No, thank you. I guess I shouldn't get so worked up about it but, well, I don't know . . . it just seems sometimes like he resents your presence in his store, and then he acts like he's doing you a favor taking your money."

"Can't say I've ever found him that bad. But then again, he doesn't have anything against me because I wasn't here when everyone killed his pig."

"He told you that story! That was years ago. And he killed his own pig, anyhow." Victoria shook her head and laughed. She couldn't believe a grown man could hang onto a twisted grudge for so long.

"Oh yeah. He sure did. First six months after I moved here I think I heard it every time I went into the store."

"And did he remember to mention that it happened fifteen years ago?"

"Fifteen years ago! No. I thought it was a fairly recent event. He's still mad as hell about it. Told me that's why he had to charge so much for bringing in special orders." Elliot laughed again at his own expense, and Victoria looked at him puzzled as to what he could possibly find so humorous about being ripped off.

"That's funny? You find that funny?" she asked, almost angered by his lack of anger.

"Well ya, kind of. I guess it's taking him a long time to offset the cost of that pig!"

"I don't know how you can see that as funny. The cheap old bugger tells you some half-truth to justify picking your pocket, and you find it amusing? I'd be furious!"

"Hmm. Well, maybe you take things too seriously. You have to try and find the humor in life sometimes. It makes it so much more, umm . . . what's the word? Placable."

"Placable?"

"Yeah. Placable. Ease up a bit, have a laugh. Hey, it was a funny story. I got a good chuckle from it. That's got to be worth something, doesn't it?"

"Well, I don't know anyone else who saw anything funny about it. The whole town was up in arms the way he raised his prices after that."

"Well, maybe the whole town needs to learn to have a laugh at themselves every now and again."

Victoria watched his mouth as he smoothly consumed his nectarine, slicing the tender flesh into large mouthfuls while his lips and tongue worked the soft, velvety edges to keep the juices from running down his chin and into his lap.

"Ya, well I'm pretty sure that's not going to happen any time soon. So . . . I guess maybe I'll have to learn from you." She dropped the words and looked out the window. Her heart pounded like she'd just stepped to the edge of a cliff and in a foolish moment peered over and realized the precarious danger of her position.

Facts used to justify one's bad behavior have a way of becoming vague and convoluted to intercept the attempts of truth; the pig story was no exception. The project had been a simple enough one to begin with. Mrs. Lyncroft's daughter Joni had decided to get married to Jimmy Smith, and the young bride was put in charge of ordering the food needed for the reception. The Lyncrofts were a sizable bunch, both in numbers and bulk, and the generally accepted notion was that they also had comparatively more money than most others in the valley. Being acutely aware of this fact and the expectation it placed on her reception dinner, young Joni had insisted on having something more elaborate than plain lettuce in the reception sandwiches. Fancy red-leaf lettuce was eventually decided upon, and Mrs. Lyncroft made the fateful mistake of sending her amply girthed but empty-headed daughter into the Lucky Dollar to place the special order.

Two days before the event, Mrs. Lyncroft was presented with twelve cases of wilted red-leaf lettuce and a horrendous bill that erred favorably in Mr. Graves's direction in several places. Furious, Mrs. Lyncroft had refused to pay, saying the order was for 12 heads not 12 cases. Mr. Graves had flown into a rage, insisting the girl had wanted enough lettuce for 250 salads and he had ordered no more than the appropriate amount. He was abruptly informed that it was 250 sandwiches, not salads, and that 12 heads would do just fine. Mr. Graves threatened to call the police, in his hysteria having completely forgotten Jimmy Smith was one. Mrs. Lyncroft had laughed rather brusquely in his wrinkled, red face and then stomped home to yell at her daughter. Who in turn yelled at her fiancé, who much to his detriment yelled back, and the whole wedding was promptly canceled, Mr. Graves stuck with the whole fancy red-leafed truckload.

Being the entrepreneurial sort and not about to throw good money after bad, Mr. Graves had the works set up as a Lucky Dollar Super Special the very next day, hoping to mitigate his losses. But the townspeople had seen plenty of lettuce in their years and were wary of this pile painted with an unfamiliar hue. The old storekeeper tried all his angles—two for one, fifty percent off, buy one get one free; but he couldn't entice them to buy. The housewives crowded around and poked at the pile. Picked heads up. Put heads down. But try as he might, they would not buy.

"What's wrong with this here lettuce?" was the inevitable question to which the visibly infuriated proprietor replied over and over: "Nothing. Nothing at all. Just a natural variation of color due to the extra vitamins in it. Very, very healthy for you."

But the townsfolk weren't fools, and it wasn't long before they'd determined the whole deviant lot had been sprayed with a toxic and probably banned pesticide. Mr. Graves, in a rare defeat, finally loaded the whole lot up and dumped it in with his pig. The pig, more than happy to oblige, gorged itself all night and promptly died, solidifying what the townsfolk had suspected all along.

"Hmm, now what on earth could that be?" Elliot leaned forward against the steering wheel and squinted into the distance. Victoria followed his gaze with mild disinterest. A lump, nondescript and gray, lay on the road ahead of them. Victoria's stomach tightened. She hoped it wasn't an animal struck by a passing vehicle—dead or, worse, left to die of its own accord. She almost prayed it wouldn't be anything that would cast waves across the calm of their day. As the truck pulled them closer, she saw the object was not sprawled out like an animal but rather sitting upright, rounded like a rock, with a stick curved as a winding stream resting against its side. To Victoria's horror and revulsion, it moved as the vehicle sidled closer to it, the gray blanket creeping back to reveal the haunted, toothless face of Mrs. Spiller, a worn black bible held tightly in her hands.

"Oh! Oh . . . it's just that old Mrs. Spiller. Just go around her. She's crazy as can be. Going to end up causing an accident one of these days," Victoria hissed, drawing her face away from the window so she couldn't be seen. Elliot put on his four-way flashers, pulled over to the side of the road and got out, either not hearing her words or choosing to ignore them. The truck, vacant without him, hissed her words back at her and, although she felt ashamed of them, it was justification that rose in her throat, not apology.

The Second World War had wreaked considerable devastation on several of Hinckly's families, but on none with such a severe vengeance as Mrs. Spiller's. Never the prettiest flower on the wall, her prospects of marriage had almost been given up for naught when a chance introduction to a second cousin once removed had salvaged her from certain spinsterhood and a barren old age. Twin babies were soon delivered and, to everyone's amazement, they grew to be handsome boys, well mannered and polite.

Mrs. Spiller, already close to forty when the twins were born, realized she'd not get another go at motherhood. She guarded over them with ten times the paranoia of any first-time mother, resulting in passive and somewhat effeminate sons who were wholly unprepared for life and as naive as two beans sprouted in a greenhouse. Army recruiters, extolling the virtues of fighting for and possibly dying for one's country, found in them a compliant cooperation eager to please. Their father was to drive them down to Fort George, where a train would pick them up and deliver them to who knew what fate. The boys could not contain their excitement, giggling and teasing each other about the fair-haired delicacies they envisioned tasting in foreign lands. Death was a strange word emitted from others' lips, a dark horse so far in the distance its color was not yet visible. It was inconceivable to them that their lives might not lay in front of them but rather behind, and they strode forward under the banner of invincibility.

So often it is the humble and unaccountable things in life that alter the course of history, and for the Spiller boys a beer bottle carelessly tossed on the edge of the road proved to be every bit as deadly as the shrapnel that awaited them. The flat tire slowed them down by a good thirty minutes. Time, with its poltergeist hand, arranged for the train to run late as well, and it caught them full-square at an unmarked crossing, crumpling the truck under its carriage like a wad of aluminum foil.

A mother's brain has no capacity to receive the news of the loss of her chicks, and for Mrs. Spiller the death of her boys, along with her husband, proved a load unbearable. From that fateful moment on, she'd become a nonentity trapped on the wrong side of death in a perpetual search for her family. She served up on the kitchen table huge meals that her flock of cats devoured convincing her that her boys had been home, and she'd only just barely missed them, again. And again and again.

Victoria watched as Elliot approached the old wretch, and she opened her window a little. She felt a little embarrassed for him, sure he had no idea what he was getting into. Mrs. Spiller had been known to fly into fits of rage, convinced somebody knew where her sons were but had conspired not to tell her. Other times she'd mortify people by bursting into uncontrollable tears, begging them with an inconsolable anguish to make her boys come home. It wasn't right, the town agreed. She put people in awkward positions, disrupting everything from suppers to funerals. Should be locked up was the general sentiment felt but seldom expressed, Mrs. Spiller's sister Doris being in strong disagreement with such opinion. Elliot walked toward her, speaking soft words Victoria couldn't hear, his manner as calm as if he were approaching a skittish colt. Head cocked to the side, the old woman watched him like a crow; Victoria half expected her to fly up and attack him.

"Hello there, Mrs. Spiller. How are you today?" Elliot asked with a charming smile, squatting slowly beside her, taking her hand in his own and stroking it lightly. The intensity in the old face dropped, and Victoria realized for the first time it was fear and not hostility that hovered there. A black grin cut across her face, weak eyes searching.

"Oh . . . oh my. Is that you, Johnny Woodstaff? Is that you, son?" Her voice creaked and cracked like old stairs in a windstorm. Victoria opened her window further to catch her words.

"It's Elliot, ma'am. Remember? Remember last week? I gave you a ride out to your sister Doris's, and she gave you some carrots and peas from her garden—"

"Her garden! Doris has got her garden in already . . . in this weather? Why, that gal's a bit of a dim bulb. It'll all freeze sure as day, I tell you." She stuck her fingers through the holes in her blanket and pulled it tight, shivering against an invisible cold, her rotted prune face contorting so violently that it looked like she would begin to cry, but she laughed instead, an old laugh from another time.

"Johnny Woodstaff, you little rascal you. You just teasing me again, ain't you? Just like your pa, you is boy." Her eyes grew serious, her voice low with concern. "How are your parents doing anyhow, Johnny? Your maw feeling any better these days?"

Elliot's hand patted the top of Mrs. Spiller's, echoing the soothing rhythm that she herself must have performed thousands of times over the years in nurturing up her young family. "There, there, Mrs. Spiller, don't you worry yourself one bit. My mom's feeling really well now. Better than ever she says."

"Oh, well thank the good Lord. I'm so glad to hear that. She's a fine woman your mom is . . . a very fine woman."

Elliot reached out and fussed with the brown toque that had slid half off the gauzy white head, smiling at the compassion she still held for these folks who had been dead and gone already for years. "Here, let me help you . . . your toque is falling off. There, that's better."

"Why, thank you, young man. I was wondering why I was catching such a chill."

"Can I offer you a ride somewhere, Mrs. Spiller? Over to your sister's maybe?"

"Oh no, that's very kind of you, Johnny, but I was just looking for my boys. Can't find them anywhere and a big breakfast I made them, too. I called all over town, but no one's seen 'em. Gone like snow in summer they are. Have you seen them, Johnny? Did you see my boys?" She turned her face up to him, hands clasped in front of her trembling in the silent prayer that he would not say no. Elliot looked down, swept the gravel with his hand and picked up a small stick, snapping it between his fingers. His head began a slow-motion nod, and Victoria strained to hear the whisper of his words.

"I did, ma'am. Yes, I did. Not so long ago in fact."

"You did! No teasing me now, Johnny. No teasing now." A forgotten joy lit her face, erasing for a moment her pain, the black void of her mouth split in a magnificent hollow smile.

"No, ma'am. No teasing," Elliot said, smiling with her, fully sharing this brief moment of lifting the cross that crushed her.

"And what did they say, my boys? Will they be home for lunch?" Her hand was wrapped around his wrist now like a claw, her eyes shiny with anticipation, eerie in one so close to death, like a cadaver awakened.

"No, not for lunch . . . so they don't want you to go to any work, okay?"

"But they got to eat, my boys do. They're growing boys, they are. They got to eat."

"They will . . . they will. Don't worry about them, ma'am. People are always saying they're the best-behaved boys in the whole valley, always helping out. People are more than happy to make them a meal when they stop by so you shouldn't worry yourself, okay?"

Mrs. Spiller sagged visibly under her blanket as if her muscles had simply given way, but she appeared serene, a look Victoria had never before seen on her face.

"Oh, they're good boys, they are. Good, good boys. A blessing from above them boys are."

"And they're lucky to have you for a mom, too." Elliot looked toward the sky as if struggling with himself. "They told me to tell you something else, ma'am."

"What's that, dear?" Mrs. Spiller asked in a small and immensely tired voice.

"They said I should tell you that . . . they asked me to tell you that . . . that they love you. Love you very, very much. More than life itself."

"They said that, Johnny? My boys said that?"

"Yes ma'am, they sure did. And they said if I saw you I was to be sure and tell you."

"Oh, that's nice. They're good boys. Such good boys."

Elliot shifted his position and helped gather her to her feet, carefully keeping the filthy blanket wrapped around her despite the objectionable heat. "Can I give you a ride, now? Over to Doris's maybe? You're a long ways from town today."

"Well, I don't want to put you out of your way—"

"No, no. Not at all. We were going right past her place, anyhow. Won't be any trouble at all," Elliot enthused, although it wasn't completely true as they'd already passed Doris's farm and would have to backtrack several miles.

"Well, okay then, Johnny. If you're sure I wouldn't be too much a bother to you. I feel dreadful tired all of a sudden. Not as young as I used to be, you know. Sometimes I think those boys are going to wear me right out."

Victoria joined in ambitiously, helping to arrange Mrs. Spiller in the cab as the old woman clutched her bible protectively against her chest. She touched the old woman's hand and bade her good day, but her nerves recoiled sharply at the crepe paper, blackened skin, and she pulled away. She'd done up her window so Elliot wouldn't think she'd covertly tried to overhear his conversation, but the stench of death radiating out from the withered carcass so vividly assaulted her senses that she opened it again in self-defense.

"We'll just take Mrs. Spiller over to her sister's. Won't take too long, okay?" Elliot looked down at the old woman, his face tender, obviously touched by the moment that had passed between them.

"Of course, no problem," Victoria rejoined, eager to offset the coarseness of her earlier response. As they returned back down the road they'd just come, she listened quietly to the conversation taking place beside her, marveling at Elliot's cheerful banter about events that had never happened and people he'd never known. Suddenly the old woman's demeanor grew apprehensive, and she began to speak in hushed tones.

"She came out to the house."

"Who did?"

"The gypsy. She snuck out to my house and stole some of my treasure."

"Hmm."

Elliot smiled Victoria a bemused glance over top of the toqued head. She'd heard the stories before as Mrs. Spiller's deteriorating memory lost money then created a host of shady characters to explain away the loss of logic.

"I had it hidden. She must have seen where, sneaking around in the dark like that, peering in my windows. She didn't think I knew she was there, but I did. The cats tell me when she comes around. They don't like her at all. Gypsies frighten them something awful."

"Were you having a nice walk, Mrs. Spiller?" Victoria said in an effort to pull the conversation back to reality.

Vitreous eyes stared back in disbelief.

"My goodness, I wasn't out for a walk, my dear. I was looking for my boys!" And then quieter, leaning aside to Elliot she giggled, "Not a very crisp pickle that one. The very idea I'd come all this way just for a walk!"

She chuckled again, and Victoria noticed Elliot struggling to suppress a smile himself. What incredibly lousy luck, Victoria fumed silently. She looked at the folds of gray and the crackled onionskin face huddled close beside Elliot and greatly resented the presence of one who so obviously had overstayed her welcome in the present world. The urge to dispose of the stinking mass in a passing ditch sat deep in her gut, and she replayed the image over and over as they trundled along.

"Have you been over to visit your sister this winter, Georgie? I hear her health's not so good these days." She looked at Victoria, expecting an answer. Normally, if she'd been accosted in town and Mrs. Spiller had begun mumbling her nonsense to her, Victoria would have simply walked on, ignoring the raspy, useless voice. Today, however, the old witch had her trapped, and Victoria began to feel sparks of panic igniting in her chest. "She's fine, thank you." She turned her attention and her body toward the side window and looked out.

Georgie. She hated the name. It was the name people had called her mother, although her Christian name had been Georgina and she had secretly despised having it altered. Victoria could recall many times when she was a young girl, her mother sitting her down and lamenting tearfully the rudeness of those who would not call her by her proper name.

"But tell them that they have to. Tell them you won't answer unless they do," an indignant Victoria had offered, hands on hips, rising to the defense of her offended mother.

"Oh, no. No, no. I couldn't do that, Victoria. That wouldn't be very nice. I suppose folks are just used to calling me that, that's all. It's fine, really. Not that important. Just a name . . . just a name," she'd digress and drop the subject, until the next time she began to suffer acutely the insignificance of her life and raised a feeble cry against the injustice of it all.

But there was one thing she was adamant about; Victoria was not to let anyone abbreviate her own name. The first time she came home from school crying, however, distressed because the teacher had reprimanded her for insisting that he please not call her Vickie, her mother had completely buckled and scolded her as well, telling her it was not a child's place to correct someone in authority. Before the school year was through, she'd been reduced from Victoria down through Vickie, and ended up just Vic: no further reduction possible short of being called nothing at all.

Doris and Tom's farm began to peek through the poplars, and Elliot idled slowly into the yard so as not to disturb too much dust. The place was quiet and unassuming, like the couple themselves. Doris's face appeared, disembodied, at the window, then reappeared attached to a lumpy frame that shuffled across the porch and over to Elliot to receive her sister like an expected parcel. Gratuitous, faded smiles were given, small words exchanged and Mrs. Spiller thanked young Johnny for his help as they disappeared back into the house. Elliot got into the truck and guided it out onto the main road, opening his window wide.

"Sorry about that. The old gal doesn't smell so good, does she?"

"That'd be a major understatement," Victoria tried to respond lightly, opening her window wider as well, hoping to blow the sobering effects of morbid reality from their space. "You think they'd do something about her."

"Do something? Like what?" Elliot questioned her loudly, adding the fan to the wind whipping wildly through the cab.

"I don't know. Put her in a home or something."

Elliot shrugged. "Well maybe, but a home probably wouldn't work, either. She's okay, doesn't hurt anyone. I worry about her, though. She gets herself a long way from home sometimes." He shook his head lightly, "I just don't know what the best answer would be for people like that."

Victoria knew perfectly well what the best answer would be but refrained from offering it. Too many people in the valley were willing to look far and wide in order to avoid seeing the plain hard truth before them, and it seemed sweet, gentle Elliot would prove no exception in this case. He drove along encased in private thoughts, and she wondered at the genuine sorrow evident on his face. Sorrow for an old woman, denied the liberty of death, who didn't even know his name.

"Who was George?"

"Who?"

"George . . . she called you George. Do you know who that was?"

"No. I don't think it was anyone, really. Just her imagination," Victoria countered quickly, anxious for the conversation to end before it got started.

"Hmm, maybe. I'll bet if you asked the old-timers, they'd be able to tell you who George was," he offered helpfully.

"Probably could. Oh, look, your groceries fell over." Victoria busied herself rearranging them, hoping to shift the conversation.

"She always calls me Johnny. Benson Ferguson told me Johnny was a neighbor boy her sons spent a lot of time with growing up. Spent so much time together people took to calling them the triplets. He said Johnny's parents forbade him from enlisting, said they needed him on the farm. I guess he was pretty shook up about the accident, went out in the field and shot himself two days after the twin's funeral. Isn't that awful? Such a waste of life. I guess you probably already knew that though, hey?"

Victoria nodded solemnly, although the tale was so familiar to her it had lost the edge of truth, Bobby dragging it up and needling her with it when he was feeling particularly morose. And it was all good and well for Elliot, a newcomer to the valley, to be filled with such patient compassion for an old soul. He had not endured endless years of Mrs. Spiller's frightful wailing as she wandered desolate streets searching for her vanished family. His was not the heart that ceased momentarily in the dead of night as gnarled fingers clawed open bedroom windows to reveal a gnarled face. There had been times, twice, that Victoria had bent to her as Elliot did now, attempted to ease her suffering and relieve her pain, but it was no good. She was eternally broken, could not be fixed. Victoria considered a bullet to the brain would be but a small mercy if one had the gumption to do it.

~ Chapter 5 ~

The rambling driveway, better maintained by far than the main road, ushered them cordially up to a quaint blue and white Norman Rockwell house. A collection of farm animals, obviously secure in their status as no more than fat pets, lounged in the shade of towering trees with armfuls of leaves. After only a year in Elliot's hands, the farm bore but a faint shadow of resemblance to its former self.

A gaggle of geese, disturbed from their resting place under an ancient maple, waddled indignantly in front of the truck as a welcoming dog woofed a hearty greeting and trotted out to hasten them along. Victoria turned her head to take it all in, amazed to see every tractor, every harrow, every hoe had its own place, and everything was put away like a toy farm set packed up for the night.

"Wow, you've done so much work around here. What a difference. I would have thought this place was a mow-down."

"Pretty much was! Sure would've been cheaper!" Elliot laughed. "Actually, it did turn into a much bigger project than I'd first envisioned. When I look at these old places, I tend to see them how they could be not as they really are, and I always seem to underestimate the amount of work required to transform them. My brother says I could dream a castle out of an outhouse, and he's not really too far off the truth." He leaned forward to gather the groceries from the floor by her feet, his head almost in her lap by the time he'd recovered an errant orange from the corner. "Want to come in and have a look?"

Victoria's face flushed hotly. "Oh, no thank you. Maybe some other time. I'll just wait here if that's okay."

"Okay by me." He winked as if he understood her dilemma. "If you change your mind, just come on in," he added as he started up the steps, which emptied onto the porch that ran across the face of the house like a wide, gap-toothed smile. He stopped briefly to chat with the cats and tousle the retriever before disappearing through the front door.

Victoria leaned her head back against the seat and watched cotton clouds puff languidly across the sky. The moment felt surreal, and she half expected to see brush marks on the horizon, wishing she herself could just be painted eternally into such a blissful scene. She did want to see the house. Wanted more than to just see it. She wanted to join Elliot in his home, explore the brilliant creations procured by his incredible, artistic hands. She wanted to sit with him on the fan-back wicker chairs that graced the porch like two Southern belles and discuss Portugal, Spain, France, the world, the universe . . . life itself. But it could not be. Even now she stood dangerously beyond her limits, and Bobby's voice lumbered up through her reverie: she refusing to acknowledge it, the pleasure of her moment being so far in advance of the displeasure of his.

A smile slipped from her heart and onto her face. She wiggled free of her shoes and pulled her long legs up onto the seat, wrapped her arms around her knees and rested her cheek against them. She felt happy. A song, bright and lively, played inside her head the words bursting onto her lips before she had a chance to quiet them. She tried to envision Elliot's life in this place. Closed her eyes and was instantly met with his, staring back through the void direct and inquisitive, his interest in her open and undisguised. Her face ran hot and she smiled again, flattered but also flustered by his attention. She tried to imagine the inside of the house. The welcoming living room, the warm bright kitchen, but her mind was filled with images of the sun streaming full into his bedroom window, gliding across the rich pine floor and onto the bed, murmuring him awake with a fiery bronze kiss. Rising from the snug embrace of his tangled sheets, she watches as he stretches his long limbs, his body painted in the white-gold hues of early morning. Behind him, asleep in the bed, she is conscious of a form, still safe in the cocoon of sleep. He turns and smiles at the figure who admits no identity, but she knows it is her, can only be her.

Bobby's voice rises loudly in her mind, his face escaping the mental shutter she had composed for him, and she shakes herself loose, reprimands herself for being ridiculous and struggles back into her shoes as she hears the screen door bang. She watches as Elliot emerges from the house with an armload of camera equipment, coos at the cats coiled in the laps of the wicker ladies and makes his way toward the truck.

"Hope I wasn't too long." He laid the camera equipment on the seat, reached for the ignition and stopped, his eyes on her face, concern on his.

"You okay?"

She was surprised by the question, confused as to its origin.

"Yes, I'm fine. Why?"

"I don't know. You just looked kind of sad. Really sad, actually."

Instantly she shrugged a smile, a practiced reaction to temporarily erase all feeling from her face. Their eyes met, a tryst between them, and she struggled to return his piercing gaze calmly. Finally he looked away, and started the truck. Whether he'd believed the lies he'd read in her eyes she could not tell, but she hoped so. She'd like to tell him the truth. Share with him just how desperately trapped she felt. How incredibly close to her heart he'd cut with his casual suggestion of her opening a studio. But what could come of it? He could listen attentively. Be compassionate, caring. But he, for all his considerable learning, all his worldly knowledge could not change the facts of her life. So what could be gained by laying herself open before him in the cold rain? His sympathy? Or worse. His pity. She rejected the very thought. Shut herself up tight. No, she thought. There was simply no point in bringing up things that couldn't be changed. Elliot, delicate to her discomfort, shifted his attention to the sky, frowned a bit too obviously.

"Hmm. Hope we can get out there before we lose too much light."

She surveyed the day, knew the strong afternoon sun would be holding fast for hours yet but understood that he knew this also, realized he was grasping thinly at ways to release her discomfort and she played along.

"There's a shortcut. Through the back of Jack Webber's place. You turn off just before his hay shed."

"Really?" Elliot said. "Through the back of Jack's place? I never knew there was a road back there."

She'd heard the words escape her mouth and instantly regretted them, cursing her inherent helpfulness.

"Well, it's not much of one. An old logging road, actually. Might not be such a good idea come to think of it. Could be blocked off or anything by now. I haven't been down it for years. Since I was a teenager. Used to pick berries down there sometimes," she added hastily and not altogether convincingly.

"Berries? What kind of berries?"

"Well, you know, like blueberries and huckleberries and stuff . . . strawberries."

Elliot nodded slowly, looked over at her and winked.

"Probably not the only berries that got picked out there, are they?"

"Elliot!" She blushed. Felt sixteen again. Giddy and beautiful. Like she actually held within her the promise of love.

Jack Webber's farm pulled them closer. The truck dipped and angled off the main road and began to follow a rutted, overgrown impression of a trail that ran along the edge of the field. Clusters of trees sprouted up and thickened until the truck was lost under a canopy of fury-armed spruce and fir, the sun reduced to an occasional twinkle through thick branches. She'd been down this road many times before. She knew it well. A false darkness closed over her with memories. It had been a game for her really. A way to divert the stifling boredom of empty summer nights. But games had rules and, as long as everyone played by them, the games could go on. Billy Bassman enjoyed her rules. Enjoyed laughing at them, enjoyed bending them and, the night the game ended, enjoyed breaking them.

The moon had hidden its face early that night, and once he'd killed the engine and turned off the headlights, there was no light at all. No light until he ripped her open with a blazing white pain that drove every last breath from her body, every seed of dignity from her soul. Afterward, he'd laughed. Told her he'd taken her for himself and every two-bit Tom she'd played for a fool and blown off like a fly. When he turned on the lights to find his cigarettes, she'd closed her eyes. Closed her eyes and wished she never had to see the light again. Later that night she'd drained the hot water tank trying to scald herself clean. But his dirt lingered in her mind, could not be washed away anymore than the irrevocable crimson that stained her panties.

She looked at Elliot. He too was occupied by his memories, but his face held the lightness of good times gone by, once lived, many times remembered. She felt sick to her stomach, couldn't wait to get back onto the main road. He felt her eyes on him and smiled.

"Little food, little wine . . . have a good time. Beautiful spot for a picnic, hey?"

"Ya. Beautiful."

"What? Don't tell me you don't like picnics."

"No, I do. Just don't feel well, that's all. This bumpy road I think."

"Know what I think?"

"No. I'm sure I don't."

"I think that you need to learn to have some fun. Loosen up, let go a bit."

"Really. Thank you, Mr. Freud." She wrinkled her nose up and threw him a toying look of disapproval. She couldn't catch if his words were meant as an observation or an invitation, so she settled on the more flattering of the two and felt herself feel better. It was nice, she reflected, being with him. Listening to his well-woven stories, laughing as he revealed his imperfections, which he laughed at as well. And she did feel better. Felt better than she had for a long, long time. Perhaps even better than she ever had. She closed her eyes, took a deep breath and, blocking her past from her future, felt better indeed.

"Whose place was that?" Elliot asked, flicking his head at faded remains stooped in the distance like sad, neglected tombstones. Victoria shrugged, not looking aside, not willing to invoke that name by her own lips.

"Oh, I know whose it was. Benson was telling me about them. An original Hinckly family. Brassmans, or something like that, right?"

"Ya, something like that," she agreed, attempting to reorganize the camera equipment which had bounced across the seat.

The Bassmans were always referred to as an original Hinckly family which, although implying some sort of great honor, actually meant little more than that the eldest surviving members of the community could no longer recollect a Bassman that hadn't originated from the town's own womb. Mr. and Mrs. Bassman had been a stiffly religious couple who, although believing all things were inherently evil, consoled themselves that some things were also inherently necessary and an uncountable sum of children promptly sprang up to give visible support to their views. The family grew as the house in town shrank and, before their fifteenth wedding anniversary Mr. Bassman had secured a sizable farm. The 160 acres, acquired off the destitute back of widow Lynch, had appeared at the time to be a considerable blessing, the perfect arrangement to gain the maximum benefit from such a large family. Unbeknownst to Mr. Bassman, however, the land, although fertile, proved to be water poor, and they'd scarcely settled in before the well started coughing up a thick, muddy phlegm. He'd searched desperately for a new source, but each new well he dug sputtered dry, and eventually the whole farm had to be abandoned as virtually worthless. The family was re-interred into a rented shack at the edge of town. Mr. Bassman had taken a job in the bush, felling trees, living all week in a stinking bunkhouse that he returned to eagerly after a weekend at home in a house that simply did not have room for him.

Slowly the whole family disintegrated, Mrs. Bassman taking to locking her kids out of the house to ease her exhaustion, nursing her depression with a self-prescribed elixir that she bought at the liquor store in one-gallon jugs. Her husband, his faith dried up completely with the last of the wells, set his own broad shoulders against the gates of heaven and was determined to gain the power and the glory for himself. He was a hard worker. Made good money. But the tribe of voracious, unruly children ate the dollar bills straight out of his hands. Although he labored a lifetime, he never overcame the loss of the farm, and his dying words were said to be a curse on the corpse of the widow Lynch.

The children, after being moved back into the confines of town, did what came natural after an upbringing of such severe deprivation; they drank. Drank like each new bottle was their savior, fearful each drink might be their last. As time moved on, the Bassman kids all grew up and coupled, creating more and more of their ilk until the whole valley was run through with them like noxious weeds.

"I'd like to explore around that place some time."

"You would? Why? Just a bunch of old junk left lying around." She wrinkled her nose, this time the distaste not playful but real.

"I don't know. I just like snooping around, I guess. I find people's histories interesting, don't you?"

"No. Not anyone around here, anyhow."

"Oh, come on, everyone has a story to tell. Even the people around here."

"No, not here they don't."

"Sure they do, they just need to find someone who wants to listen."

She looked at him with a drawn face, eyes indicating specifically how much she disagreed with him.

"You have a story, don't you?" He grinned, disregarding her eyes that narrowed slightly, warning him off. "You do, Victoria. You have a story and I'd love to hear it sometime. Everyone has one. Every single person in this world has a story to tell."

"Not one that needs to be told," she countered.

Elliot pulled the truck over to the side of the road, McCully Hill rising up to the east of them. He sighed and looked over at her with mock resignation.

"Okay. Probably you're right and I'm wrong. But I'd still like to hear your story because I'm sure you have one."

"Yup, I do. Want to hear it? Here it is. Born, lived, died. Pretty interesting, hey?" Catching the look of concern on his face, she softened her eyes, shook a wisp of hair from her face and laughed lightly. "I'm joking, okay? It hasn't been that bad living here. Come on, I'll help you carry some of this stuff."

The trail that led from the base to the top of McCully Hill started steeply then fell off to a gentle incline, and they climbed it easily, Victoria leading with Elliot following close behind. He stopped occasionally, inspected a leaf, turned over a stone, explained to her the various rocks rising up underneath their feet, each one a separate geological mystery.

"Boy, great view." He whistled softly.

A solid wall of granite rose up twenty feet above them on their right side, a barricade of trees on their left.

"What view? I can't see anything but rocks and trees."

"Really? Not from my vantage point. Best view I've seen for a long time."

Victoria stopped, turned to see what he was looking at and met his smiling eyes.

"Where? I don't see any—"

His pleased grin clued her.

"Very funny. Try to keep your eyes on the trail."

"On the what?"

"Trail."

"Oh, trail. I thought you said something else."

Her eyes sped through her armload of equipment looking for something to throw at him. But finding nothing that looked replaceable, she sent him a withering glance and continued on, a pleased grin, invisible to him, now on her face. The last three hundred yards felt like forever, the pressure of his eyes hot on her softly sashaying behind. Cresting the top of the rise, he passed her and set down his cameras and tripod then began to unpack the load from her arms.

"Thank you for carrying that up for me." His blue eyes sank into hers slowly.

"You're not welcome."

"I can live with that. Will you lead the way back down too?"

"You're bad. I thought we came to see the view up here."

"View up here's not too bad either," he winked, laughing as he made an easy sidestep from her swing.

"Elliot!" She attempted seriousness but failed, a red-cheeked smile pushing forward.

"Can't help it. I'm a guy. We only come in one model and that model is programmed to enjoy the view. It's beyond us. Primal."

"Primal?"

"Definitely."

Victoria rolled her eyes, did all but scoff. Elliot turned away from her and looked across the expanse to the indigo horizon. She watched him peripherally as the air grew quiet. His voice had fallen hushed, reverent, and she started slightly when it broke out again beside her.

"Isn't it beautiful?"

She looked out trying to catch what he was seeing, but all her eyes delivered was the valley coursing predictably between the towering hills, a muddy stream of greens and browns and grays. She closed her eyes. Tried to imagine his beauty, but it would not come. Even more vivid now in her mind, the valley lay an open wound, slit deep into the skin of the earth with Hinckly its cancerous heart of putrid decay. She snapped her eyes open looking up at Elliot, caught him looking down at her.

"No?"

"No, what?"

"I asked you if you thought it was beautiful."

"Oh."

"Do you?"

She smiled reservation.

"Here. Come over here." He walked off a short distance, moving closer toward the cliff edge. She obeyed, stood silent as he created an impromptu frame with his hands and positioned them for her to look through.

"There. That's the shot I want, right there. Can you see it?"

"Well—" She hesitated, trying not to disappoint him.

Ignoring her efforts, he slipped in behind her, his body brushing hers so softly that she couldn't be sure she'd imagined rather than felt it. He wrapped his hands over her eyes, blocking out everything, blinding her.

"Elliot. What are you doing?" She tried to duck out from under him, but his arms held her in place.

"No, just wait a minute, will you? I just want to try something. An experiment to see if I can help you see something that's so beautiful to me yet so repulsive to you."

"Not repulsive. I didn't say repulsive. I just don't see what's so amazing about it." Her voice was low and tired, her senses feeling hypnotized.

"Okay. Not repulsive. But certainly not beautiful either, right?"

She considered in dark silence.

"Right?"

"Yes, okay, you're right. Now, will you uncover my eyes? I'm getting dizzy."

"No. You know why I think you can't see anything beautiful about this valley? Because you don't see it with your senses, you see it through your memories, and your mind is so convinced you'll hate it, your senses don't stand half a chance." His arms tightened around her, pulling her in close to him; this time the pressure of his body on hers far less ambiguous. She started to protest, alarmed more by the truth of his words than by the closeness of his body, but his voice gently slipping into her ear silenced her.

"So, let's try again. Okay? Let's see if we can't get you to see through your senses this time. Through new eyes."

She yielded to his embrace. Felt the curve of his sensitive fingers, soft palms delicately framing her cheekbones. She felt like she was Helen of Troy, Cleopatra, Aphrodite in the hands of their sculptor.

His voice continued on like a soft summer day, but she could no longer distinguish his words, just the rise and fall of gentle croonings against her hair. She concentrated on the feel of his hands on her face. So relaxed. So calm and gentle. No turmoil breathed its way from his being. His were hands that were one with life, working in unison to explore and experience all that surrounded him. So different from the hands she'd known—rough and forceful. Hands like his did not rip and tear and demand their way, but rather, with a soft caress or a gentle stroke on canvas, these hands created light and life and gave as much as they received.

"That's better, Victoria. Just relax. Just listen to the quietness, feel the quietness. Can you feel it? Good, good. Just let yourself go." He continued to guide her, his sensual voice weaving itself through her body and then floating deep within her, penetrating her most secret of places.

"Okay, now look again. Can you see anything of beauty out there now?"

His voice cut into her musings and she felt disappointed, as if awakened from a wonderful, erotic dream. Her eyes flickered open. Stared straight ahead, seeing not a valley at all, but rather shapes and colors and shadows that swirled and spun and blended into one another. She swallowed. Drew in a deep breath and nodded.

"I've . . . I've never felt anything so beautiful before. Thank you."

"Hey, anytime. My pleasure. Absolutely." He gave her shoulder a light squeeze and headed back to the pile of camera equipment.

Finding a relatively flat piece of ground, she sat down and watched him set up his tripod, tilting the camera ever so slightly so as to capture exactly the perspective he wanted. He explained

things to her as he went along. Spoke of the play of light on darkness, the function of aperture, lens, focus. And all the while she
watched those beautiful hands in their dance of motion. Posi-
tioning, turning, twisting . . . touching. Tentatively, he took a few
shots. Repositioned, reconsidered, then took several more obviously delighted in his panoramic vista. The subject finally spent,
he walked back over to her and sat down.

"Done?"

"Pretty much. Just a couple more I'd like to take."

"Of what?"

"You."

"Me! Forget it." Her hands pushed aside some twigs as if
brushing off the suggestion.

"No, really. I'd love to photograph you. You have such amazing
angles to your face."

"No, I don't."

"No?"

"No."

"Well, I think you do. Come on, let me take a couple of shots.
Just a few."

"Elliot, no. Don't. You're making me feel dumb."

"I'm making you feel dumb?"

She nodded, pulled her knees up toward her chest and hid her
face.

"A man tells you he thinks you're beautiful, and it makes you
feel dumb?"

She ignored him, stayed hidden. But his opinion of her had
not gone unnoticed.

"I have to tell you, Victoria, that is a very strange reaction. A
very, very strange reaction."

"Sorry. Can't help how I feel." She turned her head on her
knees and looked at him reclining beside her.

"Neither can I," he countered, offering no apology as he lingered his eyes over her lips then slowly drew them up her face.
"Come on."

He jumped up, took her by the hand and pulled her up toward him, his other hand reaching out to steady her and coming to rest on the small hollow of her lower back. She stood beside him looking out over the valley. She felt the warmth of his hand through her cotton T-shirt. Felt it rise and fall with her body as she breathed. They said nothing, just stood silent as the heavens slowly shifted above them, contemplated neither past nor future. She felt his fingers shift imperceptibly, more of a tingling than a movement, and she stood breathless as he slid his hand further around until his arm half encircled her waist.

"Incredible, hey?" He asked the question quietly, his eyes fixed on some distant place she couldn't yet see.

She nodded. Wondered if he was planning on taking this further. Wondered if he was going to make a move on her. She'd stop him, of course. That was certain. It was a small town, and she didn't even want to imagine what would happen if Bobby were to ever find out. But that didn't mean she didn't want him to try, because she did.

They stood that way for a long moment, then abruptly he pulled away. His gaze skimmed over the valley as if searching for a place to settle. Taking a deep breath, he released it almost angrily.

"I lied to you before."

"You did? Why?"

"I don't know. Because it was easier than telling the truth, I guess."

A thin pause hung between them like a gate. She could tell that he wanted her to encourage him through it, but she resisted. Right now, he was perfect, and she did not want to hear the words that would see him changed.

Sensing this, he swung around to fully face her and forced himself to continue on. Brittle emotion constricted his words into rigid bricks.

"I guess maybe what I told you was the story of the way I wished things had been. Told you the story I told myself as a kid every time I'd get yanked out of another school that I was just starting to settle into. We did move around a lot. That was true. But it wasn't because my dad's job required it. It was because he had a big mouth and a short temper and couldn't hold down a decent job for longer than a couple of years."

"You don't have to tell me this, Elliot."

"I know. But I want to. I don't even know why I told you that other stuff. Wanted you to think I was better than I am, I guess."

An objection rose in her throat, but he continued on before she could speak.

"I was really close to my mom, though. I think it was because we were always moving. Eventually, I just gave up trying to make any real friends, and I think she did too. The only constants in our lives seemed to be the moves and each other. My dad never liked me. Resented the closeness I had with Mom. He was constantly trying to cause trouble between us. But she was too smart for him. She had a way of working things out so I didn't feel betrayed, and he got to feel he was right. When I graduated and took off for Europe, it was less for the adventure than it was just a way to get away from him.

"Mom wanted me to go. She wanted me to go more than I wanted to go. And I'm glad I listened to her. Europe changed everything for me. It changed me. When I came back home, I wasn't the same person who'd left. I'd seen and done things that my father would never see or do. And that gave me a sort of power over him. He just didn't seem so frightening anymore. He just seemed kind of sad and pathetic and insignificant.

"Anyhow, first week I was back home I was sitting with mom in the living room, having tea and looking at my pictures when he came home from the bar, drunk. He started yapping at me, but I just ignored him. All of a sudden, he reaches down and grabs the album from Mom's hands and rips it from her, spilling her tea all over her lap. I went at him with twenty years of bottled up rage. And he was so bloody stupid, he thought I was after my pictures, so he swung them up over his head like we were in a game of keep away. Lost his balance and fell down the stairs. To this day, he still maintains that I pushed him. He landed badly. Busted his neck and ended up in a wheelchair."

"Oh! Elliot, that's so horrible."

"Actually, I think it all turned out exactly the way he wanted. Ended up with my mom giving him full-time care and a justifiable reason to get rid of me. After that, I was sort of lost. Ended up doing too many drugs, drinking, wasting my days away just hating him. Then one day I looked in the mirror and realized that I hated myself just as much as I hated him. That I was becoming him. And that was the end of it, right there. I'd always had an interest in art, so I went to work, saved up some money and applied to school. I was totally shocked when I got in.

"But it was the best thing in the world for me. I felt plugged into life. Like I'd just woken up and realized who I was for the first time. And I just sort of went at it maniacally. I studied and painted and traveled like any day it could all come to an end. Then one day I clued in that I was trying to be everything that my father could never be. That paint and knowledge had just become my new drugs. And I realized that I had to make peace with the fact that he'd been a shitty father. Make peace with the fact that my own father hated me. I never actually talked to him about it. There wouldn't have been any point. But, in my own head, I knew I had to let it go."

"How'd you do that?" she asked.

"Well, that was the funny thing. Once I figured out that was what I had to do, it was as if it was already done. I just moved on. Bought a little place with some money my grandfather left me and started fixing it up. Sold it and made a profit, and so I did it again. And again. And again.

"I know people around here think I've made my money with my painting, but I didn't. Well, not most of it, anyhow. The houses are my real art. Trying to create a sense of home and stability I never had. Problem is, once they're done I can't seem to stay in them anymore. It's like I don't fit. Crazy, hey?" He laughed lightly, glancing down at her to gauge her reaction to what she'd just been told. They sat in silence for a moment as his words swirled around them like water without a place to settle.

"So, anyhow, that's the truth of it. I'm sorry I lied to you before." He looked at her almost shyly.

She smiled at him softly, and as she viewed him in this new light she decided the revelation of this imperfection only made him all the more perfect.

"Don't be. I think most people probably have things in their past that they'd rather leave there."

"Yeah. I suppose. Is that how it is for you?"

She drew back. An alarm thudded deep in her veins. Had his whole confession just been an intentional attempt to lead her up to this moment? A way to disarm her defenses so he could safely ask her such an intimate question? She tried to shrug the suggestion off as ludicrous, but she couldn't. It didn't feel ludicrous. And ludicrous or not, that is what he'd achieved, walking in comfortably and asking her a question she would not even have dared ask herself.

She realized suddenly that the air had become cool with the arrival of late afternoon and she shivered. She needed to get back home. She'd ask Elliot to drop her off at the end of the driveway under some pretense of wanting to pick some wildflowers for the table. And when Bobby asked about who'd driven her home, she'd tell him, then concoct some story about how she'd found Elliot Spencer a little bit strange.

~ Chapter 6 ~

B obby, you'd better hurry. It's almost eight o'clock; the boys will be here anytime now."

"All right, already. Relax a minute, will ya. I'm just gonna have a quick shower."

"Bobby! You can't have a shower, they'll be—" The roar of water crushed her protest mid stream.

Tears stung in her eyes as she whirled around, clenched fists powerless to stop him. Shit! He could be such a jerk. He knew how much she hated it when he came home late on Saturday nights. Hated having to fend off the abrasive, arrogant John Jr., who amused himself while waiting for his friend by tormenting his friend's wife. Frustration burned up into her throat and spread out to her limbs. She wanted to punch something, break something. Yell. Scream. But she turned her fury in on herself, swallowed her rage as clenched fists drove hard nails into tender palms. Saturday was poker night. No one had planned it that way, it just was. Started the Saturday night of their wedding. Started as a big drunken joke: the boys thinking it would be immensely funny to barge in on the newlyweds at three o'clock in the morning and haul Bobby out of bed to drink whiskey and play poker.

It was not funny, however, and Bobby had sworn vilely into the black bedroom as they thundered on the trailer door demanding in a slurred, howling chorus to be let in. She'd been sure Bobby was going to set them straight in no uncertain terms. She'd even cautioned him to remember that they were his best friends and drunk, and that he should go easy on them. Ignoring her, he'd ripped open the bedroom door and exploded down the hallway like a bullet through the barrel of a gun. But, by the time he'd traversed the short distance to the porch door, his Hyde had turned to Jekyll, and he greeted his friends with good-ol'-boy slaps on the back and an overly loud, upbeat invitation to come on in.

She'd lain awake until morning had pushed itself in around the edges of the tattered blanket nailed across the window. Lain awake listening as the four of them drank themselves into a silent stupor, and then she'd got up to repair the damage. Emptied the ashtrays, picked drowned butts out of glasses, washed the dishes, swept the floor. The first few years she'd even found blankets to lay over the comatose bodies lying inert wherever the alcohol had declared victory and the muscles had failed. The rocker, the bathtub, the floor. After a while she'd just saved herself the bother; they never acknowledged her kindness anyhow, as oblivious to it as though the blankets had just arrived on their own accord. On the good nights, they drank themselves sick before they drank themselves dead, and they could still find their way home again. It was a weekly ritual that played over and over again, like a reoccurring nightmare she couldn't escape and gradually she came to accept as her life.

Bobby had been repentant, if not apologetic, after the first night. Promised her a real honeymoon once the crops were in. Somewhere exotic. Somewhere neither of them had been, which was pretty much anywhere. But the extra cash was needed for tractor repairs that year and for trailer repairs the next. And each year brought the promise of the next, until she gave up waiting and he gave up promising.

The pounding of water joined her thoughts. Her hands whiteknuckled around a carving fork; she stuck it deep into the roast and returned it to the oven. She wiped her hands on her jeans, struggled for a full breath. Elliot was right. She was uptight. Needed to relax, have fun for a change. But relaxing seemed a foreign word to her, partially grasped but not fully understood. Relax. Have fun.

Sure, sounded simple off his tongue. But how could she relax when life kept coming undone, the whole damn thing instantly fraying every time she took her finger off the knot.

She tucked her fingertips into the softly rounded groove of the windowpane and yanked at it several times before it finally relented with a resentful crack and let itself be slid open. More and more often now, she found herself opening the windows to escape the claustrophobic closeness that pressed in on her, hoping to replenish the stagnant air that sat thickly in her lungs. Her hipbones pressed against the edges of the faded orange counter as she leaned across it to catch the fresh air stealing in through the window. Her eyes closed as the crisp night touched her face. Her mind floated backward to the day three weeks previous and began to strum serenely over its perfect chords. Pausing occasionally, she tried to retrace each word, each wink, each touch, and she grew irritated by her mind's inability to recall the vivid feelings, diluting their red intensity into a dull brown.

A slow sucking sound startled her as Bobby opened the bathroom door and emerged behind her. His towel-dried black hair glistened in a spiky disarray that would have looked boyish had it been able to overcome the ferociousness of day-old stubble.

"Hey, Vic, you seen my knife?"

"What knife?"

"My Swiss Army knife."

"Nope."

"Sure?"

"Yup."

"Well," he said slowly, "that's strange 'cause it seems to have gone missing again."

Victoria shrugged nervously. "I'm sure it'll show up somewhere. Hungry?"

She drank one more breath of fresh air, resealed the window and hurried to fill his plate with thick slabs of meat, a mound of potatoes and a forest of vegetables. The whole time she listened to his movements, feeling the air for his mood. She heard the raw

scrape of the chair as he yanked it from the table, carelessly crashing it into the wall as he cursed the confines of the trailer. She set
his plate in front of him as he lowered himself onto the chair, then
smashed a dozy housefly under his fist, flicked it from the table
and wiped his hand over his jeans.

"I think the friggin' well's drying up."

"Why would it do that?" Victoria asked, already envisioning
the extra money they would need to fix it.

"Beats me. Probably that rich bugger up the road's sucking it
all up with his fancy irrigation bullshit."

"Doesn't he pump out of the creek?"

"Don't make no matter. Water's water. You pump it outta the
creek, it'll just suck more outta the ground to fill it back up. Either
way, we gotta cut back till I can get it checked out."

"Cut back how much?"

"Five minutes for a shower, half tub for a bath."

"Five minutes? I don't think I can get my hair washed and
rinsed that quick, Bobby. How about ten?"

"Five minutes. You can't manage that, then cut your damn
hair."

Victoria opened her mouth to argue, then abandoned the
thought. Water, she realized, had become a precious commodity
on the farm—the only precious commodity on the farm.

Putting some vegetables onto her plate, she put the lids back
on the pots and sat down. She'd long since dispensed with the
notion of serving dishes. Drifting off into a solitary reverie, her
mind remained vaguely aware of Bobby's mumbling and grum-
bling but in a pre-functionary way, rolling it into the realm of background noises; ticking clocks, running toilets, the blathering TV.

"Hey! You hear me?"

Victoria quickly scrambled to recall his words, knew he'd been
talking but had no idea what about. "I, uh—"

"I don't think it's too bloody much to ask, Vic. You think it's
too much to ask? Huh? Too damn complicated for you to remember

to keep the window closed. What do I got to do? Nail the buggers shut?"

"No, I—" she started again, now remembering what it was he'd been complaining about.

"Here, why don't I get you some socks and a shirt. That'll be warmer." She slid away from the table and into the bedroom, returning with his favorite plaid flannel and wool socks.

"The problem ain't that I don't have a shirt on, Vic. The problem is you having that frickin' window wide open like it's the fourth of bloody July. Winter's gonna be a cold one this year."

"I know, I know. I'm sorry. These will help warm you up."

She gave him the shirt, watched him grunt himself into it, then handed him one sock at a time, waiting as he struggled over his belly to pull them on.

"Bad as friggin' Pearl's around here." He sat up and resumed eating, puffing slightly from the exertion. "Next thing you'll have a bloody sign up too. 'No shirt, no socks, no service.'" He paused to consider his wittiness. "Don't get no damn service around here, anyhow."

Victoria ignored him, took his plate back to the stove and refilled it. Half of what Bobby said to her she paid no attention to, having learned over the years that the words rolled across his brain and off his tongue with no depth attached, that his verbal abuse was more driven by bad habit than by any real intention to hurt her. She also knew that, if she ever dared to leave, he'd be one of those husbands who, coming home to find an empty house and his wife gone, would stand in stunned disbelief wondering what her problem was, wondering how she could just walk out when things, although not perfect, were still pretty damn good. Not that she even considered leaving a possibility. Bobby had made it abundantly clear in times past what would happen if she did. And it was a consequence she was not willing to pay.

She sat back down and pushed her food around her plate, the sound of his wet smacking filling their space in lieu of conversation. Meeting Elliot had complicated things for her. Whereas before, she could push Bobby's annoyances off to the side, they now all seemed center stage and in sharp focus, each one compared unfavorably in stark relief against Elliot's background.

"Hey! I got you something,"he said, his face brightening.

"You did?"

"Yep. A surprise. Hang on, I'll get it."

He pushed back from the table, rummaged through some bags in the porch, and emerged with a shiny aluminum teakettle.

"Here. These were on sale at Mrs. Barlow's store."

"Oh. Thank you," Victoria mumbled, as she took it and turned it over in her hand.

"Figured we could use a new one," he said, nodding at a dented kettle sitting on the back burner.

"Yeah. That one leaks a bit," Victoria agreed, both of them careful not to elude too strongly to Bobby's fit of rage, which had resulted in the kettle being crushed underfoot.

"Didn't never pour no good, anyhow. Figured it'd be best to get a new one before you ended up getting burnt again."

She looked at the red scar splashed across her left forearm. "Thanks. It's nice."

"Yup. Hey, got some milk? 'Taters are dry as hell. Not like my mama's. Now there was a lady who could cook. You gonna get in to see her this week?"

"Am I going to get in and see her? It's you she wants to see, Bobby, not me," Victoria said as she got up and poured him a glass of milk.

"I just did see her."

"When?"

"Last Tuesday . . . no, Monday."

"Hardly. You can't call that a visit."

"Can too. I was there, wasn't I? I saw her."

"You dropped off her birthday card. You could have at least gone in to see her."

"I did see her."

"Well, yes, okay. Technically you did see her. But she didn't get to see you, did she?"

"Not my fault. I was there if she wanted to see me."

"Bobby, she's an old lady. She can't help it if she was sleeping."

"Never said she could help it, did I?" He pressed the words down on her, clearly irritated.

"No."

He wrestled with his emotions for a minute, hacking at the meat, draining his milk, then looking darkly toward the door.

"Just don't like to see her that way, that's all," he said quietly. "All crumpled up and stiff."

"She's not doing so bad, Bobby. Compared to most of them in the home."

"Not right anyhow, her being stuck in that place. Once I get the house built though, I'll get her out of there. Move her back out here to the farm where she belongs."

Victoria softened as she looked at the little boy trapped inside of the man sitting across from her. After his father died, he had nearly worn himself out trying to work in the bush, run the farm and keep everything maintained so that his mother could continue to live there. Eventually, it all became too much for him. His mother had been ecstatic. She had wanted to move into town years earlier.

"Webber called today," Victoria said disdainfully.

"Ya? What he want?"

"Didn't say. Probably wants you to fix his tractor again. He ever pay you for last time?"

"Not yet."

"Not yet. Not ever, Bobby. I think you spend more time fixing his tractor than you do our own."

"Don't start, Vic. Like I told you before. I might be doing a lot of fixing stuff up for free now, but once we get to building the house all them guys are going to come out and give us a hand. Gonna save us a fortune in labor costs."

"Hmm. Seems to me we'd be a lot further ahead if you just got paid for all the mechanic work you do, and then we could afford to hire a real builder. What about, JJ? He ever give you anything from that last car he sold?"

"Why would he give me anything? It was his car."

"Come on, Bobby. Everyone in town knows he wouldn't have got near that much money for it if you hadn't rebuilt the motor."

"We all rebuilt the motor," he said defensively.

"None of them have a clue how to rebuild a motor like you do, Bobby. You've said so yourself. At least not one that can go fast enough to sell to the guys from the city. They all just do whatever you say. And then when it's done, JJ sells it and takes home a bundle of cash. Right?"

"Ya, well, maybe." He shifted sideways, trying to find a comfortable placement on the chair.

"Bobby," she chided gently. "You know I'm right. You should be fixing up your own cars. JJ's taking advantage of all you guys just because none of you are willing to stand up to him."

"Naw. It's not like that, Vic. JJ's pretty damn good with a hammer. You'll see. Once we start building our house, he'll pay me back for all the time I put into them cars. Where are those house plans, anyhow? You ever find them?"

Victoria shook her head.

"Well, we'll have to dig them out again one of these days and have another look, okay? I been thinking maybe we should add that second bathroom you wanted. Maybe I'll even get you one of them fancy dishwasher things. You'd like that, hey?"

She nodded aimlessly. The plans were really just a solitary sketch of the house they used to dream of building. During the early years, walls had been erased and expanded liberally to accommodate the imagined future growth of their family. As time wore on, reality kept revising the plan downward until one day the drawing just couldn't be found at all.

Victoria placed a pan of brownies on the table, and he devoured two and was halfway through a third before his face brightened.

"Guess what I heard at the coffee shop today. Benson Ferguson, shit . . . just like an old woman that guy. Knows more gossip about people than they knows about themselves. Anyhow, he was saying Diana's 'specting again." He shook his head with a touch of admiration. "Shit, broad's a walking, talking, baby machine, hey? What is that, her tenth or something?"

"Eighth," Victoria corrected.

Diana, it was common knowledge was, and always would be, Bobby's first love. The vivacious daughter of a relatively successful businessman, she'd been considered a good catch and Bobby, five years her senior, had claimed her as his own before she was two months into the ninth grade. With her parents openly pleased with his insular effect on their coveted firstborn and Diana herself feeling immaturely flattered, Bobby became a regular fixture in their fine home. Within the year, their two lives had been merged into one, and he decided it was time for Diana to marry him.

In typical peacock-proud fashion, he'd bought her a glittery, persuasive engagement ring and flashed it around town. So impressed was he with his exquisite trinket that he was thrown into a free fall of uncomprehending disbelief when his cocky proposal was met with cautious uncertainty. His tender ego mutilated by what he could only perceive as her rejection and open humiliation of him in front of the town, he lunged into a month-long tantrum of drunken fighting and willing women. Several times, if it hadn't been for the intervention of his friends, the situation looked like it might end quite tragically. The whole town had occupied themselves with his embittered thrashings, listening sympathetically to his endless woes before rushing out to share the latest tale of heartbreaking angst.

The weekend Victoria returned from the dance competition, however, the eyes and ears of the town swiveled around to greet its wounded hero. It was not often that Hinckly birthed an athlete good enough to compete in the important competitions held in the city. And it never seemed to matter to any of them that she had never actually competed but rather watched from the sidelines, feigning a flu. Feeling as if she were in some bizarre nightmare, she'd accepted their congratulations. She obediently rode in their welcome home victory parade, waving at dirty faces that lined dirty streets to stare as she passed by, each one seemingly oblivious to the fact that there was no victory to celebrate.

As the talk of the town shifted on a fickle wind away from Bobby and Diana's breakup and became consumed with the plight of its fallen hero, Bobby's interest shifted as well. Looking back she could never understand what it was about his swaggering boyish confidence, his tough talk and flippant attitude that she'd found appealing. Maybe it was the temporary protection she found his made-for-TV ego delivered to her own, irreparably damaged by Billy Bassman and then annihilated by the loss of the biggest opportunity of her life. Whatever the attraction had been, it was short-lived but not quite short enough. It held long enough for her, with the expectations of the town still hanging heavily across her shoulders, to accept his rebound proposal. A proposal, she later understood, that was his retaliation against Diana, who had, within four weeks of their breakup, apparently fallen in love with Tom Gainer, a long-time family friend. Diana's fall wedding was quickly planned and processed.

Victoria had never shared with anyone the truth of what really happened the day she'd withdrawn from the dance competition. Not even with Rose, who knew more about her than almost anyone. But this was a truth so deep she could scarcely share it with herself, preferring to wrap it in layers of half-truths and outright lies. Preferring to wrap it so tightly she could almost believe it ceased to be. But it remained a cold, hard, perfect pearl in the belly of the oyster, awaiting the day prying hands would push in and release it from the slimy deceit that covered but could never obliterate it. It had remained hidden in her for over twenty years now. But no matter how well she kept it concealed from the outside, it remained a constant source of irritation, pricking her at the most inopportune times: the pricking and scraping her accepted penance.

Sickness had brought her down the day she was to compete. But it was not the flu that had dug her grave. She'd watched, nauseous, as the other girls competed with the fluid lucidness of air. Watched someone with half her talent be awarded her audition, walk away with her dream. She knew with a dread certainty she could have beaten them all. Beaten them easily if it wasn't for the tiny fetal mass that had poisoned her body into worthlessness and weakness, fastened her feet firmly in the suctioning mud so well known to those cursed enough to have grown up in a place like Hinckly.

~ Chapter 7 ~

Two rivers of light spilled into the darkness, dancing a duet down the driveway. The boys had arrived. She hated poker night. Or rather, she hated how Bobby dissolved into the alcohol. How it released a cruelness in him that she otherwise seldom saw. She scraped her supper into the garbage and went into the adjoining porch, watching through the darkened window as they pulled to a stop beside Bobby's truck. A comical sight, they would have made her laugh if she'd been able to. Years ago, they had all fit comfortably into the truck, but the passing of time had slowly swollen them into puffy balloons, pressing against the doors and windows of the truck until it looked like it would burst from the pressure. Opening the doors, they oozed out into the night, completely oblivious of how ridiculous they had become.

John Jr. was the first one through the porch door. Cuddling a case of Old Style and a bottle of whiskey under one arm, his bicep bulged with bold black lettering: STAPH, a drunken tattoo attempt aborted when he realized halfway through that he didn't know how to spell the girl's name. Without bothering to knock or acknowledge Victoria, he brushed past her into the trailer. She stood quietly in the corner of the porch holding the door open for Peter and Sam. Victoria despised Peter about as much as she despised John Jr., maybe more. An insecure, fleshy lump of a man, he delighted in spurring Bobby and John Jr. forward in their pursuits of nastiness while he cleverly hung back and hid his intentions behind a baby-faced innocence. Ruled over by a tyrannical wife who constantly beat him down with a barrage of demands and complaints, he reveled in the one night a week she allowed him to go out with the boys. But it wasn't for Peter that she held open the door, but rather for Sam, who as usual, had stopped on the stairs outside to take off his filthy work boots.

Sam Billyboy was a massive boulder of a man who wore his long hair suppressed in a thick black braid that tied him to his native ancestry. A mountain of muscle, his strength was legendary. In his youth, he'd been a rough and rowdy street fighter and had routinely displaced anyone simple-headed enough to challenge him. Just short of his twenty-eighth birthday, however, he'd developed an intolerance to the liquor that fueled the fire of his fighting and was forced to give it up. As the alcohol evaporated from his life so did his anger, and he mellowed into a Goliath of a man with a heart soft as a kitten's purr. But local legends live a life of their own in a small town, and even though he hadn't lifted a combative fist for years, he still had young boys gaze at him with awe when he happened by. He lowered his head as he stepped through the doorway, smiled shyly at Victoria.

"Hi, Vic. How's it going?"

"Pretty good, I guess, how about you?"

"Yup, not too bad. Working lots, but I guess that's good."

"You should bring your boots in, Sam. It's freezing out tonight."

"Oh, no. They're okay out there. They're really muddy."

"You sure?" she asked again, noticing the mud hadn't stopped anyone else from clomping on in.

"Ya, I don't want to make a—" he started as JJ's voice thundered through and ordered him to quit yakking with the women and sit down so they could play cards.

"Hey, Petey. It was good of your mama to let you come out to play, must have been a good boy this week, hey?" Bobby boomed.

"Was ya a good boy, Petey? Did she let you have all your allowance to lose this time?" John Jr. added, not wanting to be outdone.

Peter flushed flamingo pink, an embarrassed smile jumping on and off his face as he attempted to defend himself.

"Ahh . . . get lost you guys, I don't get no allowance."

"No shit, really?" Bobby shot back with mock seriousness. "What does she do? Pay you for your services?"

A howl of laughter and then John Jr. struck. "No wonder you never have any money!"

Harsh laughter pounded the walls of the trailer, Peter's voice twice as loud and twice as shrill in the desperate attempt to prove himself part of the joke rather than the butt of it. The party had begun. Victoria quickly removed the dishes into the sink and wiped the table. Bobby and Peter had already started sucking their beers while John Jr. slowly filled his glass with a poison that could have come straight from his own heart. As the cards and insults were dealt around the table, she removed herself to the relative safety of the living room, pulled the rocker away from the wall and, her back against them, sat down facing the window. Some Saturday evenings she would read or knit, but mostly she just kept the light off and rocked, staring out into the blackness that surrounded the trailer, semi-aware of volley after volley of insulting innuendoes.

Tonight, however, she would busy herself with the task at hand. She reached down beside the chair and pulled up a floppy white plastic bag, dumped its contents onto her lap and began to sort through it. The pastel balls yielded softly to the light pressure of her hand as she stroked them, each one reveling in her pleasure like lazy cats. Eventually she settled on the gentle yellow one and put the rest away. Soon she was enveloped by the soothing click, click, click of her knitting needles as they chatted their way through another baby sweater. It was the eighth one she would give to Diana, each one made and delivered with meticulous care. The first one she'd made was actually for herself, although that too was a secret that remained buried deep in her heart. But as time had worn onward, it had become clear that the only use the little sweater would ever get would be wrapping other peoples' precious little bundles. As it became obvious that they would never produce a legacy of themselves, Bobby had become adamant that it was because of her failure and not his own. He had no reason to believe that that she knew of, no tests had ever been done. Gradually it became common knowledge throughout the valley that Victoria was barren, and before long it had crystallized into a fact.

She stopped her knitting and wiped her eyes, dismayed to find them spilling hot tears, alarmed at the prospect of being seen—the perfect target—by JJ or Petey. Once she'd made the mistake of trying to defend herself after John Jr. had taken a shot at her with one of his one-liner backhands. Instantly she'd found herself drawn into their carnage, verbally pummeled and beaten until she'd fled into the bedroom in tears, Bobby's approving laughter chasing her as she ran. She could not risk them seeing her tears, a magnet that would draw them to her pain like vultures to carrion.

Her hands tenderly smoothed the partially formed sweater that nestled in her lap. *It would have been the perfect sweater for her baby*, she thought morosely. A partially formed sweater for a partially formed baby. Again, the tears started, and she stifled them. It wasn't that she'd wanted the baby, certainly not at the time, anyway. Considered it something evil, cancerous, a tumor living inside her eating at her like a parasite. But after it was gone, destroyed, she had often wondered about it. Sometimes she'd even envisioned it, a little person she could create and carve to perfection in the studio of her mind. After the third month had passed with no sign of deliverance, she'd been almost immobilized by fear and disappointment and hatred. Her dance career was over; teenage mothers did not receive auditions. It was as simple as that.

And her father, once he found out, would have put her out on the street like a stray dog. Let her stay there until the rightful owner came along or some poor sap felt pity for her and took her in. Not willing to be claimed by the rightful owner and detesting even the thought of being held hostage by some over-sanctified well-doer's pity, she chose a rushed wedding to Bobby, hoping he would never be the wiser about why their child appeared so soon before the expected date. She suspected over the years many of

Hinckly's healthy premature babies had arrived under similar cir-
cumstances. She could have saved herself the maneuvering, however; nature had its own plans. The pregnancy had signaled the
end of everything for her that she held dear. And so, when she was
wrenched from her sleep late one night by vicious, heathen cramps
that forced her to suffocate her cries into her pillow, it was a sense
of joy not sadness that filled her.

And as she'd watched the gnarled, twisted mass of bloody tissue swirl around in the bloodstained bowl, she was elated. She'd
watched with tingling excitement as the crimson water had spun
around and around until finally the toilet opened its greedy throat
and with one swallow and a rushing gurgle devoured the whole
mess. Instantly, clear water had rushed in and calmly denied any
memory of the death that had just passed there. Her prayers had
been answered. She'd been set free. But the answer had come too
late and, now married to Bobby, freedom was more elusive than it
had ever been.

She'd never seen any reason to tell him. The miscarriage saved
her the profound indiscretion of joyously informing him she was
pregnant with his child. But when, later on, he'd made such a
point of blaming her for their inability to conceive, going so far
as to allude that he and not Diana's husband had really fathered
Diana's first child, she would have loved to throw the truth in his
face. Would have loved to remind him of what the doctor had said
regarding his childhood bout with the mumps and possible low
sperm count as a result of it. But she knew it wouldn't have mattered anyway. Bobby believed what he chose to believe, and the
truth rarely stood in his way.

The now drunken voices in the next room rose upward and
outward, riding along the ceiling until they consumed every inch
of the trailer.

"Oh yeah, shit. I knows who ya means. That broad with the—"
An adolescent gesture earned Bobby an ovation of laughter. "Forget it, you peckerhead. Even Bassman would have a better chance
at her slot than you."

"Bull-shit! That's a bunch of bull, Bobby. She ain't gonna let scum like that touch her. I could have her if I wanted to."

"Yeah, so what's the problem? Go get the bitch then, Petey. Come on, we'll even give you a ride to town."

"Yeah, well. Well, at least I'd know what to do with her if ya did. You wouldn't even know, Bobby, wouldn't know what to do even if he got the chance, would he, JJ? He wouldn't even know, would he?" Peter hurried to get this out before somebody took him down with another jab, anxious to set John Jr. on the attack.

"Hell no, Petey, I don't believe he would. Been a long bloody time since Bobby's seen a set of knockers like that. Come to think of it, I heard he didn't know what to do with the last ones he got his hands on!"

A confusion of pompous laughter joined the scraping of chairs and tables and bodies as Bobby made a lopsided lunge across the table to grab John Jr. The sobering smash of a glass meeting an undignified death cut them short for a half thought before they resumed their braying.

"Hey! Hey, Vic! We need ya in here. Stupid here dumped my drink."

She put down her knitting and sighed. Wished she could just walk out the door. Disappear into the night. Wondered what Elliot would think if she appeared on his porch seeking refuge from this war zone of twisted mentalities. But she couldn't do that. And even if she could, in reality they'd only shared a brief, mild flirtation. Probably no different than he'd have done with half the girls in town. Hardly a gesture that warranted throwing herself whole-heartedly at his feet; although for her the flirtation had been far from mild, and her heart had already chosen where it would be thrown.

"Hey!"

She rose from the rocker, walked into the kitchen avoiding eye contact, and surveyed the damage. Shards of glass littered the floor like geometrical chunks of ice; yellow liquid drooled its way down the paneled wall into a swampy pool on the kitchen floor.

Gathering some paper towels, she began to mop up, being careful not to pierce her fingers as she swept up a soggy handful and dropped it into the garbage pail. She moved with precision and care, yet the inevitable happened, so she leapt up to the sink and ran water over her finger as the wound spouted a tiny red river.

"Here. Might as well empty this while you're at it," John Jr. mumbled as he thrust an overflowing ashtray onto the counter, sending stinking cigarette butts skidding into the sink and onto the floor. She watched as the stubby projectiles hit the water then bobbed amongst the dirty dishes.

"Hey, look out!" She turned just as Peter flicked his cigarette past her, off the window and into the sink, where it snarled an angry cat hiss, then drowned.

"Bobby! Hey you dumb dickhead, put some music on will ya?"

"I gotta take a leak. Vic!" He motioned her to the stereo with a toss of his head as he crashed down the hall and into the washroom, yelling back at her. "Put on some Meat Loaf, will ya?"

Under John Jr.'s orders, Petey went into the living room as soon as she'd put the tape in and cranked up the volume, their voices rising to keep afloat of the intolerable levels of a screaming rendition of "Bat Out of Hell."

Trying to ignore the carnival behind her, Victoria stood at the sink and began picking the cigarette butts out of the water. She turned on the tap and attempted to wash the ashes and grime and filth from her soft white hands, but it seemed suddenly impossible to her that they could ever come clean and, driven by desperation, she grabbed the potato scrubber from the haze of slimy water and started frantically scrubbing the skin from her hands.

"Hey, what the hell are you doing?" Bobby's paralyzed speech dragged out like a record set one speed too slow. "Quit wasting the friggin' water."

Victoria crumpled under his yell as if she'd been struck, dropped the potato scrubber and twisted shut the faucet. Appalled, she stood in the madness of noise and looked down at the destruction she'd caused to her own hands . . . by her own hands.

"I'm hungry. You guys hungry? Samson, ya big bugger, ya wanna sandwich or something?"

Victoria turned toward the table hiding her angry, raw hands behind her back. She watched as Sam cast her an apologetic look, his lips moving slightly, but his soft voice unable to find its way over the pollution of noise. Raised on the reservation by his grandmother, he had a heritage of extremely mixed origin and, as if to accentuate this, he'd been born with one brown eye and one blue. Sometimes their eyes would find each other and an understanding would pass between them, an understanding that, no matter how much he felt for her, how much he loved her, he could never desecrate his friend's marriage. She smiled at him now and he smiled back, quickly returning his attention to his cards. She felt safer with Sam in the trailer. Although he would cross no boundaries for his own pleasure, she also knew nothing could withhold him from protecting her if the verbal abuse were ever to take a physical form.

Opening the refrigerator, she allowed her hands to tarry in its soothing coolness before she pulled out the roast and began slicing it for sandwiches. She slapped mayonnaise across slices of bread, crisscrossed it with mustard and piled on the slabs of beef. To one sandwich, she added an extra slice of meat and sprinkled it liberally with salt and pepper. The other three she sprinkled liberally with ashes. Handing the plates around the table, she became uncomfortably aware of Peter, perched precariously on the edge of his chair, ogling her, prickly sweat shining across his half-bald head. This wasn't uncommon behavior for him. As the effects of the alcohol dulled his inhibitions, his leering always became more pronounced, his hand sometimes brushing purposely across her derriere when she happened by. But tonight he seemed distracted by something other than his perverted mind.

"Hey, Vic, what'd ya do to your hair?"

"Nothing much," she answered, hoping to brush him off. Hoping someone would launch in over the top of her, ignore her like they usually did.

"Ya, you did. I can see it," he chided like a grade six boy teasing the girls at recess. "Come on, what'd ya do? You dyed it, didn't you? Didn't you?"

She wished they were in sixth grade again; she'd have no problem settling this score. She'd been tall for her age, and strong. One taunt from a half-size troublemaker like him and she'd have leveled him out across the playground with one punch. But childhood had privileges not taken with one into adulthood, and she could feel behind his hostility a latent desire to cause her real pain.

"Hey, Bobby. Bobby! Over here, numb-nuts, I'm talking to you. You ever noticed your wife's changing color on you, huh? Changing color on him, hey JJ? Starting to go kookie like her ole auntie did, hey?" He elbowed John Jr. coherent, his laugh rat-a-tat-tat like a machine gun as he pointed out his discovery.

A wave of loathing washed over her as all eyes climbed over her hair, inspecting the red highlights that had been merged with the browns and golds.

Bobby sat lopsided, a look of puzzled confusion adorning his sloppy face. "Hey! Whadda hell ya do to yer hair?"

Fear rammed her, smashed her breath from her. She realized too late she was trapped, the wolves circling into position to devastate their wounded prey. A cellophane-thin smile touched Peter's face then fled as he pressed forward to start the attack. Her eyes sought out Sam's, his holding an apology as he sat mute, immovable as the torrent of sarcasm grew around them and above them and over them.

"Hey, JJ. Can you believe that? Dip-shit doesn't even know if he's sleeping with a redhead or a brunette, he don't even know, JJ!"

"Yep, probably could have just as easy chucked the dog in with ya, ya dumb bugger. Hell! Probably did chuck the friggin' dog in with ya!"

Replying with an oafish, heavy swing, Bobby responded with all the wittiness he could muster.

"Well, shit then, mister . . . that woulda bin one lucky damn potlicker of a dog, I tell ya!"

A belt of laughter sprung up, hit the roof and it was over. Thankful none of them had taken notice of her raw, reddened hands, she cleared the empties off the table, stacked them in the sink and limped back to the sanctuary of the living room. She looked down at the yellow bundle lying beside her chair but didn't pick it up. Leaving the lamp off she sat down, stared into the nothingness and listened to their lies. Year after year they told the same old stories. Eventually they'd become so stretched and warped and twisted that she could no longer trace them back to the morsels of truth that had inspired them in the first place.

Now, as the stories grew thin, the talk turned to politics, as it always did as the evening wore on into the early dawn. Bobby, being a few drinks ahead started the ranting.

"That damn what's-his-name, should just shoot that lying bugger. Guy, he ain't got no chance of making a decent living with those bloody idiots running the country." He reached for his beer, knocked it over sideways, recovered it and continued on. "Know what I'd do? I'd fire all 'dem useless milksops and prissy faggots. Sure as hell, I'd knock some of their soft heads rolling. Bloody kid could run this here country better!"

"Kid could run it? Hell, Bobby, I'd even let Petey have a whack at it."

"I could do it, JJ, sure as hell I could. How's bloody hard kin it be, anyhow? Not hard, jus gotta know what the hell yer doing."

It was nights like this, when she sat vacantly rocking in the dark waiting for the time to pass, that Auntie May's distorted advice would sometimes find its way back to her. She'd sift through it, searching for the nuggets of truth she'd occasionally find there. When she'd been no more than five or six years old, her aunt had told her about the masks, the knowledge terrifying her sleepless. Animals didn't wear masks, Auntie May had patiently explained, didn't need to because animals don't lie. You look in their eyes and they'll tell you their souls. But people, well that was another matter. Some were well and good, but lots were evil as the devil and just as cunning. And it was hard to tell them apart because of the masks.

Frantic, Victoria had appealed to her aunt to tell her how she could tell who wore the masks, and she'd been told that although it wasn't easy, it could be done.

"You smell them, Victoria. Smell 'em a mile away. Stink like the old outhouse behind the barn. Even worse, the real bad 'uns. But you got to know how to smell for 'em. Not just anyone can tell the bad 'uns 'cause most folks never learnt to smell for 'em when they were kids, and once you're an adult it's too late 'cause your mind's too filled up. But you watch and I'll teach ya."

And she was true to her word, catching Victoria up short as they were approached on the streets by various of the town's inhabitants, sniffing the air like a dog searching for scent. Being by no means a respecter of persons, Auntie May had declared her findings unilaterally and loudly, proclaiming to both the pastor and his wife and the entire bingo hall that they stunk to high heaven. It was shortly after this that she'd been removed to a place with a pleasant name, and a reputation that fell far short of it.

Victoria smiled sadly into the dark room. If only the real world could fall so easily into the parameters Auntie May had defined for her own, but it didn't. So far she'd found no one who was exclusively good or exclusively bad: even John Jr. and Petey, whom she found so easy to vilify, went home to wives and children who loved them. And even Bobby had his reservoirs of decency that spilled over from time to time. A yawn pulled itself from her, and she glanced at the clock, its rigid black fingers pointing with disapproval at the hour. The party was playing out in the next room, the boys having drunk their flimsy backbones out of their bottles, had now almost finished solving the woes of the world with their collective wisdom. Finally, as she waited half asleep in her chair, the booze ran dry and the talk ran out. John Jr., left with nothing to conquer, rummaged for his keys and started for the door, sweeping Peter along behind him.

"See ya Monday, Bobby," he slurred as he and his tail tottered through the porch and out the door.

Silence answered him as Victoria cut the music, an empty quiet soaking its way through the trailer. Bobby had disintegrated into an inebriated lump across the kitchen table, a half-empty whiskey still in his hand. The old argument started up outside.

"Get outta here, ya stupid bugger. Ya ain't driving my friggin' truck."

"Just let me drive, JJ," Sam said evenly. "You can hardly even walk."

"I can bloody walk. Where the hell's my keys? Give me back my keys or I'll kick your ass."

"I don't have your keys. You put them in your pocket."

"I know where I put the frickin' things."

"Let me drive, JJ. Come on, don't be—"

"Petey, where the hell are you?"

"I'm taking a piss, whadda ya want?"

"This stupid Injun thinks he can drive better'n me. What the hell you think 'bout that?"

"Well hell . . . you ain't got us killed yet, JJ, that's gotta say something."

"I'll tell you what it says. It says I can drive drunk ten times better than he can drive sober. That's what it says."

"All right, JJ. You drive then, but go slow. And give me a minute, will you? I want to help Vic get Bobby into bed."

"Ya, sure, more like ya want to help put 'toria to bed, ain't it, huh? Huh, Sam, ain't it?" Peter's nasally taunt jabbed into the air but was ignored as Sam slipped off his boots and returned back inside the trailer.

In a ritual that had been performed many times before, Victoria pulled back the sheets as Sam helped Bobby, with a shepherd's tenderness, onto the bed. Together they silently worked off his jeans and shirt, then Sam turned off the light. Through the semidarkness he looked down at her.

"Hey. Thanks for the sandwich, Vic."

He dug deep into his pocket, pulled out a tiny, carved figurine and handed it to her. She felt its smooth patina. It was a wolf, head raised, howling to the moon.

"Thank you, Sam, it's beautiful," she whispered. "Thanks for helping me with Bobby again, too."

Sam looked at her, shrugged, then quietly added, "I . . . uh, I think your hair looks real nice like that."

Victoria's smile was sliced short by the angry blast of a horn followed by John Jr.'s loud threats about things she no longer heard. Sam's mismatched eyes flicked to the door then back to hers, his face struggling to release the words that grasped around his heart. John Jr. and Peter were both bellowing now, joined by the resident coyotes that'd joined in the diatribe. Twice his soft lips parted, but no words would venture forth and he finally just committed to a whispered good night and left.

Hovering beside the bed she listened as the roar of the truck melted into silence. Placing the wolf figurine on her bedside table, nestled among the other carvings Sam had given her over the years, she wrapped her arms around herself as if to hold the embrace of his kind words. Eventually, the cold laid claim to her, and she shed the skin of her clothing onto the floor and carefully slid into bed. She drew shallow breaths, laid stone still, not wishing to arouse the behemoth snoring beside her.

Luck was not to be hers tonight, however, and a rough sweaty paw groped blindly over her. Her face contorted with disgust as his hand found its way to her breasts. With a heavy grunt, he mustered the energy to hoist his hot, flaccid body on top of her ice-cold one, pressing the breath from her. She was thankful for the warmth, nothing else. His face within inches of hers, stole her breath as it rushed from her lungs, but still he did not look at her. His eyes were drawn into narrow black slits that blocked out his reality while traitorous twitches revealed the fantasy playing in his mind. His thick flesh spread out over her, his labored huffing fouling her air, so she twisted her head aside as far as she could with her body trapped beneath him. She couldn't breathe, but it didn't matter. She held her breath. Counting. Counting silently to herself, coaching her-self, *36 . . . 37 . . . 38. Hang on, hang on. Count, count. It'll be over soon.*

When they had first married, before she'd understood how things were going to be, she had moved and wriggled to let him know that there was still life left in the corpse beneath him, but she'd soon understood that it was an unnecessary, unwelcome intrusion. Slowly the pulsing faded to a rhythmic snoring, his body draping hers like death. Revolted, she realized he'd not been able to relieve himself but had succumbed to the alcohol poison-ing his brain and paralyzing his body. Anger dove out of her as she struggled to roll him off. A rancid rush of putrid air erupted from his gaping mouth as he rolled over, belched, and again began to snore. Sightless hands led her through the black hallway into the bathroom. Flipping on the light, she leaned against the door as the tiny cubicle tilted and spun beneath her. The acrid stench of urine crawled into her nostrils, her knees buckling her onto the floor as a wrenching eruption exhumed the contents of her stomach into the waiting bowl.

~ Chapter 8 ~

Rose arrived early the next afternoon, bearing a plate full of peanut butter cookies and flanked on all sides by her three children freshly starched and pressed from their morning at church. Rose had no religious inclinations, scoffed at half of what was taught there, but still felt it was her moral duty to instill in her children a healthy fear of God. That, and the fact that she found a good two-thirds of her customers there, attributed to her continued attendance even now that Steve, who'd always been a faithful churchgoer, had vaporized, and the children complained as vehemently as they dared each and every Sunday morning.

The girls, born in a rapid-fire succession that didn't quite span three years, were absolutely dutiful toward their mother but seemed a constant source of complaints for their teachers at school. Bullying and stealing lunches were occasional misdemeanors leveled against them. The biggest concern brought continually to Rose's attention, however, was their propensity for lying. Yet at home they were very good children, obeying their mother with a swiftness and respect that Rose's very presence seemed to demand, and receive, from almost everyone.

Victoria was unsure about her relationship with Rose at first, crushed under her biting criticism one time only to be restored gently on the wing of a compliment the next. But as time wore on, she began to appreciate Rose's fussing concern for her, accepting her bossiness much like one would with an older sister. Eventually, she found herself seeking Rose's company more and more; her words of reprimand offset so remarkably by her moments of kindness that Victoria would end up feeling somehow indebted to her. And, however distressing the relationship proved to be at times, Victoria knew by bare instinct that Rose was one person who'd make a far better friend than an enemy, someone you felt privileged to have on your side.

Rose handed the plate to Jennifer-Ann, her eldest, and surveyed from above as the three children presented the cookies to Victoria with clear, distinct, hand-lettered sentences that ran automatic from their mouths as if well rehearsed. She accepted the gift, fluttered gracious nonsense over the girls and wished they'd scatter off to the television. But they stood, vacant eyes placed mistakenly in cherub faces, boring into her as if they could see straight through, waiting for their mother's note of dismissal. They'd have been cute children if one discounted the condescension in their eyes. She tried to like them but found she could only accomplish this from a distance. Up close they made her feel wary.

Presently Rose clicked her tongue, flicked her head and the children turned as one and walked into the living room, where cartoon voices sprung to life and restored a sense of normality. The visits had become a regular event ever since Rose's television had quit working, and she'd promised the girls she'd drive out to the trailer for a quick visit while they watched their Sunday afternoon cartoons. Victoria settled into making tea, placing two steaming mugfuls on the table as Rose began the process of disrobing. Her penchant for display fascinated Victoria; she stood and observed as Rose unraveled from a brilliant cocoon of colors: turquoise cloak, two layers of boldly striped sweaters and a magenta scarf, all of which she piled onto an empty chair, creating the illusion of a third person at the table. Finally stripped down to her classic black turtleneck and jeans, she joined Victoria at the table and picked up a cookie to go with her tea.

"Poker night, huh?" She flashed her eyes at the pile of empties still sitting on the counter beside a stack of clean dishes.

"Oh, ya. I'd asked Bobby to take them out to the shed. Guess he forgot."

"Bobby would forget his head if it wasn't screwed on. He get your car fixed yet?"

"Not yet. This week though, I hope."

"That's what you said last week."

"I know, but he's been busy. And it took longer to get the part he needed, too," Victoria defended, even though her own mind had cursed him many times for what she knew was nothing more than his procrastination. His procrastination plus his inability to say no to the various calls he'd received requesting his help. The weeks since he'd dragged the car home passed on the back of his excuses—each one lamer than the one before—until what he'd initially said would be a one-hour job had expanded into a full day. Her requests that he fix it now seemed to him like a huge infraction of his time.

"So what's he expect you to do, stay stuck out here all winter?"

"No, he'll get it fixed. Probably this week." She sipped her tea. "How's work going? Keeping busy?"

"Work? Oh, well it's going, but barely. I don't think I'm going to keep doing it for much longer. I've just about had it with mending seams for all those old cows. You'd think they'd take a hint and quit filling their fat faces all the time." She took a bite from her cookie. "You got it easy that way, Vic. I guess if you're willing to put up with him, anyhow. Be a hell of a lot simpler. No way I could do it though. Pride's worth more to me, I guess." She sipped her tea, breathing the steam away with her nostrils, slashing the rim of the mug a rich burgundy.

Victoria felt the impact of the words, stiffened and resolved to ignore them and drink her tea. But irritation pushed itself free from her before she could raise the mug to her mouth.

"What do you mean by that?"

"By what?"

"That you have more pride than me." She'd committed herself now, suffocated anger arriving hand in hand with indignation.

"I didn't say that."

"What, then?"

"I said my pride is worth more to me. Obviously it is. Look at what you've sacrificed."

"What do you mean, Rose? I haven't sacrificed that much. Bobby's had a hard time keeping the farm going, but he feels it will do better now. It's been a—"

"Oh, come on, Vic. Get real! He's been rattling that same old chain ever since I've known him and nothing has changed yet."

The opposite of most people, who raise their voices when vexed, Rose lowered hers into a husky growl that forced her listener to pay close attention to catch each word rather than half listening while they arranged their next objection. Because of this attribute, she invariably led the conversation while the other party stumbled along to keep up.

"You must get tired of it, hey? I mean, it must be embarrassing sometimes." She looked Victoria in the eye, prepared to debate anything that she would deem a less than honest answer. Victoria tried for diversion.

"I'm not sure what you mean, Rose. Sure, I'd like a nicer place—"

"That's not what I mean."

"What do you mean, then?" she blurted, even though she desperately did not want to know. But Rose, having forced the question, now felt the only decent thing to do as a friend would be to answer it honestly.

"Well, just with the whole town knowing, it's got to be pretty humiliating for you. I don't know how you put up with it."

"Put up with what?"

Rose paused her second cookie mid-bite. She assessed Victoria's face curiously, then laughed. "Come on, Vic. Other people might fall for that, but don't expect me to believe you're that stupid. Jenny! Turn it down!" she hollered into the living room, where Woody Woodpecker had careened upward several decibels, his ricocheting laughter driving Rose's words into Victoria's head.

As sure as Rose was, this time she was wrong. She was that stupid, had no idea what Rose was alluding to. Her body felt as if it had abandoned her and her mind floated randomly, aware she was talking and breathing but without understanding how. Taking in her friend's waxen image, the drifting nonsense of her reply, Rose's features grew softer.

"You did know, Vic, didn't you? I mean everyone seems to, I thought for sure—"

"I knew, Rose. Of course I know. Only an idiot wouldn't know," she bluffed, fastened shaky hands around her cup but didn't dare lift it. "Doesn't matter to me, I couldn't care less what the jerk does. I've got plans. I won't be hanging around here forever."

"Yeah, I was sure you knew. Pretty common knowledge around town. You going to want some more tea? Hmm. See you finally got yourself a new kettle. About time. Your old one looked like someone kicked the crap out of it." Rose attempted unsuccessfully to read Victoria's averted face as she checked the water in the kettle and turned the burner on high.

"So. You've got plans. Good for you, Vic. I knew you would."

"Yeah, I've got plans," she agreed, almost believing herself.

"So, what are they?" Rose sat down enthusiastically, as if ready to partake in a verbal feast.

Victoria's mind scrambled.

"Come on, Vic, you can trust me to keep my mouth shut. You know that. Do they happen to include that artist guy?"

Victoria nodded. She didn't know why, but in having to hatch this impromptu plan Elliot seemed an ideal component. Just including his name felt like a small vengeance against whatever it was Bobby had done. "He thinks I should open a dance studio. He even offered to help me."

"I knew it! I knew there was something you weren't telling me," Rose said emphatically, jumping up to silence the kettle.

"Tell me more. Are you sleeping with him? You are, aren't you! Why didn't you tell me?"

Panicked, Victoria attempted to return the conversation back to reality. "No Rose, I'm not sleeping with him. We're just friends," she said sharply, but a self-conscious smile sabotaged the words and whet Rose's appetite for more.

"Yeah, right. Come on, tell me more." She settled back into her chair with her mug of tea and waited expectantly.

But there was no more to tell: Victoria was painfully aware that the part already told was more fabrication than fact. Fearful it would find its way from Rose's lips to Elliot's ears, she tried to think of some way she could reverse the order of what she'd done. A giggle, partly suppressed, reached them from the living room, which, she now noticed, had grown unnaturally quiet, Sunday afternoon cartoons having been shifted to a low, low volume.

"Rose! Do you think the kids—?"

"No." Rose waved burgundy-dipped fingers. "Don't worry about them, they don't pay any attention to us." And then to prove it she yelled into the living room. "Hey! What are you doing in there?"

"Nothing."

"Don't lie to me."

"I'm not lying."

"Then what are you doing?"

"Just watching TV."

"What're you laughing at then? Woody?"

"No."

"What, then?"

Smothered giggles rolled across the floor.

"Jenny! I asked you a question. What's so funny?"

"Lindsey farted!"

"Did not!" They collapsed under a fit of laughter that should have calmed Victoria's suspicions but had much the opposite effect.

"So. You going to let me in on it?" Rose pressed, her curiosity unsatiated.

"Not much to say, Rose. We're not even friends, really. God, I'm still married, Rose, can't forget that."

"Haw! Yes, I can. And you sure as hell should."

"Not just something I can forget, Rose. I'm sort of committed."

"Yeah, well, that's nice in theory, Cinderella, but what are you really committed to? Bobby? The marriage? Sounds like a good way to end up being committed to the loony bin! What the hell's a marriage, anyhow? A word? A truce? Half the time it's nothing more than a bloody lie. Just like your ring. Wasn't that a lovely way to start your life together?"

Her wedding ring had been a contentious issue from the start. Rumors had sprung up immediately after their engagement that the ring Bobby had flourished on her was the same one he'd bought for Diana. Bobby denied it vehemently, saying it was similar but not the same one. Three days before the wedding, however, Pearl Bentley had announced to Victoria and the rest of the café that she knew full well it was the same ring. She'd been in the pawn shop when he'd come in to sell it; upon hearing he'd only recover less than half of its value, he had abruptly changed his mind and stormed out, calling the shop owner a friggin' crooked kraut. Victoria moved her hands from the table as the sway of the conversation directed Rose's eyes toward them, but it was too late.

"Vic! What on earth happened to your hands? They look terrible."

"Oh, nothing. I uh, I used some cleaner without wearing gloves. Stupid, hey?"

"Yeah, really. What the hell was it, acid? Let me see."

Reluctantly Victoria slid her hands over the table where Rose inspected them and then yelled to the kids.

"Come here girls, I want you to see something. Jenny, Jessica, Lindsey! Come look at this. See what your silly Auntie Vic did? She didn't read the instructions and look what happened to her hands. Don't they look awful? You want your hands to look like that?"

Curling up their faces, the three shook their ringlets vigorously, then stared at Victoria as if her stupidity was of a considerable and possibly irredeemable depth.

"And what should Auntie Vic have done so her hands didn't end up so yucky?"

The two younger girls looked up at their sister, who glanced smugly at Victoria then delivered their answer, her oversized teeth gleaming as she snapped out the simple words.

"Worn rubber gloves."

"That's right. And I'll bet Auntie will remember to read the directions next time, don't you?"

Three heads nodded dubiously. She was not their aunt, but Rose felt it was disrespectful for children to address adults by their first names and insisted that they call her that. Victoria herself would have preferred Mrs. Lackey, but Rose deemed that far too rigid. She felt the girls would benefit from some sense of family, her own nonexistent and any contact with Steve's barred at her behest.

"Your show over? Okay then, get your coats and give Auntie a kiss goodbye. I've got things to do today."

The kids scrambled into their coats, kisses were mutually endured and Rose filed the girls out the door toward the car.

"I'll call you later," Rose winked. "For the rest of the story."

"No story to tell."

"We'll see. Talk to you later."

She wasn't sorry to see Rose's car fade into the distance, leaving her alone with her thoughts. The day was brilliant. Crisp with a hint of winter yet still held in autumn's warm hand. An exuberant celebration of color decorated the hills, garlands of red and gold running like ribbons through the black-green spruce in a glorious farewell to fall's fading days.

Pulling a sweatshirt on, Victoria crossed the rough patch of burnt grass that suggested a yard and made her way over to a slanting gray hovel that doubled for a feed shed. One rusty hinge hung valiantly onto the rough plank door, complaining bitterly as she unhooked the latch and dragged it open. Taking one step into its musty interior, she stopped and waited as the thick blackness transposed the interior first into vague images and finally into muted, though identifiable items.

Reaching down, she picked up the pitchfork that lay in front of her feet, thrown carelessly into the shed during someone's haste. Setting it securely out of harm's way, she scraped the lid off the grain barrel. She rummaged for the dented, lidless coffee can within it and scooped it deep, feeling with pleasure the silky smooth grains as they ran over her hands, the nutty fragrance rising up and soothing her like a balm. It was a strange place to find solace, here among the broken cast-offs of life, sitting quiet in the company of her hens, but it was here in this humble place that life seemed to be, for her, most sane.

She started at a noise behind her, twisting quickly to correspond the sharp snap with its source, but the contents of the shed slumped quietly against the creosote-stained walls. Twists of frayed, greasy rope hung from the solid pine beams down to the gray-powdered floor; here and there a piece of long-forgotten treasure was caught up in their sinewy arms. Two ropes, their bottom halves twisted around each other like lanky legs, swayed in the sketchy shadows. Her eyes strained into the dark corners, cautiously sifting through the humps and piles of misshapen junk, sorting fact from fiction in her mind. Slivers of light seeped in from random cracks in the old wood, cutting off the shadows and distorting her view, rearranging stovepipe into necks, gunnysacks into faces. Willing her heart to be still, she fixed her eyes on the door and listened to the quiet straining through her ears. There was no sound. But what she could not hear, could not see, she could definitely feel, its presence riveting her spine in fear. The pitchfork stood not two steps from her, and setting the coffee can softly back into the barrel of grain, she traversed the distance on the silent, fluid step of a dancer and wrapped both hands tightly around its worn handle. Brandishing it before her like a lance, she stepped toward the ropes, grasping one for balance as she stretched forward on tiptoes, peering as far as she dared into the maze of machine parts, worn-out tires, miniature mountains of rusty bolts and greasy, moth-eaten piles of rotting burlap.

Pressing gently, she nudged the sacks, and receiving no reaction, nudged them harder, the spiky tines of the pitchfork sinking into the soft folds. Listening harder, she again turned to inspect the darkness behind her. Most people, with their ill-defined sense of knowing, would have satisfied themselves already that they were a victim of their own paranoia, laughed to make themselves feel braver and rushed off to the safety of other humans. But Victoria, having spent an inordinate amount of time in her own company, knew instinctively when she was not alone, and she knew beyond a doubt she was not alone now.

A scraping, muffled yet frantic, pulled her eyes back toward the corner, the source of the sound now clearly masked under the stack of burlap. Scarcely allowing a breath, she turned toward them, the pitchfork poised in defense as images of scratching clawed hands and Mrs. Spiller's half-decayed face raged in her mind. Terrified the deranged hag would burst upon her at any moment, she gripped the handle tighter, attempted futilely to steady her voice and ordered too loudly.

"Who's there? Come out of there right now before you get a pitchfork in your guts."

Quietness met her order, a billion particles of dust rising lazily in a shaft of light beside her.

"I mean it. Get the hell out of there."

Her voice rose, a quaver giving away her position and causing her to react with an intensity that she hoped would suffice to cover it.

"Get out!"

She jabbed into the pile sharply, transforming it into a demonic thrash of motion as a blur flew from it, chased by the echo of its own scream. Flinging herself backward, she struck her head hard against a broken pulley, leaving her weapon impaled in the side of the sacks.

"Shit! Shit! You stupid damn thing. Scared the bloody hell out of me. Shit!" she exploded again, a shudder escaping up her body and forcing the words out.

The cat, a barn-born survivor, crouched low in the shadows of a motor-less washing machine as they eyed each other warily. Not wild in the literal sense of the word, the dozen or so cats that lived around the property were, however, about as close to it as a domestic animal could get. She had always liked cats, enjoyed their self-possessed arrogance, but Bobby seemed to find in it a personal statement of rebuke. Cats were good for one thing and one thing only. He'd established that right from the beginning when he forbade her two cats from joining her in her new home, saying he'd married her, not her damn pets. Either her parents could keep them, or she could give them away. Her mother had kept them, but Victoria missed having their purring security curled up in her lap when she sat alone through somber winter days. To compensate, she'd attempted to tame the barn cats, giving up quickly on the older ones but finding success among the kittens, patiently coaxing their trust from them. Turned out it was a trust abused in the end; she'd spent sleepless nights begging herself for forgiveness after Bobby and his friends decided the population was getting out of hand and arrived one day with hungry dogs and shotguns, the curious kittens making an amusing start to the rally.

The cat had finished its assessment, deemed her a minimal threat and had slunk back to its activities. Moving slowly but not stealthily, it allowed her approach as she pressed her cheek against the wall and slid her eyes down between the sacks and the barrel to a soft pocket of rags where she saw what had aroused the cat's killer instincts in the first place. A nest, plush with insulation, wriggled with a mass of sightless baby mice, like pink-skinned maggots, bumping around in a touch-and-feel search for sustenance. Revulsion clamped her stomach. Mice were a continual problem on the farm; even with a barn full of cats, their copious breeding program seemed to keep them in a plentiful supply.

Disgusted with her discovery, the thought of what she had to do with it revolted her even more. Parking her brain in neutral, she grabbed the barrel with both arms and slowly rocked it away from the wall, undermining the nest's defenses and exposing it for the cat, who pounced happily, delivering a quick destruction that, although she could not hear, she could still feel as she imagined carnivorous teeth crunching through soft skulls. Wiping her hands on her jeans, even though they had not actually been tainted by the murder, she grabbed her can of grain and stepped back into the sunshine. She paused with blinking eyes to adapt to its brightness, then creaked the door back into place.

A skittish fluster of motion drew her eyes toward the chicken pen, where her hen Tilley performed a jerky dance outside the wire enclosure. Adept at escaping the structure, once having done so, the little banty would pace endlessly and unsuccessfully for hours attempting to find her way back in. Victoria smiled, scooped out a handful of grain and rolled her thumb over the burnished gold husks raining hundreds of tiny pieces onto the ground by her feet. Tilley stopped statue still, cocked her head then scampered over and pecked greedily at the spilled morsels. Victoria stroked a finger over the cool, silky back then gathered the chicken up into both arms and sat down against the feed shed. The bird offered no resistance, held no fear as Victoria had hatched her out from an egg three years previously and from the beginning had nestled her almost daily in her arms. Tilley relaxed against her chest, translucent amber eyes blinking once, twice and then shut.

Victoria pulled in a deep breath, shifted her position slightly and, with care not to disturb the resting hen, closed her eyes. She let the breeze carry her thoughts back over the day's conversation. In the distance, she could hear the faint, plaintive honking of Canada geese, which had again made their annual pilgrimage to the valley to glean its fields. She wondered about the transgressions Rose had alluded to. She couldn't imagine Bobby being unfaithful. Sure, he talked big when he got drunk. All the boys did. But that's all she'd ever thought of it—just drunken talk. Perhaps her assumptions had been wrong. The force of the hurt that accompanied this revelation both surprised and annoyed her in unison. A stream of familiar faces drifted in front of her: blond-brained bartenders and unhappy housewives not unlike herself. She cautioned herself against jumping to conclusions. Rose's facts were often far from infallible, and Hinckly itself was well versed in misconstruing and distorting innocent events. But she had to concede the possibility of an affair, Bobby having the perfect situation in which to pull one off. A wife who seldom accompanied him anywhere, half the time stranded at home waiting for him to arrive, the other half waiting for him to leave.

She was beginning to feel cramped, the warmth of the hen and the long rays of the sun making her sweat beneath Bobby's sweatshirt, but she sat still and endured her discomfort, unwilling to alter her position and disturb the sleeping Tilley. Brushing her lips over the banty's glossy head, she kissed it lightly and smiled. Since she was not permitted to have a conventional pet, the bird had in many ways, become like a treasured friend, providing the calm comfort of another beating heart on lost and lonely days. Bobby laughed at her protective attachment toward the hen, more than a little embarrassed that others might find out his wife had made a pet out of a dumb bird. But eventually he left her alone and more or less forgot about it. And besides, the chickens were useful to him, providing eggs, or at least used to until about a month ago when for some reason they had quit laying. Victoria had taken care that he didn't find out, though, transferring a weekly dozen from the store into her egg basket.

Tipping her head back against the shed, her eyes rolled across buckskin fields, searching for the farm machine that wearily droned in the distance as it earned its keep. She contemplated briefly whether she should confront Bobby about what she'd heard, then nullified the thought before it was even finished. Whether the words were all true or only partially, he would deny it either way. And then he'd spin the conversation and berate her for being stupid enough to believe Hinckly's gossip when she herself knew the kind of bullshit it could pull from the sludge of its suspicious minds. And probably he'd be right. But still she ran over the last few weeks, mentally flagging late nights and missed meals that grew in importance when weighed in this new light. Late nights and missed meals that had all been explained away with the excuse of helping JJ with his latest car. With perhaps five absences duly noted, she wondered about him no more and let her thoughts slide to Elliot.

True, she hadn't seen him since the day he'd offered her a ride home, but it was also true that her mind had been filled with little else. After the first week, she'd had to forbid herself from letting his name cross her lips, finding it constantly pushing into every conversation, Bobby scowling at the mere mention of it. Not because he suspected anything, but rather because he didn't feel any priss-ass artist from the city had anything worth saying, much less repeating. Now, as she searched her fading memory for his face, the sound of his voice, she knew she had to see him again. Not that it could go anywhere, lead into anything beyond an affair of the mind. She'd already determined that much. Elliot moved through life, someone who coveted his freedom as much as his next breath. Someone who did not want, could not live with the oppressions of responsibility, duty, dependents—the oppressions realized in someone like herself. And she, acrid as the thought was, had to admit that Bobby's explosive insecurity hung an invisible noose not only around his own neck but around hers as well. If she was very careful, she could still spend time with Elliot. Talk and laugh and linger. What would it hurt, really? She would just play a little bit. Have fun and loosen up like Elliot had said. Not that she could ever let it lead to an affair. She was just so mortally weary of compressing her every feeling.

A vague sound touched her subconscious and drew itself forward into her ear. Straining to hear it, she closed her eyes and held her breath, but it eluded her with faintness. Turning her head slightly toward the trailer, she caught it and jumped up, Tilley scrambling for balance with a perturbed flapping of wings as Victoria flung open the pen door and set her in.

Sure the insistent ranting would quit just before she reached it, she flew into the trailer and literally fell onto the phone, seizing the receiver in her hand.

"Hi! Hello. Still there?"

A fuzzy static answered back.

"Hello . . . anyone there?"

Nothing. Dropping onto the floor, she let the receiver slide into her lap, disappointed she'd missed the call. Spending the better part of most days alone in the trailer, she relished the impromptu interruptions of a phone call, enjoying the company of another human's voice. Flipping the receiver upside-right, she reluctantly began to replace it on the cradle when an unintelligible mumbling spilled out. Instantly she had it back to her ear.

"Hi! Sorry, I didn't think you were still there—"

Her voice trailed off as she waited for a response to her words that didn't come.

"Rose?" Rose had said she was going to call. She tried again. "Rose, is that you? We seem to have a bad connection. I'll hang up and you can try again, okay?"

Static answered her back as she pressed the hard smoothness of the receiver against her cheek listening intently for any identifiable sound, then abruptly the noise quit.

"Oh there, that's better," she offered, but still her words were met with a strange silence. "Hello? Hello, can you hear me now?"

Motionless, she listened carefully. The line was not dead. A thin breath was lightly perceptible on the other end: someone was holding their receiver close, listening to her. Annoyance closed over her. Stupid kids and their stupid pranks. She again went to disconnect, and again, just before she severed the connection, a muffled voice emanated into the room. Raising the phone once more to her ear, she tried again.

"Look, can I—"

A gravely voice thick with disguise cut her off along with the renewed static, and she had to listen intently to decipher the words spoken.

"What? What did you say?" She was answered by a soft click.

Electricity sizzled through her as she set the telephone back in place and sat staring at it. Her mind reeled in a dizzy attempt to understand what had just transpired. Who would do such a thing? Say such a thing? What sort of silly prank was that, to phone someone in the middle of the day and say such a thing? She raised herself slowly onto a chair and sat stiffly staring at the demure black box, which suddenly seemed to possess gargantuan proportions. She did not move, did not blink, the silence pounding in her head. She waited, terrified it might ring again. Terrified it might not.

She sat that way for five minutes or fifty, she couldn't tell, but eventually she reasoned that whoever had called was not going to do so again. She closed her eyes and attempted to resurrect the words, chipped and broken as she'd received them. Only a few stood out undeniably, and these she gathered up, savored, and let flow freely over her before she gathered them up again. A truant smile engaged her and she stroked her face lightly with her fingertips, wondering at the words that had been whispered into her, recalling them over and over: "I think you're beautiful."

Disbelief bolted out and pounded on her heart. What if the call had been a joke? A cruel joke. Probably right now someone lay laughing at her naiveté, amused by her foolishness. She sprang up through the porch and closed the door, the mirror catching her as she whisked by. Yes. That's all it had been. Someone's idea of fun. Or a wrong number. She seized upon this thought, wanting to believe the words spoken had been true; she'd been the victim of nothing more invasive than a wrong number, a simple wrong number. But even this thought, although better, caused disappointment to flood through her. She didn't want the call to be meant for someone else. She wanted the words to be hers.

She grabbed a chair, hurled it against the pressboard cupboards, delivering a satisfying gash across their tired brown faces.

Seizing it again, she raised it up, wanting to send it flying through the window with every frustrated ounce of strength that flowed through her. Catching herself, knowing that she could never explain such an occurrence to Bobby, she sat it back down, biting her lip until an appeasement of blood tasted on her tongue. The phone rang, jangled fiercely against her nerves. Paralyzed, she looked at it, hesitated, then lifted it quietly to her ear.

"Hello?"

Silence met her.

"Hello?" she repeated louder, a little more desperate.

"Oh, hi Vic. Sorry about that. Just had to grab something. So anyhow, Bobby home yet or do you have time to talk?"

"Oh, Rose! Hi. I wasn't expecting it to be you."

"You sound disappointed, who *were* you expecting it to be?"

"Oh, I don't know. Not anyone really. Did you get all your stuff done?"

"Almost. I have to have that Mrs. Miller's seam fixed by tomorrow, and I still have two rows of potatoes to dig. I think I'll get the kids to do them tomorrow, getting dark already. I hate it when the days get shorter, don't you?"

"Yeah."

"What's the matter?"

"Nothing. Why?"

"I don't know. You sound upset. I didn't upset you by what I said, did I?"

"No, it's not that. I just . . . I just had a really strange call before, that's all."

"Really? How strange?"

"I don't know. I guess it wasn't that strange. Probably just a wrong number."

"What did they say?"

"Oh. Well, I couldn't really tell for sure. The line wasn't very clear and—"

"Who'd it sound like? Anyone you know?" Rose barged in, eager to get on with the details.

"Not really. I couldn't tell. I think maybe he was disguising his voice or something."

"So it was a guy?"

"Yeah, I think so. Like I said, it was hard to hear."

"Well, what did he say? You must have heard some of what he said."

"Not very much. Just a few words . . . and I'm not even sure I got those straight. There was a lot of noise on the line."

"Well, what do you think he said?"

"I don't know, it was too hard to tell for sure," Victoria hedged, suddenly unsure herself if she'd actually heard the words or just imagined them out of the garble. "I think it was just a wrong number anyhow."

"Why do you think that?"

Victoria hesitated, feeling herself being backed very adroitly into a corner she knew she didn't want to be backed into.

"Was it something he said? It was, wasn't it? Come on Vic, tell me."

"Well, okay, but I'm not even sure I heard it right. I probably didn't. I think he was saying something about thinking someone was beautiful . . . or something like that."

"Thinking who was beautiful?"

"I don't know, whoever he thought he was talking to I guess."

"Well, maybe he thought he was talking to you. That thought ever occur to you, Vic?"

"Yeah right Rose, not likely. I'm pretty sure it was just a wrong number. The line was bad, could have even been long distance."

"Hey, maybe it was that Elliot guy."

"No, Rose. It wasn't Elliot. It wasn't anyone. Anyhow, forget it. It's not a big deal. Just scared me a little bit, being out here all by myself and getting a call like that." She glanced at the darkening windows and flipped on the light.

"Bet it was him. Maybe he's out of town somewhere, sitting in his hotel room all lonely, finally works up his courage, gives you a call—"

Victoria rolled her eyes and laughed as she listened to her friend pick pieces out of the air and create a suitable scenario.

"Rose, forget it. It wasn't Elliot, and besides I can't quite imagine him having to sit around working up his courage. He's not exactly lacking in the self-esteem department."

"No? Well what department is he lacking in then?" Rose asked laughing, flipping the conversation back to Elliot before Victoria realized it.

"None that I know of."

"Really? And which ones do you know of?"

"Rose! We're not talking about him."

"Why not?"

"Because there's nothing to say."

"I hear your words, Vic, but I'm not believing them."

"Rose, why are you so stuck on me liking this guy?"

"Oh, well let me see. Because he's good-looking, has a great body, obviously has some bucks and he's nice. Oh, yeah, and also because your husband is a selfish jerk who treats you badly."

Victoria laughed again as Rose ticked through her list. "Okay. I can't argue with most of that. But it's not going to happen. Why don't you go for him if you think he's so fascinating?"

"Love to, darling, but there's one fatal flaw."

"What's that?"

"Too much bohemian blood in his veins. Can't tie a guy like that down with three kids and a dog."

"He has a dog."

"Maybe so, but you watch. When the time comes for him to fly, the pets will be given away to the neighbors and he'll be gone. Can't very well do that with kids."

"You think so, Rose? You think he'll just up and go one day?" She knew Rose's words were an echo of what Elliot himself had told her, but still she resisted them. They didn't fit with what she wanted to believe.

"Absolutely. Leave just as suddenly as he arrived. He doesn't belong here; you know that. He knows it, too. Just kind of playing the farm life thing for a while and then on to something new. That's why I think you'd better just hang on and talk to him next time he calls."

"Rose. It wasn't him. Really. I'm sure of it. It wasn't a normal call; it was sort of creepy. Like whoever it was was just sitting there listening to me most of the time. Kind of scary, actually."

"Yeah, well, trust me, Vic, people are weird. You never know how they might get their kicks. Or maybe he was just unsure how you'd react, or maybe he just wanted to be sure it was you on the phone and not Bobby. Who knows? Next time just talk to him and find out."

"Well, I'm sure there won't even be a next—"

"Whoops. Sorry Vic, gotta run. Jenny just dumped the milk. Catch you later."

"Okay, bye, Rose."

Victoria hung up the phone, sat in silence except for the slow, steady hum of the yard light as it threw a patch of yellow onto the ground where Bobby parked his truck. The clock ticked out 6:45. She placed leftovers into the oven to warm and started a bath. Shedding her sweatshirt and jeans into a lumpy pile beside the hamper, she closed her eyes and listened for the familiar rumble of an approaching vehicle. Hearing nothing, she disappeared down the hall and into the bedroom. Leaning against a stack of unread mail-order books, a lopsided chair buried under five years of household procrastination blocked her entry into the left half of the closet. There a myriad of obsolete clothes with washed-away patterns hung hidden from Bobby's view so he would no longer wear them. Edging the chair off to one side, she slid the door open and began to flip through the shirts and pants, her hands feeling their way to the back of the closet. She wondered at how quickly the years had stolen by since she'd first hung the dress up, never dreaming it would remain buried for the next twenty years. Her fingers found it first, dangling in the gauzy film that encased it. She pulled it from the closet, tore away the plastic and twirled it lightly on the hanger, the brilliant green glowing vitality into the room.

She slipped it on, smiling as she once again felt the perfection of its silky caress. Studying herself in the closet door mirror, she twisted to survey her backside, the skirt swishing playfully around her thighs as she inspected first from one side and then the other. Running her hands along the gentle taper of her waist she found the dress still fit with ease, was if anything a shadow too big. Watching the mimic of her reflection, she performed well-rehearsed movements, her limbs remembering themselves in the confident elegance of the dance and responding with grace. Slowly, she twirled herself to a stop, dropped her head and raised her eyes coquettishly to assess the vision she created and smiled, pleased to see the dress still presented her with the elusive charm of provocative innocence.

Stepping lightly across the unmade bed, she slunk into the living room on a sweeping step, her skin and the silk slipping against each other igniting her as she went. Twisting her hair on top of her head, she held it there with one hand as she moved to the motion of the music in her mind, the accompanying steps ones from the dance she never performed. She had lived to dance. Loved the feel of appreciative eyes on her as she moved in synchronicity with the music. Flowed across the stage as she lost herself in the passion of her love, becoming not a body moving to the music but a body moved by the music. Stepping carefully in the cramped room, she performed a minuscule version of her routine, remembering rather than executing the full flying leaps and intricate spins. Drawing to a close, she curtsied deeply to herself and favored her audience with a smile. With exquisite balance, she raised herself up on tiptoe and slipped the dress off in a fluid arc, letting it dissolve into a pool around her feet soon joined by a black bra and white panties.

Critically she examined her nakedness in the hollow eyes of the windows, spun a slow pirouette to view herself from all sides. In spite of how she'd come to feel about herself, she had to acknowledge her own image did not bear her out and, although the dynamic strength of her youthful body had left her, its shape had not. Scooping her clothes off the floor, she looked again at her reflection. The uncomfortable realization settled over her that she was also fully visible from outside, and instinctively she covered herself as best she could. Quickly, she crossed over to the porch door. For the first time in almost twenty years she locked it, then retraced her steps back down the hall and into the bathroom.

She twisted off the faucets, the steaming bath scarcely an inch short of overflowing onto the floor. Wiping a blurred swath across the medicine cabinet mirror, she pulled her hair away from her face and gazed openly at herself. She supposed she might be thought beautiful, although the presence of her mother's diminutive mouth overpowered by her father's stark green eyes disqualified her ability to judge herself that way. But her jaw was strong, her cheekbones set on an angular cut, giving the impression of a strength of character she did not feel she possessed. She released her hair and watched as it swung forward crowding her face, the steam forming once again over the mirror slowly fading her out.

Sliding deep into the bath, she smiled as the displaced water swelled up and over the sides. Screw Bobby and his water restrictions. Tonight she was going to pamper herself. Sliding even lower, she closed her eyes and felt the warm lapping of tiny waves against her nipples. She set her thoughts free to run wild and they ran at once to Elliot. She searched back through her memory of the time she'd spent with him, looking for evidence that perhaps he'd heard the rumors of Bobby's alleged unfaithfulness toward her, but nothing presented itself. If he'd been a longtime resident of the valley, he'd have heard for sure, gossip being passed among the locals like colds and flu. But Elliot was still considered an outsider, and as such was kept just outside the most intimate sins of the valley.

The soap in one hand, she raised her left leg upward, admired it and drew it toward her. Elliot was right; she should open a studio. No. She was *going* to open a studio. Her studio. Her very own studio. She would make the suggestion lightly to Bobby this time in order not to upset him. Plant the seed and let it take root. Perhaps, if she went slowly enough, he might even agree to help her get a place set up. Cupping her foot with both hands, she pressed the soap into the hollow of her sole and slid it slowly back and forth in a gentle arc, the motion evoking sensual feelings within her. Gradually she worked the bar over to the top of her foot, massaging her toes and slipping a pinkie deeply between them as she went, slowly spreading them apart until they almost signaled pain. Dropping the soap beneath her, she dipped her leg into the water, found the soap and again began to lather her calf, her knee, her thigh into a bubbly white stocking of silk champagne. Closing her eyes she continued up over the smooth flatness of her stomach, traced a slippery curve over first one breast then the other. Raising the other leg she again began the slippery ascent, the bar of soap settling against her inner thigh where, pressing it tightly against her she slipped it upward and over to the other leg, the pressure catching her with a stifled cry.

The glide of the soap against her skin became Elliot's lips. Her breath, his voice. Her hands, his. His hands that had obsessed her every waking hour for the last few weeks, haunted her dreams, reaching in and drawing her toward nocturnal ecstasy. The hands that materialized before her in the branches of trees stroking the wind, became the caress of her hair as it kissed her neck. She sucked moist air deep inside her, continuing to run the soap firmly and quickly over her body, then froze. Her eyes flashed open as she attempted to reconcile in her mind the unmistakable roar of Bobby's truck coming down the driveway.

~ Chapter 9 ~

They sat silent as the truck grumbled its way toward town, the radio providing the entertainment with sketches of static occasionally interrupted by music. The slate sky stretched tight and serious across the valley, darker clouds threatening at the edges and hinting at more snow. Bobby had been right: it was barely the end of October, winter arriving early and with such severity it made one wonder if the earth could ever again find its way into full bloom.

"Heard Gainer's got himself a new truck. Brand-new '78 Ford. JJ says it's decked right out, got all the bells and whistles. Bet Diana's old man helped him out with it."

He yanked a cigarette from the pack on the dash, lit it angrily then flicked the dead match into the garbage littering the floor. Taking a forceful drag, he expelled it sharply.

"Shit! Bet that dumb bugger's mortgaged right to the bloody nuts. Won't be thinking he's so damn smart once those peckers at the bank start jerking his chain."

He smiled at this thought, paused to savor a couple more squinty-eyed pulls from his smoke then continued airing his complaints.

"Any dumb-ass can drive 'round in a new rig if they're willing to be mortgaged to the hilt. I sure as hell wouldn't do that. No way those crooked buggers gonna think they've got me by the balls. No blee-oody way. Nope. Don't owe a dime on this here truck and that's how it's gonna stay. Man can be damn proud of owning what he owns."

He stamped this declaration with a heavy fist brought down emphatically on the dash, sealing his words with the dusty print. Snatching his red Finning cap off his black curls, he scratched his head then pulled it back on decisively, as if he'd settled the matter.

"Yeah, Gainer ain't near so smart as he thinks. Potlicker'll be kissing ass before he knows what hit him."

He took another drag, harder, longer, and the cigarette flared viciously. A frozen pothole jarred them off balance, breaking away the ash, which exploded softly across the top of his thigh.

"Shit!" He immediately rubbed the ash into the light beige dress pants, where it refused to disappear but rather transformed into an unsightly gray smudge down the length of his femur. "Shit! Damn, useless, faggot pants. Look at that. Just bloody lovely."

Pressing harder, he scrubbed his palm against the mark as if he could, by causing enough friction, reverse the damage done. Checking his progress and seeing none, he abandoned his efforts and returned to his former laments even more irritated, as if his trials were a direct consequence of Tom Gainer's new truck.

"And you know what else? You'll never believe what color that dumb mother bought. Petey says it's this real puke green. Uglier than snot, he says."

Pulling the last bit from his smoke, he tried to open his window to flick it out, but it was stuck, frozen shut. He jammed the butt into the overflowing ashtray, sending several others out onto the floor. A litany of defenses had jumped to her mind as Bobby spoke, but she'd let them slide away. Tom Gainer was by no means dumb, and everyone, including Bobby and his friends, knew the truck had been purchased with the gains of wise dealings and hard work and not on the back of bank credit as Bobby would have wished. But she held her words and ignored his tirade knowing a confrontation with the truth would do little more than enrage him. She didn't want him enraged; she wanted his cooperation. Wanted an answer to the questions that prickled in her mind.

"Bobby, do you . . . do you think I'm . . . beautiful?"

Her voice faltered, hesitated with the words, not sure if she wanted to commit herself to the question, and the roar of the engine and rattle of the truck consumed her soft voice. Bobby, talking around a fresh cigarette stuck in between his dry lips continued on, unaware she'd even spoken.

"Paid way too damn much for it, too. JJ says he could've got that exact same rig for at least a grand cheaper. I betcha—"

"Bobby, I asked you a question."

"What?"

"I asked you a question."

"*What?*"

She shifted her position, uncomfortable to have gained his full attention. She'd become accustomed to their cursory conversations, both of them applying only nominal resources, instinctively knowing each turn in the dialog, filling in their parts as if on cue, thoughts elsewhere and not sharply required. She took a breath and pushed the words out one behind the other before she could hesitate or think about his response. She wanted to know. Felt that since the question had been raised she needed to ascertain the answer. Needed to uncover the caller's motive, which seemed to her more important even than his identity. Had it been merely a prank call or was it possible someone actually felt that way about her?

"Well? Do you?"

"Do I what?"

"You heard me, Bobby. Would you describe me that way?"

"What way?"

"Beautiful." She forced the word out yet again, even though they both knew he was well aware of what she'd said.

He caught the word with a scowl and grunted, uncomfortable at being put on the spot.

"What kind of asinine question is that?"

"It's not asinine. I was just wondering that's all, you never—"

"Don't even bother saying that I never told you that, Vic, 'cause I did and you know it."

"When?"

"I don't know when. I told you lots of times. Ain't my fault if you can't remember."

"I remember once, Bobby. No, twice. But it was a long time ago, before we were even married."

"Yeah, well, you was good looking then."

"Then? You thought I was good looking then?"

"Course I did. Wouldn't have married you if I didn't."

"But what—" she started then stumbled, fiddled with the zipper of her coat. It surprised her, this sudden nervousness in the face of his verdict, having long believed herself immune to his judgment. "Well, what about now?"

"Now?"

She nodded, forced her eyes to hold his face as he lit his cigarette with agitation.

"Right now? This very bloody minute?"

"Well, no, Bobby. Not exactly right now. Just in general. Now that I'm older and everything."

"Now?"

She nodded, her eyes fleeing to her hands, which continued fussing back and forth between her coat zipper and the snap closure on her purse. He looked over at her, slid solid eyes over each feature, a frown wrinkling together his brow as he struggled toward a conclusion. He gave a cursory nod, expelling two bursts of smoke from his nostrils as he did so.

"Yeah. Yeah, I guess you ain't too bad looking yet."

"But, would you say I'm beautiful, Bobby?"

"Blee-oody-hell woman. That's what I just said. Is that not what I just bloody said?"

She could feel his discomfort at being cornered. Recognized his brewing frustration in the bunching of his shoulders, the defensive angle at which he'd set his jaw, the way his hands gripped the wheel and harassed it back and forth.

"Well, why do you think it is you never tell me that?"

"Tell you what?"

She felt foolish. Knew she was pushing beyond his comfort zone, but she continued anyhow, wanting more than anything to hear the words she longed to hear.

"What we were just talking about, Bobby. That you think I still look nice. Why don't you ever tell me that?"

It was too much for him: the pressuring, the cornering, the unfamiliar intimacy of the conversation. Even the irregular scratching of the radio combined to form one massive provocation that flew at his face, sending him into a flailing-armed fit.

"I did tell you! I did! What the hell I got to do, woman, tattoo it across my bloody chest? That make you happy? Huh? Or maybe across my forehead. Yeah, that's what I'll do. Tattoo it straight across friggin' here." He ripped off his cap and knuckled his forehead hard. "Then every time you look at me you'll see it. That be good enough for you, Vic? Huh? That work for you?"

He rattled on over this line of attack, amused with his ingenuity, minuscule beads of sweat working onto his reddened face as he notched his way up through several degrees of intensity.

"Problem with them tattoos is that they don't ever go away. Here you'd be all dried up and wrinkly, and me going round still with this damn tattoo across my bloody forehead. I'll just tell 'em—"

He attempted his speech several times, but his internal image dissolved him into laughter. He laughed across at her, slapped his leg and actually expected her to join him. She sat stiffly, eyes straight ahead unseeing and ignoring while she waited for him to realize his amusement had not been shared.

"Hey! What the hell's picking your ass?"

"Nothing. Just forget it." She tried for flippant, but hurt slipped across the consonants and dripped from the vowels.

"No, I ain't gonna just forget it. You got a problem, I wanna hear about it."

"It's not a problem."

"Yeah, well it feels like a problem to me. Just having a little fun, that's all. Man, you get your pyramid every friggin' day of the month or what? Seems you're always pissy about something."

This snagged her temper, drew her back into the arena. Not because it was true, but because it was not, being both grossly unfair and a reversing of the truth.

"Not true, Bobby. Not true and you know it."

"I do, eh?"

"Well, you should."

"Should I?"

"Yes, you should."

"And why is that?"

"You've been around other guy's wives. You've said yourself you're glad I'm not like most of them."

"I said that?"

"Yes. You did. You know you did, Bobby. You've said it lots."

"Yeah, well I'm glad you ain't like Webber's wife, that's for damn sure. Look what happened to him."

"Webber?"

"Yeah, you know Webber. JJ's cousin—"

"Of course I know Webber, Bobby. What happened to him?"

"Oh, you know his wife leaving him and all. Own bloody fault, though, I'd say, always flashing her around like a big-titted Barbie doll, yakking about her looks and stuff. Right in front of her, too. Sure as hell didn't surprise none of us when the bitch up and left the dumb prick. Run straight back home to her mama like a spoiled kid."

"Bobby, that's not why Melanie left him—"

"That's exactly what it was. Just look where she ended up. Goes down to that fancy-ass college, ain't two months before she's moved in with some old bugger twice her age . . . Dr. what's-his-face. Ain't even a real Dr., just some bloody English teacher. Would've never happened if she hadn't got so hopped up on herself. Still be with Webber minding her own damn business."

"Come on, Bobby. That's not fair. Mel just got caught up in a bad situation."

"Situation? What the hell's this situation crap? Ain't no bloody situation, just a pile of bull-shit gossip."

"How would you know?" she challenged, her mind cautioning her to stop while the gullibility of his words provoked her simmering anger.

"I know. I talked to Webber myself right after she ran off. Poor bugger was in Trappers having a beer because he couldn't stand going home and being all alone again . . . selfish bitch." He angrily dragged a quarter of the life from his cigarette, squinting thickly to protect his eyes.

"Webber. How credible is his story going to be?"

"Sounded good to me. But ain't no one going to expect you girls to take his side. Bunch of bloody victims, every last one of you. Drive a man to drink . . . or have a one-night stand with the ole Enfield."

Victoria flashed him a look. "Not something to joke about, Bobby."

"Who said I was joking?"

"Well, I saw what he did to her."

"Oh, bullshit! Webber told me she was always making up shit just to get people to feel sorry for her. Said she bruised real easy, bumped into a chair and she'd come up with this great big friggin' welt, blame it on him. Was all just bullshit."

"Well, I saw her face that last time, Bobby, looked awful. What did Webber say about that? She throw herself down the stairs?"

"Probably did, the crazy bitch. Wouldn't put it past her. She wasn't all there, Vic. You wouldn't believe the shit Webber says she used to pull."

"No, I'm sure I wouldn't," she said quietly, hoping to put an end to the conversation. She had more questions she needed answers to. Answers that would be found not so much in his words but in his unspoken reactions.

"Well, that's one thing for sure. I pretty much stay out of your way. Probably have an affair and I would never even know."

She placed the words before him, watched intently to perceive the telltale defensive clues that would give her her answer. But his body withheld its information and he, seemingly untouched, scoffed at the idea.

"An affair! Shit, what the hell would I want with an affair? Two women to nag me and spend my money? Not bloody likely." He turned his attention back to his cigarette, french inhaled and blew a couple of jaunty smoke rings into the mirror. "No sir, you're safe on that front, Vic. Least while you still got your looks." It was the best he got to giving a compliment, but she recognized the effort and, feeling the feeble base of a conversation forming, decided to pursue it further.

"You know, I've been thinking. I've been thinking maybe it might be good for me to find something to do other than just help out around the farm."

"Something wrong with just helping out around the farm?" he bristled.

"No," she countered quickly. "I sometimes just think it might be nice to be around other people a little bit more, that's all."

"You talking 'bout getting a job? Ain't no wife of mine needs—"

"No, Bobby. I wasn't thinking about getting a job. Not really. I was more thinking of . . . of . . . of opening a dance studio."

"A dance studio? Absolutely not! Why the hell you digging up that nonsense again, anyhow? I told ya before. Ain't no way we can afford to rent a place and have you driving back and forth to town just to play around at teaching a bunch of little kids something they ain't never gonna use anyhow."

"But, what if I could get enough students signed up to pay all the expenses?"

"Ain't never gonna happen."

"But, what if I could?"

"You can't. Rent alone would cost ya a fortune."

"Well, I was thinking maybe I could get that empty space beside the Lucky Dollar. It never gets used for anything anyhow so it probably wouldn't cost much, and if you helped me fix it up a bit, I could—"

"Hey! I ain't bloody helping do nothing."

"Why not?"

"Because you ain't bloody doing it, that's why!"

"Bobby, please. Listen, this is important to me. I've always wanted—"

"Well, you ain't always get what you want, Vic. So forget it."

"Bobby—"

"No!" he yelled.

"You no!" she yelled back defiantly, surprising both of them. "Look, I've wanted to do this for a long, long time. It doesn't hurt anything if I can get enough students to pay the expenses. I'm doing this, Bobby. Whether you want me to or not."

He looked across at her, momentarily stunned. "Well, I ain't bloody helping you, so don't think you'll be asking."

"Fine. I'll do it myself."

"Good luck with that."

"Thank you," she chirped sarcastically, surging dangerously on the adrenaline current racing within her. She could hardly believe she'd actually said what she'd just said. Or how quickly Bobby had folded in the face of her defiance.

"Hey! Hey! Look at that. A friggin' buck, too." He pointed excitedly out the front window and into the field running adjacent to the road. A small herd of deer had slipped just beyond the tree-lined fringe and grazed peacefully with dainty movements and watchful eyes. Bobby eased the truck to the side of the road, holding his breath as if by doing so he could restrict the buck's ability to look up and flee. Quietly as possible he opened his door, stepped with a squeaky scrunch onto the snowy road and unharnessed his rifle from the rack hanging across the truck's rear window. Shifting the gun under one arm, he scrounged amongst the paper chaos on the seat in search of his clip. His eyes darted intensely from the seat to the buck and back again.

"Shit! Where's my bloody clip?"

"Bobby, what are you doing? You can't shoot from here, someone could be back in those trees."

"Give your head a shake, woman. You think that buck would be standing around if someone was in those trees? Not bloody likely. Shit. Where is that friggin' thing? Check the cubby will you? Hurry up before the damn thing gets a whiff of us."

She obeyed slowly, but the glove box was stuffed beyond full and jammed shut. She gave it a couple of good shots with her fist.

"Shut up! What the hell you doing? Trying to scare the bugger off?" His head jerked up to see the deers' reaction, but they ate on, peacefully unaware of the warning they'd been issued. He snapped his eyes back to hers, wildness glaring in his pupil. "Could you be any friggin' louder?"

"Well, it's stuck, Bobby. I was just trying to get it opened. Maybe if you didn't shove so much crap in—"

"Ha! There it is, knew it was on the seat."

He squeezed the clip out from between the seat, snapped it in place with a cold click and moved with a surprising stealthiness to the front of the truck. Supporting his torso across the hood, he raised the rifle to his eye and pulled the buck into his sights.

"Ya. Ya, four pointer. Right on," he murmured, a smile touching on his lips but missing his eyes.

Victoria sat frozen, waited for the boom that would sound with the force of shock waves and miraculously level the demure taupe statue onto the soft white earth. She watched as the deer picked their way through invisible tufts of grass and scraggles of roots poking through the early snow. She watched their gentle beauty and waited with dread as unbearable seconds crawled by to form one unbearable minute, then two. She looked back to Bobby, briefly thought perhaps he'd been persuaded by the sheer beauty of the animal, but he remained inert, hovering passionately over his rifle, grease-blackened knuckles anxious but steady around the trigger. She slid over the seat and whispered out his opened door.

"What are you waiting for?"

"Shhh! Bugger's in behind. He'll come out though. Just got to wait a bit."

"Bobby, you sure Patterson doesn't have anything in that field? Last year I think his horses were in there for the winter, weren't they?"

"Shht! Shut the hell up, will you? I don't want to lose this one, it's a beaut."

She sighed and crossed back over to her own seat, whispering under her breath for the deer to look up and run back into the protection of the silver birch, and was startled to see first one head rise then another, followed by tentative steps toward the trees. Bobby, snarling with disbelief, squeezed off a quick shot in a last ditch effort to at least pull one down with an injury if not the simplicity of instant death, but the trees foiled him as white flag tails bounded past silver-blue trunks and out of sight.

"Shee-it! Damn it all, anyhow. Couple of more seconds and I'd of had the mother. Shit! Nicest damn buck I've seen, too."

He stamped some warmth back to his toes and jostled the rifle into place, flipping the clip back onto the seat with hard-frozen fingers. All the while he cursed his incredibly bad luck. "Shit, froze my ass off for nothing. I suppose that makes you happy, don't it?"

"Well, neither of us is exactly dressed to drag a deer back to the truck."

He remembered what he had worn, against his will, to try and simulate respectability in the loan manager's eyes. "Ah, shit. Don't give a damn 'bout these ugly faggot pants. Look good with a little blood on 'em, set that priss-ass banker back in his place a bit."

Grabbing the wheel with both hands, he pulled himself behind it, lit a smoke and gunned the engine, snatching first gear with a spray of snowy gravel that spat up behind them as they careened back onto the road. Victoria seized the dash to steady herself, swallowed a burst of retaliation and settled her eyes on the blur outside the window as the truck picked up rattles and speed in accompanying degrees. The trees flickered past, blends of coniferous and stark deciduous that paused off and on for ponds and pastures and roadways. A quarter of a mile down the road two toque-topped Patterson grandkids bounced out from the trees astride the long, strong back of the family's old buckskin mare, waving and laughing as if they'd not a care in the world. Victoria returned a stiff wave. She held her thoughts, her chest heaving with anger at what might have been, at how close Bobby's actions had been to causing a possibly horrific tragedy. She slid him a sideways glance and saw at once the possibility hadn't occurred to him. He was intent on picking something from his teeth, checking the mirror, picking some more.

A west wind greeted them with the stench of the dump as they closed in on town, traffic increasing to the point where everyone was forced to acknowledge two lanes and keep to their own side of the road. Hands and fingers and hats began to tip and nod and wave between vehicles, practically every driver knowing the identity of those they met. Bobby, still peevish, pretended not to see the waves, feigning preoccupation with papers on his dash as he drove by, as if he was searching for a document of profound significance and was too busy with important matters to notice those around him.

"Where you wanna get dropped off?"

"Oh, well, maybe Mrs. Barlow's store. Then I can walk down to the feed store."

"What you need at the feed store? You ain't outta grain yet, are you?"

"Well, no, not quite. But we might as well get some more since we have the truck in town. Would you mind picking it up for me?"

"I suppose. What do ya need?"

"Not sure, that's why I want to go down there. I need to talk to them about my laying hens."

"Why's that? What's wrong with them bloody things now?"

"Nothing really. Just not laying as well as I think they should be. I just want to ask one of those guys what they think."

"Those dumb asses? Don't know shit-all about nothing. Just feed them more."

"Feed them more?"

"Yeah, feed them more."

"Will that work?"

"How the hell would I bloody know? Ain't no chicken farmer. Just try it and see, then you'll know, right?"

"Hmm, well maybe. But I think I should still ask around a bit. Doesn't hurt to get opinions."

"Stupid damn chickens. More trouble than they're worth. Should just butcher the bunch of 'em and buy your eggs. Probably be cheaper."

He'd cut off a brown Chevy and pulled to an abrupt stop outside the department store, his truck blocking the whole lane.

"Why don't you just pull in, Bobby? There's a spot right up there."

"Don't need to pull in. I ain't staying."

"But you're blocking the road."

"Well, quit your yapping then. Where you want to be picked up?"

She scrambled to find her purse, her gloves, her thoughts, the first horn already sounding behind them.

"Oh, um, let me think. I'm meeting Rose for lunch at Pearl's, so maybe there if you're done with your appointment by two."

Irate tires spun gravel and sand and snow as driver after driver grew impatient and veered into the other lane to get past the obstacle Bobby had parked in the middle of the road.

"Won't be done by two. JJ's got a new tranny for the 'cuda. Wanna go have a look and make sure he got the right one."

"Today, Bobby? We don't have time. Still got to get groceries and stop by to see your mom."

"Oh shit, yeah. Forgot about that. We got to do that today?"

"She's expecting us, Bobby."

"Well, can you skip lunch with Rose and drop by the home instead? Tell her I'll be in next week."

"Bobby! She wants to see you. You haven't been there for ages."

He grimaced into the rearview mirror. "Guess it has been a while. But I told JJ I'd be by to see his tranny today."

"Well, tell him you'll see it next week."

"Shit." He frowned darkly. "All right, where you want me to meet you? How long you need to get the groceries, half hour?"

"At least." She slid from the truck as another horn blared and a whiskey-voiced woman yelled epithets foul enough to wilt a dandelion. "Maybe give me 'till about three. Pick me up at the grocery store . . . and don't be late, okay? Mr. Graves gets grumpy if I hang around too long after I'm done shopping."

"All right already, I got it. Hurry up and grab your purse. People getting right pissy back there."

"Don't be late, Bobby, okay. Please," she added, as she pulled her purse out of the truck sending a snowstorm of wrinkled invoices and candy wrappers onto the street. She bent down and hastily gathered up a handful of what seemed somewhat important and shoved it back into the truck.

"Hurry up and close the frickin' door," Bobby bellered, bull-like, as she did so, dropping her purse in the process and spilling its contents onto the road, a super-plus Tampax rolling to a flattened death under the tires of a black four-wheel drive. Gathering up papers, lipstick and most of her change, she stuck frozen fingers into her thin parka pockets, set her jaw and walked past the gawking eyes and whispered exchanges on the sidewalk.

"Victoria, wait!"

Her heart soared then sunk. Whirling around she saw Elliot crossing the street toward her. She searched his smiling face as he got closer, trying to ascertain whether or not he'd witnessed the embarrassing fiasco she and Bobby had just created on Main Street.

"Hi! Hey, how've you been?"

"Fine. You?" She kept her smile controlled, her face neutral, aware that the town's eyes were on them, observing, speculating, judging.

"Great! Busy. Took a little road trip this fall to do some painting."

"Oh. Where?"

"Up north, mostly," he answered vaguely.

She looked at him sharply, trying to imagine him on the other end of that strange call, whispering through the static of a bad connection from a dingy hotel room.

"Hey, I ended up with a really nice painting from that day we went up McCully Hill. You should come out sometime and see it."

"Um . . . sure."

"Bring your husband, too, if you want."

Averting her eyes, she shifted her purse from one shoulder to the other, hoping to obscure a confused frown.

"Sure."

"I've been thinking about you a lot this last while."

Panicked, she scanned around them to ensure no one had come within hearing range.

"You have?"

"Ya. Been wondering if you're going to open that studio."

She felt a tinge of disappointment.

"Still thinking about it."

He grinned gently. "That's good. Be even better when you quit thinking about it and just do it."

She grinned back at him, a shiver rippling through her.

"You're cold. I should let you go."

"Ya. I probably should get going," she agreed, knowing the more they stood there and talked the more questions started arising in people's minds.

"It was really good to see you again, Victoria." His eyes lingered softly on hers.

"You too," she said lightly as they waved goodbye and continued going their separate ways down the street.

Pressing open the door into Mrs. Barlow's department store, she was announced by a melancholy door chime that long ago had used up the best of its vocal cords. This department store was somewhat of an anomaly, containing no departments, no sections and very little in the way of even a basic order. Better described as an ongoing garage sale, items not sold were shuffled, turned and rearranged until they were either covered over by oily dust or buried among new and more enticing stock. As such it was a difficult place to actually shop in, and most people resorted immediately to Mrs. Barlow's assistance, which was given, but never offered.

"Well, look what dragged home the cat. Ain't seen you a long time fer. What's bin keeping ya?"

Mrs. Barlow's voice, thick as January molasses, flowed out from the shadows. Her peculiar form of verbal dyslexia forced Victoria to hesitate before answering as her brain flip-flopped the words back into place.

"Oh, hello, Mrs. Barlow. I haven't been up to much. A little knitting lately. Need some more wool."

She said this into the general direction from which Mrs. Barlow's voice had emerged and waited as her eyes adjusted. The gloom slowly revealed a menagerie of burned-out bulbs dotting a water-stained ceiling that appeared to be supported by precarious pillars of junk piled the length and width of all four walls. An Armageddon of flies dried on the wide sills of two filthy display windows looking out to the street, and a stinky brown dog, alive or dead was anyone's guess, lay sprawled in front of a snorting, snuffing little wood heater.

"What kind of wool wanting ya?" the voice replied, pulling forth the apparition of large, lumpy Mrs. Barlow. She sat in a recliner behind the front counter. Her blue-daisied polyester dress formed an almost perfect square as she rolled up onto her feet. "Your crops this year, how did they come?"

"Not too bad, really. Prices were down though."

"So I hear. Joe and Phyllis didn't git much fer their's either. A tough year be it. And Phyllis that girl spends money like trees. My poor Joey, wishing he listened me to now, I tell ya. Hard-working boy, is he. Just like your Bobby. Work himself to the bone. Not like yer maw's family, no-sir-ee. Now there was some shiftless bunch.

And weak in the head, too, somes them." She eyed Victoria suspiciously, as if checking for any emerging signs of insanity. "Darn lucky to get yer pa, she was. Even if he were a touch mean. I tell that Phyllis just yesterday—"

Victoria sighed, resigned herself to hear again Mrs. Barlow's painfully slow and lengthy summation of her daughter in-law's many faults. An outsider would have assumed she had no use for her son's wife at all, but the opposite was true. She quite liked the girl and had a self-replenishing list of odd jobs she'd have her do and redo, then do over again. Victoria waited impatiently as Mrs. Barlow droned on, her nerves still zinging excitedly after her unexpected encounter with Elliot. She thought again about how triumphant she'd felt when she had challenged Bobby about opening a studio, but now an insidious shadow of doubt began to crawl up her spine. Maybe he'd been right. Maybe it was impossible. Maybe she wouldn't be able to get enough students to have her own studio. Maybe she should have left well enough alone. Fortunately, Mrs. Barlow could only talk so long without breaking for a cigarette. She smoked as regular as most people breathed and any long-term disruption in her pattern left her short of breath. Sure enough, midsentence she began to wheeze and gasp and broke off to light up. Victoria jumped in to repeat her request, time ticking off in her head as she mentally ran through the list of errands in her purse.

"I think I'll just need one ball of wool. Are they still in the back corner?"

Mrs. Barlow inhaled a quarter inch off the cigarette then stood stroking the hanging folds of her double chin as the smoke slowly seeped back out of her nose. She tilted her head to one side, examined the roof for guidance.

"Wee-ell, let me remember. Some is. Some ain't. What color wants you?"

"Yellow. But it's got to match this." She fished into her purse and produced a pale yellow strand. Mrs. Barlow bent toward it, squinted, then scrunched up her piggy nose.

"What's fer it?"

"Pardon?"

"What's fer it?"

"Oh. A baby sweater. For Diana Gainer. Guess you heard she's expecting again?"

Mrs. Barlow received this question as a bit of an affront, feeling herself somewhat of an authority on the town's gossip. Being best friends with Millie Miller, the doctor's secretary, clearly gave her a hands-down advantage in the medical department, and with her husband Bill behind the counter at the local bar, there wasn't much happening in Hinckly where she wasn't one of the first to know.

"Course'n I knew. Knewed fer a long time, I did. Due early March." She moistened her lips to receive the cigarette, slowly took a drag then shook her head as she expelled it. "Heard you about Diana and Tom's eldest, did you? Got caught up in Benny Olson's hay barn and his daughter with." She stopped for another long drag followed by an even longer shaking of her head. "Is a bad one, that boy. Chased him straight off with his shotgun, Benny did." She fell into a wheezy chortle that ended in a gut-wrenching hack she appeased with the last of her cigarette.

"Come here to the back with me. Some have I, maybe for sure."

Victoria followed in the slowly waddled path, picking up and replacing pots and clothes pegs and books as they were rubbed or bumped or hip-checked onto the floor. Mrs. Barlow swayed to a stop. She looked under, over and through the cluttered shelves then shook her head quizzically, tugged at her chin fat and pursed her wet lips.

"So. Did ya heard about Mrs. Spiller's latest bad guy?"

Victoria nodded her head quickly but to no avail.

"Nutty old bird thinks her money the gypsies are stealing! Gypsies! Not gypsies tell you me. Nope. Old man Graves, now he's a stealer. Selling that crazy old coot all them groceries, them damn cats just to feed. Should arrest him, I say." And with this proclamation her energy was depleted, and she slumped against a stack of boxes trying to recall what it was she'd been looking for. "Let me think now a minute."

They stood silent, listened to Mrs. Barlow's nasal wheezing and waited for the reluctant revelation to reveal itself. After a non-productive moment, the older lady pulled a pencil from her scraggly faded red bun as if hoping to joggle the memory loose.

"Oh! Now I know. Over here, come." And she again waddled forward on stumpy legs that called up visions of bloated bratwurst. She traversed one aisle then the next with the speed of a glacier, finally stopped and began rummaging between cans of paint and some toasters.

"What color?"

Victoria again scouted out the piece of wool from her purse and again was met by Mrs. Barlow's disapproving scrunched up face.

"Not such a nice color that."

She turned to the box of wool in front of her, and Victoria noticed her push past several balls that may have worked, obviously intent on finding a color that was more in accordance with her own tastes.

"How about that one, Mrs. Barlow? Looks pretty close."

The suggestion was cast off with a grunt as she pulled up a lime-green ball and turned to Victoria, quite pleased with her find.

"This one, how's about?"

"Hmm. That's nice. But maybe a bit too bright. I think it needs to be a bit paler."

"Paler? Pale enough babies are. Dead you make 'em look with pale. Here, this one how about?"

She pushed an equally atrocious fuchsia into Victoria's hand, a smoke-stained smile splitting her fat cheeks.

"Good, huh?"

Victoria held her temper, smiled through gritted teeth. "Okay, and maybe if you don't mind, I'll also take that one back there, back behind the toaster."

"Sure," Mrs. Barlow beamed agreeably as she reached back and grabbed the soft yellow ball, happy in the knowledge she had just doubled her sales for the day. Cheerfully she led the way back up the aisle to ring in the purchase.

"You ain't no kids got ya, strange thing sure enough. But not all bad it is. Spoiled these days kids are, get by with too much. A smack's the thing, it is. I tell you, my boys—"

Victoria tapped her foot impatiently through several minutes of advice on how to raise the children she'd never had followed by almost fifteen more of Hinckly gossip old and current, but certainly not new. By the time Mrs. Barlow paused to light up her third cigarette, she all but lunged for the door with a backward goodbye.

Her exit was impeded by Diana, her bustling entourage of children stampeding noisily through the door Victoria held open.

"Oh, hi Vic. Thanks for getting the door. Girls, you can look, but no touching, okay?"

Turning back to Victoria, she shifted a youngster from her hip into the waiting arms of an older sibling as she prepared to make small talk.

"So, how are you? Haven't seen you in ages."

"Me? Oh, I'm fine. How about yourself?"

"Good. Crazy busy, as usual. Preggers again, did you hear?" she asked happily, smoothing down her shirt to expose a rather obvious belly.

"Wow! Congratulations. Must almost have enough for your own baseball team by now, hey?"

"Well, maybe if the girls played."

"I don't want to play bayth-ball," lisped a young girl who had entwined herself around Diana's left leg.

"And who is this?" asked Victoria, smiling down at an irresistibly cute little girl who blinked back with shy blue eyes.

"This is Lily. Lily wants to be a ballerina when she grows up. Don't you Lily?"

"Really?" Victoria smiled, surprised at her fortunate timing. "That's wonderful. I was just—"

"No, mommy," Lily interjected seriously, a look of consternation on her face. "I don't want to be a baw-weena. I want to be a prayee-princess."

"A prairie princess?" Diana frowned.

"Fairy princess," Victoria corrected.

"Yeth, mommy! A prayee-princess!" the little girl squealed, delighted she had been understood.

"And do fairy princesses dance?" asked Victoria, her hand unable to resist the bubbling brown curls which bounced with the child's enthusiasm.

"Yeth. An they can flies, too!" the girl returned earnestly, eyes wide with innocent amazement.

"Well, maybe I can teach you to dance like a fairy princess. Would you like that?"

The child nodded and giggled with excitement. "Can you teach me to fly, too?"

Victoria stroked a petal-soft cheek with the back of her hand. "Well, I don't know about that, sweetie. But, I will try my very best, okay?"

"Okay," she agreed, her face flowering as she scrambled off to tell her siblings.

"Well, that was easy," Diana laughed. "I didn't know you were teaching, Vic. That's wonderful! Where's your studio?"

"Uh . . . I, uh . . . I don't have one, yet. But, I will pretty soon. Bobby and I were just discussing that on the way into town. I was thinking maybe I could rent that empty space beside—"

"Hey, I have an idea," Diana beamed enthusiastically. "What about the ballroom at the hotel? It never gets used. Might need a few repairs, but I'm sure Bobby could help you with that."

"Hmm. Maybe. It's a good idea, but I doubt if Pearl would agree to a reasonable rent."

"Well," Diana looked at her fingers for a moment, mentally counting up figures. "Look. Pearl owes us some money I'm sure we'll never see, so how about this? I'll talk to her about letting you use the ballroom and maybe you can teach my girls for free? Does that sound fair?" Not used to handling business negotiations, she looked at Victoria uncertainly.

"That sounds fantastic, Diana. Do you really think you can get Pearl to agree to that?"

"I think so. She's not really so bad underneath it all, Vic. Oh-oh. Got to run. I'll phone you later to let you know how it goes, okay?" Diana said, already hurrying off in the direction of a loud and rather ominous crash.

Victoria's mind swung between excitement and trepidation. She hadn't intended for things to materialize so fast. She wasn't even sure she had really intended them to materialize at all. In calling Bobby's bluff, she'd inadvertently called her own. And now she'd promised sweet little Lily she would teach her how to dance. She couldn't bear the thought of being the one to paint disappointment onto that angelic face. She had no idea how she was going to do it, but she did know she was at least going to try.

Benson Ferguson and his brother-in-law bade Victoria a quick hello as she met them on the sidewalk, relinquishing their perpetual debate just long enough to pass her by, then resumed, each empowered with a renewed vigor after the temporary cease-fire. Both retired farmers with little to do, they'd learned to make sport out of argument, and if one said it was a fine day, the other would set off to prove unequivocally that it most certainly was anything but. She walked behind them, found herself listening not to their words but to the inflection of their voices, the variances of their speech. It could have been anyone who'd phoned her. Anyone. Suddenly the whole town was under her suspicion, every male voice that drifted by her as she walked caught her attention, and she found her pace slowed several times as she tried to superimpose static and disguise over them. She waved at those who waved to her, but she also tried to catch their eye, see if any secret was hidden there. She felt exposed.

Glad when she finally gained the smooth plank stairs of the feed store, she double-stepped up them and slipped into the comforting aroma of grain and straw and the peachy-sweet smoke of

Mr. Miller's pipe. A brass cowbell clanged overhead as she shut the door, summoning no one and leaving her waiting in its echo. She walked to the counter, picked through a magazine on sheep and then examined the names on the delinquent checks taped to the cash register. Eventually two voices emerged from the back where the stacks of feed were stored, joined together in a hushed giggle and subsided. She couldn't be sure but one had sounded like a girl's, and it wasn't long afterward that she saw Benny Olson's third-youngest daughter slip across the loading dock and disappear down the street.

A good-looking kid sauntered rather than walked in through the back door, flashing her with smirking green eyes and a kick-ass smile.

"Help you, ma'am?"

A grimy white telephone attached to a wooden post beside the cash register rang shrilly over her reply. She jerked back awkwardly, her gaze darting back and forth as she waited for him to silence it. Instead, he casually roved freely over her face with his eyes.

"Go ahead," she offered, gesturing toward the telephone.

"Thanks," he grinned as he picked up the receiver, dropped it back down to disconnect the call then let the handle dangle loosely down the post.

Victoria stared at it. The plaintive tone of the severed line reached back to her.

"Don't worry about it, ma'am. They'll call back. What can I get ya?"

Her attention was fixated on the dangling telephone, ears straining for the sounds of static, mind tumbling with why he'd been so reluctant to answer that call.

"Umm, I need to get some grain, Mark," she stammered. "Bobby will pick it up later. And I want to talk to Mr. Miller about my laying hens. Is he in?"

"Nope. What's wrong with them?" he asked, but his concerns were clearly already elsewhere, appraising her up and down.

"You know about chickens?"

He swaggered out in front of the counter and leaned against it, crossing arms grown massive from chucking fifty-pound bags and eighty-pound bales and winked her a challenge.

"Try me."

She smiled back, middle-aged respectful as if she hadn't caught his brazen, double-edged invitation. A piece of flattened gold straw fell from his shoulder, and she noticed more trapped in the glossy black curls escaping from under his red cap.

"Um, okay," she stammered dryly. "Well, they used to lay fine. Up until a couple months ago."

"Ya? What happened a couple months ago?"

"Nothing."

"Hmm. Something must have." He helped himself to an overt sampling of her reflection in the store window. "You try amping up their light?"

Victoria nodded uncomfortably. She could feel the heat of his body beside her. Smell the rut of his sweat. "Ya. Didn't seem to help."

"Maybe they're just too old." He smirked down at her.

"They're not that old," she quickly defended.

"Got a rooster?"

"Ya."

"In with them?"

She shook her head impatiently.

"Why not?"

"Well, because I don't want the eggs fertilized."

Mark threw his arms up in an exaggerated gesture. "Well, that's your problem, then."

"What is?"

She eased backward as he leaned toward her, ran a slow search over her body then fixed her with an audacious stare.

"Ain't no fun happening in your hen house, ma'am. Hens no different than chicks. You want 'em to give up the goods, they're gonna want a little something in exchange. Right?"

"Uh . . . I . . . Um . . . maybe. Maybe I should call back when Mr. Miller's here."

"Whatever cranks ya."

Winking, he took a step closer to her and for a moment she thought he was going to slap her ass. But his hand fell to a feed sack behind her and he hoisted it onto his shoulder like it was lightly stuffed with cotton. She tried desperately to scramble her memory backward over his words, feeling for similarities, convinced for a moment she'd found her anonymous caller. But something about it didn't make sense. He was so brazen, so comfortable with himself. He hardly struck her as the type to hide behind a blank wall of static.

"Anything else I can help you with?" He smiled, knowing full well he'd successfully seen her undone.

"No. Yes, yes, I mean. My grain. I didn't order my grain."

"Oh, right. What do you want, same as usual?"

She nodded even though she had planned to try something different. But she needed more advice for that, and she sure as hell wasn't anxious to begin over again from where they'd left off.

"How many bags? Five do you?"

She nodded, fumbling her purse open as he scribbled some figures onto a pad. Pressing the bills into his thick hand, she was careful not to make contact, but he curled his fingers up around hers brushing them softly, deposited her change with a firm touch then wished her a good day.

"Been a pleasure, ma'am." He tossed her another wink, obviously pleased with his performance.

Walking back down the stairs she retroactively felt offended. The smart ass, who did he think he was, parading around like a virile young bull? Feeling drained, she stopped on the bottom step and leaned briefly against the peeling white post that held up the feedstore's sign. No wonder Diana was having trouble with him. Hollywood looks, a testosterone-inflated ego and muscles to pump it up with. The perfect heartbreaking combination: deadly not only to young girls but to his distressed mother as well. And she had to admit, at least to herself, that his self-assured cockiness had gotten to her in no small degree.

~Chapter 10 ~

The telephone shrilled incessantly and Victoria hurried down the hall, her fingers working dexterously with the clasp of her bra, hoping to have one hand free by the time she got to it. Twice she'd almost had the bra fastened before it sprung loose again. She cursed mildly as she debated missing the call altogether or sacrificing her breasts to a few more moments of freedom. Choosing the latter, she let them fall free as she grabbed for the phone. She'd been rushing for it all week, waiting for Diana to call to say whether Pearl had agreed to let them use the ballroom for a dance studio. Ragged bits of static greeted her breathless hello.

Jolted, she just barely stopped herself from slamming the receiver back down. Watching it carefully, as if it might suddenly come alive in her hand, she slowly inched the handset up toward her ear. She shot a glance through the porch window to make sure Bobby's truck was still gone. Holding her breath, she listened. Fear began to palpitate her heart as her mind raced with images of who might be breathing into the other end of the line. But, slowly, as she returned her thoughts back over the delicious memory she held of the previous call, her anxiety began to transform into anticipation. Really, there had been no harm done. He had not been crude or frightening, although the strangeness of the call, coming when she was stranded all alone out at the trailer had unnerved her. Maybe Rose was right. Maybe, she should just hang on for a bit. What would be wrong with just listening to what he had to say? Inching a chair toward her she slid into place.

"Hello? Anyone there?"

She closed her eyes and tried to concentrate her senses into the line. Focusing deeply, she attempted to listen through the erratic pop of static to glean any wayward background noise, which might inadvertently offer a clue to the caller's identity. Soon tiring of this, she resorted to more obvious attempts to draw him out.

"So, did you call to talk to me or not?"

Silence.

"I have to go pretty soon, you know. Did you have something you wanted to say to me?"

She waited briefly, growing irritated at the noisy silence that crackled in her ear, then decided to beat him at his own game. Two could sit in silence just as easy as one. He was the one who had called her, let him work up the courage to speak. She pulled her knees up onto her chair and began to work the telephone cord through her bare toes like a curly black snake. It was a silly little standoff; she knew that. As immature and petty as those that spice the earliest interactions between young lovers and young love. But it gave her an almost sexual pleasure to imagine his attraction to her could be so strong that her silence could actually coax him out beyond his anonymous security. As the two of them sat silently stalemated in their cat-and-mouse game, a smile played lightly on her lips. She imagined him to be doing the same: imagined his mouth—full, generous and responsive—framed by features worn into being by the wind and waves rather than the sharp, steady chip of a sculpture's tool. Craggy rather than chiseled.

"I think you're really beautiful," the voice cut forcefully through the line, penetrating her thoughts so deeply it was as if he had stood right inside her.

"Oh! What? No, I'm not. I'm not. I'm just me. Just me." And then, prodded by the habit of good manners, flustered, "But thank you anyhow for saying so."

Suddenly she became aware of the coolness of air against her breasts and, grabbing Bobby's jacket up from where he had hung it on the floor, she wrapped it around her shoulders. It was as if the image of the caller that she had created in her mind were so real it suddenly seemed possible he also might have the ability to imagine her sitting there, curled up on a chair missing half her clothes. The thought was erotic and ridiculous at the same time, yet for some reason she could not push it away. She rolled the cold, black telephone cord tight across her breasts, pleased as the nipples sprang back up like hungry brown hatchlings.

"Is that why you phoned me?" she prodded. "Just to tell me that?" She managed to coax casual into her voice, but she was like someone who, having tasted a new delicacy for the first time, suddenly realizes they cannot live without a second bite.

"You'd probably really like the way I look right now," she teased playfully. "I had to run to catch the phone and I never had time to get dressed."

She felt a little race of panic as she released this half-truth, but it was short lived, alleviated by the real power she felt imagining him imagining her. Listening carefully, she waited to catch his reply until finally it came to her not in words, but in a slow pulsing sensuality that began to seep back to her across the line. She closed her eyes and breathed it in as if it were a stream of loving caresses and soul-searching kisses. She was about to offer more of herself when a scattered spray of words stopped her cold.

"Are you lonely?"

"Lonely?" she repeated defensively. She blinked her eyes as if casting off a daydream. "I'm not lonely. Why would you think I'm lonely?"

They were not the words she had been expecting and no more fit into her moment than an elephant into a canary cage. Yet even as she denied their truth, loneliness began to emerge all around her as if it had always been there but as faded and dingy and unnoticed as the wallpaper. Unobserved and unobtrusive until somebody turns on the light and makes a point of imprinting its unmistakably dismal existence onto your brain.

Victoria pulled Bobby's coat tighter as these new feelings began to focus around her. She would not have described herself as lonely because to her this feeling was normal. She had never felt any other way. Always lonely. Always alone. She put her feet on the floor and sat up straight. It annoyed her to be forced to see herself in this light. She preferred to think of herself as a loner: someone who chose not to waste her time in the gossipy presence of the other wives, someone who was comfortable in her own space. Not lonely. Not alone. Not these strong, desperate, glaring words that illuminated her back upon herself.

"I should go now," she whispered flatly, shocked to find the caller already gone and the line dead. Pulling her knees up to her chest, she buried her head and began to cry as if she had just received news of the death of an old friend.

~ Chapter 11 ~

Victoria glanced quickly behind her as she grappled with the mangled ring of keys Pearl had given her. Her hands trembled visibly as she searched for the long-unused one that would unseal the ballroom doors. She was irritated by her nervousness. It wasn't as if she were doing anything wrong, she chided herself. Bobby knew full well what her plans were for the studio. They had discussed it again just the night before. Vehemently. Now, standing alone outside the massive double doors of the ballroom, she began to wonder if she shouldn't have considered his objections a little more seriously.

Fumbling the key ring, she accidentally scraped the ornate carving beveled into the thick oak panel of the left door. A sprinkling of filigreed gold fell to the burgundy carpet. Rubbing it invisible with her foot, Victoria suddenly became aware of the complexity of the doors. Over the years she must have walked right past them hundreds of times. But, she had never really paid them any attention, saw them without seeing them. The way someone who grows up in the shadow of a mountain may never truly encounter its raw majesty.

That seemed impossible to her now as her eyes explored the imposing and intricately carved doors. They rose at least three feet above her head. Even with both her arms stretched out, she would not be able to encompass their span. Stained a depthless indigo, the carvings in the raised panels had been brushed with a now-crackled and flaking gold. Sturdy brass hardware held the doors firmly in place.

Her fingers toyed with a long, jagged key. Even without looking she knew it was the brass one that would unlock the door. She hesitated, her mind raging with a searing question: Who was she to open these doors? Who was she to disturb these hopes and dreams and fears, so silently sealed away? The carefully carved pictures on the door captivated her as she vacillated between expectation and anxiety. Demure ladies in kimonos, ferocious dragons, snow-capped mountains, a collage of symbols she could not understand.

The key slid easily into place, but she could not turn her hand. She felt paralyzed. Suddenly, she wanted the whole crazy idea of the studio to disappear. She thought about sliding the key back out. She could return it to Pearl. Say the room was unsuitable. It was too big. That it would be impossible to control the children in such a large space. It would be pandemonium at least and chaos at best.

She would simply tell Bobby she had changed her mind. Not that the idea couldn't work, as he insisted, just that she didn't feel like pursuing it yet. And Elliot. She felt an unexpected rush of rage course through her. Why had he even suggested such a thing in the first place? He knew nothing about her. She hadn't danced in years. Not really. Not since she'd come home from the failed dance audition, thrown her shoes in the basement, buried her albums and pictures in a bottom drawer and hissed to her mother that she never wanted to dance again. Even to herself it had been a surprise how perfectly able she had been to alienate herself from the only thing that caused the blood to course through her veins. She had felt she had no other choice. Bassman had stolen far more from her that night than he would ever know. Her dignity, yes. But far worse was that without the protection of her arrogant facade, he'd managed to expose her to herself.

Her eyes lingered on the gently spiked motif in the center of the door. A flower: foreign, mystical. Certainly not anything that could ever survive in Hinckly's inhospitable climate. *A lotus flower,*

Victoria thought, surprised she could identify it. She wondered at the workings of the mind, how it could hold so many random bits of information, able to dislodge and float them forward at seemly obscure, unimportant moments.

Her thoughts turned to Lily. Fresh, beautiful, innocent Lily. Her protective affection for the child puzzled her. She felt her hand turn the key. She knew she turned it not for herself. She turned it for Lily. For a promise made which she felt compelled to keep.

The door slid open easily. As if it had been merely awaiting her decision. A gust of damp, musty air escaped past her like a desperate sigh. She wondered again how many half-lived dreams had been sealed up behind these doors. For a moment she again faltered, then the sound of someone entering the lobby coaxed her quickly forward. Sliding inside, she closed the door behind her and was instantly encased in darkness.

Keeping her hand on the cold doorknob, the sound of her shallow breathing filled the room with a rapid, audible pulse. Shadows evolved into shapes. Gloom hung as tangibly as the tattered blankets nailed across the tall windows. She was surprised to discover the room was not expansive at all. A dividing wall, unpainted and none too straight, had been slapped up somewhere over the years, consuming at least half of what had once been a palatial space. The room was suffocated with boxes, crates, bottles, jars, bed frames, sagging mattresses, broken televisions and bent bicycles. Partially used rolls of silver duct tape littered the floor. Like the elephants' elusive graveyard, Victoria realized she had just solved the mystery about what Bud did with the copious amount of stuff he was constantly dragging home from the dump. Sinking onto a broken-backed chair, she pulled her knees up to her chest and closed her eyes.

A soft tap on the door startled her upright, hands swiping hastily at tears. She held her breath, heart thundering as she stood transfixed, eyes riveted to the doors, willing them not to open. Another tap, firmer this time, then a sliver of sharp light shot in at her. She froze, praying the darkness was capable of transforming her into just another piece of inanimate junk. Her lungs strained wildly for air. She allowed herself a thin whisper of breath as the door opened wider, and a silhouetted figure stepped toward her.

"Hey, you in here?"

"Um . . . ya. Hi," she ventured, voice gravelly with emotion. She barely suppressed a giggle as Elliot flinched ever so slightly.

"Jeez! Scared me. Didn't see you there. What are you doing standing in the dark anyhow?"

"Well . . . I don't know where the light switch is."

"Has to be around here somewhere," he murmured, hands already sweeping over the wall like quick black spiders. "Here."

Victoria ducked her head as a tight snap brought the room to life. The addition of light did little to brighten her mood.

"There, that's better," Elliot congratulated himself. "Oh. Maybe not. Wow," he whistled an exhalation. "This place is a bit of a disaster."

"No argument there," Victoria agreed wryly.

"I saw your car out front. Thought I'd stop in and see how it was going. Rumor around town has it that you're going to turn the ballroom into a dance studio. That true?" He grinned over at her expectantly.

"It was. Until I came in here and discovered it's Bud's dumping ground for his dump treasures." She hated the thin scrape of her voice. The way her words so easily extinguished the playfulness from his face.

"Ya," he frowned as he surveyed the piles of debris. "It's going to take quite a bit of work, that's for sure. He's quite an interesting old character, Bud, isn't he? You should see some of the things he's got welded together back of his garage. He's actually pretty clever in some ways. How you figure he manages to get all this stuff back here from the dump with just his bike?"

Victoria shrugged. Discouragement was stealing over her thoughts as she looked around the room. So, Bobby would again be proven right. *Maybe the studio had been a stupid idea after all,* she thought. And rising thickly on the tide of her disappointment, she was surprised to feel an enormous sense of relief.

"This will make a fantastic studio, though. Won't it?" Elliot offered, edging his way through the maze, stopping to flip open a box, thumb through a magazine.

"Would have."

He ceased his rummaging. "What do you mean, would have?"

"It's kind of obvious, isn't it?"

"Not to me, it isn't."

Victoria sighed and nudged a basketful of ratty towels with her foot.

"Well, obviously I can't have a studio in here. Look at this place, Elliot."

"You want me to look at it? Okay, Victoria. I'll look at it. And then I'm going to do you the profound favor of telling you exactly what it is I see, because apparently your vision is still impaired by the darkness."

Victoria started to object, but he softened his remark with a wink. Swinging around theatrically, he opened his arms expansively and silently surveyed the room. She grinned nervously at his antics, half fearing he was going to break out in song.

"What I see is twelve-foot ceilings iced with moldings as ornate as hoar frost on a wintery window. A delicate center rosette giving flower to an exquisite crystal and brass chandelier, which will once again sparkle after it is unburdened from decades of dust." He pointedly ignored her amusement as she looked up at the bare light bulb dangling from the center of the yellowed ceiling. "Oh, and look over here," he continued, as he leaned over to her, gently took her hand and guided her toward the shabbily draped window. Picking up half of a broken crutch from the floor, he swooped the tired blanket aside and revealed a rather ornate but filthy window.

"Have you ever seen such a resplendent Gothic arch? And do I have to note how incredibly rare it is to find such masterful stained glass outside of a cathedral?"

He grinned down at her, releasing the blanket and handing the crutch to her with great flourish. Moving quickly, he scooted several items away from the center of the room and gestured to the floor.

"And, just in case you were not sufficiently impressed by all that opulence, have a look at this."

Victoria shook her head and laughed as she glanced at the floor.

"No, you have to look at it."

"I am looking at it."

"You have to really look at it. Up close."

Victoria held his eye until she realized he was actually quite serious. Bending over slightly, she again looked at the floor. Slowly, it began to dawn on her what Elliot was trying to get her to see. The floor, although abused and water stained, was a lovely oak parquet.

"This is perfect, Elliot! This would make a perfect dance floor!"

Victoria laughed wondrously. It was as if Elliot had created a different world by the mere force of his enthusiasm. They stood grinning at each other for a long moment, their eyes sparkling with excitement before Victoria felt compelled to look away. She wondered if he had any idea of the strength of his charm.

She surveyed the wreckage of the room again slowly, her mind flipping between Elliot's vision and the reality staring her in the face.

"Your brother is right. You really can dream a castle up out of an outhouse, can't you?"

"I consider it a gift, thank you," he smiled, stepping directly in front of her, placing his hands softly on her shoulders as he held her with his eyes. "Okay, so you want to tell me what you see now?"

"Elliot, I . . ." she stepped back, unnerved by a sudden urge to slip her arms around his waist. She felt both frightened and intrigued by the casualness of his touch. With him it was as if the traditional, unspoken boundaries that should have prevailed simply ceased to exist.

Sensing her confusion, Elliot busied himself rearranging some boxes up against the wall, producing a makeshift chair. "Come here. Let's sit down and you can wax poetic about the many fine attributes of this exquisite room."

"Wax poetic? I doubt it."

"Try," he whispered dramatically as he positioned himself on top of the boxes and patted the empty space beside him.

A million cautions crackled in her mind. A million desires snuffed them out. She grinned over at him, her mind vacillating, her body tense. She marveled at his easy composure.

Propped on top of the broken boxes, his lean blue-jeaned legs swung loosely to an inaudible song. He again patted the empty space beside him and raised his eyebrows.

"Your turn."

Mentally, she glanced around. The windows were covered; the door was closed. Taking a deep breath, she stepped toward him, maneuvering somewhat awkwardly through the maze of items as she felt his eyes on her. Edging gingerly past a looped anaconda of rusted chain, her foot toppled over a chipped mason jar displaying a morbid collection of dried spider carcasses.

"Oh," she said distastefully and almost instantly felt Elliot's hand hot against her back as he steadied her. He helped her over a pile of pails, and they sat down in a perfectly choreographed move. They burst into laughter, dissipating the tension sparkling around them. Sitting silent for a moment, their legs swinging in tandem, they pretended to study the contents of the room. A wafer-thin line of respectable space ran between them.

Surreptitiously, she slid her eyes up his legs to the navy T-shirt loosely tucked into his jeans. She scanned his denim jacket for bleached-out grease stains, mended tears or resewn buttons. Finding nothing, she wondered how long it had been since Elliot had had someone in his life to take care of such things. A stab of jealousy flashed through her.

A dangle of dark laces flicking out from his pant hem caught her attention.

"I think your shoe is undone," she offered.

"Yup. Both of them are," he said as he pulled up his pant legs to reveal the loose laces of his brown suede shoes.

Victoria scrunched up her nose. "Doesn't that bug you?"

"Nope. It bugs me when they're tied up and my feet feel like they're choking. I'm actually more of a barefoot-in-the-sand kind of guy."

"Ha! Well, what on earth are you doing in Hinckly, then?"

"Not quite sure, yet. But I think I might be very close to finding out," he twinkled her a grin. She shifted her position, slightly increasing the space between them.

"You have really long legs."

"What? Oh, ya, I guess so," Victoria murmured, pulling them up toward her and wrapping her arms around them tightly.

"You guess so? Well, look at them. I have to be a good two inches taller than you and our legs are almost the same length."

"Maybe you just have short legs," she cracked.

Elliot nudged her softly sideways, his arm remaining pressed up against hers.

"Okay. Quit stalling," he grinned. "What do you see?"

"Junk."

He nudged her sideways again, a little farther this time and she reached out and grabbed onto him to keep from tumbling to the floor. "Okay! Okay!"

She turned serious, skimming the room in a desperate attempt to see beyond the tangle of cast-offs. They sat in comfortable silence, Elliot patient as she struggled to form her thoughts. Finally, she cleared her throat and spoke aimlessly into the room.

"I'm sorry, Elliot. It just looks impossible to me."

"Why impossible?" he asked, laying his arm along her leg and gently squeezing her knee.

"Just with all this stuff," she mumbled, her thoughts heavily distracted by his casually placed hand. "I'll never be able to get it all out of here."

"Are you serious?"

Victoria frowned at him, confused.

"You mean you would seriously let all this junk stop you from pursuing your lifelong dream?"

Victoria bristled.

"Have I offended you?"

She shrugged one shoulder.

"Good."

Snapping around to face him, she was met by the smooth stroke of his fingers across her prominently protesting lips.

"Look, the last thing I'd want to do is offend you. But it's good that you felt that way."

"Why?"

"Because now you know where to look for the truth."

She flicked her hair away from her face. "That was the truth, Elliot. Look at this mess. It'd be impossible for me to ever clean this up."

"Impossible? Or just difficult?"

Her mind raced to all the other errands she wasn't getting done. Bobby would be furious if she missed the grocery store and she had to drive all the way back into town again tomorrow.

"Okay, well not impossible, I guess. Look, I really should get going. I have to stop by the Lucky Dollar before they close."

"Friday today," Elliot smiled. "They're open late."

He reached over and she watched as her hand disappeared inside of both of his. He held her eye steadily. "So. What do you think might really be holding you back, Victoria?"

She shrugged, her mind a maze of confusion.

He sat patiently, cupping her hand in his, waiting for her answer. Finally, he sighed gently as he slowly spread open her fingers and began to analyze her glistening palm.

"Okay, well maybe we can find some answers in here," he whispered secretively. She leaned her head against the wall, lulled into a hypnotic trance by the butterfly touch of his middle finger as he stroked the telltale lines of her palm.

"Oh, my. There are definitely some mysteries written here," he said with playful seriousness.

Struggling against a deep desire to curl up into sleep, Victoria closed her eyes and smiled as he continued stroking down over her wrist and began to trace the inky veins which branched up the inside of her arm. Drifting in a moment of soft pleasure, she suddenly sat bolt upright, snapping her arm from him.

"Oh! That . . . tickles," she gasped, roughly rubbing away the electrifying sensation which had erupted when his finger had found the small, concave depression at her elbow.

Elliot shook his head and cast her a sidelong look. "Well, that's really a shame, Miss, because I think I almost had the answer there. Now, I guess it's up to you again."

Victoria chewed her lip, struggling for a full breath. A racing fear replaced the calm in her stomach.

"Maybe I'm just scared a studio won't work out, that's all."

"Or, maybe you're scared it will work out."

Their eyes met abruptly. "At any rate, I don't think we can reasonably hold all this junk here responsible for holding you back. Right?"

Victoria shook her head slowly.

"Besides, we can get this place cleaned up in no time . . . with a little help."

"We?"

"Ya. We can get your husband and his buddies, a couple of trucks and we'll have you Swan-Laking in here in no time." He snapped his fingers to accentuate the simplicity of his plan, jolting Victoria's senses back to reality.

"No. That would never work, Elliot."

"Of course it will. Believe me, I've cleared out worse situations than this one."

"No, it's not that. It's just . . ." she hesitated, nervous about revealing any more of the intimate details of her life. Part of her was convinced that the more Elliot found out about her, the less attractive he was likely to find her.

"What?"

"Well, it's just with Bobby. I don't think he would be able to help."

Elliot frowned a question.

"He, um . . . he doesn't really want me to have a studio, at all."

She waited for Elliot to say something, but in the void of his words her own tumbled out.

"He just doesn't think it will be a success. Says he doesn't want me to end up disappointed. I don't know. Either way, he definitely won't help me with it." Her foot toyed abjectly with a rusty bread pan filled with orange nails.

"Well, I'll help you then."

"Elliot, no. I can't ask you to do that."

"You didn't ask. I offered."

Victoria released the tension between them with an exasperated laugh.

"Don't you ever take no for an answer?"

"Only when I think someone really means it," he grinned.

Victoria took a deep breath and allowed her eyes to follow the caves and mounds that littered the room. She felt like she stood on a free-floating bridge with elation and fear seesawing manically at either end. Finally, she shook her head.

"Thank you, Elliot. It's very nice of you, but I really can't accept your offer."

"Because . . .?"

"Because, well, because Bobby is kind of protective sometimes."

"Protective?"

Victoria nodded.

"Well, that's fine. Because I don't plan on hurting you, I plan on helping you."

"Okay. Maybe protective isn't quite the right word."

"And what would be the right word?"

She twirled a long, silky strand of hair around her index finger and shrugged.

"Jealous?" Their eyes met in a steely gaze.

"Look, I really do have to get going," she said brusquely as she edged off the boxes and stood up.

"Okay, wait! I'm sorry. It's not my business, right?"

She looked down at his softly restraining hand on her arm. "It's just that it's complicated, Elliot. I'd rather not talk about it."

"Might be good for you to talk about it," he said quietly.

Victoria laughed mirthlessly. "Spoken like a true out-of-towner! It's best to keep things to yourself here in Hinckly, Elliot. If you haven't learned that yet, you just haven't been here long enough."

"Maybe. Maybe you just need to learn to trust people more. I find most everyone confides in someone, whether they think of it that way or not. Think of how often people bare their soul to the semi-listening ear of a hairdresser or bartender. It's good for you."

"Well, it might work that way in the city. Bare your soul around here and it'll be served up with Pearl's lunch special by the next day."

Elliot shook his head and laughed. "Pessimist."

"Delusionist."

She looked at him curiously, thinking back over their conversation. Was it possible he had been the one who'd called her? That he'd called because of some altruistic concern for her? She displaced the thought at once.

"Fair enough. Still, I want to help you with this. I have an idea I think could work."

She cast him a dubious glance.

"You know, I bet Pearl has no idea that Bud has been sneaking all this junk in here through that back door over there. And I'll also bet she'll be more than happy to pay me to haul it all away."

"Elliot, I can't let you do that. Pearl will have you working for a pittance."

He nodded thoughtfully. "True. But there are other ways you can pay me back, you know."

"Elliot!" she flushed hotly.

His rippling laughter filled the room. "Hey, get your mind out of the gutter, young lady. That's not the kind of favor I mean."

Victoria crumpled her burning face into her hands. "Okay, well I feel silly."

"Don't. I completely set you up for that."

She looked up at him quizzically. "Why?"

"Because I love it when you blush. It's a truly lost art form."

She blushed again and pushed his leg playfully.

"There really is another way you can return the favor, though."

Apprehensive green eyes flicked his way. "How?"

"First, you have to promise to hear me out."

She held his eye, stalling as she tried to ascertain where he might be leading her. Finally, she shrugged her consent. "Okay, I promise."

Elliot sprang to his feet, facing her, his features animated. "Okay, great! I want to do a painting of you . . ."

Victoria erupted, arms wildly waving away his words. "No way, Elliot! Forget it."

"Victoria, wait," he pleaded. "You said you'd hear me out."

"Well, there's no point in hearing you out, Elliot, because it's just not ever going to happen."

"Why do you insist on slamming doors shut before they've even had a chance to open?"

"I don't," she defended hotly, crossing her arms and bracing for an argument.

Nodding his head in apparent agreement, Elliot slid back onto the boxes, steady and silent as he closed his eyes and rested his head against the wall.

She stood watching him, coiled inside herself, searching for any sign of hostility. In its absence she started to become acutely aware of her own, percolating ferociously through her veins. Standing in the presence of his peaceful demeanor, she began to feel self-conscious and foolish.

"So, are you going to finish telling me or not?" she asked, twirling her hair back into a thick ponytail and then letting it go.

"Are you going to listen?"

She wished he would open his eyes. She felt blind when she couldn't at least try to see what he was thinking.

"Okay. Okay, I'll listen. But, just as long as you know that it won't change anything."

Elliot's blue eyes sparked open as he shook his head and laughed. "You are quite possibly the most infuriating woman I've ever met, do you know that?"

"Well, that's not much of a compliment," she said, making a face at him.

"Wasn't intended as one," he grinned. "Here, come sit down and I'll tell you my idea."

Reluctantly she got back up on the boxes and looked at him.

"Okay, so this is my plan. I want to do a painting of you . . ." he paused to intercept her objection with his eyes. "And then I'm going to sell it and use the money to set up a scholarship fund for your studio."

Victoria's face crumbled with emotion, and she instantly hid behind her hands as tears pushed free. She had not expected this. Something as foreign as a scholarship fund had never even graced her thoughts. Memories of her own constant struggles to find ways to keep dancing swirled around her. What a gift this would be for her studio. Perhaps it could one day even enable one of her own students to dance forward with the flag of her own dream to perform on some of the most esteemed stages in the world.

She looked up at him through blurry eyes. "Elliot, I don't know what to say. That is such a wonderful offer . . ."

Elliot sighed. "But?"

She took a deep breath, her mind scrambling for words that could help him understand the predicament in which he had unwittingly placed her.

"This really is such a wonderful offer, such an amazing thing for you to do. And having a scholarship fund would open up so many opportunities . . ."

"But?" he grinned half-heartedly.

"But, I can't have you paint my picture," she whispered, looking down at her hands.

"Why not?"

She picked absently at a hangnail, embarrassment creeping over her.

"Your protective husband, again?"

Victoria nodded softly.

"Well, I won't tell him if you don't tell him. I can just slip in that side door after your lessons are finished and no one will be the wiser."

She looked over at the side door, which led into a deserted alley. "But, what if he sees the painting after it's sold and recognizes me?"

Elliot laughed out loud, startling her. "Victoria, I can promise you that the place where this painting will be sold is not a place your husband or anyone else from Hinckly is ever likely to be."

"But . . ."

"No. No buts. Just trust me on that one."

She allowed herself a small moment to consider this. She thought of what a scholarship would have meant to her when she was full of dreams and short of finances.

"But still, Elliot, it's not impossible that someone could see it and recognize me, right?"

"Right. Not impossible, just completely unlikely."

"Oh, I don't know," she murmured, dropping her head forward.

"There!" Elliot said excitedly, as he turned toward her. "Just like that. How about if I paint you like that, with your hair falling in front of your face. No one would ever be able to recognize you like that. What do you think, Victoria? Why couldn't that work?"

She played the question over and over in her mind, then slowly smiled up at him. "I don't know, Elliot. Maybe it could."

"Perfect! That's great," he exclaimed energetically. "We can get started just as soon as I can get this stuff hauled out of here."

"No, wait, Elliot. I don't know if I feel good about you going to all this work for me. Let me think about it, okay?"

Elliot slid off the boxes and looked at her. "Nothing for you to think about. I'm going to be working for Pearl."

~ Chapter 12 ~

The car was a '64 Barracuda, sanded down to a January gray and, with a generous fistful of imagination, just oozing with potential. She was permanently parked among the greasy spare parts and stacks of empty bottles that littered the floor of JJ's toolshed. Three pairs of work boots poked out from her undercarriage: Bobby, JJ and Peter already hard at it, ripping out the transmission JJ had just put in so they could spend the next weekend replacing it with the new one Bobby had ordered. JJ was forever second-guessing Bobby about each new part he suggested, constantly wondering if something else wouldn't be better. Although he denied it, the boys had heard that he already had a possible buyer lined up for the car and, if it was fast enough, that he'd be willing to pay him top dollar. The on-going dissension between Bobby and JJ was one of the reasons it was turning into a never-ending project, the half-empty case of beer sitting next to the toolbox being the other one.

"You guys drinking already?" Sam asked, careful to mask his dismay. The boys had no patience for any do-gooder raining on their good times just because his own had come up dry.

Three grimy, black faces popped out from under the car and peered up at him.

"Yeah, we're drinking already, Grandma. What the frick's it to ya?"

"Ain't nothing to me. Just early yet, that's all."

"Early? Ain't early. You just frickin' late. Us guys been working half the morning already. What time is it anyhow, ya big pecker-head?"

"Don't know. 'Bout nine I guess."

"Nine!" shot JJ, jumping to his feet, eyes wide as if he'd forgotten something vitally important. "Bobby, ya hear that? It's nine bloody o'clock already."

"So?" Bobby frowned back thickly, mopping at his face with a rag and smudging grease over the spots that had initially been clean.

"So! So, you pinhead. Ain't that tell you something?"

Bobby's black face crumpled up like the rag he held in his hand as he strained to find an answer. He stood up, Peter's snide chuckle mocking him quietly from below but, unfortunately for Peter, not quite quietly enough. Whirling around, Bobby seized him by his chicken neck, hoisted him up against the side of the car and dangled him just high enough so he wouldn't need his feet.

"What you laughing about, asshole?"

Peter's eyes bulged from rage and a serious lack of air. He screwed up his face and winced as if the answer was so obvious it was painful. He looked at JJ and rolled his buggy eyes, hoping to inspire JJ to barge in and avert Bobby's attention, but to no avail. Amused, JJ leaned back against the wall, wrapped a sarcastic smile around his cigarette and settled in to watch the show.

"Hey?" Bobby gave Peter a sharp shake like a dog would to a cat held by the scruff of the neck. "Hey, dwarf-pecker? You tell me, huh? You tell me what's so special 'bout nine o'clock, huh?"

Peter squirmed and wriggled, finally worming his way free. "How the hell would I know, ya asshole? You wanna know, ask him." He jutted his chin toward JJ, who received the gesture with a nasty grin, amused at Peter, who was usually fish slippery, getting caught in his own net. Peter's eyes shot hot darts at all of them in turn as he clambered back under the car muttering foul things.

"So," Bobby turned his attention back to JJ, who was reaching down for a bottle of whiskey lying beside the sack of beer. "What is the frickin' big deal 'bout nine o'clock?"

JJ stood up slowly, stretched and yawned loudly, his hairy black stomach puffing out from under his shirt like a pregnant porcupine. "Johnny time, you moron," he announced, draining a stiff drink straight from the bottle. "Petey, ya little cockroach! Get out from under there before you get your finger stuck up some place it don't belong."

Peter offered no reply.

"Peter, come on! Time for a drink that'll put a little hair on your scrawny chest. Hell with your chest! You need a drink that'll put some hair on your baby-ass head."

Still no response filtered out from under the car, Peter's legs sticking out as motionless as if they'd been chopped off at the knees. JJ offered the bottle to Bobby as they exchanged looks. Catching their meaning, Sam sighed. Pulling a chunk of wood and his carving knife from his coat pocket, he resigned himself to a spectator's seat on a pile of dusty tires. Clearly, work was not to be the order of the day. He half watched out of one eye as Bobby and JJ stealthily lowered themselves on either side of Peter's legs and gathered up his feet into tight handfuls.

"Come on, Petey!" They gave a good hard tug but didn't even budge him. Repositioning themselves, they grappled on a bit tighter and attempted to winch him out from under the car. Again, he stayed fastened tight. A squeak snuck out from below, and it was obvious the little bugger was laughing at their efforts.

JJ's face reddened. "Let go that muffler, dickhead," he warned, then gave the leg he was holding a vicious jerk hoping to snap Peter loose.

"Screw off!" Peter's voice muffled out as he reaffirmed his grasp and pulled himself up tighter. "I ain't bloody drinking with you assholes!"

"Whoo-ee!" JJ whistled, rocking back on his heels. "You hear that Bobby? Little whistle-prick's got too good to have a drink with

us. What you think 'bout that? Sounds to me like we's mighty overdue to bring the bugger down to size, hey?"

Sam watched as JJ let go of Peter's foot then wrapped his fist
around a handful of frayed jean bottoms. Catching on, Bobby
grinned and did the same.

"Hey! Hey, frick-heads! What're you doing? Don't you dare!
Don't you friggin' bloody dare—" Peter hollered, panicking to grab
at his belt a split second after a massive, coordinated effort ripped
his pants and shorts clear down to his knees, leaving his nether
regions unceremoniously exposed to the uproarious hoots of his
friends.

"Frickin' peckers! Frickin', perverted peckerheads! Sick sons-a-
bitches," he fumed over himself as he struggled out from under the
car, face flare-red as he tried to quickly cover himself up.

"What's the panic, Petey? I didn't see nothing. You see anything, Bobby?" JJ crowed, taking a deep slug that dribbled out the
corners of his mouth and ran down to the crease in his chin.

"Ain't much to see. Hey! Hey, maybe our little Peter's a friggin'
'morphadite."

"A friggin' what?"

"'Morphadite."

"What the hell's a 'morphadite?"

"You know. 'Morphadite. Like a dually."

"Not 'morphadite, you idiot."

"Bloody is too."

"No, it bloody ain't."

"What then?"

"It's a—" JJ hesitated for a fraction of an eighth note. "It's 'aphrodite, you ignorant moron."

"Bloody is not!"

"Is too!"

"Bullshit!"Bobby proclaimed, picking up a wrench and firing it
into the toolbox next to JJ's feet.

"Hey! Bloody watch where you're chucking that thing."

Bobby ignored him, snatched his cap off and scratched his head with some agitation. "Well, maybe it ain't friggin' 'morphadite, but it sure as hell ain't 'aphrodite neither."

"No? You think not, hey? Well, tells you what. Why the hell don't we just ask Petey then? Petey!" He looked over at Peter who looked away pointedly, arms wrapped up tight, legs crossed, a steady creak coming from his jaw as he slowly ground away his back teeth.

"Peter!" JJ tried again but was again stonewalled. A sardonic smile slipped onto Peter's face.

"Hey! Dick-face! I'm bloody talking to you," JJ bellered again, but this time with as much velocity as he could muster, straight into Peter's ear. Peter's hands flew up to defend against certain deafness, his body flinging involuntarily around to face John Jr.'s growling grin.

"Hey! What're trying to do, ya asshole? Trying to make me go completely friggin' deaf?"

"Naw, I ain't trying to make you go completely friggin' deaf, worm-dick. I thought ya's already was completely friggin' deaf 'cause you didn't seem to be hearing me when I was talking to you." He offered Peter the bottle of whiskey but pulled it up above his reach at the last minute, laughing as Peter's hand-grasp closed around a fistful of air. "Unh-unh Petey. First ya answer the question, then ya get a drink."

Peter pretzeled himself back into his defensive stance, clamped his jaw shut and focused on the floor.

"Come on, Petey. Help us out. What are you? An 'aphrodite or a 'morphadite?"

"Piss off!"

"It ain't bloody Aphrodite," Bobby said, grabbing back the bottle. "Ain't that some bloody Greek god or something?"

"Some bloody Greek god or something!" JJ scoffed. "Yeah, he was some bloody Greek god. The bloody Greek god of dual friggin' citizenship! That's who he friggin' was. That's why they call it 'aphroditism, ya moron."

"Ya? Really?"

"Ya! Really friggin' really."

Bobby slid off his cap, scratched his head with greasy fingers. "Makes bloody sense, I 'spose."

"Course it makes sense, genius. It's the frickin' bloody truth."

JJ snapped the top off a beer and clanked it against the whiskey bottle in Bobby's hand. "To our friend, Petey! The best little 'aphrodite in the valley."

"An' now we knows why he was always dressing up in his mama's clothes," added Bobby as they chugged a cheer.

Peter's face wriggled and seethed like a pocket-load of worms, but he held his tongue.

Sam sighed. "We gonna work on this thing or just stand around and b.s. all day?"

"Why? What the hell's your panic?" fired back Bobby.

"No panic. Just got some stuff to do, that's all."

"Ya right! Like what?" chided JJ.

"I don't know. Just stuff."

"Just stuff! What kind of frickin' stuff?"

"Just some stuff I said I'd do for Vic, that's all."

Bobby's eyes narrowed as JJ and Peter shared a malicious glance. "Vic? What the hell you doing for my old lady now?"

"Not much," Sam reassured slowly, looking down at his boots. "Just gonna fix up the dance floor a bit at the hotel."

"Now why the hell you gonna do that?"

"She asked me to, Bobby. Since you're too busy and all. It isn't much. I don't mind."

"Ya? Well, maybe I mind, Sammy. Ever think of that? I told her right from the get-go I didn't want her wasting a buncha money on some stupid studio."

Sam shuffled his feet. "I wasn't 'specting her to pay me—"

"No? Then what was you 'specting?"

"Nothing, Bobby. You know I don't mind helping you guys out. Besides, she seems real excited about it. She was telling me she's already got eight kids signed up."

Bobby shrugged the surprise off his face. "That right? Well, that still don't mean she's gonna make any money."

"Maybe she's not really doing it for the money," Sam started, then hesitated. He knew he shouldn't continue on. Knew he should just lay the words back down and let the moment slip away as he usually did. But for some reason he didn't. Maybe the planets had perfectly aligned that day. Or perhaps Zeus had chosen to pass overhead in a flaming chariot, baptizing him with a brief moment of courage that clouded his judgment. Whatever it was, it proved to be a colossal mistake as he let his words trip on.

"Maybe sometimes she gets a bit lonely out—"

"Lonely!" flared Bobby. "Why the frick would she be lonely, asshole?"

Sam sat quietly but Bobby was pissed.

"You wanna hear about lonely? You should read the bloody paper, Samson. Story in there 'bout some poor bugger locked up for eight years for something he didn't never do in the first place. You want friggin' lonely? That's friggin' lonely. Here, ya wanna read it? It's in my truck. I'll even go get it for ya."

Sam said nothing, his eyes sliding away to the ground.

"Hey, it ain't no problem, Sammy. I don't mind. I'll jus' go an grab it for you," Bobby shot as he headed for the door. Slamming the truck door behind him he reappeared in the shed, pranced over to Sam and flung a ratty paper in his face. "There! Read it for yourself, Sammy boy," he stabbed, his grin breaking into a nasty snicker as Peter and JJ's voices joined in from behind.

Sam took the paper from Bobby's hand and set it down on the workbench beside him.

"Oh, that's right, ain't it? You can't read. Now why am I always forgetting that?"

It had always been this way for Sam. Raised in the earthy tongue of his Cree grandmother, he'd been deposited at six years old into a classroom of strange people speaking strange noises, which they assumed he understood. But he hadn't understood and, unsure of what was expected of him, had quickly developed the lifelong habit of looking away and smiling shyly whenever he was spoken to. Which had, along with his unnatural size, helped to fasten a permanent label of *slow* across his young back. Sam was however, not slow.

And yet somewhere between conceptualization and delivery, there existed a dark moment that swallowed his sentences before he could deliver them back out his mouth. The problem, simply enough, was that while Sam spoke in English, his thoughts were in Cree. Alcohol had set him free. Freed his tongue and his lips and his fists so that even if his words got too jumbled up, a right hook could still adequately convey his expression.

An older model Dodge truck spun around the corner and screamed up the street toward them. They watched it with disguised interest as it pulled toward the big open door of the shop.

"Now, who the hell might that be?" JJ asked into his next drink.

"Miller's truck, looks like," offered Peter helpfully.

"Obviously it's Miller's truck, you moron. But that sure as piss ain't Miller driving it."

"Looks like that kid that works for him."

"Hmpff. Wonder what that little pecker wants," added Bobby as they watched Mark swing free of the truck and saunter toward them.

"Hey!" he tossed by way of greeting. "You old men give me a hand with this here tranny, or will it aggravate your hemorrhoids?"

"Only hemorrhoids get aggravated around here'll be the one hanging where your face should be, ya smart ass. Thought Miller said he couldn't get me one of these till next week."

Mark shrugged. "Don't ask me. He just said to bring it over, so I'm bringing it over. Can ya give me a hand?"

"Sammy," JJ ordered. "Give the candy-ass a hand with it, will ya?"

Setting his carving aside, Sam walked over to the truck, gathered the transmission up in his arms and set it easily on top of the workbench.

Mark's face sprung a cocky expression.

"What's this piece of shit?" he chided, thumping at the 'cuda's front tire with his foot.

"Hey! Watch your mouth, punk. This here car's about the finest piece of mother you'll ever see cruising atop four wheels."

"Ain't look like it'll be doing much cruising for some while yet."

"You think not, hey? Well, that just goes to show how much an ignorant pup like you ain't know. Ain't that right, Bobby? Got plans for this bitch, I do."

"Oh yeah? Like what?" asked Mark, losing the edge off his chippyness.

Everyone had heard how much JJ had got for the last car they'd fixed up. How some hot-shot rich kid from the city had dropped a fistful of money on it so he could be king of the drag-racing strip. Rumor was Mark and some of his buddies had plans to begin fixing up a car of their own.

"Like what? Like what, he says." JJ rolled his eyes at Bobby. Pulling a new case of beer out of the backseat, he snapped one open and thrust it at Mark. "Here, sit down and have a barley sandwich while I tell you, like what."

"Can't. I'm 'sposed to be working."

"Oh, shee-it!" hollered JJ. "I think I hear my freakin' granny calling. Hey, Bobby! You hear that? Someone sure as hell sounding a lot like my freakin' granny 'round here."

"Aw, shit," Mark mumbled, grabbing the beer JJ was waving around in front of his face. "Give me the damn thing then. But I gotta hurry. 'Sposed to get the truck right back so's Miller can make a delivery."

"Miller's delivery can wait. You got the important one of the day done right here. By the time we boys get done with this here car, the bitch'll be so hot punks like you'll bow down on yer knees and worship her every time she passes by."

"Not friggin' likely! Only bitch I bow down on my knees to worship is the one I'm about to lay," Mark shot back, provoking laughs and a cheer.

"We're taking the 'ruf off too," piped in Peter.

"The what?" asked Mark, looking down at Peter as if he'd only just now noticed him.

"The 'ruf. Whole thing."

"Ruf?" Mark's eyes bypassed Peter altogether by the six inches of clearance he had over his head and directed the query to Bobby. "What the hell's a ruf?"

"Roof! He can't never bloody say it right. Friggin' 'aphrodite."

Mark's face twisted up as he tried to make sense of this, then let it go. "Ya gonna cut the roof off?"

"Ya. You know, like a convertible. Broads dig that."

"Broads? Ain't you guys forgetting yer married?"

"Might be married pus-head," John Jr. retorted stuffing a beer into Mark's other hand. "But we ain't friggin' dead."

Mark took the beer, drained his first one then pried the cap off with his teeth and flicked it out the window and into the sandbox. "What color ya painting it? Red?"

Three answers collided together. JJ silenced the other two with a dirty look then started again. "I'm thinking orange. You know, real bright tomato orange. With big bloody yellow flames licking up the sides—"

"Sounds like shit," Mark spat, laughing at the insulted fury that bristled across JJ's face.

"No . . . not orange, JJ. You said I could paint it purple. You promised," whined Peter, using his sleeve to catch a dribble of snot hanging off his nose.

"You promised . . . you promised," JJ taunted back gleefully. "Well, I'm changing my promise piss-ass 'cause I don't bloody like purple no more."

"Hey!" interjected Mark. "Got an idea." He strode over to a shelf full of mismatched cans of spray paint and started rooting through them. "Here, why don't you each take a section and give it your best shot then we can decide what looks best."

JJ pushed in beside him and grabbed his colors first, promptly scoring off the hood and the car's best side while Peter and Bobby scrambled over one another to carve up what was left.

"Wait! Wait, you guys! No fair!" Peter squealed as he struggled to snap off the top only to find that the purple the can's lid had promised was really more of a cotton candy pink.

Mark found a derelict chair where he deposited himself so he could watch and jeer in comfort. Soon tiring of this, he hoisted himself back up and proceeded around the car slowly, his swagger starting to stagger as he got down to work on another beer.

A piercing scream snapped their attention over to the wood-pile where Peter was scrambling to zip his pants up, his eyes locked to the ceiling.

"Ooh! Look you guys! Look! Up on the 'ruf. Friggin' bat! Scared the frickin' piss outta me!" He shuffled back quickly as the others crowded around to see. A tiny, furry brown mound hung motion-less from a rafter above them.

"Maybe it's dead," Peter offered hopefully.

"Ain't dead, ya idiot."

"How's you know? Looks dead to me."

"'Cause it'd fall on the friggin ground if it was dead, ya moron. It's just pretending."

"How come?" Peter asked, scrunching up his nose in disgust.

"Just trying to trick us," answered JJ.

"Chuck something at it."

"You chuck something at it, piss-ass."

"Here. Look out," a voice ordered from behind them, Mark stepping forward with a wrench and winging it at the rafter, bounc-ing it off the little creature's gauzy wing. Instantly the bat snapped to life, mouth wide in a silent warning to its invisible tormentors. Hanging limply, its injured wing quivered lightly.

"Eek!" screeched Peter, tripping backward over Bobby and roll-ing across the floor. "Gross! It hissed at us. The friggin' thing hissed at us. Knock it down, JJ! Knock it down!"

JJ looked around him for a weapon, seized upon a rusted shovel leaning against the wall, lifted it high and gave the bat a quick poke. Again the bat's mouth sprang open as it tried to ward off an attack. The boys cringed in spite of themselves. Sam watched his friends curiously. There was something about this audacious creature's response toward them that provoked them to fury. How dare it, barely a hand big or a pound heavy, open its mouth to hiss and try to drive them away. Any of them could kill it with one blow. And yet it held sway over them, held the power of aversion. Mark grabbed the shovel from JJ's limp hand and swept the bat onto the floor, all of them stepping back quickly to give it wide berth even though they knew the creature was essentially harmless and totally helpless with its damaged wing. Hitting the ground hard, the bat scrambled upright and turned again to face them, its mouth now permanently splayed wide open. Bobby picked up a long stick, crept forward and poked it in the mouth.

"Eek!" Peter screamed again, this time receiving a hard clout on the back of his head for yelling in JJ's ear.

"Hey you guys," Sam's thick voice tumbled up from behind them. "Leave it alone, hey. It ain't hurting nothing."

If any of them heard, they paid no attention and Peter slithered through the crush of bodies, leaned as close to the bat as he dared and doused it with a spray of purple paint. Anxious, boisterous laughter broke out above him as the bat recoiled, gagging. Encouraged, he let it have it again.

"Come on, you guys," Sam spoke a little louder. "Just leave it alone, okay?"

Bobby grabbed a can of silver spray paint off the shelf and joined Peter on the front lines. The bat lay crumpled on the floor unmoving, its soft fur layered with a sickening purple. Feeling brave, Bobby eased forward and prodded it once again. The mouth flared open in an automatic response and excitedly he quickly filled it with toxic silver. A heavy hand knocked the can rolling from his grip, and he looked up to see Samson standing over him, shovel in hand. Raising it slowly overhead, Sam hesitated as he caught Bobby's eye then brought it down hard, crushing the bat dead.

~ Chapter 13 ~

The refrigerator was offering her nothing, and she flung the door shut on its frosty interior just as the telephone jangled behind her. Whirling around, she lunged at it even though she was the only one home in the trailer. She'd grown skilled at beating Bobby to it, often snatching it right out from under his hand just before he closed down on it. Word about the studio had spread quickly, and although she finally had to cap the class at 16, she still received a few calls each week from mothers who'd initially scoffed at the idea but were now anxious to have their daughters put on the waiting list. Bobby, feeling vilified by the studio's apparent success, viewed each call as a personal affront and answered the phone accordingly, offending people with his sarcasm and neglecting to give Victoria her messages. And, besides trying to intercept Bobby's abuse of her possible future customers, Victoria could also never be sure when static would suddenly fill the line. The growing indiscretion of her words had left her feeling as anxious and guilty as if she'd actively welcomed a lover into their marriage bed and found him irresistible. Half expecting the call to be from Rose, she answered it with a distracted "hi," then brightened visibly as static greeted her.

"I was thinking of you."

"Of me? Really?" She felt flattered and flustered, off-center. "And what's so special about me that you were thinking of me?"

"Everything."

"Everything?" She laughed gently, encouragingly.

"Your eyes."

"My eyes aren't—"

"Your lips."

She dropped her lashes and skimmed her tongue over her lips.

"I—" she started then stopped, paralyzed into silence by a sudden crushing ache of emotion. Squeezing her eyes tighter, she wrestled internally, forbidding herself from bleeding her desperation into the line. Biting her lip hard she sealed away how much she had missed him, how insane she had been for him to call again. Hot tears singed her face as she pressed the receiver to her cheek, taking strength from it as if it were a lover's hand. They sat silent like this for measureless moments as she soaked in the comfort of his presence and felt it slowly dissipate the cold isolation within her. It occurred to her suddenly that his calls were nothing less than a gift. A kindness that needed to be repaid.

"Do you remember what you said?" Her voice, encumbered by emotion had choked itself to a throaty whisper. "A while ago. About me being . . . lonely?" Flickering her eyes open, she spotted a warm sliver of sunlight on the living room floor and settled herself into it. "It's true, you know. I am. Except when I'm at the studio. With the children. I feel happier there. Happier, but still a bit lonely, I guess. It's like it comes from the inside. Like it's a part of me. I think it's always been there. Even as a child I always felt out of place. Like a stranger in my own home. Do you think . . . do you think it's possible to be born into the wrong life?" She punctuated this last thought with a self-effacing laugh in case he found it as ridiculous as it sounded.

The caller did not return her laughter or an answer to her question, but as they sat joined in mutual silence she began to sense that he could understand how she felt. He was a good listener, sympathetic, compassionate. The kind of person that heard beyond the boundaries that words set in the way. Encouraged by his patient silence she continued on.

"I think of you too, you know. All the time."

She closed her eyes again, tighter, and felt the almost instant response of her body as she entered the freedom of her dark cocoon. It was as if here, with the outside world blocked away, she could finally be alone with him. As if she'd stepped into a moral no-man's-land where thoughts and feelings and even rabid desire could linger in safety, no longer under the constant threat of reprisal or consequence. Pulling her legs up toward her chest, she let them fall away from each other then pulsed them gently with the slow, rhythmic beat of giant butterfly wings as she searched the line for the caller's breathing. Impatience began to work its way toward her as she willed him to speak to her again, hungry to feel the delicate stroke of his word's feathery touch.

"You're so beautiful," the words finally rushed through to her, erupting inside her head like an emotional orgasm. She clung to the receiver. Wanted to crawl right into it. To touch him. Feel him. Kiss the salty pleasure from his back as they swam into horizonless sex. She moaned a mix of physical and mental anguish into his ear as she felt the jagged impossibility of their desire cut through her.

The swoosh of the porch door startled her upright with a gasp, and she turned to face Bobby as he kicked free of his boots and stepped into the kitchen. She stood, receiver in hand, the long black cord leading past Bobby's legs to where the telephone sat on the table.

"Who you talking to?" he gestured to the phone with his chin.

"No one."

His eyes narrowed as he raised a dark eyebrow.

"No one?"

Blood rushed hot to her face. She pressed the handset hard against her leg.

"Well, no. Not anymore. It . . . it was just one of the mothers."

He eyed her sharply for a moment, turned and walked down the hall into the bathroom. Waiting for the click of the door, she took a quick listen. Thankfully, the line was dead. She could only hope it had been that way for some time and that her and Bobby's conversation had not been overheard. Hurrying to place the telephone back on the cradle, she began to straighten up the trailer although not one thing appeared to be out of place.

~ Chapter 14 ~

Christmas was coming to Hinckly. A few attempts at decorations had been made by the local businesses, only to be vandalized by kids who enjoyed the spoils of naughty over nice. Mrs. Barlow's Santa had lost his head, and Mr. Graves's Rudolph had been strung up by his horns with a silver garland and shot full of arrows. Pearl and Bud's lights had been enlisted for target practice, but fortunately the young hooligans proved to be terrible shots: only a few lights were smashed and a couple were even jolted back into service.

Victoria pushed her way through the resistant hotel door and hurried through the lobby. She felt half-prepared and disorganized. Her plan had been to arrive early at the studio so she could make out some bills before the parents arrived with their kids. But by the time she had realized the kitchen clock was way behind accurate, she'd had to drive as fast as she dared all the way into town just to avoid being late.

The excited chipmunk chatter of small voices greeted her as she made her way toward the ballroom where the children waited outside the locked doors. Enjoying their enthusiasm and perhaps feeling overly optimistic, she had planned and choreographed a Christmas recital. Now, with performance night looming, she was feeling somewhat anxious about her decision and contemplating postponing it until spring. Shrieks and squeaks filled the air when the children saw her, a cloud of tutu-ed little girls clamoring around her like frilly, miniature marshmallows.

"Hello, hello, hello," she said, laughing at their sprightliness as they twirled and whirled around, each one eager to show off to their beloved teacher.

Scanning across their antics, her eye caught on a small, dejected form hunched down in the back corner of the lobby. Walking over, she tried to read the troubled face partially hidden beneath ribbons of brown curls.

"Hey, Lily. What's the matter, sweetie?"

"I'm sad."

"Sad? How come you're sad?"

"Rufus said prayee-princesses can't fly."

"Who's Rufus?"

"My bow-ther's friend."

"Your brother's friend?"

"Uh-huh. He's nine."

"And so why does your brother's friend think fairy princesses can't fly?"

"'Cause they're girls."

"Girls can't fly?"

"Nope. Just Superman."

"Really?" Victoria felt herself bristle protectively. "But who do you think taught Superman to fly?"

Lily looked up brightly. "His dance teacher?"

"You bet. Now, come on, put on your shoes. We have lots to do."

Imbued with a new sense of resolve, Victoria gathered the children into the studio and coaxed them through one of their more successful practices. Watching them, she began to feel it might just be possible to pull off the Christmas recital after all. Teasing and laughing with the children after the lesson, she waited patiently for parents to retrieve their respective charges. As usual, a few chronically late ones arrived well after the class had ended. Hastily waving them goodbye, Victoria quickly locked the ballroom doors from the inside, eyes dashing anxiously back toward the simple, unobtrusive side door that led into the deserted alleyway. Her stomach had twisted itself into a tight knot. She wasn't sure whether she was more nervous that Elliot would show up or that he wouldn't.

With a self-conscious glance around, she hurriedly shed her jeans and T-shirt and pulled her dance dress from a bag lying next to her purse. Her hands glided over the silky green fabric. It hung flawlessly against her body, her still-muscular, long bare legs forming a vivid contrast to its flowing smoothness. Grabbing her ballet slippers from the bag, she crossed to the center of the room and stared back at the reflections staring out at her. She ran a critical check over her body, searching out any defects, wondering how she could have been so gullible as to agree to let Elliot do a painting of her in the first place. She felt as exposed and nervous as a Victorian virgin on her wedding day. Twirling around, she checked her images from behind.

For a brief moment she considered that she could just not answer when Elliot's knock came at the back door. But, as her gaze took in the colossal reformation of the ballroom, she knew it wasn't really an option. Elliot's vision had proved correct. Freed from years of neglect and misuse, the room had been transformed into a truly marvelous studio. Even its size felt more airy and spacious than it really was, thanks to the addition of a row of mirrors along one wall, which folded the room outward into itself.

The bottom half of the tall window had been blacked out to discourage curious onlookers, but the top half of its resplendent Gothic arch welcomed in the mid-morning sun, flooding the room with exuberant light. She looked down and smiled warmly at the barely visible filling and patch job Sam had insisted she let him do on the damaged part of the floor. All in all, she had been surprised by the generosity of people's support for the studio. Pearl had even dropped by occasionally to offer advice, sending Victoria into a panic when she offered for Bud to hang up the mirrors. Bud, for his part, lurked about grudgingly, making it silently clear what he thought of the damage Victoria had wreaked upon his storage room.

The scrunch of shoes on snow jerked her attention toward the alleyway, and she followed the sound blindly as it made its way past the blacked-out window, up the three stairs leading to the side door and culminated in a sure knock. Heart fluttering, she rechecked her images, worked down a full smile then glided back to let him in.

Her smile was met with an armload of painting apparatus shoved her way.

"Hi! Here, can you take some of this stuff for me while I take off my shoes?"

"Shh!" Victoria whispered. "No, don't take them off out there. Come in before someone sees you."

"And a good day to you, too," Elliot grinned, peeking around a large canvas.

"I'm sorry, Elliot. Hi. Been kind of a hectic morning. And I guess I'm just nervous someone might see you."

"Well, don't worry. I was careful. Besides, the amount of times I've been in and out of this place the last while pretty much makes me a natural part of the landscape."

Victoria flushed. She was still uncomfortable with the amount of work he'd done to help her out with the studio. And she was still unsure as to exactly why he had done so.

"Wow! Look at this place. You've done a great job pulling it into shape, Victoria."

"Well, I've had lots of help," she answered, suddenly remembering that Elliot, asked by her to make himself scarce once other people started showing up to help, hadn't actually been in the ballroom since he'd hauled away the last bent bicycle frame.

Slipping out of his shoes, he wandered breezily around, admiring the improvements and smiling at her in the mirrors. He turned and looked up at the waterfall of light pouring through the arched window.

"This place turned out just perfect, Victoria. Don't you think?" he asked as he squatted down to inspect the repairs that had been made to the floor. "Who fixed the floor?"

"Um, Sam. Samson Billyboy. He's a friend of Bobby's. Have you met him?"

Elliot shook his head without looking up as he continued inspecting the floor. "No. Not really. Heard about him. Pretty good with his hands, I'd say. This repair is really well done."

"Is it?" Victoria asked, bending over to take a closer look. She wished she had had time to at least sweep before this formal inspection. "Not too surprising, really. Sam loves wood. He's always carving little statues of animals and birds and stuff."

"Hmm," Elliot murmured as he stood up, his sparkling eyes pulling her thoughts back from Sam.

"Hey, look at you," he said, walking a slow circle around her. "That's an absolutely exquisite dress. Fits perfectly."

"Thanks," she answered distractedly. She didn't like him apprising her so closely, and she turned with him, holding his intent gaze. "What are you doing, Elliot?"

"Well, if you would stand still for a moment, what I'm trying to do is look at you from different angles to see how I'd like to set up the painting."

"Oh." She looked away. "Well, let me put my dance shoes on first, okay?"

"No," he said authoritatively. "No shoes. Bare feet."

"Bare feet?"

He nodded firmly.

"But no one dances in bare feet, Elliot."

"Sure they do," he said, a smile sliding over his face as he looked too deeply into her eyes. "Not in the studio, maybe. Definitely not onstage. But when they're all alone, just them, the moment and the music. There'd be such a freedom in it. Right?"

Victoria couldn't help but smile back at him. "Maybe. I guess I just thought you'd want shoes on for the painting."

"Nope. Bare feet," he said simply as he walked to the back door, stripped off his coat and picked up his sketchpad and pencils from the floor. Returning to the center of the room, he took her hand gently and turned her slightly into the light, studying the lines of her as if she were marble.

"Beautiful," he murmured quietly.

She snapped around to face him, ears humming with his inflection of the word as she struggled desperately to align it with her memory of the caller's voice. She studied his face intently for any sign of unease, any awareness of what the word had triggered in her.

Elliot looked at her curiously. "Problem?" he asked, his face and body giving no sign that anything was amiss within him.

Flushing, she shook her head and looked away. Seeing his paints and canvas still propped up against a chair at the back of the room, she rushed over to collect them. "Here. Don't you want your paints?"

Taking them from her, he leaned them against the wall then slid cross-legged to the floor across from the arched window, flipping through his sketchpad to find a fresh sheet.

"Well, aren't you going to need them?" she asked, confused.

"Not yet. Later. First I want to do some sketching."

She felt a little rise of disappointment. "Oh. Okay. Of what?"

Elliot threw his head back and laughed heartily as Victoria hastened to quiet him.

"Of you, silly! That's how it works. For me, anyhow. First I do a few sketches, try to find the right feel until the picture presents itself."

She stood quietly, feeling a little admonished. "Oh. Okay. So, what do you want me to do?"

"Dance."

She felt herself brace against the suggestion. She hadn't anticipated that she might have to actually dance in front of him. "Oh. I thought I'd just have to pose while you did your painting."

Elliot ran long graceful fingers through his hair as he leaned back against the wall.

"Victoria, we are in a dance studio, you are a dancer and I am a painter looking to express the essence of the dance in you onto my canvas. Does it not seem reasonable then that I should, at least once, have the pleasure of seeing you dance?"

She considered this for a moment. "Yes, I suppose so. But, I can't put the music on. Someone might hear."

"You don't need the music. Just close your eyes and remember it."

She wrinkled her nose up and grinned at him. "It'd be easier for me if you closed your eyes, too."

"No doubt. But that really makes it so very difficult for me to see anything." He grinned back at her.

Seeing he had no intention of giving in, and with their time slipping by, she took a deep breath and closed her eyes. The disconnection of their gaze left her feeling instantly vulnerable and exposed. She flashed her eyes open again. "Wait! It makes me nervous having someone watch me."

"Victoria," he said with exaggerated patience, "you *have* had people watch you dance before, right?"

"Yes, of course. But, that was a long time ago. This feels different."

"How?"

"I don't know how to explain it. Just different."

"More intimate?"

She thought about this for a moment, then nodded.

"Good. That's what I want to bring to the painting. That sense of intimacy."

Victoria frowned.

"Well, think of it this way. A dancer dances for an audience. But to the individual watching, the audience is an illusion. They cannot feel as an audience. There is only the interchange between each individual and the dancer. The dancer's body becomes a work of art expressing the emotion of each scene. It's really an intercourse or, say, interchange of intimate connection between the dancer and her viewer."

Victoria looked at him wide-eyed. "Well, if that explanation was intended to make me feel less nervous, it wasn't a major success."

Elliot laughed loudly. "Okay, fair enough. Forget what I just said. I know what I wanted to say, but I got lost in there somewhere. Maybe that's why I paint," he added, uncharacteristically flustered.

She smiled lightly at his discomfort. This was something of a revelation, that he wasn't always quite as comfortable expressing his thoughts as he had seemed. Again, she wondered if it were possible that he was in fact the one who'd called her. Suddenly the idea seized her that perhaps he thought she knew that it was he who was calling. That they sat in mutually agreeably anonymity in order to keep things simple and eliminate barriers. She panicked at the possibility. Maybe he had no idea his phone was so full of static that she could barely make out the few words he ever spoke. Maybe he felt he was doing her a favor, listening to her pathetic outpouring of self-indulgent talk. She clamped down over the erratic barraging of her mind. No. It was not like that. She was letting her imagination carry her away. Whoever the caller was, she was almost positive it was not Elliot. The thought disappointed her, and she adjusted it slightly. Anything was possible. She didn't really have a clue about whom it might be. She knew it could just as easily be some grotesque old wanker from down at the home as it could be Elliot. She strongly resisted the idea. Deep inside her, she knew she'd felt a connection as they'd sat in silence. Anything was possible. Anything. It could be Elliot, she conceded protectively. It could be anyone.

Her compulsive thinking was distracted by the wall clock. "I guess we'd better hurry."

Elliot spread his hands open and gestured for her to begin. She stood quiet for a moment, eyes closed, refusing to give reign to all the thoughts clamoring through her head. She pulled deeply at a few strains of music, allowed them to calm her, then to fill her with their rapturous, weeping chords. She felt the movement of air, cloud-soft against her skin as she began to move. Slowly, conscious of his eyes on her, her movements became richer and fuller as the music continued to possess her. And then she felt no more. She simply was. A resplendent note dancing in the symphony of life. A capriccio of motion, glorious in her belonging.

Her eyes fluttered open, her awareness of Elliot total and yet wholly unconcerned, as if she were drugged by the dance. He was peripheral and yet central to the pleasure fueling her moment. Lost in an ecstasy of movement, she danced into exhaustion finally twirling into stillness, extending a vibrant, long left leg toward him as she tipped forward in a slight bow.

He stood up quietly and stepped toward her. She straightened, eyes blinking as if suddenly awakened as she felt his warm hands across her shoulders, lightly encouraging her back into the position she had ended with.

"Like that, Victoria. Perfect. That's the way I want to paint you." His voice sounded oddly altered, moved with emotion. He again began to circle her, slowly nodding his approval. "Yes, definitely. That's the one. Can you hold that for me while I do a quick sketch?"

She stood full in the streaming light, her chest heaving from the exertion of the dance. The raw, sizzling energy coursing through her veins made it all but impossible for her to be still. It had released her to dance so freely. It had released her to dance so freely in front of him.

He stood against the wall for a moment observing, then walked back over to her. She drew up, afraid he was going to admonish her for her inability to stand in stillness. Instead, he walked behind her, searching fingers slipping lightly into her hair, seeking out the little hairpins that fastened her hair into a tight bun. Gently he worked them free until her hair hung loosely down her back. Gathering it over to one side, he finger-combed it lightly, then arranged it forward so it partially shielded her face.

She looked up at him shyly. "Thank you."

Taking a deep breath, she allowed herself to become more pliable under his hands as he gently shifted her position, delicately molding her fingers beneath his own. He tipped her still further forward, her left strap sliding down until it hung precariously close to slipping right off. She tried to imperceptibly raise her shoulder to keep it in place, but Elliot's palm gently pressed it back down. Suddenly, the strap released its tenuous hold and slid part way down her arm, openly exposing the top part of her breast. Automatically, her other hand flew up and snatched the strap back into place.

"No," he said firmly, his hand covering hers as she held the strap up. "Leave it. I like it that way. It's . . . unexpected."

Struggling deeply within herself, she tried to remember why she shouldn't listen to him, but her thoughts refused to cooperate as her attention was circumvented by the feel of his hand on hers. Overwhelmed by the intensity of the moment, she gently withdrew her hand out from under his.

"Thank you," he whispered as he softly slid the strap back over her shoulder and down her arm.

Victoria said nothing, her mind a flurry of conflicted emotion as Elliot easily sauntered over to his easel, put his canvas in place and immersed himself in his sketch. She tried to relax into the moment, but her senses were hyper-alert to the sounds of the comings and goings outside the ballroom doors. Twice, she imagined she heard Bobby's voice booming out over the din coming from the steadily growing lunchtime crowd filling the café. Victoria's heart started to flutter manically, her breath pulled away from her. She cursed herself as she bit her lip nervously. Why had she ever agreed to do this? If word ever got out, Bobby would go ballistic.

"What was that?" she asked suddenly, yanking her strap back into place, eyes fixed on the window behind him.

He looked up trance-like. "What?"

"That noise," she whispered, as she made her way over to the blacked-out window and listened intently.

"I didn't hear anything."

"Shh," she said. Waving him off to one side, she softly padded toward the back door, opened it slightly and peeked out. A large yellow tomcat, beat-up and mangy, flew off the stairs as she did so. "Oh! It's just a cat," she exhaled with obvious relief.

"Victoria, I think you're letting your nerves run away with you a bit," Elliot offered kindly.

"I know. You're probably right. It's just, you know, I'm still not sure that this is such a good idea."

"It'll be fine," he grinned. "I promise."

Victoria smiled back at him. "I hope so. Anyhow, I'd better go. I still have some errands to run."

"Okay," he agreed. "Where do you want me to put my stuff? In the broom closet?"

She looked around. "There's a broom closet?"

"Well, not anymore. You're using it for a coat closet. But, that used to be where they kept the brooms and mops and stuff. How about I put some hooks up on the wall by the doors for the kids to hang their coats on and then we can use the closet to keep the painting?"

"But . . . we can't keep the painting here."

"Well," he said slowly, "I can't very well be packing it in and out of here if we're trying to be discreet about things, can I?"

Victoria shook her head, her mind racing. She could not believe she hadn't thought this through.

"Listen," he said quietly. "It's not a problem to keep it here. I had to get a key from Pearl to empty out that room when I was cleaning up. She made a big fuss about making sure I didn't lose it because she only has one. Why don't you see if you can get it from her again, and we'll just keep it while the painting is in there."

"Okay," she sighed with relief. "That'd work great. Otherwise, I'd be worried sick about someone going in there and seeing it."

Elliot reached his arms around her and gave her a quick hug. "You shouldn't worry so much, Victoria. Trust me. Everything is going to work out fine."

~ Chapter 15 ~

Sorry," she apologized, joining Rose in a corner booth. "A couple of the parents didn't get there until late."

"No problem. Gave me time to balance my checkbook." Rose waved her off with a smile. "How've you been? Too busy with the studio now to call, I suppose?"

"I'm sorry, Rose. Went and planned this Christmas recital . . . I don't remember them being so much work. The kids are trying really hard, though. I think we might just pull it off."

"That's good. So, you're enjoying it? Not too busy for you?"

"No, it's not too busy. I love it. Other than Bobby trying to sabotage me every chance he gets. Last week he actually set the clock back so I'd be late. Denied doing it of course, but the batteries were just fine when I checked them. I keep hoping he'll just get used to the idea and quit being so difficult."

"Hmm. Well, aren't you just the eternal optimist?"

"I guess you could call it that," Victoria sighed.

"The girls have been pestering me about joining, too. You've become quite the celebrity with the elementary school crowd, you know. None of my girls ever had a bit of interest in dance before, but now that it's become de rigueur, I've suddenly become like the evil stepmother for not signing them up. I told them maybe in the spring . . . if you have any room. Coffee?"

Victoria nodded. Undoing her sweater, she wrestled for a moment with the stuck zipper and finally pulled it off over her head, sending her hair into early morning chaos. She finger-combed it calm and muttered thanks as Pearl wandered over, filled up her mug and dropped two menus on the table. She stood waiting expectantly, a wad of pink gum receiving brutal treatment between her jaws. "So, how's them kids' dance lessons comin'?"

"Good. You going to join us again?"

"Naw. Wasn't fer me."

Victoria suppressed a grin as she remembered the tittering giggles that had broken out the first time Pearl had shown up in her homemade pink tutu.

Victoria reached for her menu. "Could you give us a minute, please?"

Ignoring the request, Pearl ran her quick eyes off to the back of the café and waited for Victoria's to follow. Stuffed into the back corner sagged a ragamuffin fake tree fastened by duct tape to the wall like a weary prisoner of war. Pearl had found a way to save the bother of redecorating each year. With the first good thaw in March, she would holler at Bud, and he'd cut the duct tape off the wall and drag the tree back down into the coal cellar till the time came to pull it back out the next year. Not exactly of the nature to get overly extravagant just because it was Christmas, Pearl still expected people to appreciate the effort she did make. She glowered at Victoria, waiting for her to respond.

"Oh, I see you decorated."

"Yup. Bud taped it up yesterday," she agreed, snapped her gum, waited.

"Looks nice. Very festive," Victoria lied as she had every year since Bud discovered the tree at the dump, dragging it home behind his bike.

Pearl scowled, pressed the gum out between a gap in her front teeth almost to the point of losing it, then sucked it back in with a little slurp.

"You don't think it's getting a little worn out?"

It was a trick question. Victoria had almost fallen for it once but had watched others get taken in time and again. Anyone agreeing quite honestly that it was perhaps looking a little bedraggled was instantly seized upon for a donation to cheer it up, Pearl supplying the decorations at three times their original cost. Honesty at Pearl's was synonymous to stupidity.

Pastor Jack was her favorite victim.

"No. No, it looks just fine to me, Pearl. Same as last year."

Disappointed, Pearl turned on her heel and marched back toward the kitchen where Bud had just come in.

"Buddy! What you doing in my kitchen with those dirty rubbers? No! No siree, mister. You ain't bloody well washing them in my sink. Git outside with you. Git out 'fore I grab my broom and git you out."

A screen door screeched and banged, and one could just imagine Bud slinking off like a dump dog with its tail tucked between its legs. Bud was one of those fellows very seldom seen but evidenced everywhere by the work he left behind. Duct tape was his trademark, and judging from the fact that it seemed to hold most of the hotel together, he must have purchased it by the truckload.

Pearl walked back out from behind the counter, glared at a few customers in case they'd had second thoughts about lunch, then came back up to Rose and Victoria's table to take their order. The snapping of her gum indicated she was in no mood for patience. She shook her head vigorously.

"That Bud! No more brains than a bitch in heat, that man. Bring his dirty rubbers into my kitchen . . . gonna wash them in my sink. Dumb I tell you! Dumb, dumb, dumb, shit-fer-brains dumb. Whadda ya wanna eat?"

Pearl was possibly one of the only people around who still thought rubbers were something people wore on their feet. Rose and Victoria avoided each other's eyes, carefully placed their orders and suppressed laughs until Pearl had left and disappeared well out of ear range.

"So?" Rose raised her sweeping brows and batted her lashes dramatically.

"So, what?" Victoria countered, but they both knew all that "so" represented, and she smiled coyly.

"So, anymore anonymous calls from your secret admirer? Or are you too busy for him now, too?"

"Rose. I told you. It was just a prank."

"Nothing?" Rose pressed. "Nothing at all?"

"Well, not really. Just a couple times, but he didn't really say much. And there's been a few times when I picked up, but no one was there." She threw it out like she hadn't given it a second thought. But the aborted calls had seemed odd in light of the other ones, and she'd felt a thrill crushed by disappointment each time.

"Happens how often?"

"Pardon?"

"How often? How often do you get those calls?"

"Oh, I don't know. Not often, really. Maybe four or five times. It's nothing Rose." She wished Rose would just leave it alone. She felt protective about the calls. They were not something she wanted to share, and she felt annoyed at herself for telling Rose about them in the first place. Speaking about them aloud unnerved her, thoughts crowding in about how badly things could go if Bobby were to ever overhear.

"Four or five times? Sounds like something to me. Who do you think it is?"

"Rose, it's no one."

"Ya, ya. Okay, fine. But hypothetically, just for fun. Who would you want it to be? If it could be anyone in town."

"Don't be ridiculous."

"Why is that ridiculous? Oh, come on, Vic, loosen up and have a little fun with it. What's it going to hurt? Come on, just for fun. Who?"

Victoria stirred her coffee and watched the miniature whirlpool she'd created spin. She smiled, looking around quickly. Rose smiled in return her eyes expectant, encouraging.

"Well? Who?"

"Just for fun?"

"Of course."

"Do I have to be limited to just one?"

"Ha!" Rose clapped her hands together. "Greedy girl. Yes, one. That's all you get. Make your choice."

Victoria grimaced, rubbed her forehead and was on the verge of answering when she felt Pearl pattering up behind her to deliver the sandwich and cream of broccoli soup they'd ordered, which had, through one of Pearl's mysteries, been replaced by a thin and tepid cream of potato and corn made without a trace of cream or corn. A quarter step from the table, her left shoe stuck momentarily to the floor, slopping a good part of the soup into the accompanying saucers. She set the soup on the table, wiped her fingers on the napkins and tucked them in beside the bowls.

"Damn that Bud, don't do nothing right. I told him to pull that tape tight."

She leaned her hipless body against the table and tugged off her shoe, holding it out for them to examine the evidence of Bud's poor workmanship. The orange canvas runners that she'd pretty much walked right out of during the summer had obviously spent some time in Bud's repair shop. Copious bands of duct tape wrapped them first one way then the other, then executed a beautifully maneuvered crisscross switchback over the toe and wound up fastened tightly with, well, more duct tape. But an error had been made, and Pearl was not pleased to discover it. In his exuberance to do a bang-up job, Bud had inadvertently twisted the tape, and every here and there a maniacally sticky, silver tongue lay in waiting.

"Dumb ass," she growled as she unstuck the shoe from her hand and put it back on her knobby foot. "Got to put up with this now till the dirt takes the sticky away."

And with that she hobbled off, the duct tape grabbing every second step, throwing her a hesitation off beat as she stepped and stuck her way back into the kitchen. They fished their spoons into their soup, determined it passably safe and Victoria took a swallow only to be stopped by Rose's interjection.

"Vic!"

"What?"

"Well?"

"Well, what?"

"Well, who. Who?"

"Oh, yeah. Okay, but I just want you to know this is stupid. And it doesn't mean anything."

"Of course not." Rose smiled and started into her sandwich, her eyes not leaving Victoria's face.

"Okay. But it's not just one guy—"

"Whoops, wrong answer. Against the rules."

"Well, okay, it is one guy then. But he's sort of a blend of three. Is that against the rules?"

"Oh, the hell with the rules. Who is it . . . they?"

They laughed, lowered their voices and peeked over the booths to make sure they weren't being eavesdropped on. Victoria blushed.

"Can't tell anyone."

"Fine, like who would I tell?"

"Promise?"

"Yes. Cross my heart and spit to die and all that shit."

Rose sat poised, sandwich in hand, waiting for Victoria to release her answer. Her dark eyes grew impatient as their soup slid from tepid to cold.

"Come on, Vic. What's the big deal? Out with it."

"Okay. Shit, this is embarrassing."

"What's so embarrassing?"

"I don't know; it's stupid."

"Don't like divulging your secret fantasies, hmm?"

"Oh shit, Rose, it's nothing like that."

"Who then? Come on, give me Hinckly's best."

"Okay. But don't laugh."

"Wouldn't think of it."

They stared at each other. Rose mouthed a silent—*who?*

"Elliot. Obviously."

"Obviously."

"Sam." She shot Rose a look and giggled.

"Aha! Not so obvious. You know I always thought he had a thing for you."

"Rose, it's just pretend remember? The perfect combination."

"Oh yes, right. The perfect ménage à trois."

"What?"

"Nothing. And number three would be?" She held her hands and face in an open question.

"Shit. I can't, Rose."

"Why not? You already told me the first two."

"Because I can't, that's why."

"Why? What's so bad about number three? He married?"

"Hardly. He still lives at home."

"Ohh . . . young hottie, is he?" She touched her mug to her lips and took a sip. "How young?"

"Young enough I could probably go to jail for even thinking about it."

"Akk! Okay, tell me. Do. You have to."

Victoria took a deep breath, looked into her soup and whispered out the name.

"Mark."

"Mark?"

"Tom and Diana's kid. Works at the feed store."

"Oh, yes! Good one. I wouldn't mind showing him a thing or two myself. He's not that young, is he?"

"Not quite twenty. Looks older than he is. And he's built like a brick shit-house. Sure didn't get that from his dad. Anyhow, that'd be it. The perfect blend. Too bad we don't get to choose in real life, hey?"

"Who says we don't? A perfectly good imagination can be a very useful tool."

"What do you mean?"

"Oh, I don't know." She teased the words out slowly, a wide-eyed smile suggesting that she very much did. "I guess just let your mind run free if whoever it is calls again. That's what I'd do. Play it for all it was worth. Have a little fun. Why not? Guys do it all the time."

"Do what?"

Rose laughed, helped herself to Victoria's sandwich.

"Mind if I have a bite? I'm actually enjoying this, if you can believe it."

"Do what Rose? What do guys always do?"

"Fantasize, baby. You think that's you Bobby's been rocking for the last twenty years? Not a chance. It's a little of Denise, a little of Francy, a little of Diana, a snag of *Penthouse*, a snatch of *Playboy* and a little of me. No, a whole lot of me, all stirred up with a little whatever else happened to catch his eye that day."

"Well, you know, if you really want him, Rose—"

"No thanks, got three kids of my own already."

The content of the words whispered from their lips must have reached Billy Bassman like a subliminal message. He swung around on his stool at the far end of the bar, planted an elbowless elbow on the counter and leered at them, his greasy head propped up by a grimy hand. Rose glared back at him, eyes like flaming spitfires, but he was just amused and upped the ante by licking his cracked lips and noisily smacking them together as if he could already taste her. Riff-raff like him were a huge source of irritation for Rose. Possessing neither pride nor secrets, she viewed them with an unredeemable scorn.

"Quit looking at us, you pervert."

"Kiss my ass, sweetheart," he responded with a puckered-up kiss into the air and a sloppy grin. "I look where I want to look, when I want to look and ain't no one telling me different."

"Well, I'm telling you. Turn your ugly head around and quit spoiling our lunch."

"I ain't spoiling Vic's lunch. She likes my ugly head . . . don't you, Vic?"

Victoria ignored him, concentrated on piling up the dirty dishes, her half-eaten lunch tightening into a cement fist in the pit of her gut. She wished Rose would just ignore him as well rather than engaging in a derogatory argument. She could never be too sure what might fall out of Bassman's mouth. And even though she'd always been able to hide her reactions well enough to refute his claims and convince most people, Rose knew her better by far than most people.

"You know, Bassman, you really should try to stagger over and look in a mirror some day. You never wonder why your mother didn't want you around? Had to drink her face off just so she could forgive herself for bringing such a useless piece of crap into the world in the first place."

If Rose's insult had bothered him, there was no outward evidence. But his reply suggested she may well have found her mark.

"Go to hell, bitch. I was talking to 'toria."

"Well, she doesn't want you to talk to her, creep, so turn around and leave us alone."

"We goes way back, me and little Vicky does. Don't we, Vicky? Way, way back." His drugged eyes groped over her as he remembered just how far back they went and with the knowledge that prefaces fact, she knew he was about to sketch in the lurid details. Her eyes panicked to his and held fast, frantically begging him not to. He hesitated, grinned. He was unaccustomed to finding himself sitting in the seat of power, and he'd be damned if he was going to lose his position without at least the benefit of a few earthly spoils.

"You got some money, Vic? 'Cause I need some smokes and my check ain't here till tomorrow."

"Screw off, you friggin' bum. She isn't—"

Relieved, Victoria reached for her purse and slipped a ten across the aisle into his grubby, outstretched hand.

"Vic, what the hell are you doing? Don't do that. He's just a bum; let him buy his own damn cigarettes." Rose sat back, visibly indignant and completely mystified by the transaction.

"Don't worry about it, Rose. He'll pay me back."

"Like a rat's-ass he will. Are you nuts? His check'll be pissed away before the ink even dries on his X. You can kiss that ten goodbye."

Billy Bassman, acting out her outraged accusations, held the bill up to his lips and wet it with a soggy kiss, bent it in half and gave it a french.

"Where the hell's your head, Vic? Why'd you give the puke money? You just encouraged him."

"I don't know. Christmas spirit, I guess. My yearly donation to the poor and underprivileged." She attempted unsuccessfully to make light of it.

"Poor and underprivileged, my ass. Well, if you think that pig'll be happy with a once yearly contribution, better think again because you're going to be in his debt forever now. Come on. Let's get out of this hole. I've got to get home and get some work done."

Victoria gathered herself quickly into her coat and gloves, paid the bill and followed Rose out of the hotel. They waved off good-byes, with Rose promising to call, and Victoria carried on down the street immersed in thought about what had transpired. Rose, as usual, was absolutely correct. Billy Bassman would never pay her the money back, and she would remain eternally in his debt. But then again, she already was.

* * *

The early morning storm had continued its onslaught, the snow mounding up on her car like a Russian hat of white ermine. It was frigid out, the weak sun having abandoned its attempt to alter the day. Shivering, she pulled some papers from her purse, pretending to be engrossed in them as she waited for Rose to sweep her car free and drive away. Pushing up the sleeve of her parka, she checked the time. The week before, even with life running at a frenetic pace in advance of the Christmas recital, she had again let Elliot charm her into meeting him for another session of painting after her lunch with Rose.

Although he still steadfastly refused to actually show her the painting, carefully draping the canvas behind a sheet and locking it in the closet between sessions, he did assure her that it was coming along very well. She was apprehensively anxious to see it. Although a fear of being found out was never far from her thoughts, the extra dance practices she'd scheduled to prepare for the recital had provided the perfect opportunity for her to spend more time at the studio without provoking Bobby's suspicions.

Reaching for an air of nonchalance, she entered the hotel, discreetly scanning the stairway for Bassman's distasteful form. It infuriated her that even now, after all these years, such an indecent speck of humanity still could hold such power over her. Their brief lunchtime encounter had stolen away the delicious anticipation she had secreted away knowing she would be meeting Elliot later on in the studio. She had always hoped she would eventually outgrow the hold Bassman had over her. Or, preferably, that he would just die a conveniently early death like his older brother.

Quickly closing the door of the ballroom behind her, she locked it then drew a deep breath. She felt safe here. This was her world. Her sanctuary. Here, Bassman didn't exist. And yet the heaviness of her mood refused to lift. He had destroyed the delightful lightness that had propelled her through the last few days. She felt cheated.

She sensed that Elliot was at the back door before he even knocked. There had been no sound of him walking up the alley, and suddenly it dawned on her that he had been standing out there, waiting for her in the bitter cold. She rushed back to let him in, feeling at once both apologetic for being late and leaving him waiting on the steps, and annoyed that he had risked exposing their secret meetings by having done so.

"Quick! Come in," she said urgently after she had cracked the door and peered out to ensure the alleyway was empty.

Elliot swept through the door wearing his characteristic, bemused grin.

"Relax, Victoria. No one saw me. Wouldn't have mattered anyway. I was pretending to fix the railing on the stairs." An involuntary shiver rivered through him as he slipped free from his jacket and blue plaid scarf, hanging them neatly from the knob of the door.

Feeling ashamed for her lack of compassion, she envisioned herself reaching up and warming the fierce redness from his cheeks and ears with her hands. Relishing the thought of it, she braced against actually moving toward him. The sheer physicality of such a gesture would be far too intimate. Too close.

"I'm sorry I'm so late, Elliot," she offered instead. "Trying to get Pearl to hurry lunch today was like trying to get tomorrow's news. Look at you. You're freezing."

"Ya, I am. It's biting cold out there today," he agreed as he stepped free of his shoes and attempted to wriggle some warmth back into his toes.

"You should dress warmer," she advised as she eyed his fashionable but wholly inadequate leather jacket and snow-packed brown suede shoes.

"Well," he grinned mischievously, "if I had known I'd be standing outside for twenty minutes, I most assuredly would have."

Heat fueled Victoria's face. "I can't believe you waited for so long," she added quietly.

"Well, I have to admit, I was beginning to think you'd stood me up."

She couldn't imagine anyone ever standing him up and said so.

Elliot rippled laughter through the ballroom. "Believe me, Victoria, I've been stood up before."

He was met with a dubious face.

"What? You think I've lived some kind of charmed life?"

The contrast of their lives rose before her. Him: free as a leaf blown from the tree, exploring the world, successful, confident, free. And her: grounded in the town of her birth, oppressed by a ubiquitous history that refused to die.

"Well, ya. Don't you?" she shot back petulantly. Dropping her eyes to the floor, she glanced back up at him, briefly allowing the black swamp of her emotions to flood across her face.

He was not insensitive to the depths of her pain and stepped toward her softly.

"Hey, what's wrong, Victoria? Something I said?"

She shook her head and looked away, savoring the tenderness in his eyes as he'd looked deeply into hers, searching desperately to discover the secrets hidden away there.

"Victoria, please. You can talk to me. I promise you, I'm a very good listener. Not when I'm working, mind you, but other than that," he added wryly, trying to ease the weight of the moment.

She smiled in spite of herself. It had been one of the things she'd been most surprised to discover about him. Originally, she had envisioned their painting sessions would be loose chatty times, the conversation slowly opening up as they got to better know one another. But Elliot didn't like to talk while he painted, and he preferred her not to as well. Once his focus was drawn to the canvas, he became like a man possessed, consumed by and taken from her into the creation of his work. At first she'd felt disappointed, even a little rejected. But she'd rapidly found a place of pleasure, reveling in his intoxicated desire to re-create her.

Now, with tears threatening, she imagined for a moment what an indescribable release it would be for her to finally take down the wall that surrounded her and let him in. Sharing with him each brick of hurt and betrayal and self-loathing as she did so. She looked into his clear blue eyes, willing herself to speak. His face was fully open to her, calm and willing and receptive.

And yet she remained silent. For, although the emotions floated freely near the surface, like tortuous ghosts haunting her, the words themselves were buried too deep. She battled herself. How could it be that she spoke so freely into the void of an anonymous call—all the while wondering if it were really Elliot receiving her offerings—when face to face with him she could not utter even one word of her pain? Perhaps he was right. Perhaps sometimes a person really did need the dividing screen of the confessional in order to exorcise their demons.

Seeing the brief flash of vulnerability fade from her, Elliot gave her shoulders a tight squeeze, nodding his head as he accepted her decision to keep her pain private.

"So. I have some very good news to share with you." He smiled cautiously, not sure where Victoria's mood had left them.

"What's that?" she asked, surprised by the peevishness of her tone. She had expected him to try a little harder to unearth the source of her discomfort. Not that she had any intentions of revealing it, but she craved the soothing balm of his intense concern.

"Remember that gallery that I said was interested in taking the painting?"

She nodded slowly, already knowing she didn't like the direction in which the conversation was taking her.

"Well, they finally got back to me. They want it. They want it in two weeks."

Their faces mirrored each other in polar opposite: Elliot's enthusiastic, Victoria's stricken.

"What? It's what we wanted. Right?" Elliot flailed about like a man caught in a sudden ice floe, struggling desperately to find some solid ground.

Emotions dive-bombed Victoria from every angle. It had been one thing to hold the thought of actually ever releasing the painting but quite another to be confronted with the reality of such a plan. The thought of losing their clandestine weekly meetings at the studio, however, fueled her most overwhelming panic: she had not prepared for that. Had not allowed herself to think how diminished her life would once again be when she could no longer bathe herself in the river of his desire.

"I . . . I . . . it's not ready, Elliot. We can't have it ready that soon. I'm far too busy. I've never even seen it. I have to make sure no one can recognize me," she babbled, words tangling together as she attempted to reel the situation back under control.

He smiled calmly as he waited for her to talk herself out.

"You really don't trust anyone, do you, Victoria?" he asked, the faintest hint of hurt tingeing his voice. "I promised you that I'd paint you so you were unrecognizable. That was our agreement. Right?"

Her eyes left his as she nodded.

"So, why do you think I'd do anything other than what we'd agreed upon?"

Uncomfortable now under his intense focus, she shifted her position and shrugged tightly. "Well, I'm sure it's fine, Elliot. But I still want to see it to make sure."

He lowered the intensity of his gaze. "Of course you get to see it, Victoria. I actually can't wait for you to see it. I just wanted to wait until it was far enough along so that it felt like something more than just sketches on the page."

Even just talking about the painting bloomed his voice full of passion, and she looked up at him, fascinated.

"Okay," he said huskily, "let's get it out of the closet and have a look then, shall we?"

He stood looking down at her expectantly, and she started a bit as she realized he was waiting for the key. Retrieving the key ring from her purse, she walked over to the closet door, sifting through to find the correct one.

"It's the shorter one," he offered gently from behind her after a few abortive attempts.

"There's a shorter one?" she asked, holding the keys in a line to see for herself. "How do you notice things like that?"

"I just notice details, that's all. Wouldn't be much of a painter if I didn't, would I?" he asked, walking past her into the closet as she opened it and bringing the fully draped canvas out to the center of the room.

Nerves began to dance through her as he turned to face her, one hand holding the edge of the sheet that still covered the painting. They smiled at each other shyly. Like two platonic lovers about to consummate their union, suddenly hyper-aware of their separateness, the illusion of their perceived knowledge of each other about to be unceremoniously exposed.

And then it was done. The painting erupted into the room, drawing Victoria's breath into itself. A powerful creature—primal, tangible and exotic with long, languorous, full-moon luminous limbs—dominated the canvas. Explosive in its quiet wanting, the green dress quivered with the vitality of the animal coiled within, the left strap tantalizingly low, offering a curve of porcelain breast, sensual in its simplicity.

The ghost of the gothic arch window hovered in the distance. The figure was surrounded by the murky moodiness of the background. But it could not touch her. It served only to further radiate the dynamic contrast of her being. She was a creature-goddess, birthed free. A creature with no thought to look beneath it for the depleted sack, the afterbirth that had held it for so long.

They stood in silence as she struggled to absorb the pure raging emotions the painting had set off within her.

Finally, Elliot cleared his throat, breaking her trance. "So? What do you think? Is it okay?"

She wrenched her gaze from the canvas, forcing herself to look at him, surprised to hear the unfamiliar note of self-doubt in his voice.

"Elliot . . . it's just . . . it's just, unbelievable. It's just incredible. It's just . . ." she hesitated as her attention was pulled back to the painting.

"What? It's just what?" he replied nervously. "Didn't I cover your face up enough? I can fix that."

"No, don't worry about that, Elliot. That's just the thing. Even I wouldn't recognize myself. I *don't* recognize myself. I mean, it's a wonderful painting, Elliot. Incredible. But, I don't know who you've painted there. Certainly not me. That's not how I look. Not really."

Regaining his sense of composure, Elliot laughed with noticeable relief.

"Yes it is, Victoria. That's exactly how you look. That's exactly how you look . . . to me."

~ Chapter 16 ~

Sleep numbing her brain, Victoria miscalculated the extent of her reach and sent the receiver sprawling across the floor. Barely a week had passed since the last call, and the spray of static shooting into the room snapped her instantly alert. Her mind scrambled for Bobby's whereabouts. He was going to be in town late working on JJ's car. Wasn't that what he'd said?

"Hi. Sorry about that. I was just lying down. Guess I fell asleep."

She strained against the darkness to make out the wall clock and was surprised to see she'd slept away the afternoon and on into the night. Curling onto the couch, she nestled the telephone beside her and pulled the comforter into place.

"Mmm," she murmured warmly. "I was having the most amazing dream."

She waited for a signal to carry on, juggling against her fears of sharing such an intimate moment with a stranger. And yet, she argued with herself, really he was not a stranger. He understood and sympathized with her more than anyone she could put a face to. And she felt more comforted in his anonymous presence than she ever had in Bobby's physical one. If a relationship were to be judged on how it made her feel, then she judged this one as far stronger and deeper than any she'd ever known. It had become obvious to her that the caller, whoever he was, meant her no malice. So far, she'd heard no talk of the calls around town, a fact that made her feel insular, her secrets safe. And besides, she wanted to share the delight of her intimacies with him. It was the least she could do, she reasoned, after all he'd done for her.

"It was sort of terrifying, but also kind of, you know . . . erotic."

She tossed the word away quickly, as if it might be found deviant and she would be rejected for using it. She sat tightly, held her breath until she was assured of his calm acceptance.

"I was all alone, in this dream, putting makeup on in front of this big mirror. Or trying to, anyhow. I had this tube of lipstick. Bright, bright red. Brilliant red. And I was trying to put it on so I could go out, but I couldn't get it to work. I kept dropping it and it wouldn't go on and I was getting incredibly frustrated about it . . . could you hold on a minute? Don't hang up, okay? I just have to check something."

Setting the phone down carefully on the floor, she slid out from under her blanket and tiptoed to the porch window. She surveyed the spot where Bobby's truck should be, scanned the horizon for lights then opened the porch door and listened into the flat distance for any sound. Somewhat satisfied, she hurried to sit back down and closed her eyes with an almost prayer of relief as the static reached back out to her.

"Oh, you're still here. Good. Anyhow, like I was saying, I was late for something. In my dream. I don't know what . . . you know how dreams are. They never seem to make any sense, do they? But I was really getting irritated because I had to get ready and I couldn't. Nothing was working. I felt like screaming and crying and having this big fit, and then the next thing I know I'm sitting in this huge concert hall. Up on stage and the place is packed and everyone's looking up at me like they're waiting for something. Like they were waiting for me to entertain them." She paused as she reflected back over the moment, fully aware that reality had diffused it of all its power and that her words were impotent to bring it back for him.

"I know it sounds silly now, but it really was quite terrifying. And then, as I was sitting there filling up with panic, I realized there's this huge guitar in my lap. So I pick it up and start to play, but I don't know how. I can't figure out a single chord." She settled deeper under the blanket and continued on in a whisper as if the walls themselves might someday bear witness against her.

"Then, all of a sudden something strange started to happen. Something . . . you know. There was this pressure building inside me as I sat there not knowing what to do. And it just kept getting stronger and fuller and pressing up inside of me until I thought I'd explode. And then I did. Do you know what I mean? It was like I exploded out of myself. Something had to let go, you see. And it was me that finally did. Do you understand what I'm trying to say? It was me letting go. Me."

Quietness fell over her as she tried to trace her way back to the pure, raw sexuality that had been born inside of her. Imagining him sharing her pleasure as she celebrated herself she danced on, emboldened.

"I could never tell my husband anything like this. I mean, sure he talks big, but the truth is sex embarrasses him. Stuffs it away for some cold, dark night then never mentions it again. An animal act. That's what it's like with him. An animal act without the intensity."

A caustic laugh escaped her as she considered her choice of words and, in an almost reflex reaction, she ran her tongue over her lips like a salve.

"I want to tell you something. But you have to promise me you'll never tell anyone else, okay?" She listened for a moment then continued on. "Everyone thinks I can't have children, you know, but I can. I was pregnant once. A long time ago. Before I was even married. I've never told anyone that. Never. Not even my husband. It wasn't his. It was someone else's . . . Bassman's. He forced himself on me—it wasn't anything I wanted. I lost it anyhow, which was good, but it ruined my chance to audition. I was so sick I'd thought I'd die. Sometimes I wish I had—"

A quick confusion of noise scattered across the line, and she felt as well as heard the line being severed. She sat frozen for a moment with the receiver still against her face as something unsettling attempted to work its way into her mind. The sharp burst could've been anything. A radio, TV, even the fractured yelp of a small dog.

She debated with herself over whether it could have been anything else. A voice maybe. The voice of a young child. Standing up suddenly, she shook away the thought, wrapped the comforter tightly around herself and turned on the light.

~ Chapter 17 ~

The knock came too early. And it came to the wrong door. Victoria placed the chair she was holding into the row she was creating. The swirling list of things she still had to do froze in her mind as she riveted her attention on the ballroom doors. She was not expecting anyone. Other than Elliot, that was, and he would be knocking at the alleyway door. Shortly. Her mind leapt between answering the knock or just ignoring it altogether. A sense of duty finally propelled her forward. What if it were one of the mothers, fledgling dancer in tow, in need of their teacher's encouragement before their first dance recital?

Taking a quick listen for any sign of Elliot walking up the alleyway, she pressed a smile onto her face and hurried over to answer the door. She would make this quick. Obviously, everyone would know she would be busy preparing for that night's recital. No one could reasonably expect too much of her time.

Opening the door, she was greeted by the long-fingered branches of a spruce tree, reaching in toward her as if to shake hands. The smell of Christmas instantly swaddled her. Too late, her hands flew up to stifle a delighted cry of surprise. Large logger's hands, roughly reddened and bulky jointed, wrestled the tree in place.

"Sam! Hi. You brought me a tree?"

Peering through the maze of branches, she just managed to catch his flashing grin before he looked away.

"For the show tonight. If that's okay."

"Of course it's okay," she gushed generously, shooting a look toward the back door. He'd looked so absolutely pleased with himself that she hadn't the heart to turn him away. "Here, let me open the other side of the door so you can bring it in."

"Thanks," he said, lumbering through the door, bear-hugging the tree, which was anchored into a five-gallon pail of wet sand.

Victoria attempted to keep the tree from capsizing as he struggled free of his work boots. They stood grinning up at the tree, then back at each other, then back at the tree.

"Got it off the block we been logging."

"It's perfect, Sam. Thank you."

Surreptitiously, she checked her watch, alert to any sound of movement from outside. A thin metallic coil of blood tasted in her mouth as she slowly bit her lip, cursing her stupidity.

She had trapped herself. How on earth could she ever explain Elliot's arrival to Sam? Not that Sam would say anything to Bobby about it. She knew with absolute certainty that he would not. For once, the growing sense of dread swelling within her had precious little to do with her husband. Quite simply, she did not want Elliot's unexpected arrival to cause any more suffering to her noble, horse-hearted, Sam.

"You really shouldn't have gone to so much bother."

Towering above her, one hand holding the tree upright, his mismatched eyes quickly roamed the now-shrunken space. Ten rows of chairs gobbled up most of the floor not sectioned off by a pink ribbon for a stage. A long wooden table holding foam cups, snowflake serviettes and a garish little blue tree with flickering lights consumed the better part of the back wall.

Sam stared down at his heavy wool socks, flecks of chainsaw shavings clinging like yellowed insect husks. She noticed a black rim of grease embedded around each cuticle. Clearly, in his excitement to bring her the tree, he had not even stopped by at home to clean up on his way in from the bush. He leaned the tree over sideways a bit, as if trying to mask the sheer enormity of it. Somehow, right in his hands, it had twisted from a gift into an imposition.

"Maybe Rose can use it," he murmured as he hoisted the tree up roughly and turned for the door.

"No! Don't be silly, Sam. We can find room for it. How about . . . ." She scanned the cramped room desperately. "How about right back there?"

Following him back to the alleyway door, she actually shook her head at her own careening flirtation with impending disaster. Heart hammering, ears alert for the cardboard crunch of Elliot's footsteps, she watched, anxiety-ridden, as Sam anchored the tree further into the sand and pulled at its branches in an attempt to get it to stand up straight.

"How's that?"

"Perfect," she lied. "Thank you, Sam. The children will love it." She smiled up at him energetically, willing him to say goodbye. Instead he brought their attention to a pool of melted snow forming beneath the tree.

"Thought I knocked all that snow off of it. Got a mop in here . . . ?" he asked, whirling one giant step around and seizing the handle of the closet door. Victoria's life clasped at her throat, the old lock rattling ominously then holding fast.

"No, don't! Don't . . . worry about it, Sam. I have to run the mop around later, anyhow." Her panic sizzled into the room. He withdrew his hand, eyeing her closely.

Avoiding his gaze, she attempted to ignore the multitude of questions dancing around them. With some clever maneuvering she might be able to shuffle around Elliot's impromptu arrival at the alleyway door. But she knew no combination of words would ever be sufficient to explain away the intimate painting locked away inside that closet.

A curious silence hovered around them. Sam looked down and questioned his hands, growing lumbrous with thought. Victoria grew more anxious. She recognized this in him. This uncomfortable fullness of emotion without expression. Despite the state of her own frantic inner turmoil, she wanted to reach in to him. To help ease his pain. She smiled encouragement. With agonizing slowness, he unzipped his parka and reached inside. Their eyes did not meet as he withdrew a brightly decorated package and tentatively handed it to her.

Her own emotions were a stew of intensity simmering inside a too-small pot. She took the gift from his outstretched hand, his bullrush fingers a stark contrast to the intricately laced knot and bow that wove together and bound the package. As a small child, she had momentarily felt special when her mother was wrapping presents and would enlist her tiny finger to hold the knot so that she could execute the perfect bow. Her mother had taken special pride in wrapping her gifts. Victoria could see that Sam did as well. Unraveling it, she felt brutish and careless, the paper crumpling in her hands, a long lacy ribbon of red refuse curling by her feet. She wanted to apologize.

An exquisitely graceful carving emerged, a seemingly impossible union of solid wood and implied flow. Richly touchable waves undulated freely from the high breast, creating a beautifully draped mahogany gown. Breath almost seemed possible from the deftly carved features of the delicate face. Of all the carvings Sam had previously given her, none had come close to resonating such a visible life force as this one.

Victoria's eyes dashed to the marvel of Sam's hands.

"It's an angel," he said redemptively, shoving his hands into his pockets. "For your tree."

Turning it over, she traced a finger, fish-like, down the illusion of feathery softness suggested there. "Sam, this is wonderful. You could sell these."

His face rose and fell simultaneously, the shadow of hurt left behind a clear sign: this gift presented to her had traveled deeply through the Hades of his soul. Their eyes met in instant apology and forgiveness.

"Can you put it up for me?" she asked softly.

Easily reaching to the top of the tree, he fastened the angel in place. Awkwardness began to balloon around them as they stood staring up at it, the imminent punch of Elliot's inevitable knock reverberating through Victoria's mind. Anxiety finally squeezed her manners from her.

"Well, I really must get back to work, Sam."

He ducked his head, the embarrassment of having overstayed his welcome like a physical slap.

"Yup. I got to get going, too. Just wanted to drop this off for you. See you later, Vic."

"You coming to the recital tonight?"she asked hopefully.

He avoided her gaze as he stepped back into his snow boots and refastened the laces.

"Would," he mumbled, "just it being poker night and all . . ."

"Oh, yes, of course," she hastened to aid his discomfort. "Well, maybe next year. Thanks for the tree, Sam. And the angel. She's beautiful."

"Yup," he nodded as he tossed her a half-smile and left.

Locking the door behind him, her huge sigh of relief was cut short by Elliot's knock. The event was so synchronized she wondered for a moment if Elliot hadn't been standing outside listening, waiting for Sam to leave. Cursing her stupidity and thanking her lucky stars, she skitted back to the rear door, where she was confronted by a wall of greenery. Elliot's tentative second knock was answered by a whispered hiss to hold on while she moved the tree.

"Hol-ee!" he exhaled, as he slid with difficulty through the partially opened doorway. "Father Christmas bring you that?"

"Sam. He just dropped it off," she said, choosing not to elaborate on how close his *just* had been to a three-way meeting.

The abundant addition of new snow had managed to persuade even Elliot to graduate to winter boots. Victoria noticed that even though they remained unlaced, they still managed to steal some of the freeness from his limbs. He walked out of them, his attention diverted.

"Wow!"

He whistled appreciatively, stepping around the tree, inspecting it and the finely hewn angel crowning it. A playful smile began to toy with his face.

"What?" Victoria demanded nervously.

"Sam carve you that?"

She let the obvious answer speak for itself.

"It's you."

"What?"

"The angel. It's you."

"Is not!"

"Is," he challenged back lightly. "Look."

Her eyes met the blank almonds staring back at her from the steadfast yet delicately carved wooden face. The similarity was so brazenly obvious now she couldn't believe she hadn't seen it right away. Her face mutinied into a blush.

"Seems you might have yourself a secret admirer, Victoria," Elliot whispered.

Not able to catch the tone of his words, she looked over at him for more information.

"Don't be silly. Sam and I are just friends."

"Well, *you* might be just friends," he replied, looking her straight in the eyes. "But I can recognize the blunt-force trauma of unrequited love when I see it and it looks to me like this guy is bleeding internally pretty bad."

"Oh, Elliot. It's nothing like that. He just likes to carve stuff, that's all."

She attempted to sweep the suggestion aside, but Elliot held her eye until she looked away. She felt trespassed upon.

"That melted snow isn't going to do your wood floor any favors," he said, gesturing beneath the tree.

Glad for the juncture in the conversation, she turned to the closet. "I'll give it a mop while you get out the painting."

Unlocking the closet door she stepped back and checked her watch. The day was flying by hopelessly beyond her control. Elliot swept past her into the tiny room, his movements briskly agitated. She looked in after him. He stood directly in front of the canvas, tense and immovable. Coiled in a twisted heap upon the floor lay the old sheet they used to cover the canvas between their meetings.

Clearly something was wrong. She wanted to scream at him to move out of the way. She wanted to scream at him to stay that way forever.

Panic vomited inside her. Elliot slowly stepped aside, the incomprehensible sight of the painting assaulting her. It was ruined. A collage of uninspired red finger-swirls and random yellow splatters defaced it.

Victoria gasped, her eyes racing like wild animals to Elliot's.

"This makes no sense, Victoria. Absolutely no sense." He spoke like he was stunned of feeling. "Did you give the key to someone?"

"Of course not!"

"But, it's supposed to be the only one, right?"

"That's what Pearl said. Obviously, she was wrong."

They stood staring at each other, their minds consumed in a search to find the illogical answer that eluded them. How could anyone have known about the painting? Had someone been watching them? Had whoever was calling her also been watching her? Had he become jealous over Elliot's attentions? She leaned heavily on the doorway, mind manic, heart racing. The painting, exposed now and no longer just the domain of their private exclusivity, seemed to her far more intimate, far more damning than she had remembered. She looked up at him hopefully as he turned to speak.

"You know, Victoria, this isn't so bad. I think I can fix this."

Her face brightened. "You can? How?"

"Ya. Ya, with a bit of time, I think I might just be able to salvage this." He inspected the painting closer, picking at a glob of paint with his fingernail.

"Are you crazy?" she spat. "You can't salvage it, Elliot. You have to destroy it."

"Destroy it? Why?"

Victoria bolted up at him. "Don't you get it? Someone knows about this. If it gets back to Bobby . . ." The words slid away from her but their impact remained on her face.

Seeing the depth of her panic as he turned from the painting, he stepped toward her protectively. "Victoria. I'm sorry. Truly, I am. The last thing I wanted was to put you in harm's way."

She looked up at him, incredulous. "It's not me you have to worry about, Elliot."

A question narrowed his eyes. "But, it's not like we've done anything wrong. I painted your picture to raise some money for the studio. So what? I've painted plenty of girls before."

The remark stung.

"Actually, I think it'd be best if you don't come around for a while," she said defensively. "At least until I find out who's been in here."

"Victoria. You think that's really . . ."

"Yes. It is."

"And the painting?"

"You have to destroy it. Tonight."

"Tonight?"

"Yes. Promise me."

"Okay. If that's the way you want it to be."

She looked up at him, searching for understanding.

"It's not the way I want it to be, Elliot," she whispered. "It's just the way it has to be."

~ Chapter 18 ~

Christmas came and passed as usual, with full-throttle parties and obligatory visits to the home where they had again endured reruns of Bobby's mother's life told through the meager accomplishments of her husband and only son. The dance recital had gone far better than Victoria had expected, with only one case of stage fright other than her own and the occasional misstep. Bobby, true to his word, had refused to attend. Although frustrated over his lack of support, Victoria had also been relieved; she hadn't had to monitor his simmering hostility on top of everything else. She had been an anxiety of nerves: every random look and snippet of conversation knocking her sideways, dreading the moment when someone would come forward and expose her and Elliot's intimate secret to the whole town. Nervously, she had scanned the crowd for him. He had not shown up. Not that she could have expected him to. She had asked him to disappear from her life, and he had honored her wishes. But still, disappointment had floated heavily among her fears.

January had blown the valley solid until the middle of February when ferocious storms took over, paralyzing it under a straitjacket of wet and hazardous snow. Expectant mounds had grown higher and heavier with each passing day until warm March winds began to moan and the valley heaved and groaned until winter finally gave birth to spring. Victoria anxiously watched the slowly retreating ice and snow. Shortly after the Christmas recital, her car had suspiciously refused to start. Bobby, declaring the roads too

dangerous for her ancient bald tires, had refused to fix it, grudgingly taking it upon himself to drive her back and forth to town
each week to teach her dance class and gather the supplies needed
to keep life sustained.

The rest of her dull, dark days had been spent in the confines
of the trailer, shuffling things from drawer to drawer and closet to
closet. The hens had continued their barren ways. Victoria still
kept them alive by smuggling store-bought eggs into her basket.
Every Thursday her neighbor stopped by to pick up a dozen, have
a little chat and provide a break to the daily monotony for each of
them. Other winters would have found her almost desperate with
boredom, but this year she had settled in, let her imagination run
and waited for the phone to ring.

After the painting had been exposed, she had sat through the
first few static-filled calls listening with anxious hesitation. Once
Bobby had even answered it and had sworn vilely about how stupid
people were to dial wrong numbers. But for the most part he was
out when the calls came, and she began to wonder if whoever it was
knew when she was alone. As time wore on and no word of her tres-
pass had filtered back to her, either through the telephone line or
town gossip, she began to lower her guard and trust again that the
caller meant her no harm.

The calls had relaxed, their duration increasing, with the conversations mostly one-sided, if they could be called conversations
at all. Somehow over the months she'd transgressed from listener
to speaker, and the details of what she divulged slipped from the
general and mundane to the secret and intimate. The caller proved
to be an attentive listener, never interrupting or criticizing, just
listening to each word as though what she said was of the utmost
importance. Listened to her like no one else ever had. Listened to
her as if she mattered, as if she existed. And occasionally he would
offer a delicious stroke to her confidence, tell her she was fascinating, intelligent, beautiful.

For a time she was convinced she was talking to Elliot. In her
mind seeing his gentle hands holding the receiver he was breathing

into, almost feeling them against her cheek, tasting the touch of his lips. But then she'd heard he'd been out-of-town, gallivanting somewhere warm and exotic, far from her and the frigid valley. Then she'd thought perhaps it was Sam, bound by his boyhood loyalty to Bobby, restricted by the fearful knowledge of the magnitude of his feelings toward her, knowing any tangible expression of them would send him reeling to a place he could not go. Would not start what he could not finish. Other times, it was Diana's son Mark who she envisioned breathing into the other end of the phone. But most of all she imagined the caller to be all three. Elliot's sensual worldliness, Sam's protective, unfaltering love and Mark's cocky brazenness. And it was the thought of their hungry eyes that stirred her to distraction, pressing a warm glow against her cheeks that she panicked to hide when Bobby unexpectedly came up the steps and through the porch door.

Slowly her curiosity about the caller's identity waned, and she asked the question only as a formality, a way to placate her conscience when it pricked at her, warning against the folly of setting such intimate knowledge into the hands of a stranger. But her reality was that the caller no longer was a stranger, but had become like a dear and trusted friend. Her confidant. Her lover. And she knew her trust would not be taken in vain, that this person who, for whatever reason chose to remain cloaked in anonymity, would not forsake her but would continue to cherish her so deeply that he was willing to have her in the only form he could.

Spring sang the valley into vivid, fresh colors, and for the first time she heard its hopeful song. Today she'd already changed her shirt five times, searching for something that matched her mood. Finally she settled on a breezy lavender, billowy soft and sexy. She hoped the weatherman was worth his paycheck, and the day would stay unseasonably warm as he'd promised. An estate auction was to be held, one of the biggest events of the year so far. It was highly probable Elliot, along with most of the town, would be there. The thought of seeing him again brought a smile into her eyes as she traced her lips a glossy red. She was anxious to hear what he'd been up to. Where he'd gone, what he'd seen. Although she hadn't been with him for nearly five months, she felt as though no time had passed, as if she had talked to him almost every day, like the glow of her skin still tingled from the touch of his hands.

She stepped into the kitchen and checked the time. Twelve-forty five. With the sale starting at one and a forty-minute drive to get there, they were already late. Bobby finally had found some spare time to work on her car, and even though he proclaimed it fixed, he had also cautioned it was far from road-safe. As such, she found herself still at the mercy of his erratic schedule. Having second thoughts about the jeans she'd chosen to wear, she slipped back into the bedroom to change them once again.

She heard Bobby clumping up the porch stairs.

"Vic?"

"What?" she yelled back from the bathroom, where she was now redoing her hair.

"Come here a sec, okay?"

"Why?"

"Just come here a minute, will ya?" he said, exasperation tingeing his voice. "I got something for you."

"We don't have a minute, Bobby. In case you haven't noticed, we're already going to be late for the sale."

"Really? What time is it?"

"Quarter to."

"Aw, shit. Why didn't you call me?"

"I didn't know you wanted me to call you," she yelled back angrily. "Where's your watch?"

"I don't know. Damn thing disappeared. You ain't seen it?"

"Nope."

"Sure? Cause I'm positive I left it on the table and now it ain't there."

"Maybe it fell behind."

"Didn't fall behind," he said loudly. "More likely you put it somewhere when you were fussin' things around. Wish you'd just leave my stuff alone."

"Well, maybe you shouldn't just leave your stuff lying around all the time."

"Hey! Don't even start with me," he hollered down the hallway. "I ain't got the time or patience for any of your attitude today."

"What attitude? What are you talking about? Attitude? I'm an adult, Bobby. Not a friggin' teenager."

"Yeah, well maybe you should start acting like one then, hey?"

She heard him struggling with the door then heard it slam angrily.

"What do you mean by that?" she yelled, flying into the porch to confront him.

"Oh shit, I wonder. Look at all that makeup you got on . . . just like a bloody floozy. Who you trying to impress, anyhow?"

"Oh, give me a break, Bobby. A little bit of lipstick and now I'm a floozy?"

"Not just the lipstick. Look at that shirt you're wearing. Pretty obvious what you're advertising."

"What are you talking about? What's wrong with this shirt?"

"What wrong with it?" His voice was rising along with the color in his face. "Look how bloody low it is, shows half your bloody tits."

"Oh, it does not."

"Sure as hell does!"

"How come you never had a problem with it before then?"

"Who says I didn't?"

"Well, you never said anything if you did."

"Yeah, well that's 'cause you weren't so shit hot on yourself before, that's why. Now you all hopped up on yourself like you think you're something pretty bloody special."

"And I guess I'm not anything special, right?"

"Not to me you ain't. Lots of chicks out there got a lot more going for 'em than you, Vic, so I wouldn't be getting so impressed with myself."

She held his eye, her blood raging in her veins.

"Well, just so happens I like this shirt," she challenged.

"That so? Well too damn bad, 'cause ain't no wife of mine going out dressed like that."

"You can't tell me what to wear, Bobby! You don't own me. I'm your wife not your bloody kid."

"Yeah, well if you want to be staying my wife you'd better be changing your attitude. Or is that it, Vic? You too good to be my wife all a sudden? You think you do better off on your own, huh? Huh? Well you better think twice, sweetheart, 'cause ain't no one in this valley gonna mess with a wife of mine."

He was furious now, and as he pushed past her into the trailer, she cringed her eyes shut against the slap that surprisingly, didn't come. Although she should have credited it to him as decency, she saw only his weakness instead. Ranting his way into clean jeans and a shirt, he'd bellowed himself into an absolute frenzy by the time he'd grabbed a half bottle of whiskey and walked back through the porch in search of his cap.

"Where's my frickin' cap?"

"Don't know. I wasn't wearing it."

"Don't get smart with me. And if you're coming you'd better hurry up and get changed 'cause I ain't waiting for ya."

"I'm not going with you."

"That right? Who you going with then?"

"Myself."

"In what?"

"My car."

"You can't. Ain't ready yet."

"I'll go slow."

"You think so, do you?"

He stepped back into the kitchen and pulled the car keys off the hook on the wall, jangled them above her head and laughed.

"I don't think so," he said, shoving them in his pant's pocket.

"Bobby, give them back! It's my car."

"Yeah, it's your piece-of-crap car, Vic, but who fixes it for you, huh? Think you better just sit a spell and remember all the stuff I do for you."

"Bobby, give me my keys. I want to go to the sale."

"You do, huh? Well, maybe you should have thought about that a little sooner, before you started acting like such a bitch."

He held her powerless and, as usual, his voice had taken on a merry, singsong mockingness, which she despised.

"Bobby. Please. I'm sorry. I'll change if that'll make you happy. Just give me my keys. Please?"

"Nope. Afternoon alone to think will be good for you."

He pushed her aside from the porch door, slammed it behind him, climbed into his truck and spun out of the yard.

Attempting to kick the door, she tangled her feet in his overalls, lost her balance and crashed to the floor. Cursing, she scooped them up, shoved them into the wood stove and lit the fire. A smile flickered on her face as the flames took over, growing stronger and higher as they consumed the greasy material. Jumping up, she flung open the porch door and bolted for the feed shed. She shook off a momentary flush of guilt as she spotted a magnificent pile of spiky purple lupines and fresh yellow buttercups that had been discarded under the porch steps.

Searching for the shovel she finally found it under the tractor and, leaving the door as wide open as she could without it falling off its hinges, she rocked the grain barrel aside and began to dig. The box came unearthed easily, and she quickly pulled it loose, shook the dirt from it and opened the lid. She dug through it frantically, looking for her spare key. Pushed aside the Swiss Army knife and the faded sketch of their house plan. Searched under the various nuts and bolts and screwdrivers that Bobby had set down somewhere and never seen again. Finally she found the key, hidden under his watch, nestled in her wedding rings.

~ Chapter 19 ~

Auction sales were familiar rituals in the valley and always well attended. But an estate auction was the best attended of all. Whether friend or foe in life, a resident's death was sure to bring all together to sift through their humble remains: friends coming to secure a memento, foes delighting in the chance to snitch something at a bare fraction of the cost their enemy had to pay for it. Today's auction was a dispersal of the lives of Mutt and Joe Fisher, Mutt being not Joe's dog but rather his loyal wife's nickname. Joe had passed on years earlier but, to the valley's dismay, Mutt stubbornly clung on to every inch of his life until she passed away as well. When the contents of the house were evacuated into the yard, it proved a bit of a resurrection of old Joe Fisher himself. On a make-do plywood table a pile of stiffly pressed pants rose beside a half dozen carefully folded dress shirts. Underneath, a wicker basket overflowed with black dress socks while vacant shoes and boots stood patiently at attention waiting for a pair of size elevens to step forward and give them expression. Fluttering above them on the clothesline were prim floral dresses with Pearl announcing to everyone that she was buying the brown one, which had been Mutt Fisher's best.

The sale had wound halfway down by the time Victoria finally arrived. A flock of young girls ran up and enveloped her excitedly as she exited her car, each one trying to outdo the others in a verbal wrestling match as they all tried to speak. Patiently, she chattered with all of them until an older boy happened by, pulled a pigtail then ran away with the bunch of them in shrieking pursuit. She watched them go, then continued walking and talking and waving her way through the collage of people and faces and random piles of household junk, working her way toward the only item that had caught her interest. A huge box, broken down on three sides, lay shoved up against the porch railing, spilling books onto the stairs. Rummaging through it, she pulled out a heavy, leather-bound black one and filtered through its pages, trying to gain a sense of what two schoolteachers might have deemed appropriate reading material through seventy-odd years, five children and sixteen grandchildren.

"You thinking about buying some them books?"

She was startled from *Treasure Island* into the suspicious eyes of Pearl.

"Oh! I don't know, maybe. I was just looking."

"Hmmph. Well, maybe look at the little ones then."

"Why, Pearl? You planning on buying Bud some books to read?"

Even Pearl found this thought amusing, and she burst out in her peculiar laugh so loudly that people turned to stare and a herd of goats answered her back from the neighboring field. Victoria ducked her head behind her book, embarrassed for Pearl even though she wouldn't have thought to be embarrassed for herself.

"Books for Buddy, ha!" She snorted and snickered herself back into a scowl, remembering she had serious business to do, laying claim to what would soon be her belongings.

"No, I ain't buying nothing for Bud. But them big ones are mine. You can have the little ones. They don't do me no good."

"Well, some of the ones I want might be big ones, Pearl. Like this one." Victoria gestured toward her with *Treasure Island*, which she was beginning to feel even fonder of now that Pearl had claim-jumped it.

"Well, that don't make no sense!" Pearl leveled back.

"Why not?"

"Why not? I'll tell you why not. Don't make a spit of difference what size book you read, little one's just as good as a big one."

"Well, then I guess it shouldn't make any difference what size book you read either then, should it, Pearl?"

"Read 'em! I ain't gonna read 'em. Need something to prop my chesterfield up with."

A microphone screeched, sputtered and generally assaulted their ears, fortunately drowning out most of Victoria's reply. Pearl cast her another well-practiced glare then scurried off into the knot of bodies forming in front of the auctioneer, both elbows working her into an advantageous position. Victoria sat on the steps and scanned the bustling of bodies over the top of her book. Her eyes searched for blond hair and clear blue eyes but found instead three bobbing caps and an intoxicated commotion. The boys, cheering on the arrival of spring, were celebrating with flasks full of whiskey, and Bobby, in intoxicated exuberance, had tackled Mutt Fisher's dresses and pulled the whole clothesline to the ground. Raising her book, she pretended to be duly occupied and completely oblivious of the fiasco her husband was performing before her. Suddenly, warm hands slipped over her eyes, and her body instantly responded as a smile leapt onto her face.

"Guess who?"

She twisted around into Elliot's grin and barely restrained herself from responding as she wished to.

"Elliot! How are you?"

"Couldn't be better. You? Everything been . . . okay?" His eyes searched into hers, asking the question that had occupied both of their minds for the last few months.

"Ya, everything's been fine." She discreetly scanned the crowd for any unwelcome gawkers staring their way and lowered her voice. "I don't know what went on with that painting, Elliot, but so far I haven't heard a word about it."

He was noticeably relieved.

"You know, I was wondering, do you think it could have been Bud?"

"Why would Bud want to wreck our painting?" he asked.

"Well, I don't know. Maybe it was just his way of getting even with me for taking his junk room."

Elliot considered. "I guess it could have been. He could have probably picked the locks without too much trouble."

She looked up at him.

"Well, if I had to *choose* who went in there, Bud would be a good choice. He doesn't really seem to say much of anything to anyone, does he?"

"No. He pretty much keeps to himself."

"You have no idea how many times I wanted to call to make sure you were okay."

Her eyes questioned him.

He twinkled a smile at her, his explanation cut off by a chorus of drunken rollicking in the yard. They looked over to the tables where Bobby and JJ had wrestled Petey into a huge white brassiere and were stuffing it full of black socks. Elliot grinned, but his face fell silent when he looked back at her and saw pain muffled behind her eyes.

"You okay?"

"Yes, I'm fine. It's just embarrassing." She nodded toward Bobby, who had now stood up, lost his balance and collided with a shelf full of shoes.

"He's just having fun. Don't worry about it."

"He's drunk."

"Hey, that's him. It's not a reflection on you."

"Easy for you to say; you're not married to him."

Elliot laughed, squeezed her shoulders and winked.

"Quite true, I'm not. Hey, you want something? Can I get you a coffee?"

"Okay, sure. Thank you."

"Cream or sugar?"

"Both. One sugar, please."

"Perfect. Same as me."

He stepped off the porch and crossed the yard, mingling with the old-timers as he passed by. She held the book in front of her as she watched him go, covering a smile that swallowed her face. She wanted to reach up and kiss the sky. Resting her head against the porch railing, she blurred all the sights and sounds of the auction into a steady, dull murmur as she waited for him to come back. The touch of his hands had not lost their magnetic draw and, as before, he'd left her with every light in the house on.

"Here you are. Whoops, spilled some."

She let him place the foam cup into her hand then slid the tip of her tongue up the side of it, recovering the drip.

"Thank you. So, how was your trip?"

"My trip?"

"Yeah. This winter, where'd you go?"

"Did I go somewhere?"

Victoria looked at him curiously as she sipped her coffee. "Didn't you? I heard you had."

"Really? Where'd you hear I went?"

"I don't remember. The Bahamas, Barbados . . . some place like that."

Humor crossed with surprise mingled on Elliot's face. "Interesting. Did you happen to hear if I had a good time as well?"

Victoria shook her head as she joined him in a laugh. "You know, I'd really like to know how these stories get started."

"Probably just a misunderstanding. No harm done. Kind of funny actually."

Victoria nibbled delicate teeth marks around the rim of her cup, pondering the avalanche of questions this small shift of information sent tumbling her way.

"So, you've been here all winter? In the valley?"

He nodded a smile, questioning her question with his eyes. "Well, I guess that's not quite true. I spent a week at Christmas down on the island visiting my brother."

"The island?"

"Ya. South end."

Victoria smiled knowingly. "Oh, south end of the island. Now I know where that rumor came from."

"You do?"

"Island. South. More than enough information to get a story started around here."

"Come on! You're joking!"

"Afraid not."

"Doesn't take much, hey?"

"Nope."

"Things must get pretty twisted in a place like this."

"Consider that a serious understatement. You wouldn't believe the stories I've heard about myself."

"And what . . . people just sort of believe whatever best suits them?"

"Pretty much."

He paused to consider this, imprinting a happy face into the soft foam of his cup with his thumbnail. "Regardless of the truth?"

"If it works for them, ya." She swished her coffee around and watched as it swirled into a slow eddy.

"Kind of like you?"

She felt her back stiffen as she bristled against the words. "What do you mean?"

"You know."

"Do I?"

"Yeah. I'm pretty sure you do." He sat on the step below her and leaned back against the porch railing, turned his cup toward her and pressed the happy face into a sad one. "Correct?"

She rolled her eyes and pushed lightly against his shoulder with her knee. "I wish I'd never even mentioned that. Don't you ever forget anything?"

"Not if it's important to me, no."

"And me being happy is important to you?"

"Your being honest with yourself is important to me."

"I am being honest!"

"How honest? Honest enough to admit you're not being honest?"

She put her coffee down beside her, met his eyes and held fast. "I'm fine, Elliot."

"Uh-huh. You're the Queen of the Fine-Fine."

Victoria laughed. "Okay. Fair enough. So, let's say I'm that honest. Where would it get me?"

He set his coffee down beside hers and rested his hand lightly across her foot.

"Everyone has options, Victoria."

"Really? So what are mine?"

"Don't know. That's something only you can decide."

It wasn't the answer she was hoping to hear and her body, her mood, even the air around them seemed to grow agitated.

"Well, maybe I've decided my options don't look so good. What then?"

He squeezed her foot. "Well, maybe then you just need to look a little deeper. Try to see things from a different perspective."

"Well, right now what my perspective sees is my husband and his friends staggering this way."

"Is that a problem?"

"When Bobby's drunk, everything is a problem." She smiled as if it were a joke and shifted her leg away from Elliot's arm.

"Should I leave?"

"Too late. It'll look like you're running away."

Bobby knocked his way through the crowd, saw her sitting off by the house with Elliot and attempted to fix her with a damning stare as he made his way closer, but the interference of people and potholes and a gut full of booze made it all but impossible to maintain. Avoiding his eyes, Victoria examined her cup and concentrated on carving it full of nervous Xs. Looming up on her, he nudged her foot with his boot, focused his frown and spit into the lilac bush beside the stairs.

"How'd you git here?"

"In my car."

"How the hell you git it started?"

"The key."

"Bullshit! I got the frickin' key."

"Well, I got the frickin' spare," she jousted, feeling somewhat insular surrounded by the polite restrictions of social mores.

"That right? You thinking you're pretty bloody smart, ain't ya?"

She kept her head bowed, the foam cup slowly imploding inside her fist. "Hey! I'm talking to you!" He nudged her again harder and the cup collapsed completely, spilling the coffee over her hand and down her leg.

Elliot rose up beside her, the easy looseness gone from his limbs. "Hey Buddy, hold on there. Let's just—"

"Keep your face outta where it don't belong, pretty boy," John Jr.'s voice warned with bitter amusement.

Wisely Elliot ignored him, touching Bobby's arm, which was attempting to steady him against the rails. "Come on, Bobby. Everyone's just having a good time. Let's just—"

"Let's just you mind your own friggin' business how's about!" He tried to square off with Elliot, but the step beneath him tottered under his weight and kept him off balance.

"Better watch that stair. Doesn't seem too safe." Elliot reached out to help steady him, but Bobby pushed his hand away, lost his balance and half-fell, half-sat beside Victoria. He wrapped an arm around her shoulders and tipped her toward him, the sweat of his underarms cold and rancid against her cheek.

"Bobby," she whispered. "Let go. You're hurting me."

"That so?" he returned evenly as he fished a half-chugged mickey from his pocket, squeezing her tighter as he took a swallow. "Drink?"

Elliot declined the offer, held his coffee up in defense. He tried to catch Victoria's attention, but she kept her eyes riveted to the stair beneath her, mortified at having Bobby join their conversation, furious at finding herself trapped beneath his arm. But the situation reeked of explosive potential, and the mere thought of what might happen should Bobby be set off was enough to internalize her fury into shame.

"Heard ya was gone this winter." Bobby mumbled the words and finished with a loud belch.

"Pardon?"

"Heard ya was gone. Where'd ya go?"

"Nowhere really. I just—"

"Heard ya went to Bally or somewhere."

"Bali?"

"Ya. Where 'bouts is that anyways?"

"Well, it's a part of Indo—"

"It's part of India, you nitwit," Petey volunteered.

"Not India you jackass! It's just below Africa," John Jr. cried decisively, the matter settled and Bali relocated. "What the hell you do down there all winter, anyhow?"

"Actually I wasn't down there this winter. Haven't been down there since I went with my brother, oh man, I guess almost ten years ago."

"I heard ya was down there most the winter," Bobby challenged as he took another guzzle.

"Hmm, well, not that I remember. I spent a few days on the island though."

Bobby slapped his thigh. "That damn Ferguson. Potlicker ain't never got his stories straight. Whatcha do on the island?"

"Stayed with my brother. Fished a bit."

"You got a brother?"

"Yup. Two of them. This was my youngest one. The one I went to Bali with."

Bobby glared up at him suspiciously, not too sure he wasn't being played for a fool but eager to show himself up for the challenge.

"Thought you just bloody said you didn't go there."

"No. I said I did go there. With my brother. The one who lives on the island."

"I just bloody asked you that and you just bloody said you didn't."

"Asked me what?" Elliot returned evenly, without a trace of emotion, so innocent in fact that Victoria had to look up and catch the devil in his eye to be sure he wasn't.

"Asked you if ya went to friggin' Bali this winter!" Bobby took an extended pull from his bottle in an attempt to clarify things.

Elliot shook his head. "Nope, not this year. Maybe next year I'll get back down there. Hey, I need a coffee. Anyone else want one? Victoria, can I get you something?"

She slipped him a smile as she shook her head. Bobby, still confused scratched his.

"You bin lots of places?" John Jr.'s words ran across Peter's just as he, not one to refuse a free anything, was on the verge of accepting a coffee.

"Yeah. Yeah, I guess I have."

"Ever bin on one them safaris?"

"Couple times."

"Git anything?"

"Just photos. Not really a hunter in the true sense of the—"

"Ever seen a lion?"

Elliot's nod brought the boys closer around him. "Oh ya, lots of lions. One time we were going down this trail and—"

And he was off. Leading them down a sunburned trail, creating for them a mystical beauty that they could never, not even in their deepest dreams ever fully imagine. Victoria relaxed as Bobby's arm slipped from her, and he and the boys dissolved into Elliot's tale, slack-jawed and daze-eyed as schoolboys at story time.

So. He had been home for the winter. Or for most of it anyhow. She watched his lips play as he spoke, tried to imagine his voice traveling a static-filled line into her ear. It was possible, she conceded. But just as possible it may have been Sam or Mark or Billy Bassman, for that matter. The voice had offered her little in the way of clues. And what purpose would there be for Elliot to hide behind anonymity? He seemed to have no problem speaking

to her directly, perhaps even a little more directly than she appreciated. Then again, maybe Rose was right. People could not always
be accounted for. Sometimes they did strange things. She searched
Elliot's face, turned and found Sam doing the same to hers. Embarrassed, they both looked away quickly, he back to Elliot's oracle and
she back to the sale.

The pressure cooker was on the block now, and the right to
its title was brewing into an all-out war. Mrs. Lyncroft and her
twin sister, Hilda, deadly competitive since they'd fallen in puppy
love with the same boy in sixth grade, had both set their hearts
on owning the heavy silver pot. Pearl, having arrived at the sale
earlier than either of them, felt by rights the pot belonged to her.
Unwittingly underestimating the powers of twinship, she set about
warning them off of it and unintentionally combined their efforts
against her instead.

The price of the pot had started justifiably low and risen frantically on waving arms and seething faces to where it was now trad-
ing at a multiple premium of its worth. No one appeared to care.
The crowd cheered or jeered each new bid, the three women froth-
ing with the quest of attainment. Finally, the competition tired and
Mrs. Lyncroft surged into the lead, captured her prize and raised
it overhead like Olympic gold. Today was a day to celebrate. Never
mind tomorrow when she'd search through the catalogue and find
she could have ordered a new one for less than half the price.

Bobby was butting in now, Elliot's story reminding him of one
of his own, although he didn't seem to make the connection that
while Elliot's had stemmed from the adventures of a real life, his
own was nothing more than an old joke.

"Hey. Hey. I got one. There's this guy, eh. Jus' bin married and
him an his wife they's driving down the road—"

"Naw, not that one, Bobby," Peter whined. "Tell the other one.
That hooker that worked as a nun one."

"It was a nun who worked as a hooker, peckerhead," corrected
John Jr.

"Whatever. Tells him that one, Bobby."

"Can't never 'member that one."

"Can't 'member it? Ya got shit fer brains or what?" John Jr. spat beside Peter's foot and slapped Bobby's arm for a drink of his whiskey.

"You jus' never bloody mind what I got fer brains." He reached over and retrieved his bottle, attempting without success to straighten himself on the stair.

"So anyhow, they's driving along and all-a-sudden his dog starts howling and whining and carrying on in the back of the truck, eh? Bugger hollers back at it to shut the hell up an sure 'nuff the bitch settles right down. Guy turns to his wife. 'That's once,' he says. Keeps on driving."

He paused here to fumble a cigarette into his slack mouth. "All a sudden, you can't bloody believe it, eh, friggin' mutt starts up again. Whining and crying an' carrying on. Well, that's it. Bugger's pissed right bloody off now. Pulls the truck over, jumps out—"

"Hey, Bobby . . . pass me a slosh will ya?"

"Petey, ya dumb-assed dickhead! Will ya shut the hell up? You're wrecking my friggin' joke!"

"I jus' wanted a—"

Bobby answered him with a smack that knocked his cap into the lilac bush and scattered what little was left of his hair.

"Now, where was I?"

"He just got out of his truck," Elliot replied as he retrieved Peter's hat and handed it back to him.

"Did he have his rifle?"

"Don't think so."

"Okay. Well, he grabs it eh, goes to the back of the truck, BOOM! Blows the friggin' dog away. All over hell and back, hey?" The edges of his mouth began to fan upward with the promise of expectant laughter. "Gets back in the truck and holy shee-it if his woman don't start freaking out on him. Whining and crying and carrying on. Bugger takes one look at her, hollers 'Shut up bitch.' Pulls the bloody truck back on the road says, 'That's once.' Ya get it?" He exploded with laughter. "'That's once,' he says. Same's the dog!"

Elliot smiled dryly, looked at Victoria his eyes opened in mock exclamation. Bobby's mood soured dramatically when he found himself laughing a solo.

"Hey! What's the matter with you? Didn't ya git it, or what?"

"Ya. Ya, I think I got it."

"Why ain't ya laughing then? You got a problem with my joke?"

"No. No, I don't have a problem with your joke. I just didn't find it particularly funny. Do you have a problem with that?"

"Ya just didn't git it, did ya?" Peter sneered. "He jus' didn't git it did he JJ? Dumb as that other potlicker we hadda explain it to."

"That was you ya dumb-shit," John Jr. shot back.

"Bullshit JJ! Wasn't me. Was that friggin' what's-his-face. I got it first time I bloody heard it I did." He jutted his chin accusingly at Elliot. "You didn't git it though, did ya?"

Elliot looked around, assessed the situation and nodded. "Yep. Guess you're right Peter. Maybe I didn't. Anyhow, looks like this sale is about sold."

The group of them started to make their way across the emptying yard toward the vehicles, Peter still questioning Elliot on why he didn't shoot the lion when he had the chance. Bobby kept his arm locked around Victoria in an iron embrace.

"You guys need a lift back to town?" Elliot offered.

Bobby squinted at the others thickly to see if any of them had understood the question. "What fer? We got my truck."

"Hmm. Don't think you might have had a tad too much to be thinking about driving?"

"Whoo-ee!" Bobby bellered like a bull-calf on branding day. "You sound just like my friggin' granny. Us boys drink twice the hell as much as a fella like you, still drive ten times as good."

"Hope so," Elliot replied as he slipped Victoria the hint of a wink.

"Drive ten times better'n any city boy anyway, drunk or sober. Ain't that right, Petey?"

"Oh ya, Bobby. You're friggin' Superman. Just won't mention what the hell ya did to my garbage cans." Peter, after a lifetime of abuse was not one to forgive and forget, not one to concede when a point could be taken.

"Hey, asshole. Leave the buggers in the middle of the road . . . whadda ya expect?"

"Ya managed by them just fine on your way into the yard," he challenged back, moving just beyond belting distance.

"You criticizing my driving skills?"

"Criticizing more than that. You got stuck in the garden twice for ya got your ass turned around."

"Wasn't stuck, ya little dwarf pecker. Ya ain't never stuck long as ya still's moving."

"Ya was only moving 'cause Samson an me was pushing ya."

"Ya. Wasn't stuck then, was I? You wanna criticize my driving maybe ya better put some money where your yap is."

Victoria looked up quickly into Bobby's drunken, frozen face.

"Bobby, don't be stupid. You're way too drunk to—"

"Yee-haw," whooped Peter, "even your woman don't think you can drive!"

"That so?" Bobby lurched sideways toward his truck, roughly pulling Victoria with him. "Guess she best come along and see how much she don't know then, hey?"

"Bobby, don't. Please," she pleaded quietly as she tried to twist away without drawing any more attention to herself. "I have my car, Bobby. I have to take it home."

Seeing the pain in Victoria's face, Elliot stepped forward, his body steeled, jaw tight.

"Hey, Bobby. Come on now. Let her go. I think she's made it pretty clear she'd rather not ride with you right now."

"That so?" Bobby snarled back in surprise. He was not used to being openly challenged on his own turf. "So, just what the hell you planning to do about it, huh?"

"Not planning on doing anything about it, okay? She has her own car here. Why not just let her drive that home?"

"Cause it ain't safe. She ain't even bloody 'sposed to be driving it yet, that's why!" he hollered violently.

Victoria avoided Elliot's eyes.

"Well, look. Why don't I give her a ride home, then? If you don't mind."

"Mind! Why the hell should I mind?" Bobby blustered, fear boiling up alongside the rage filling his mind. "Hey, Vic. That what you want to do? You want to get a ride home with this here guy, huh?" His thumb bruised hard into the bones of her wrist and she bit her lip so she wouldn't cry out. Then suddenly, he let her go. For one fragile breath freedom bloomed within her then perished just as quickly.

"Hey, Vic. You wanna play cards?"

"Bobby, no—" Victoria whispered frantically.

"No? Why not? You liked it last time we played, didn't ya?"

"Bobby, please. Don't—" she pleaded, Bobby ignoring her as he swung open the door of his truck and dug something silver out from behind the seat.

"Holy shit, Bobby," exhaled John Jr. "Put that frickin' thing down before someone gets hurt. You goddam crazy?"

"Don't know, JJ. Maybe I am. Whadda you think, Vic? You think you're married to a crazy man or what?" He loosely waved the revolver around and laughed.

"Oh, my god, Bobby. Don't. There's kids—" Victoria whispered, hysterical voices rising around her as horrified parents shoved crying children into vehicles and quickly drove away with one frantic eye on the rearview mirror.

Electricity sizzled around them, tense breathing driving like pistons through the constricted air. Seeking out Sam's face she held his gaze for a desperate moment. A thousand words could not have hoped to articulate what passed silently between them, and slowly Sam's head began to lower, his mismatched eyes sliding shamefully away.

"So? Whadda ya think, Vic?" Bobby sneered, the gun now nestled into the folds of his crossed arms. "You wanna play cards again or not?"

"No, Bobby. You know I don't."

"You sure?"

Dropping her head, she nodded back tears.

"You think you're married to a goddamn crazy man or what?"

Victoria looked at Elliot helplessly, then shook her head. "Of course not, Bobby. Now, just put the gun down, okay?"

"You still thinking of going home with this here joker?" Bobby flicked his head toward Elliot who stood in appalled disbelief at the scene unfolding before him.

Hot tears slid free of her eyes as she looked at the ground and shook her head.

The air began to move again as Bobby finally lowered the revolver and took a drink of his whiskey. She heard Elliot clear his throat and speak softly, his voice imploring her to look up at him, but she could not.

"This isn't right, Victoria—" he said gently.

"Leave her alone, priss-ass! She's fine," Bobby yelled. "You're just fine, ain't you, Vic? Ain't you?"

Victoria's head gave an almost imperceptible nod.

"Victoria, I can—"

"You can't do nothing!" Bobby fumed, snapping the gun up toward Elliot.

"Jesus, Bobby! Come on. Settle down with that thing—" Sam ventured carefully.

"I'll settle down once this city-prick gets out of my face."

"Think you better get outta here," Peter advised from his hiding spot behind the truck.

Elliot stood his ground. "You deserve more than this, Victoria. I hope you know that."

She listened as he began to walk away, his words crucifying her heart with each step he took.

Pushing her toward the truck, Bobby commanded her to get in while he rummaged in a case on the floor, found a warm and somewhat skanky beer, and cracked it open with his teeth. Crawling across to the middle of the seat she scraped a patch clear to sit in and hugged her arms around herself as she started shaking, Bobby and John Jr. crushing into the spaces on either side.

John Jr. looked hard over at Bobby.

"What?"

"What? What the frick you think, *what?*"

"What? That?"

"Yeah. That."

"Wasn't nothing, JJ. I was just jerking that priss-ass's chain."

"Yah? Well, don't be doing it again."

Bobby laughed edgily. "Okay, grandma," he said in an attempt to make light of the situation as he started the truck, spun a donut then accelerated out of the yard.

The sign was a local landmark erected by optimistic forefathers to mark their town's growth. Following the main road, it'd take about three-quarters of an hour to reach, but Bobby, adrenaline still pumping furiously, was impatient to prove what he considered was his legendary status as a marksman with a beer bottle. Roaring across several cow pastures and straight through one fence, he created his own shortcut instead. Someone, no one could remember exactly who, although the boys each claimed responsibility, had taken a can of spray paint and whited out part of the sign, leaving the population at a grand total of two. Years of abuse by projectiles hurled from passing vehicles had slowly chipped away at the center of the sign until Hinckly's N was completely obliterated.

"How much?" Bobby slurred over at John Jr.

"How much you wanna lose, numb-nuts?"

"Case . . . two cases. An a mickey if I git the N."

John Jr. expelled a gritty laugh, snapped the cap off a beer and flicked it across the cab. "Ya stupid potlicker. You be lucky to even hit the friggin' sign, never mind the N."

"Hey, I think you's forgetting who nailed the bitch last time. Hey? Who was that, huh?" Bobby had pulled the truck around to face back toward town, and they sat in the middle of the road now, Bobby gunning the motor till the truck shook.

"Quit revving the shit out of her, or we'll end up walking back to town."

"Rev the shit outta her, iffin I want. Shut up and pass me a beer."

John Jr. hammered his fist on the back window and an opened beer was dutifully passed forward and chugged down by Bobby as the others hooted and cheered and egged him on. Enjoying a sizable belch, Bobby slid his foot from the brake and the truck fishtailed angrily, almost throwing Peter clear out of the back.

Stomping the gas pedal into the floor, he pressed as hard as he could, as if by sheer force he could propel the vehicle faster. Slowly the road, the trees, the gravel began to swish by in a blur as the sign began to come into focus before them. Leaning his bulk into his door, Bobby pressed as much of his flesh through the window as he could manage, the empty bottle held tightly in his left hand.

"Grab the wheel, Vic!" he yelled as he took aim, leaning still further out the window until Victoria was certain she felt the whole truck following his direction, felt it slowly begin to lean toward the opposite side of the road. She watched hypnotically as the ditch opened below them and revealed its entrails: blurred swipes of cardboard boxes, unsprung mattresses and a long-dead deer. He hollered again, commanded her to take the wheel, but something in her sat rigid and her limbs refused to obey.

"Grab it!" John Jr. shrieked at her then grabbed it himself when he saw defiance had rewritten her face. The crackle of tires on gravel filled their ears as John Jr. wrenched the truck back onto the road, a sharp thwack signaling Bobby's bottle had indeed found its mark. Raucous applause pounded the cab roof as Bobby whooped and hollered and congratulated himself.

"Two cases and a mickey!"

"Bullshit! Ya didn't git the N."

"Bloody did too. Didn't ya see it? Nailed the bitch dead on!"

"Naw, I didn't see 'cause someone had to keep the friggin' truck on the road." He shot a glare at Victoria. "Let's go to Trappers, I'll buy you a beer."

"Screw that! You bet me two cases an a friggin' mickey to boot."

"Tough shit for you numb-nuts. Didn't shake on it!" John Jr. grinned victoriously.

"Ah, shit, that ain't fair JJ! Deal's a deal."

"Not if ya don't shake on it. Ain't nothing but negotiations lessen you shake on it."

"Shit!" Bobby pounded the steering wheel. He could see when he was defeated. "Damn shit! Well, least you owes me a beer iffin nothing else."

"Sure, I'll buy you a beer. Swing by Trappers."

"Bobby, I don't want to go to Trappers. I want to go home, okay?" Victoria's voice barely rose above the roar of the motor. Bobby looked down at her, surprised, as if he'd forgotten she was even there. Instinctively he began to deny her request, but John Jr. cut in before he had a chance.

"Ya, send her home, Bobby. We can pick up my rig."

Bobby sped down Main Street, swerved around two corners and tried to hit a sleeping dog before roaring to a stop outside John Jr.'s bedraggled house, where a clutch of equally bedraggled children offered up grubby hands in a tentative wave, which their father ignored as he left Bobby's truck and clambered into his own. Grinding into reverse, Bobby zigzagged back out the driveway, down the street and all the way over to the bar. Victoria felt completely sick to her stomach now, and she wished Bobby would just get out so she could go home and be alone. But he sat making no attempt to move, watching the rearview mirror like he was waiting for something to happen. And when it did happen, he abruptly popped the clutch causing the truck to jump ahead and send Peter sprawling like a sack of potatoes. And each time Peter made a renewed attempt to get out of the truck, Bobby sent him sprawling again, squealing and cursing like a stuck pig, until finally he

became annoyed at being the amusement and refused to cooperate, hunkering down in the back of the truck and glaring at anyone
who caught his eye. Bobby, having had a good laugh, fell out of the
truck, grabbed Peter by the scruff of the neck and hauled him out
as well, easily sidestepping a few weak blows as they staggered off
into the bar followed slowly by Sam.

Victoria scrounged through the garbage on the floor, found a
semi-clean rag and wiped slopped beer from the driver's seat. Slipping behind the wheel, her eye caught the forms of two men leaning against the garbage bins breathing hair spray from paper bags.
Coaxing the truck into gear, she bucked and lurched into motion
then, despite herself, looked over and caught the unmistakable
gesture of a feeble wave.

~ Chapter 20 ~

S he picked up the phone apprehensively, profoundly relieved when no one answered her tentative hello. The calls had come in a trickle at first then developed into a torrent as word got out about Bobby's gun-waving performance: apologetic or angry mothers calling with translucent excuses why they had to immediately pull their children out of dance classes. In less than a week the studio's roster went from over-full to annihilated. Victoria looked down at her half-empty glass, absently pulled the whiskey bottle from the cupboard and topped it up.

"Oh, hi. I was wondering when you'd call again. I was beginning to think you'd forgot my number. Or forgot about me . . . or something like that."

She fished the words carefully into the line, desperate for a bite, a nibble, a response however small that would reassure her that it was not possible for him to ever forget her, or even her number. She hesitated a moment but didn't wait long. She'd long ago learned his words either erupted in a short burst or not at all. Pressing the small of her back against the refrigerator, she slid unevenly to the floor, twirling her fingers in the black cord. She found a pen lying beside her and, pulling her knees up to her chest, causing her nightie to slide down across her hips, she began doodling on her thigh.

"Guess you heard about my husband? Out at the sale? Sure everyone has by now. Well, he's managed to get his way. Again." She stopped, licked her lips as she carefully etched a leafy tree up her left thigh. "He never wanted me to have a studio in the first place, and now he's scared off every mother in town."

She blossomed apples onto the tree, "Sometimes, I wish he would just do it." The words held an ice that froze her, but considering them, she let them be. "I do. It's true. Don't tell anyone, okay? Never. I know it sounds awful to say. It *is* awful to say. I'm sure I don't really wish it. I don't. It's just that I'm so confused. He makes me feel so trapped, so useless. I just don't know what to do anymore."

She listened for a response, gave up and stretched her legs out, admiring her artwork from a different perspective. She added three blue and flesh daisies at the base of the tree, reconsidered and rubbed one away with her thumb.

"Doesn't love me, anyhow. Not really. More of a possession thing. Bobby's wife. You know? Apostrophe *s*, as in the wife belonging to Bobby."

"Leave him then," the voice and the static spilled out together.

Starting a little, she dropped her pen. Even after all the time she'd spent in these solitary conversations the caller's few, infrequent advances still unnerved her.

"What?" she asked, but carried on without waiting for an answer, knowing he never repeated himself no matter how long she waited for him to do so. "Easy for you to say. Easy for everyone to say. But not everyone knows Bobby the way I do, do they?" She coaxed the pen back toward her with slender fingers. "He wasn't just messing around out at the sale, you know. He's pulled that stuff on me before. Like the night with the cards. We'd only been married about a year then, but I'd already had enough. Told him I was leaving. I actually thought it was that easy. Ha! Made me stay up all night. His Dad's old Enfield and a pack of cards on the table between us. Him ranting and raving about every little injustice anyone had ever done him. Then every once in a while he would stop and make me pull a card from the deck. 'Don't pull that Ace of Spades,' he'd yell. 'You pull that Ace of Spades, I gonna blow my goddam head off.' All night long. Until he finally passed out. There were only five cards left. Five. I can't even begin to tell you what an insane hell that was. Anyhow, wasn't till a week later I found that goddam Ace of Spades, crumpled up in the pocket of the jeans he was wearing that night. Never forgave him for that. He destroyed something in me. Something that can't ever be fixed again, you know?

"Runs in his family. That's what makes it so hard for me to know what to do. It's like he got a bad gene or something so how can that be his fault, right? Like his great-grandfather hanging himself and his uncle Johnny blowing his brains out. And you know his dad's hunting accident? You can't ever tell anyone this, okay? Never. The thing no one knows about there is that Bobby found his dad at the bottom of the rock bluff, wearing nothing but his pajamas in minus forty degrees. It wasn't any hunting accident. It was the family disease." Taking a deep swallow from her drink she squeezed back the tears. "So, what am I supposed to do?" she whispered, starting to cry silently. "I mean, he frustrates me beyond belief. Sometimes I think I even hate him. But I can't just take off and have him kill himself, can I? I mean, what kind of a person would that make me?"

Sketching a flock of "v" birds above her tree, she landed a few in the apples. A leaf fell from the tree, and she quickly etched it into a bird then surrounded it with a larger bird, confining it within itself. "Anyhow, even if I could leave, what would I do? Don't have a job, a place to stay. Nothing." Hesitating, she hoped for an answer and grew angry when she received nothing but static. "See! Not so easy, is it? You can't give me any answers, either. You can't even give me your name."

"You want my name?"

This caught her off guard. Her accusation had been empty, driven by the frustration of her situation and not by any real desire to discover the caller's identity. She pulled her legs crossed and reflected soberly on his proposal. Did she want to know? She had spent countless sleepless nights in pursuit of that answer, offered to her so simply now. But to know, really know, seemed anything but simple and fear began to bubble at the edges of her curiosity. She felt a sudden protectiveness toward the person she had created. Not Elliot. Not Sam. Not Mark. Not one, but all three.

"No. No, don't tell me. We know who we are, right? I think it works better this way anyhow, don't you? At least for now." She resumed her sketching, adding the framework of a house beside the tree. "I'm sorry if I sounded rude. I just get so desperate sometimes. You're right though. I could leave. I mean who even knows if he'd ever really do anything, right? He's been threatening me with it for years. He doesn't think I'll ever leave, but one day he might come home and I'll be gone. Love to see his face then." She fumbled with the phone as tears surprised her, and she angrily wiped them away. Reaching for a tissue, she blew her nose, took a couple of deep breaths to calm any tremors from her voice and continued speaking.

"He'd probably be fine, anyhow. Have me replaced by the weekend. Replace me with Rose in a second if he thought he had half a chance. Ha! Good luck there. She can't stand him. Even thinks I should leave him. And maybe I will. Some time. But not yet. Who knows—"

"I dream of you."

"What?"

"I want you." The words struggled through the static, lost their way and for the first time were repeated. "I want you—" the static again overwhelmed them and the sentence ended with a sharp click.

She sat still, breathing into the dead line, a self-conscious smile slowly edging shock off her face.

"Me? You want me?" she questioned, then answered herself. "He wants me. Me."

Night drifted slowly around her as she sat running his words back and forth through her mind. Eventually she rose to her feet and stretched her legs, thighs almost completely tattooed with little ink hearts etched secretively with *? loves Victoria*. So. He dreamt of her. Desired her. She tipped her nightie straps off her shoulders and let it slip onto the floor.

Walking into the bathroom she flipped the switch on with a tight snap and remained in the dark. She spat Bobby's name like a curse. He'd gone into the bathroom that morning and discovered the light bulb burnt out, so he'd told her about it. Told her about it as if it was beyond him to replace it himself. She turned to find a replacement bulb then stopped, set her jaw and decided she was not going to fulfill his expectations. He wasn't coming home until later anyhow. Errands to run in town, then a stop by JJ's to help with the 'cuda. He'd told her not to wait up for him, and she'd quietly marveled at how lost his touch of their reality was. She'd given up waiting for him more than a decade ago.

Leaving the bathroom door ajar, she groped the darkness and patted her way to the faucet controls. Feeling the water until it was comfortable on her palm, she popped the shower lever and stepped into the beating stream. Closing her eyes, she relaxed under the warm massage of liquid velvet hands as they pressed the tension from her neck and shoulders. Leaning against the wall she drew moist air deep inside herself and exhaled slowly. The blackness wrapped her in a silky robe, slipped its arms around her and enveloped her. Delighted itself in her, teasing fingers seducing as a thousand silver-tongued devils licked lacy patterns down her body. Clenching her fists against herself, she attempted to alleviate her suffering, but the time was past. She could no more stop the storm within her than press back the rays from the sun. Sinking on weakening knees, the water pounded her lower, pressed her down on top of herself until her heels, rising up to meet her detonated an explosion that shook her spirit and rocked her world.

Hovering in a universe distorted, she watched as she felt the planes around her shift, then solidify and eventually reconnect. Discomfort began to seep in and register on her brain and she straightened up, still seeking support against the wall to steady herself. A new sensation began to emerge, uncomfortable and intrusive, and her senses were sharpened back to assess it. The water was turning cold. Instantly reason and intellect seized their positions, and she twisted off the faucets. Her hands fluttered like delicate twin butterflies as they searched through the darkness for a towel. Pulling one to her, she rubbed herself roughly, kept rubbing long after the dampness was gone.

Cool air met her as she stepped into the hallway, and she was startled to find the porch door ajar with a night breeze stealing through it. The strong, steady thrum of a million crickets announced a brilliantly sequined indigo night, and she took a seat on the top stair to admire them both. She marveled at the blessing of the crickets. So humble an existence and yet lucky enough to be deeply stamped from the moment of creation with a song to be sung in unison and a purpose they knew without knowing. And she considered her own life, a dull flat prairie with a song unknown. The river of youth having seeped through her hands long before it could even begin to find its course.

The air swirled around her and beckoned her onto the dance floor, and for a hesitation she resisted before abandoning her inhibitions and running free toward that which she knew. Alighting at the edge of the freshly sown field, she listened carefully into the darkness, released her towel and crossed to center stage, the earth soft, cool flour beneath her feet. An orchestra began to moan in the soft whisper of the wind, spread like wildfire across the meadow and ignited the night. Curtsying deeply to the moon, she emptied herself at its feet and felt the music run back through her, consume her, become her as its expression carried her limbs in an orgy of pleasure, and for the first time she danced with the pure joy of life.

Her spirit would have danced for eternity but, still shackled to her body, found it could not, and eventually the two parted, and she fell heavily back to the earth. She stretched herself full under the glittering stars and smiled back at them. Tonight they had all been one. All brilliant. All stars. A wash of color spilled across the sky, shimmered stronger then faded only to reappear on the undulations of a wave. She watched in awe as the northern lights claimed the stage, illuminating it with the precious laughter of all the unborn children. Relaxing against the cool thighs of the earth, she watched them play, shades of pink and green and yellow rolling over and under and through one another in a beautifully choreographed dance.

Exhaustion pressed against her, and it was with reluctance that she began to hear the sound tapping inside her head. She forced herself to sit upright, her body half painted with soil, hair hanging down her back in long, dirt-encased shrines. Rocking gently in her tranquil peace a low, rumbling noise picked deeper into her consciousness, then verified its existence with a single headlight slicing toward her forewarning that the Cyclops was returning to his lair, effectively silencing all the woodland nymphs.

~ Chapter 21 ~

As summer drifted by, Victoria found herself rebelling at her habit of waving at everyone who happened across her path during her infrequent trips to town: inherited acquaintances and childhood classmates. It became absurd to her that she should still consider someone a friend when the last thing they'd shared had been wallpaper paste in kindergarten. She hadn't intentionally begun to snub people, but once she had, it quickly developed into an obsession, each time infusing her with a tiny injection of power. And, as might be expected, people responded poorly to her condescension and began to erect stiff barriers of resentment, some even going so far as to start feeling sorry for Bobby as he had such a difficult wife. One fellow in particular chafed at her attitude, believing himself of elevated status in the valley and therefore entitled to a certain amount of gratuitous respect.

Gavin Hackett had a gift some said. He could find water under the earth with no more than a green willow branch. And it was a gift, too. A gift turned lucrative after he realized people would pay not only for the location of water but just to follow along and be entertained in the process. Whenever Gavin Hackett set about finding water with a stick, he stirred up a good deal of dissension as well. Old-timers popped around to pay their buck and watch the ceremony, swapping tales of previous times when Gavin had found water even though the experts had claimed there was none. Some of the stories had grown so ludicrous Victoria wondered how long it would be before Gavin Hackett was credited with turning water into wine. But people swore by him. Or at him, depending on whether or not they were true believers.

Victoria found it preposterous that people treated him with either fawning admiration or reverent fear, or both. And although she did have to admit that his ability to find water with a stick was pretty strange, she'd gone from grade school to almost graduation with him, and she found it impossible to revere someone who she'd seen snort spaghetti up his nose and cough it back out his mouth. The one thing about him, though, that wasn't in question was his ability to find the location of a new well, so Bobby had scrounged together the money and set a date for the show. Victoria had told him flat out she wasn't hanging around while half the town came out to snoop around their place but quickly changed her mind when she considered the possibilities of whom that might bring her way.

Saturday afternoon was set for the witching, and the day had started out bad and blown itself worse. She wondered if Gavin Hackett could have gotten a more theatrical sky even if he'd special ordered. Bitchy storm clouds spat down darkly, and the growl of thunder and slashes of lightning that should have raised people's caution, electrified their excitement instead. Victoria stood back from the window and peeked outside at the familiar strangers milling in loose groups. All the usuals were already in place, men and women splintered into separate factions as a legion of boisterous children ran up, over and around her car in a squealing game of tag, leaving muddy footprints and dents across its already muddy, dented hood. Slipping away from the window, she hid in the bedroom wishing Bobby would hurry back from town. Gavin Hackett had insisted Bobby drive into town and usher him back out to the trailer. Never mind that half the town was headed that way anyhow, and he could have easily hitched a ride with almost any one of them. He had a reputation to uphold and mixing with the mortals was not the way to do so. Bobby had complained about the unnecessary trip almost daily for the last two weeks. But when he woke up and got dressed to go that morning, she could see that he was excited and even felt a little proud to be the one delivering the guest of honor.

She started going through the closet, searching for the wrapping paper and bows to wrap Diana's baby sweater. The months had slipped past, and the gift, now months overdue, had to be unraveled and made larger so it had a chance of still fitting. She searched her way through two closets and three drawers before the multicolored teddy bears finally peeked out from under a pillowcase. Tucking and patting limp arms across a nonexistent pale yellow chest she carefully wrapped it up and decorated it with a bright pink bow.

Pulling back the edge of the blanket that covered the bedroom window, she scanned the vehicles parked and pulling into the yard, and felt disappointment mixed with relief. Elliot hadn't come and, while she yearned to see him, she had no desire to see a repeat of his and Bobby's confrontation. She noticed a klatch of women over by the chicken coop where Diana stood back against the fence, clutching her baby as old women clucked and cackled and cooed, secretly glad their own reproductive days were long over. Victoria picked up her package, rearranged the bow and walked into the porch to put on her parka and rubber boots. She glanced back outside and noticed Rose had joined the ladies, settled Diana's baby into her arms and was full barrel into the heart of the gossip. Chatting vivaciously, she was unaware of the blanketed shadow slowly drawing closer behind her. Foul looks were cast around as some of the ladies craned their necks to see if Doris's husband was close at hand. Mrs. Spiller was an infringement on their day, and they were not happy to have her infiltrate their group. They began to split ranks as the old woman settled in beside them, not able to stomach the smell of her. Bent and silent, she hovered motionless for a while as if she were listening to Rose's story. Suddenly, and with surprising speed a clawed hand sliced out at Rose's shocked face. Momentarily stunned, the women erupted into motion. Diana leapt forward to save her baby while several of the others grabbed onto a thrashing Mrs. Spiller and pulled her backward away from Rose.

"Get that crazy old witch away from me," Rose seethed, touching the mark on her face, which had started to bleed.

"Filthy gypsy!" Mrs. Spiller screeched, her white hair dancing wildly atop her head as she struggled to get free. "That filthy gypsy stole my treasure," she howled. "Stole it and hid it away in her house. She did. She did. I saw her last night through the window. I know where it is. I know. I'll get it. I will—"

The old woman was furious. Eyes flashing like pistol shots, she was spitting mad and more alive than Victoria had ever seen her. Slivering the trailer door open, she poked her head out to get a better view, inadvertently diverting Mrs. Spiller's attention her way.

"And that one! She stole my painting!"

Victoria's mouth gasped open as she tucked her head back inside the porch, banging the door shut behind her. Standing beside the window, she slid it open and listened intently to the confusion of conversations swirling around Mrs. Spiller.

"What painting? What's she talking about now?"

"Don't be stupid. There is no painting. She's just making it up like everything else."

"I'm not!" the old woman screeched hysterically. "She stole it out of my mop room!"

"Agnes! Don't be silly." Doris tried desperately to bring some sanity to the situation. "You haven't cleaned the hotel for over forty years now. Your mind's just getting you all jumbled up again."

Victoria leaned heavily against the wall. So that explained it. Mrs. Spiller must still have keys from back in the days when she used to clean the hotel. She breathed a massive sigh of relief. Perfect. The old woman's mind was so addled that no one gave any credence to a thing she had to say.

Apparently Doris's husband had been alerted by the commotion and was now hurrying over in his shuffling gait to attend to things. Rose redirected her anger toward him, and he ducked his head low as he made his way past her.

"This is beyond ridiculous. Crazy thing snuck up and attacked me from behind. And I was holding Diana's baby! You're just damn lucky I didn't drop it. It's past bloody time you locked her up before someone really gets hurt."

An approving murmur slipped through the crowd as he mumbled worn apologies. Gathering up his sister-in-law, he directed her toward the car where Doris already sat waiting in stony silence, her gaze leveled off across the fields. What could he say? He agreed with the crowd, but in the end it was Doris who warmed his bed at night.

The eyes of the crowd followed their departure down the driveway, indignant conversations jumping up all around. Concerned appraisals were made of Rose's face. It was a small wound surely. But blood had been drawn. Who knew what the old woman was growing capable of? Dementia had been eroding her mind for years. What was stopping her from becoming increasingly violent? And this time there had been a baby involved. Mrs. Lyncroft had been standing the closest, and she thought she was almost sure Mrs. Spiller had been eyeing up the child before she'd struck. Clearly something would have to be done. They were good citizens and had been patient. But this was too much. This would have to end.

In the distance, Victoria could see Bobby's truck barreling down the road, barely keeping pace with itself. A few heads turned, then more and she began to feel a shift in the crowd's energy. She knew once Gavin Hackett arrived he'd wrap the crowd's attention around himself, and she could slip unnoticed from the trailer. As the truck slowed to turn into the driveway, the intensity of suppressed excitement grew louder in the circles of conversation, and the children's squeals turned to shrieks as they started to fight.

Bobby pulled up importantly, splashing through mud puddles and spraying several people before he jerked to a stop, banged his door open and swung himself onto the ground. Although everyone had a watchful eye on his mood, no one had sacrificed a Saturday afternoon to see Bobby perform. They'd come to see the divine deliverer: every eye was fixated on the dark form hunched in the passenger seat, each one eager to be the first to spot any new additions to the act. Feeling a bit cheated, Bobby hesitated briefly then strode over and flung Gavin Hackett's door open with a dramatic flair.

And the divine deliverer was not one to disappoint. Flying abruptly from the truck, he sent Bobby stumbling backward, drawing a hysterical scream, upon which appeared from the back of the truck the grubby form of recently awakened Billy Bassman. The stage set and the show ready to roll, arguments began breaking out as to whether army boots had in fact made their debut at Potter's witching, and whether the rabbit's foot dangling from his hat had indeed been a gift from an authentic Indian medicine man. Always a showman, Gavin whirled like a dervish through the crowd, his long black trench coat billowing out behind him like a prehistoric bird. Pulling a black felt cowboy hat low over shifty eyes, he stuck a fat cigar in his mouth but did not light it. Smoke made him sick. Mumbling something unintelligible, he began to stroke the odd assortment of necklaces hanging around his neck. It was the necklaces that had gotten him into trouble. Alert church-goers had immediately reported them back to the clergy and soon there had been suspicion that the devil himself had somehow gotten involved. Which of course had added greatly to Gavin Hackett's fame as well as his fortunes. Overnight it spread through the valley that if you needed a fortune told or a message sent to the other side, Gavin Hackett was the man for the job.

Determining all fees had been paid in full, he raised a slow, ring-encrusted hand into the air. He spoke not one word, but the conversations around him crumbled, then collapsed. Reaching into a scarlet velvet case, he withdrew three willow sticks grown in the shape of a Y. Raising them to his face, he fluttered his eyes as he first smelled, then tasted each one. Suddenly dropping two, he pressed the other one to his ear, appeared to listen then rocked himself into a high-pitched wail before snapping his arms out in front of him, fists gripping tightly as the willow appeared to drag him out across the field.

The crowd all but ran to keep up as it streamed behind him. Victoria scoffed as she watched them race off like a pack of hounds after a fox. Wondering if Gavin still snorted spaghetti up his nose, she laughed out loud then stopped abruptly as she remembered she hadn't seen Billy Bassman get out of the truck or join the crowd. Quietly she made her way as close as necessary to the truck and peered over the side of the box. Sure enough, there he lay sprawled out like a dead dog, passed out cold. A shiver crawled over her, and she walked off quickly toward the field, zipping her parka in an attempt to keep herself warm.

Diana had fallen back from the group, the weight of the baby and roughness of the field providing a more daunting task than she had anticipated. Slowly gaining on her, Victoria assessed her from behind and noted with satisfaction that the production of eight children had not come without sacrifices. The satisfaction, however, was hasty and ill-formed, evaporating rapidly as two curly-topped cherubs raced back from the others to place bouquets of wildflowers into their mother's already overburdened hands. Emotion choked Victoria. She so missed being surrounded by her dance students that it felt like the blood had crusted in her veins.

Diana stopped to reorganize and regroup her armload of baby and blanket and bottles and bouquets. Victoria noticed that even now, wearing girlish florals and lace over two decades of good cooking and her mother's genes, Diana still managed to look sprightly rather than matronly. Victoria felt at once both annoyed and ashamed for feeling so.

"Hi Vic," Diana smiled, her face a portrait of snugness.

"Hi."

"How's it going?"

"Okay. You?"

"Oh, good. Busy," she gestured unnecessarily toward the baby.

"Yes, I'd imagine."

"Vic, I . . ." Diana began nervously. "I'm really sorry how things went. With the studio, you know?"

Avoiding eyes, Victoria nodded.

"I'm sure there wasn't anything to it. He was probably just being silly. Too much to drink and all. You know how people in this town are, though. I didn't want to pull the girls out, but Tom said I had to. I'm really sorry, Vic."

The baby began to whimper, and Victoria was relieved as Diana immediately responded to that central force of all mothers holding their newborn and abruptly shifted the conversation onto the child.

"I didn't realize Gavin was going so far across the field. At the last witching he found water just back of the house. If I knew I'd have to pack her all the way out here, I'd have at least brought her stroller, although that probably wouldn't have worked either, the field being so rough and all. Can't believe how heavy she's getting already. She's really big for her age. Last time the health nurse checked she couldn't believe how big she was already. Last month she was above average on the chart and this month she was right off of it. Gonna be a big girl just like her brothers and sisters I guess."

Diana smiled keenly at Victoria as if waiting for applause or at least a pat on the back for a job well done.

Victoria smiled back, made the appropriate noises and wondered to herself how accurate these mysterious charts could be. She'd heard the same boasts of superior growth in relation to each of Diana's children over the years, and all had grown up to be strong and healthy but certainly not outside the parameters of normal.

"Did you see what Mrs. Spiller did to Rose?"

Victoria nodded.

"It's so sad, really. But Rose is right. Someone needs to do something about it. She's completely off her rocker. Thinks Rose is some gypsy who stole some treasure or something. Must be awfully hard for Doris. But still . . . really, they need to do something about her."

Victoria nodded again. There was no use talking about it. Things had come up before. Nothing had been done then, and she knew nothing would be done now.

"Hey, my teacher, my teacher!" Lily squealed as she ran up and coiled herself around Victoria's leg. "I mith you teacher. When are you not going to be too bithy to teach me again?"

"Oh, I . . ." Victoria stammered.

"Mrs. Lackey will be busy for a while yet, Lily. Go play with your sisters," Diana swept her off easily.

"Look at me, teacher. I'm flying," called out Lily as she whirled off in figure-eight circles, arms outstretched, her eyes closed tight.

"I can see that, Lily. Good for you," Victoria called back, struggling against the tide of emotion surging within her. But even as she spoke she saw an older boy descending on the small frame, his loutish hand reaching out and pulling a brown piggy-tail.

"Rufus! I'm telling," Lily wailed.

Victoria stepped forward, then caught herself. She wanted to grab the boy by the arm and squeeze until it hurt. Until it more than hurt. She looked at Diana.

"Oh, boys. Always teasing," Diana excused. "Would you like to hold her?" She passed over the blanketed bundle as if an affirmative reply were the only one possible.

Victoria tightened noticeably. "Oh, I don't know Diana. I'm not very good with babies."

"Nonsense." Diana waved off her objection as if Victoria was simply being modest. "Here. Is that for me?"

She gestured to the gift Victoria still held in her hand, and Victoria passed it to her, somehow receiving the baby in return. It felt surprisingly heavy and solid folded into her arms, and she tried to soften her grip to appear more comfortable. But despite her efforts, she continued to cradle it tightly.

"Oh! Oh, Vic! Thank you, it's so sweet. And she looks beautiful in yellow." Diana caressed the little sweater lovingly, as if it were the most splendid gift she'd ever received, and even though Victoria had knitted identical ones for each child.

"I hope it'll still fit her. Do you think it will?" Victoria asked, suddenly seized by a desperate desire that it *must* fit. She fought against an impulse to wake the child right there and fill the empty yellow sweater with the soft plumpness of new life.

"Oh yes, it'll still fit. Definitely," Diana responded decisively, knowingly, as someone intimately aware of each square inch of her child's flesh. "Here, want me to take her?"

Victoria looked at Diana's face with some alarm. Had she done something wrong? Held the child too tightly? Had her face let slip the secrets of her mind? She responded carefully, hesitatingly.

"Do you mind if I hold her a little longer?"

"No, of course not. Hold her all day if you want," Diana laughed. She knelt down, attempting a reorganization of her diaper bag to include one more item, happily chattering about one or the other, then eventually all of her children.

Victoria focused her attention on the baby, cradled it to her closer and felt the warmth of its sleeping body against her chest. Slowly she edged the blankets back to reveal the soft round forehead, the little flip nose and the gentle curve of black lashes protecting innocent eyes. She peeled the blanket back further to reveal a tiny white hand and traced it lightly with her own, marveling at the buttery softness of the fingers as Diana continued on below her, her voice a stream of words lost to the wind. Feeling inside the blankets, Victoria cupped each pudgy foot in the palm of her hand, watching the faint rise and fall of the blanket as a tiny heart beat next to her own. Emotion filled her thickly, and she wrapped herself even closer around the child, felt her breasts grow full and heavy as she began to sway with the innate rhythm of motherhood. She lightly touched the angel-kissed mouth with the tip of her pinkie and felt sure that all of life would stand corrected if she could just forever stay there and hold that child.

But life does not stand corrected. It simply makes its mistakes and moves on, and the moment was fractured by a frilly, high-pitched giggle. Their attentions were instantly diverted to a couple crossing toward them, completely oblivious to all but their own immediate world. Mark, dressed in his standard jeans and muscle-emphasizing T-shirt, led the conversation, which was occasionally punctuated by the girl's giggles. He held one arm protectively around her as she shivered and shimmered beside him. Dressed for weather ten degrees warmer, she wore a dress made for someone two sizes smaller, revealing a bodacious cleavage that explained a great many things.

They sidled up together, Mark tossing out a hello while his girlfriend could only respond with a muffled giggle to their greetings as she buried her face into his bicep. Victoria judged her with an immediate and irrevocable dislike. Frivolous and stupid creature; even her blond curls seemed to giggle down her bare back. One look at Diana confirmed the verdict was unanimous. Victoria studied Mark as he whispered something into the girl's ear, wondered, as she occasionally found herself doing, if it were at all possible that Bobby's suspicions about being his father might indeed have had some chance at truth. Again assessing his dark curls and green eyes, she had to concede they were features that easily could be attributed to Bobby. But then again, they could easily be attributed to Diana as well, her and Bobby sharing enough similarities to pass as siblings, possibly even twins.

"I thought you were supposed to be working today," Diana demanded in a voice Victoria could not readily connect to her, that seemed to come through somebody else.

"Nope. Called in sick."

"Sick?"

"Yup."

"Don't exactly seem sick."

"Am. Sick of work." He grinned down at the girl, who failed to suppress a giggle then honored his wit with a quick kiss.

"Mark, I've told you a hundred times—"

"Hey! Save the lecture, maw. Ain't got time today. Came out to see the town crazy con the village idiots . . . no offense, Mrs. Lackey. Hey, you ever get your hens laying?"

She avoided his eyes, nodded her head.

"New rooster?"

She nodded again, kept her eyes fixed on the sleeping baby as she felt his on her face.

"Yes! I knew it!" He punched the air with his free arm. "Damn, I'm good, hey?" he crowed, and was confirmed by a coy tiddle and a press of flesh against his side.

"Mark, ssht! You'll wake the baby. Here, see what Mrs. Lackey made for her. Isn't it adorable?" Diana asked as she unearthed the sweater from the diaper bag, spilling the rest of its contents onto the ground.

"Yeah. Nice," he replied as he ran his hand down the girl's chirpy behind until she blushed and slapped it away.

"You had one just like this," Diana continued after cooling the girl with a disapproving glare. "Except blue. And Jamie's was green, and Lily's and Amy's were pink and peach. She's made one for each of you kids. Isn't that special?" She asked the question in that simple, plaintive tone one reserves for talking to the very young, the very old, or the very stupid.

"Made one for me?" He raised his eyebrows with genuine surprise, paused to consider then laughed out loud, startling the baby awake. "Damn, that's twisted!"

Victoria instantly began to bounce and rock as if by bouncing and rocking she could juggle the child back into sleep. She twinged self-consciously as Mark's words hung over them, and she hoped Diana was too preoccupied by the commotion of the baby to question their meaning.

Diana had already moved forward to take the child and restore order to the situation but in the same moment the child's fist found Victoria's finger and pulled it eagerly to its mouth, slobbering profusely on her knuckle. Victoria relaxed for a second; the child's agitation seemed to disappear as it attempted to latch on, then returned with a vengeance when no milk was forthcoming. Quickly she yanked her hand from its mouth, and the tiny face that was but a second before the epitome of angelhood, now contorted, and reddened and began to shriek in protest.

Not knowing what else to do, Victoria looked up at Diana, the panic that filled her body spreading rapidly across her face. Diana smiled calmly and looked at Mark.

"Mark, could you help Mrs. Lackey with the baby for a second? I just have to get this diaper bag back together."

Mark shrugged and unhitched his arm from around his girl-friend, who instantly sprouted a pouty lip as he stepped closer to Victoria than was necessary. He ran his eyes purposefully across her own as he leaned over her, trying to distract the child. But as he cooed and kissed and whistled a hairsbreadth from her breast, the only one distracted was Victoria, and she wished the child would shut up before she became completely unglued. Realizing he was having no effect whatsoever on the child, he straightened up and amused himself in Victoria's embarrassment as the little head, trig-gered by an ancient response, twisted toward her breasts, its hot, red mouth open in a frantic search for sustenance. Holding the fussing bundle awkwardly away from her, she looked helplessly at Mark who leered into her, grinned and tossed a suggestion to his mother.

"Looks like you gotta handle this one, Mom. She needs some tit—"

"Mark! I've asked you not to use that word."

"Oh, come on maw. Tit, breast, boob . . . all the same to me. All the same to her, too, long as they got lunch in 'em."

"Well, just a sec'. I'm just about done. Could you take her for a minute, Mark?" Diana asked, looking up now and seeing the ris-ing panic inflicting Victoria's face. Mark's hand slid between Victo-ria and the baby, lingered unnecessarily, then lifted the child easily into the crook of his arm where, as if on cue, the screaming ceased and shifted to happy smiles instead.

A cheer broke out across the field. They turned to see hats being thrown into the air and backs being slapped as the crowd congratulated itself on a successful witching. Gavin Hackett was already strutting defensively back toward the trailer, the bark of the willow ripped and shredded as it had twisted violently toward the pull of water. Bobby, flanked by the boys, lumbered along at his side, arguing vehemently that something was unfair. As they drew closer, she caught enough to understand that although water had been found, and quickly, it was so far from the trailer that it would take them two years' worth of saving just to run the pipes. Bobby demanded a refund. Gavin Hackett resolutely declared he'd said what he could find, not where and a refund would not be forthcoming. Perhaps Bobby should have read the fine print he suggested, which was as ludicrous as the rest of the act. There had been no written contract to begin with. Bobby looked around him and saw the sentiment of the group fell with Gavin, who had delivered a spirited if somewhat limited show. And, after all, water theoretically had been found. Feeling beaten, Bobby ordered Peter to give the cheat a ride home.

The storm had proven somewhat bogus as well, fizzling out by the end of the show; a stroke of blue was beginning to split the cantankerous sky. Stripping off her parka, Victoria walked with Diana back to the vehicles, noticing as she passed Bobby's truck that the effigy of Billy Bassman had been removed. She scoured the line of vehicles already making a slow exit down the driveway, squinting to focus on the figures bouncing roughly along in the backs of the trucks. Unable to accurately pick out his grizzled form, she could only hope he'd passed out somewhere else, and someone would haul him back into town.

She stood and watched with amazement as Diana gathered her children and somehow shuffled them all back into the car. Waving them goodbye, she turned to find Rose sitting on the trailer step, secretively waving her over.

"You okay?" she asked, walking over to join Rose.

"Oh yes. Of course. Just a scratch, really. But it could have been worse. I'm just glad she didn't hurt the baby."

Victoria nodded, thinking about how truly disastrous the situation could have been.

"What painting was she talking about?"

Victoria braced herself. "No idea."

"I'd forgot about that."

"What?"

"That she used to clean the hotel. Pearl told me sometimes they find her in there at night wandering around."

Victoria shook her head, her thoughts on the unnecessary stress and conflict the old woman's actions had inflicted on herself and Elliot.

"What?"

"Umm . . . nothing. It's just sad, right?"

Rose eyed her a question, then let it go.

"He's gone you know."

"Who's gone? Bassman?"

"Bassman? Who gives a shit about Bassman?" She flicked his name away from her like a squashed fly. "Elliot. He's gone. Did you know?"

"Gone? No. What do you mean, gone?"

"Dog to neighbor left, cat to neighbor right, exit center stage . . . gone. Just like I said. Didn't you know?"

"No. I didn't hear anything. When?"

"Couple months ago. Just after that big blowup between him and Bobby out at the sale."

"Are you sure, Rose?"

"Well, I'm sure Millie's watching his house till it sells, and I'm sure she said it was going to be almost impossible to keep in contact with him because he just stuck a pin in the map to decide where he was going to. Have you ever heard of anything so bizarre? Didn't he even call you? Least he could've done. Knew he was too good to be true. They always are."

"Shit. I can't believe it." She sat down absently on a rotting stair. "He didn't even say . . . unless." She stopped, looked as if someone had reached down her throat and crushed her heart.

"What? Unless what, Vic?"

"I got a call a while ago . . . two of them, actually, but they were different somehow."

"Same guy?"

"Yeah. But it was different. He said some things—"

"You think it was him? Elliot?"

"I didn't, no. Not really. But he said a couple of things the one time, and that was unusual because usually he doesn't say much at all. And then the last call he didn't say anything. Just listened like maybe he was waiting for something." She flushed as she remembered the intimacies she'd laid out before him.

"Vic!" Rose demanded. "What did he say? Tell me!"

"Well, it's hard to be sure. The line is always bad, static-y, and he speaks so seldom I'm never prepared for it and then I always have to try and fit the pieces together."

"Why don't you just ask him to repeat himself?"

"He won't. I've tried. I guess he knows I would be listening then and maybe I'd recognize his voice. He never repeats himself."

"Never?"

"No. Except for that one call. He did just once."

"What did he say?"

"Not sure. The damn line is always so broke up."

"Well, what do you think he said?"

"Well, we were just kind of talking about whatever, or I was anyhow, and all of a sudden he says—" She hesitated, the unexpected words still flooding her with hot emotion.

"What? Said what?" Rose prodded impatiently.

"He said . . . or I thought he said . . . that he wanted me—"

"Whoo . . . you little sexpot you. You were probably driving him bonkers. No wonder he had to leave."

"Rose," Victoria turned to her serious, tears rising in her eyes. "Rose, what if he was asking me to go with him? What if he'd said that he wanted me to come with him and I just didn't hear him because of all the static?"

"Come on, Vic. Assuming it was him, if that was what he had wanted, wouldn't he just come straight out and ask you?"

"But maybe he thought he did, Rose. Twice. He said it twice. And he's never done that before. Never. Maybe that's why he phoned back, to hear what my answer was—"

"Oh." Rose laid a warm hand over her friend's cold one. "But that wouldn't have been fair. How the hell could he expect you to know who was phoning? Could have been anyone asking you to run off. Even Bassman, for all you knew."

"No. I told him that I knew who he was."

"You did?"

Victoria nodded.

"Did you?"

"No. Not really. Well, kinda. It just didn't seem important anymore." Her voice fell off to a whisper. She didn't want to talk. She felt utterly defeated. How could things always turn out so wrong for her? It was as if life itself held her a grudge.

"Maybe it wasn't even him, Vic. Maybe it'll turn out to be someone else after all. Someone who just doesn't up and leave without even saying good-bye."

"No. It was him, Rose. It was Elliot."

"How do you know? You can't be certain."

Her silence affirmed she could be.

"How?"

"He hasn't called, Rose. He hasn't called since spring."

Perceiving the anguish in her voice, Rose swung an arm around Victoria's shoulders and rocked her gently. "Shh. It's okay, Vic. It'll be okay."

"What am I going to do, Rose? Everything is such a mess."

"Come on now, Vic. It's not all bad. You still have Bobby, your place."

"I don't want Bobby, Rose. And I hate this place . . . hate it. At least when I had the studio I had something to look forward to every week. Now he's taken that away from me too."

"Well, maybe it's time to leave then."

Victoria shook her head despondently.

"Well, why not? If you hate it here that much, why stay?"

"What choice do I have, Rose?"

"As much choice as anyone does."

"It's not that easy."

"Why not?"

"You know why."

"Oh, come on, Vic. You think he'd actually do it?"

"Don't you?"

"Well, maybe you guys can get some help, try to work things out."

"There's nothing left to work out. He doesn't even like me anymore, much less love me."

"That's not true." Rose pulled a package of tissue from her pocket and offered them to Victoria. "Not true at all, Vic. He does love you . . . he does."

"Well, he has a crappy way of showing it."

"I know. You're right. He does, but it's because he's worried about you. Scared he'll lose you."

"Rose—" Victoria objected.

"It's true, Vic. He told me so himself."

"He told you? When?"

"Oh, we talk sometimes."

This caught Victoria completely blind side, and she turned to assess Rose's face, her own a page full of questions.

"You do? When?"

"Oh, just the odd time we bump into each other around town. Relax, Vic. I'm not after your husband. Just trying to help out. Give me a little credit, will you?"

They laughed politely to erase the suggestion, and then Rose turned serious again. "Vic, you don't have to worry about him on that end."

"I don't?"

Rose shook her head.

"But, I thought you said he was—"

"Bobby? I didn't say that. When did I say that?"

Victoria's mind raced to bring back the conversation, but she couldn't hold the thoughts as they raced past her and all she could snap were remnants of what she'd assumed Rose had been alluding to.

"I thought you said . . . I guess I . . . shit, I don't even remember why I thought that you said that."

"Vic, listen to me. I mean obviously Bobby's got his things, right? But, if there's one thing I know for certain, it's that your husband is faithful to you and will be as long as you live under his roof. You're lucky that way, you know. The man is faithful to a fault."

Victoria laid her fingers against her temples and pressed hard to slow the tornado spinning in her mind. How could her timing be so completely wretched? Discovering it had been none other than crazy old Mrs. Spiller who had destroyed their painting was a giant swath of bittersweet relief. Although she was ecstatic to know their secret was safe, the knowledge had come far too late. Suddenly it all fell clear in front of her. It became obvious to her that Elliot had been on the other end of those calls. She'd told him things about herself he shouldn't know, and it had poisoned his opinion of her. Of course it had. Who would want someone who was willing to deceive their own husband by getting married when they were pregnant with Bassman's bastard child? Someone who wished her own husband dead? She'd thought, carelessly, that somehow he would understand. But he hadn't. Who could? She'd been a fool to think such a possibility could exist.

"I have to go in. I don't feel well . . . want to lie down a bit."

"Of course you do. Poor girl. Here, let me help you up. I've got to go anyhow, Millie's watching the girls for me, and she'll be driving them nuts by now."

* * *

Victoria laid her head on the pillow, but it refused to stay there. She popped a couple of Bobby's sleeping pills, but each time the gift of sleep began to filter through her a dull, insistent ringing cried dimly through the haze. Drawing herself onto her knees, her head fought to connect the noise into reality and, failing to do so, she collapsed in despair onto the bed. A sullen darkness filled her eyes when she finally awoke, and she sensed that night had fallen. She blinked at the red-eyed clock beside the bed. Half past eleven. She closed her eyes and listened for noises in the trailer, but it was dead. Bobby hadn't come home. For the first Saturday in twenty years the orangutan crew had not descended on the trailer to play poker. Elation should have filled her, but a dread uncertainty stole its place. She pulled her knees up to her chest and tried to squeeze away the pain inside her, but it broke free and she cried into the pillow until her hair clung to her face in strands.

Shuffling through the dark to the kitchen, she poured herself a whiskey and dumped it down her throat. The harsh liquid ran like lava, igniting her unaccustomed stomach, erupting her eyes to tears. She shuddered, caught her breath and delivered herself another blow. The hot, centered pain felt good. So easy to identify. She drank another and another until the liquid ran clear and cool down her throat and floated her into euphoria. A movement caught her eye, and she turned to see her reflection watching her. She stared back, became aware of Bobby's black sweatshirt covering her and fired the glass into the window, cracking the pane from side to side. Ripping the sweatshirt off, she grabbed the bottle of whiskey and paraded naked through the trailer, stumbling and cursing between drinks. A thought occurred to her, and she stumbled purposefully into the bedroom, dumping the contents of the closet onto the floor, once more exhuming her dress and pulling it on.

Turning on the light she admired the several images of herself that floated in the mirror and laughed.

"You see. Plenty of me to go around. One Victoria for each of you. All you had to do was ask . . . all you had to do was ask. Elliot, I would have gone with you. I would have. Just phone again, just one more time. I'll go, I promise. Just phone again." She sank onto the bed, her images sinking with her as they slowly wove back and forth listening for the phone. "Forget it, then," she hollered down the hall. "Don't ever phone. Don't ever come back. Don't ever even think of me again. I hate you! I hate all of you! All you ever do . . . all any of you have ever done is let me down. And I don't need you, anyhow. You think I do, but I don't. I know who I am. Don't need you to leave this shithole of a place."

Invigorated by her own pep rally she roughly navigated the hallway, grabbed her keys and a pack of Bobby's cigarettes from the drawer and headed out the door. Tonight it seemed the car would be an ally and sputtered more or less instantly to life, and she pulled a cigarette from the package, burning her finger as she struggled to light it. The last cigarette she'd smoked had been a stolen butt out behind her father's woodshed. Pulling a huge drag into her lungs, she perversely savored the coarse harshness of it. Spilling across the edges of the driveway as she drove, she rolled her window wide open even though the night was cool. Singing at the top of her lungs, she yelled out words to songs, supplemented her own additions when memory failed to supply the originals and basically created a whole new tune.

Attempting to steady her arm, she tried to read her wristwatch as she barreled along, but many things were not cooperating and the hands seemed to jump from 1:30 to 2:30 to 3:30, and finally she gave up as the car crashed through a pothole, challenging her to slow down and reassess where the road was. Slowing the car to a stall in the middle of the road, she clambered out and slipped down the bank, losing her footing and falling against a fence post. A dull thud against her skull suggested pain would be imminent, although none arrived. Grabbing the wire with both hands, she steadied herself somewhat and started to pee. The barbed wire bit into her hands, and she unfolded one to see the sharp teeth imbedded in her palm, the glow of the moon illuminating glossy black saliva as it dripped down her arm. Wiping it on her dress, she toppled over sideways and scrambled back up the ditch into the car. Again it sprung to life, and she felt like she'd acquired a silent partner. She roared the engine, spitting gravel up behind her as she picked up speed and swerved her way toward town. She kept her foot locked on the gas pedal; knew she had to gather enough speed so that the momentum could fuel her up the last leg of the hill even if the car's engine could not. Knew if she could go down Main Street fast enough, cause enough of a blur, maybe she could just sweep the whole place from her memory. Cause her whole life to be a sad, forgotten dream.

Town was around her before she knew it. She puzzled over when she'd rounded the corner, crossed the bridge and gone past the dump, but it was beyond her. All she knew was that they were behind her and somehow she'd made it this far and now Main Street was streaming past her window like a watercolor in a rainstorm, the base of the hill rushing up to defeat her. The car rose into the hill valiantly, but was quickly subdued as if a giant hand had reached up from the valley floor and grasped her by the tail. She searched the rearview mirror, cursed the fading lights and drank a victory salute as her vessel crawled toward the crest of the hill. She watched as the summit became visible above her. Watched as her life faded behind her, folded out before her. Suddenly, angrily, she pulled to the shoulder, parked and began to cry.

~ Chapter 22 ~

None of them had seen the headlights. Nor the vehicle as it veered off the side of the bridge, shot through the air and landed on its back in the shallow part of the river. For a brief, stunned moment they just stood and stared at the rusted undercarriage, black tires spinning useless as the waving appendages of an upside-down beetle. Slowly reason began to trickle into their stupefied brains and one, quickly followed by several of the others abandoned their drinks and ran toward the car.

Victoria could hear voices and water slurring together, felt the push and pull of her body as strong hands attempted to free her. Annoyance swirled with the water in her mind, and she wished they would just all go away and leave her alone. Let her sleep. The rushing current twisted her hair and her dress around her as it begged her to slip free, flow with it into oblivion, but the hands holding her tightly pulled her back and she cursed them. She felt from a distant place as her body was hauled forcibly from the wreck and dragged through the water toward shore. Hard arms locked around her and raised her upward, floated her in a time without place. Maybe her luck had changed after all. Maybe she was being born backward, God finally realizing his mistake and calling for her speedy return in the arms of Gabriel. A sensation occurred faintly against her face and a dim memory told her it was fire. Perfect. Just her luck. The promise of heaven, then she's delivered to hell.

A young girl, sober with fear, yet drunk with the effects of the night, almost hyperventilated as she tried to speak.

"Oh my god . . . oh my god. Is she okay? Is she dead? Oh my god . . . I should go get help. Someone go get help."

"Sit down, Amy! You can't even bloody stand much less go fer help. She's all right anyhow, just cracked her head. Just got to get the bleeding stopped that's all."

Victoria felt a thick pressure against her head and wondered whether she was seriously hurt. She felt no pain. No fear. Felt no connection between her body and her mind whatsoever. Instinctively she knew she should be able to gain access into the world surrounding her, but she couldn't remember how or why she would want to do so. She hovered at the periphery of her self and listened to the voices, tried to discern the entities around her. Even with her eyes closed and her mind lost somewhere between two dimensions, she knew exactly where she was. She wondered if this was how it was to be a ghost, a spirit trapped between realities, observing one yet existing in another.

The sandbar had been the traditional partying spot for years. Her, Bobby, Diana, John Jr., their whole generation had hung out there, explored things best left unexplored and hurled themselves into adulthood. And before them, her own parents and before them, only the guttural voice of the river knew for sure. And now this new group had sprung up to replace them, add their tales to Hinckly's history.

"Is that that Bobby's wife?"

"Ya, looks like," affirmed the slurred and heavy voice above her.

"No, it ain't," challenged another voice, a male's but high-pitched, tipping toward hysteria.

"Ya it is, ya dumb shit. That's her car, ain't it?"

She felt something soft and rubbery under her cheekbone, the toe of a sneaker as it nudged her head over to reveal the other side of her face. Immediately a chorus of horrified shrieks rained down on her.

"Ohh, gross! Look at her face . . . that's so disgusting."

"Oh my god . . . her eye. Ohh, what happened to it? That's so sick!"

She felt pressure against her temple as someone lolled her head over further and examined her face.

"Shit! That don't look so good, do it?"

"It's gross! Turn it back the other way. Makes me want to throw up just looking at it."

She felt the sensation of the fire creep across her face as her head was adjusted so as to appease the delicate sensibilities of the girls in the group. She felt like a dead fish, washed up and rotting along the shore, foul and disgusting to those who gave a wide berth as they passed by. A maze of confusion claimed her thoughts, and whether she lay there dead or asleep she could not tell until the voices, all husky now began to return to her, even more slovenly and tinged with anger.

"Should take her in to the doc, I tell ya."

"No! I told ya already. Ain't no need to wake the doctor. She'll be fine once she warms up. Ain't nothing broken."

"How you bloody know? You ain't no bloody doctor."

"Ya, well I worked a whole summer with Doc Feribee asshole. Don't be forgetting that."

"That ain't the same. That ain't the same at all."

"Screw you it ain't the same. It's all the same shit. Bones are bones, don't make no matter whether they're animal or human. Where the hell's my beer? Virgil, where the hell you put my beer?"

"Ouch! What the hell you cuffin' me for? I didn't take your friggin' beer."

"You gonna sit next to the case, you got a job to do. You gonna slack off, you gonna get smacked. Now give me one 'fore I smack ya again just for fun."

"Last one."

"Shit! Where the hell they all go?"

"I don't bloody know. Girls I guess."

"Four sacks of beer and the bitches all go home without us. Bloody poor investment I'd say. Gotta upgrade to pantie-remover."

"Pantie-remover?"

"Yeah, pantie-remover, numb nuts. Don't you know nothing?"

"Screw you. I know stuff. I know she ain't got none on under that dress."

"And how the hell would you know that?"

"You kin see. Right there. See?"

"Wholly shit! I think you might be right for once."

"Where ya think she was going, anyhow? Pretty slinky getup to be driving around in in the middle of the night. You think she's dicking someone on the side?"

"Naw."

"How'd you know? You ain't bloody know everything."

"She ain't."

"How you know?"

"Just do."

The voices ceased, replaced by the crackle of the fire and the murmur of the river. A spray of orange fanned above her as someone took a stick and provoked the coals.

"Bet I could get it in up to there."

"What you talking about?"

"Bet I could. Ya wanna bet I could?"

"Forget it jerk-off. That far and it'd be coming out her friggin' mouth."

"There?"

"In your dreams lard ass. Try about three inches back."

"That's it? Bullshit! Bet I could get it least up to there."

She felt a short, hot stab shoot through her as someone stumbled and fell across her legs. Her eye flickered open, delivered the image of a bulky form hovering above her, fat hands between her thighs.

"Virgil, you perverted son-a-bitch! Get off her!"

"I just wanna see. In the interests of medical science?"

"Medical science?"

"Ya. Didn't I ever mention I always wanted to be a pussy doctor?"

"Every guy wants to be a pussy doctor, you moron. Get off."

"Come on. In the interests of science?"

"In the interests of your face. Now get your fat ass off her 'fore I kick it so hard it takes you two weeks to shit again."

"Aw, come on."

"Get off, Virgil. Now!"

"Aw, shit. All right already, sit down! I gotta get home, anyhow. My old man gets up pretty soon, and if he catches me out with his truck I won't have an ass left to kick. Whatcha gonna do with her?"

"Don't worry about it. I'll take care of her."

"Ya need some help?"

"Have a think, Virgil. Do I look like I need some help?"

"Just asking."

"Well, don't. If ya wanna help, take Monty home. Saves me a trip out to his place."

"Monty? Where the hell *is* Monty? I thought he left with the girls."

"Naw, he's passed out in your truck."

"In my truck? He'd better not be! Shit, I'll kill the bugger if he pukes in there! My dad'll kill me if he pukes in there. Man, my old man's gonna kick the beejeezus outta me."

"He's not in the cab stupid. I chucked him in the back."

"Oh. You coming?"

"Not yet. Gonna let the fire die down a bit first. I get home when I feel like it. Be a sad day for my old man if he ever tried to kick the beejeezus outta me."

Victoria listened to the irregular crunch of cowboy boots on gravel, heard the tinny slam of a door and a motor growl as a lonesome song drooled away into the night. Slowly the soft rumbling of the water and the warm glow of the fire settled around her, and she felt the slip of her consciousness drift into their gentle undertow. She felt the presence of a body parallel to her own and strong arms encasing her from behind as she struggled within herself as to whether it was real or fantasy. Hope or delusion. She felt the warmth leave her face as he crawled over her, began to nurse and nuzzle against her breasts then pressed himself into her, pounding her to a place beyond time.

~ Chapter 23 ~

The horses had spotted her first. Stamped and snorted and steadfastly refused to approach any closer until finally the Patterson grandkids had given them full rein, and they'd raced all the way home, the children screaming hysterically that they'd found something dead. And their grandparents, after first scolding them for running the horses so hard, had finished up their chores then driven down to the river expecting to find a dead deer or at worst a bloated cow, but had found Victoria Lackey instead. The doctor had stitched her up, held her overnight and then sent her home to let time mend her wounds. The superficial ones. The ones that could be seen and touched and healed by the mere passage of time but were but scratches when measured against the emotional ones which could not.

Bobby had arrived late to pick her up, and she had hidden behind a magazine of smiling female faces as the passage of time swelled into public humiliation. She watched silently when he finally made his entrance and was updated on his wife's condition, just beyond her hearing. Nodding his head grievously, he cast a long, woeful look in Victoria's direction, purely for the benefit of the perky nurse who had, by her unamused, no-nonsense attitude already made it perfectly clear she had thrown her lot in with the unfortunate husband. The long ride home proved excruciating as well, every jar of the truck twisting the knife imbedded behind her eye and forcing her mouth open in a cry of silent agony.

Bobby fumbled with his cigarettes, stuck one in his mouth and struck a match.

"So . . . what exactly *were* you doing, Vic? All dolled up like that, driving around in the middle of the night?"

"I wasn't *doing* anything."

"Ya, right. Who you 'specting to meet?"

"No one."

"And you 'spect me to just believe that?"

"Believe whatever you want, Bobby. I don't care."

They drove along in heavy silence.

"You know, Vic, I been thinking maybe we should get some real plans drawn up for the house. What you think about that?"

She looked out the side window as she placed her fingers against her temples and tried to press away the pain.

"I been thinking maybe I can get a start on it next spring. Once the crops are planted."

He looked over at her, but her eyes were closed tight.

"Thought maybe once I get it done, I can get my mom moved back out here with us. Give you a little something to do. Looking after her a bit. Wouldn't be by yourself so much anymore."

He looked over at her again, sighed, then notched down a gear as they approached their driveway.

The truck swung onto the driveway and, as they crawled toward the trailer, she looked at it as if for the first time. Faded to the hazy blue of a cataracted eye and improved only by a crinkled glazing of tin foil across the living room window to counteract the summer heat, the trailer did not do a disservice to the other abominations that littered the yard. A smattering of old tires had been thrown on top of its tin roof in an effort to hold it down, and the wind, unable to unearth them, had blown them full of dirt instead, a motley array of thistles and grasses and stink weeds sprouting up from their centers. Victoria helped herself slowly from the truck and made her way up the stairs and into the trailer, a tattered throw rug tangling briefly around her feet like a mangy mongrel welcoming her home. She leaned against the porch wall to slide out of her shoes, looked around her and observed wryly, but without amusement that, like it or not, she was home.

Bobby attributed his wife's insolent behavior to a belated teenage rebellion. He responded by clamping his fist down tighter, watching her warily for any seeds of resistance that would need to be crushed before they again found root. He need not have bothered. She felt deflated, no more able to envision flying free than a scrap of paper stepped firmly into the mud. She walked forward through the days, each one identical to the one past, the one future, save for the constantly changing date of the wall calendar. In the evenings she placed herself into the rocking chair and rocked herself into the night when at last sleep would claim her, and Bobby, finding her bent and broken as a discarded doll, would carry her off to bed.

Life had become a spectator sport, observed from a distance. From the outside looking in. She moved through it methodically. Ate. Drank. Sometimes even laughed. But her reactions were born of an almost involuntary response toward life rather than any real desire to participate within it.

Bobby had taken to rising before her in the morning, and she lay in bed waiting as he ran through his morning routine. Listened to his brushing and showering, peeing and farting before he moved on into the kitchen. Her mind was as sluggish and thick as the fog hanging outside the dark morning windows. She tried to convince herself out of bed, her body feeling as if it had magnetized toward the earth. Dragging herself into the abused bathroom, she brushed her teeth, washed her face, then gave a halfhearted struggle against tangled hair before giving up and stuffing it away in a bun.

The static of the TV crackled through the air as Bobby settled himself in front of the morning news with a cup of instant coffee, the instant intended to placate him only long enough for her to get up and brew him a real pot. Shrugging into yesterday's clothes she wandered into the kitchen, reaching to turn on the light that was all ready on. She was greeted by a wall of unwashed dishes that somehow kept managing to elude her. Indeed, it seemed more and more that the mundane tasks of her life kept eluding her, stacking up against her, the simple requirement of folding a basket of laundry more than enough to drive her back to the comforts of bed at four in the afternoon. Slowly she made Bobby his breakfast and delivered it to the floor by his feet, receiving a guttural grunt in lieu of a thank-you. She watched as he gulped down the food like a half-starved husky, barely bothering to chew even the long, greasy strips of bacon, which he choked on in his haste to devour. The sight of it nauseated her, and she hurried back into the kitchen, her stomach making little leaps at her throat. Rummaging through the cupboard, she found a dry cracker to pick at as her mind slogged through the absolute redundancy of her life. Her life's work: the work she'd sacrificed her strength and time and purpose to each day. A constant, revolving circle of futureless effort. Meals prepared, consumed and eliminated. Clothes washed only to be resoiled. Dirt chased from the trailer only to creep in again at its leisure. And it struck clearly in her that life was no less than a farce. A pathetic, humorless farce, full of self-induced delusions of purpose and meaning and false attaining.

Bobby walked in from the living room, disrupting her thoughts. "What are you up to today?" he asked, a hopeful eye on the grungy mountain growing out of the sink.

She shrugged, walked into the living room to retrieve his dishes then, struggling to recall what day it was, added hesitatingly, "I think Rose might be coming out for coffee."

"You think?"

"Well, I can't remember for sure what day she said. Monday or Tuesday. What day is it today?"

"Friday."

"Oh. Well, maybe it was Friday."

Bobby raised his eyebrows and stared at her for a moment as if trying to understand, then, giving up, shook his head and scowled at the sink full of week-old dishes.

"Well, you better clean this mess up if you're having company. Starting to stink in here."

He turned away from her to reach for his jacket, but not before she glimmered the trace of embarrassment that ran across his face. The idea of his feeling embarrassment over her mortified her, and she struck back defensively.

"I know, Bobby. I haven't been feeling well . . . in case you haven't noticed."

"In case I haven't noticed," he spat. "Got news for you, Vic. That's all I have noticed lately. You moping around and complaining dawn to dusk 'bout how shitty you feel."

"Bullshit, Bobby! You never hear me complain. You're not around enough to even know what I do all day."

"Pretty friggin' obvious what you do all day, Vic. Bo-diddley-squat. That's what you do. Sit around on your friggin' ass all day and do piss-all. Look at these socks," he hollered, stumbling against the wall as he tore a dirty sock from his foot and flung it at her face. "Been wearing the same friggin' pair for the last bloody week. Last bloody two weeks, probably. I don't even bother remembering anymore."

If he had accused her of anything but the truth, she'd have easily found the fuel to fight him, but the accuracy of his accusation derailed her and, to her absolute horror, she began to cry. It was not something she did, cry in front of her husband, and the sight of her tears filled him with such an uncomfortable helplessness that he raged at her to get them to stop.

"What the hell you bawling about? Ain't no use bawling," he yelled desperately, as if she'd struck out at him with an unfair advantage.

Covering her face with her hands, she slid down the wall and sat crumpled on the floor, shoulders convulsed by silent sobs. She lifted her head slightly and pleaded up at him. "I'm sick, Bobby. Can't you understand that?"

He fished his sock from under the table and struggled it back over his foot with exaggerated effort. "Ya, well maybe I'm getting sick of you being sick, huh? Ever think of that? Ever think maybe it's time you snapped out of it and got with the program?"

"Can't just snap out of it, Bobby. I'm sick. I don't feel—"

"Well, what about that shit the doc gave ya? Ain't that 'sposed to fix ya up?"

Victoria picked at a noodle dried to the floor beside her.

"Hey? Ain't that shit helping none?"

She shook her head.

"Not at all?"

She concentrated hard on the noodle.

"Well, why the hell not? You tell the doc?"

Sensing a collision course with a conversation she would rather avoid, she pulled herself back up and started past him into the hall.

"Hey! I asked you a question. Did you tell the doc they ain't working or not?"

Looking at the floor she shook her head.

"Well, why the hell not?"

"I haven't taken any."

"What?"

"You heard me."

"None? Ya ain't taken none of 'em?" he yelled, his face incredulous.

She silently looked out the porch window, wished he would follow her empty gaze down the driveway and leave her alone.

"Well, why not? Can ya just tell me that much, Vic? You like being sick? Ya like moping around here all the time having everyone feel sorry for you? Is that it, Vic? Huh? Ya like having an excuse for feeling sorry for yourself?"

"Bobby, don't," she rushed in trying to end his tirade before he blew himself into a storm. "I don't know why I haven't taken them. I guess I just don't think they'll help, that's all."

"Well, that's pretty twisted bloody logic. Ya ain't ever take 'em, how the hell ya ever going to know?"

It was twisted logic, but her reality was twisted and unless the pills could untwist that she knew they offered her no hope. A dulling of the pain perhaps, but definitely not a cure for the hopeless mistake of her life.

Bobby jabbed his hands into his coat pocket irritably. "Now, where the frick did my bloody keys go? You put them somewhere again?"

"No. I didn't touch—"

"Well, find the damn things then. 'Sposed to be in town a half hour ago already."

"What're you doing in town?"

He stopped rummaging through the heap of miscellaneous junk covering the counter and stared at her hard.

"Like I told you yesterday. First I'm going by to help JJ. with his carport then I gotta stop by Rose's an fix up her plumbing. Now, can ya remember all that or I gotta write it down for ya?"

She made no attempt at an answer, just watched silently as he unearthed his keys, snubbed his cap into place and exited goodbye-less out the door.

The pills he alluded to had been a small shopping list of tranquilizers and sleeping pills and antidepressants the doctor had prescribed when she had gotten her stitches removed and made the grave mistake of mentioning her mental distress. She hadn't appreciated the doctor's condescending chuckle as he wiped away her self-diagnosis of asthma to explain the crushing tightness in her chest and her sudden inability to draw a full breath of air. Anxiety. Not asthma, he'd proclaimed too carefully, as if she were a child. She'd listened to him politely, received his list of prescriptions with a trite thank you, but she didn't believe it. Didn't trust him or his casual diagnosis. She didn't feel anxious. Quite to the contrary, she felt utterly desolate. And she hadn't even bothered to tell him the rest of her symptoms, mainly because he hadn't seemed bothered enough to want to hear them. And how could one describe them anyhow? Or when they had become a part of her, stealing inside and becoming one with her as seamlessly as senility and old age.

She'd noticed it first as a soft, pulsing flutter at the base of her throat. Like a small injured bird or a heartbeat, discordant and misplaced. At times, for reasons she could not distinguish, the gentle fluttering rose into a frenzied pounding as if there were a bird trapped within her, desperate to find its way free. The way she'd seen them do among the rafters in the barn, crashing aimlessly into the windows and battering themselves to exhaustion as the cats slunk below and licked their lips. Sometimes she'd opened the big doors wide and sat watching silently as she tried to coax them to their freedom. Every once in a while, although not often, one would find its way out, their sudden escape making her want to laugh and sing and shout. She wished she could do that now. Wished she could open her mouth and let the tiny creature rise up through her throat and find its way free.

She looked around her. Blinked. She turned to check the time on the clock. Two hours. Gone. Vaporized in thoughts. It happened so often now that it failed to raise her concern. Although it did raise a warning that Rose would be arriving soon, and the trailer was far from ready to receive her. It felt like ages since Rose had last been out to visit. Having finally broken down and bought a new television for the girls, she had abruptly ceased her weekly trips. Victoria turned to the disaster of the kitchen, but the complexity of the mess stymied her. She didn't know where to start, or even how. She picked up a plate and a mug then set them back down. She gathered a pile of cutlery from one side of the sink and sat them down on the other side. Above her head the clock kept taunting her with its cheery ticking until finally she yanked it down, ripped out its batteries and fired it in a drawer.

Still, time would not come over to her side, and she wandered helpless and aimless through the trailer until the roar of Rose's car coming down the road jolted her into action. Opening the cupboard doors, she crammed them full of dirty dishes, and what wouldn't fit in there went into the oven. Victoria slammed the cupboard door just as Rose burst into the porch without the formality of a knock. She had emptied out the mailbox that stood at the end of Victoria's driveway and was busy skimming through a handful of envelopes.

"Gross! What stinks in here?" she demanded, her nose instantly offended upon entering the trailer.

Victoria flung around and laughed, embarrassed. She hadn't noticed any odor. "Oh, hi, Rose. I don't—"

Rose's corkscrewed face abruptly led her to the source of the problem. Mortified, Victoria scrambled uselessly for an explanation. The garbage can under the table had risen through the stages of full to over-full to spilling-over-onto-the-floor full without garnering itself the least bit of attention.

"Holy shit, Vic! This place is an absolute pigsty. You been sick, or what?"

Defense was the first thing to rush to Victoria's mind, but as her gaze followed Rose's over grimy, stuck floors and counters and chairs lost beneath mounds of unfolded laundry, she bit her lip. The extent of what she saw shocked her. She knew things were getting behind, but she had absolutely no recollection of how or when the trailer had become so disgusting.

"Why didn't you call me? The girls and I could have come out and helped you if you were feeling that bad," Rose offered, although it was obvious to both of them that it would take more than just general malaise to explain the total deterioration of Victoria's life. "Here, you sit down. I'll make tea."

"No, that's okay. I'm fine. I can—"

"Sit!" Rose ordered, pointing at a chair like an irate mother, refusing to move until Victoria shuffled some laundry onto the table and complied. "Why didn't you call?"

"Uh, I was going to but I started feeling better. Actually, I feel a lot better this week. It's just going to take a while to get caught up again, that's all," she lied.

"Well, what about Bobby? Is it beyond him to clean up a little?" Rose went to set the mail on the sticky counter, decided against it and threw it on the couch instead.

"You know Bobby, Rose. There's men's work and there's women's work and the two don't cross over. He figures he doesn't ask me to fix his truck, and I shouldn't ask him to clean my house."

"Oh, shit! I forgot. I asked him to come by the house today to fix my toilet. Damn it! And I locked the door, too."

"Since when did you start locking your door?"

"Since that crazy old bird got it in her head that I stole her mythical treasure. I've warned the girls about her, too. Poor kids are scared senseless. Have to make sure I'm back home before they get out of school. It's absolutely ridiculous that someone doesn't make them do something with her."

Victoria nodded absently.

"We could try calling Bobby at JJ's if you want," she offered, already dialing the number. "He's stopping by there first." She listened as the phone rang, then finally gave up. "No, guess not. They're probably outside."

"Shit. I guess I'll have to get him to stop by this weekend. Cups in here?" Rose asked, her hand already moving toward the cupboard door. Victoria jumped up and rattled the door of the china cabinet open, seizing two of her mother's dusty teacups and clattering them onto the table.

"These! Let's use these for a change."

"China? What's the occasion?"

"Nothing, really. I just never use these, that's all. Not much point having nice things if you never use them, right?"

"Whatever. Where's the sugar?"

"You don't take sugar."

Rose gave her a queer look. "I know I don't Vic, but you do. Where is it, in here?" She turned back to the cupboard, her hand just starting to open it as Victoria almost shouted.

"No! No, I don't anymore. I don't take it in my tea anymore. I . . . I just like it plain now."

Rose shrugged, reached into a canister sitting against the wall, pulled out two tea bags, dropped them into the steaming water and leaned back against the oven door to let them steep, her hand busy picking at something indescribable stuck on the handle. Victoria's breath caught in her throat as the door made little halfhearted attempts to open, knowing full well there was simply no sane explanation to be offered for an oven load of grunge-encrusted dishes. Finally, Rose settled herself at the table and Victoria began to breath again as the conversation slipped into other people's lives.

"So, did you hear the latest?" Rose asked, then continued on without waiting for an answer. "Sounds like Joe and Phyllis are going broke. Don't know if it's true, you know how those stories go, but I heard Joe owes half the town money."

"Really?" Victoria asked without caring, almost without hearing.

"Yep. That's what I hear. Phyllis even bounced a check at Pearl's. Pearl was right pissed. She had Bud tape it up in the window facing the street so everyone could see until Joe finally went in and cleared it up and got them to take it down. I got to see it though. And you know what? It was only for sixteen dollars. Can you imagine? Not having sixteen dollars to your name?"

"Hmm."

"I guess Joe tried to say it was just a mix-up in their accounts, but nobody believes him. Everyone knows they've been having trouble for years. I bet Phyllis will leave him. She can't live without money. Only reason she married him in the first place is because she thought he had lots. I don't think she ever did catch the difference between credit and cash." She stopped to sip her tea. "Oh yeah, you know that Sanderson guy? Jack, I think his name is."

Victoria shook her head.

"Yes, you do."

"I do?"

"Yes. You remember. He's related to . . . oh, what's her name? That skinny woman who works at the Lucky Dollar."

"Hazel?"

"Yeah, her. He's related to her, somehow. Brother-in-law or cousin or something. You know—"

She looked at Victoria eagerly, encouraging her to remember, but with no success. Blowing her tea cool she continued on, somewhat irritated at Victoria's lack of cooperation. "He's a real tall, skinny guy. Kind of ugly. You know him Vic, I'm sure you do.

He used to drive that old beat-up station wagon with no muffler, remember?"

"Oh," Victoria agreed, just to get Rose off her case. "Yeah, kind of."

"Yeah, see. I knew you knew him. Anyhow, turns out his wife's pregnant."

"Hmm. That's nice."

"Not for him it's not," Rose trumped. "Millie told me he got snipped last year. Oh. Hey. Got something for you," she said as she reached across the table and grabbed her large black purse off of the chair opposite her. "The girls made it for you. Just a little thank-you for letting them come out and watch cartoons."

Unzipping her purse, she struggled for a moment to unearth an oversized paper folded up into several layers. Impatiently working it loose, she gave it a tug, pulling it and a cascade of old one-hundred-dollar bills onto the table. Looking up quickly, she saw that Victoria had not missed them and her face grew hard in defense.

"Rose!" Victoria sputtered, absolute shock crossing her face, "Did you take her money?"

Rose laughed, flipping her hair behind her and twisting it up into a nervous knot.

"Oh, just a little bit. Old bag has more money than she'll ever need. Just wastes it all feeding those stupid cats of hers, anyhow."

"But still . . . Rose! I can't believe—"

The jar of the phone snatched their focus, and Victoria spilled her tea as she jumped up to answer it. Grabbing a washcloth off the floor, Rose kept an eye on Victoria's face as she mopped up the mess, both ears attentive as she tried to eavesdrop on the conversation. She watched with mounting curiosity as Victoria's features softened around the receiver then grew pale and hard as if she were turning to ice from the inside out. She nodded stiffly once, then twice as her mouth worked uselessly to form the words her brain was trying to send. Setting the receiver back into place, she stared first at it, then at Rose, then back to the receiver.

"Problem?" Rose pressed, excitement alive in her eyes.

Victoria stood motionless, unsure of whether to nod or shake her head as she wrestled with words that as yet made no sense to her.

"It was Bobby," she whispered, as if this in itself should hold some meaning for Rose, some meaning for herself.

Rose shook her head, not comprehending the significance. "So?"

"He's at your house."

"So?" Rose countered again, but coherency was beginning to shift itself uncomfortably to the forefront of her brain.

"He called from the workshop, Rose. From the extension in Steve's workshop." She searched her friend's face wildly to find a denial of the truth that was marching toward her but was met instead with a self-conscious laugh.

"Rose? Was it you?"

Jaw set and eyes hard she leveled Victoria with her answer.

"Of course it was me, Vic. Don't even try to tell me you didn't know."

"Rose! I had no idea it was you. I thought it was . . . I believed it was—"

"You believed what you wanted to believe, Vic."

"I believed what you said, Rose. I believed what you told me."

"Wrong!" Rose shouted, clearly happy to be accused of something she knew she was innocent of, seizing on the opportunity it afforded her to turn the tables on Victoria. "Totally wrong. I offered to tell you several times who your mysterious caller was, but you didn't want to know. Did you? It was you who chose to keep your little fantasy going. I just played along to keep you happy."

The room was spinning inside Victoria's head, and she gripped the edges of a chair to keep herself from reeling off into space. Anger, fear, hurt, sadness, rage each raced in on her, but she couldn't grasp one. She didn't know what she felt other than bewildered, and she looked searchingly at Rose, hot tears accompanying her words.

"But why, Rose? Why would you do that to me?"

"Hey! Don't blame me. You did it to yourself. The first time was just an accident. I tried to call you from the shop and couldn't get through because of all the static. And then when I called back from the house, you started telling me this big fantasy about some guy calling and saying he thought you were beautiful when what I'd actually said was 'I think you'd be a fool not to pursue that thing with Elliot.' It was kind of funny actually."

"It wasn't funny, Rose. It was my life. Why didn't you just tell me right then that it was you rather than let me carry on and make an idiot of myself?"

"Why? You want to know why, Vic?"

"Yes. Yes, Rose, I do want to know why."

"Because you were so damn pathetic about it, that's why. Because it was so bloody obvious you needed a little something to hold on to." Rose shrugged, then drained her tea casually. "And then it all just kind of got carried away. Or I should say . . . you got carried away."

"Me? I got carried away? You almost ruined my marriage, Rose—"

"I almost ruined your marriage? Better back up the bus on that one, Vic. From what I heard coming across that line, I'd say it was pretty much screwed already."

"You bitch! You fucking, fucking bitch!" Victoria erupted, boiling toward Rose with her arm raised to strike before reason grabbed her with the realization of the precariousness of her position.

Her mind flooded full of the details of their conversations, and her heart began pumping insanely as she remembered her unrestricted outpouring of confidences so intimate she had hardly dared share them with herself. She'd spilled her most secret of secrets across that line. Her frustrated blurting that Bobby should go ahead and kill himself. Her ill-fated confession of having been pregnant with Bassman's child. Rose stood up and stretched leisurely.

"So, that whole thing that happened with Steve? Was that you, too?"

Rose shrugged.

"How could you do such a thing? You ruined his life, Rose."

"Well, he was ruining mine."

"How?"

"He annoyed me."

"Why didn't you just divorce him then?"

"Divorce is an expensive option, Vic."

Wrapping herself back inside her cloak, she leaned across the table and tapped Victoria's hand gently.

"So. I guess we both have our little secrets that need keeping. Right?"

Victoria felt as if the whole puzzle of her life had just been scattered hopelessly across the floor. She looked toward Rose and nodded. But she couldn't make their eyes meet.

She sat silent at the table until long after the roar of Rose's car faded into still air. Her mind was wild. Frantic collisions of thoughts that finally drove her from her chair and sent her racing through the trailer. Rose held everything in the grip of her hand. And clearly that hand could not be trusted. Every one of her most intricate secrets had eventually found their way through that phone line and into Rose's gluttonous ear. Suddenly, she understood Pearl's uncharacteristic tolerance of Rose. The quick flicker of fear that sparked in her eye whenever Rose voiced any displeasure. How could she not have seen it before? How could she not have understood that Rose held the most damning of Pearl's secrets as well. She felt sick. Like poison was slowly filling her.

She slumped onto the couch, pushing newspapers and mail to the floor. Her hand stopped over a small envelope, embossed in beautiful script like black lace over a white dress. She flipped it over and over, then held it in her hand as she curled her knees up to her chest and rested her head.

The discovery of the caller's identity, or lack thereof, was no less than a death to her and many degrees more jagged. The thought could find no place within her, no nook or cranny in which to settle. Finally she rejected it. Him, Rose could not take from her; she would not allow it. She could no more deny his existence than if she had looked into the fullest of nights and tried to believe it day. Within her mind, he lived. And beyond that, in her senses. She had heard his voice. Felt his hands. His hair. She had smelled the warm, sensual pleasures of his skin and tasted his kisses. He had moved over her and in her. Became one with her. And she with him. All of this she had felt and, at the drop of her lashes, she still could.

She stood up, crossed to her rocking chair and sat down. She did not rock. Did not wait. Just sat quiet and empty watching out the window as creation slowly reversed itself. Softly, she stroked the envelope until her hands found their way inside.

Her fingers traced the lettering as she read it. Strong, slanted consonants and soft, feminine vowels joined together with promises of true love, godly unions and happiness eternal. Reaching under her chair she pulled long handled, sharp scissors from her knitting bag. She began to make quick, intricate cuts. Consumed with her task she didn't notice when she cut herself and her blood was smeared along the sharp, tight creases and folds. She worked intensely until her shoulders began to ache so convincingly that she had to stop. In her lap lay a tiny square box and an exquisite origami crane. Taking the lid off of the box, she placed the bird inside and tried gently to make it fit until finally her patience failed her and, taking it back out, she clipped short its wings and forced it into place.

~ Chapter 24 ~

It was raining. Not a driving, healthy rain but a sick, miserable drizzle that had eventually overwhelmed the potholes and transformed the fine, powdery road into a greasy, gray paste. As they approached the church, Victoria was surprised to see a steady stream of muddy vehicles pouring into the yard as the valley's inhabitants, most of whom had forgotten Bobby's mother in her life, now came out to remember her in her death. She kept her eyes riveted to her feet as Bobby slopped the truck through the puddles and bounced it to a stop. As usual they were running late and Bobby immediately rushed off into the church, leaving her standing alone as she struggled with her umbrella. Shielding herself from curious stares, she held her umbrella low and made her way into the vestibule. Pastor Jack's wife spotted her immediately and waved pointedly from across the room. She was a hawkish woman, brittle as last week's toast, and she fit no one's ideal of what a good pastor's wife should be. As if to counteract this sentiment, she'd taken to fluttering her lashes helplessly, as though she had a constant irritant in both her eyes. Her smile, perfect, open and painted, never left her face, and Victoria wondered if she removed it at night and dropped it into a glass on her bedside table along with her false teeth. Despite her attempts to appear otherwise, no one ever had any illusions that a hand other than hers puppeteered Pastor Jack's every move.

"Well, well, well. And how are you doing, Vic? Tsk. Wasn't it just a pity about Mrs. Lackey's passing?" gushed Pastor Jack's wife.

She grabbed Victoria's cold hand, patting it vigorously as if checking for life. "And how are you yourself, dear? After the accident and all? Trust you're doing better now?" She crushed her face into a question mark as she left off, hoping Victoria would fill in the story.

Victoria returned a stiff nod. "I'm fine, thank you."

"Oh, well praise the Lord, dear. Praise the Lord. Our ladies group prayed for you every Wednesday, you know. Not a Wednesday went by when we didn't raise our voices to the throne and beseech the Father on your behalf."

"Oh. Well, thank you," Victoria offered dryly. She knew the more likely truth was that they had bantered around the latest gossip about her, then quickly offered up a prayer to appease their guilt. Nausea was beginning to disrupt her stomach again and she gently tried to retract her hand, but the older woman held on.

"And so . . . what was it that happened again, dear? Goodness sake, you hear so many different things. Most of it such nonsense." She shook her head and fluttered her lashes with manic exaggeration.

"Nothing happened," Victoria shot back coldly.

Pastor Jack's wife dropped her hold on Victoria's hand and leaned back slightly. "Oh. Well, of course I wasn't meaning to imply anything . . . um, well. Well, you're sure looking good now, anyhow. Isn't she, Sara?" she said to an elderly woman just passing by.

"Ay? What's that?" crackled the old lady as stiff fingers fumbled with her hearing aid. "What's that you say?"

"I said—" intoned Pastor Jack's wife loudly enough to draw several stares, "—that she's looking well, now. Since the accident. She's looking much better now. Wouldn't you agree?"

"Accident? Who had an accident?"

Victoria shifted uncomfortably as the women's loud interchange attracted several, rather obvious, eavesdroppers.

"Tsk. Well, Vic did, Sara. Down by the bend in the river. She drove off the bridge. Remember?"

"Drove off the bridge?"

"Yes. Down by the gravel bed in the river."

"Well," the older woman hrumphed. "Now what in tarnation did she do that for?"

Pastor Jack's wife again seized Victoria's hand and patted it consolingly as she whispered below the other woman's hearing. "Don't pay her no mind, dear. She's getting a little daft in her old age."

"Hrumpff! I most certainly am not getting daft!"

"Oh. No, no, nooo. I didn't say daft, Sara. I said deaf. And that's mostly just the fault of your hearing aid not working so well sometimes. Remind me to check those batteries for you." She slipped Victoria a sly wink as she took the older lady's hand and began to pat it like the withered back of a spotted, yellow frog.

"Now, anyhow, Vic, we just want to welcome you to our little church and to invite you to join our Wednesday night prayer group." She paused an extended moment as she melted her face into an image of pained compassion. "Just remember dear, the Lord is faithful to those who worship him and no matter what you may have done . . . His grace is sufficient for all, and all one needs to do is throw all of themselves, mind, body and soul at the Father's feet and beg for forgiveness. Praise God!" She ended with an inspirational glance at the vestibule's stained ceiling, and for a moment Victoria suppressed the urge to applaud.

Instead, she excused herself. What her mind, body and soul were begging for right now was a washroom. Pressing the bathroom door open, she was relieved to find both cubicles empty. She flipped down the toilet lid, sat on it and locked the door. Resting her head in her hands, she closed her eyes and tried to will the swirl in her stomach down. Failing to do so, she flew onto her feet, smashed open the lid and erupted with painful dry heaves. Sitting back down again, she loosened the button of her skirt and ran a soothing hand over her stomach. Cold pricks of sweat glistened on her forehead. She had to get back upstairs and find Bobby. Make sure he didn't drink too much before he had to pack his mother's coffin across the slippery churchyard to the gravesite. Although he tried to hide it, his mother's death had winded him like an unexpected punch, his steady injections of alcohol deepening his moroseness.

An organ began to wheeze a dusty hymn and she looked at her watch, trying to calculate how long it would take to bury the dead. Not long at all if most people had their way, she knew, but Pastor Jack rarely saw fresh faces to preach at and was sure to take full advantage of the situation. She stiffened at the sudden irritated squeak of the bathroom door, instinctively pulling her feet up from the floor so no one could see she was there. She followed the other person's movements with her ears, heard their shuffling about, opening and closing cupboard doors, then stop. The footsteps came closer and Victoria held onto her breath as she waited for the woman to enter the plywood cubicle next to her but instead she started as a hard push rattled her own door against its lock.

She sat very still, her legs cramping against the discomfort of their position and knowing it was only a matter of time before she had to set them back down. Closing her eyes, she willed the other woman to use the empty toilet and leave. She had no desire to talk to anyone, even less so to have to try to explain why she was holed up in the toilet with both feet off the floor. The other woman, however, appeared to be making no effort to either use the toilet or leave but rather seemed to have positioned herself outside the cubicle to wait and see who would come out of it. Her thighs beginning to scream, Victoria edged herself over to peek through the gap in the door and was shocked to meet two shiny brown eyes staring in at her. She darted away in an instinctive movement that came far too late. Clearly she had been seen, and now felt as trapped as a rabbit in a one-way hole. In a somewhat belated attempt to save face, she coughed, grabbed some toilet paper and blew her nose loudly.

"Who's that in there?" the eye's voice demanded.

Victoria ignored the request, struggled to refasten her skirt button, wiped the black smudges under her eyes into gray ones, and opened the door.

"Oh," Pearl said. "Just you. What you doing hiding in there?"

"I wasn't hiding, Pearl," Victoria countered peevishly. "I was blowing my nose. What are you doing here? Cleaning up?"

Pearl stepped her stick legs in front of her bag, which sat on the floor, straining with its bounty of pilfered toilet paper rolls. "Naw, I came in to check my makeup." She snorted with sour humor. "You don't look so good."

"Well, thank you, Pearl. Neither do you. Could you move please, so I can wash my hands?"

"Be my guest," Pearl said, gesturing to the sink behind her without budging an inch. She looked at Victoria with unflinching intensity. "Yup, Pastor Jack's wife was right. I figured she was carrying on a bit but, nope . . . you really do look like hell. What's wrong with ya, anyhow? Got cancer or something?"

"No, Pearl. I don't. Just picked up a flu bug, that's all."

Pearl visibly shrunk, pulling herself away. "Well, don't be breathing no germs on me, then. I sure as hell don't want it."

Victoria moved toward the sink and Pearl, grabbing her bag up quickly, sidestepped out of the way.

"Too bad about the old girl, hey?"

Victoria looked glassily into the mirror, not comprehending a word being said as waves of nausea again started to spill over her.

"About Mrs. Lackey," Pearl offered again loudly, thinking Victoria hadn't heard her. "It's too bad, hey? About what happened to her."

"What's so bad about it? She'd have been better off if she died years ago. Lying there in that home just waiting for life to go by—"

Pearl's face combusted with disbelief. "Well, ain't that a nice thing to say."

Victoria looked at Pearl's combative position in the mirror. It irritated her, this sudden misplaced concern, but she was far too tired to care. She silently pushed past Pearl and escaped up the stairs.

Pastor Jack had droned on through the Beatitudes and several more hymns, threatened all the nonchurchgoers with a fate worse than hell, then summed up by inviting everyone to join

him in the church basement for coffee, cakes and tea. She barely
made it through the service, the church wreaking of old wax and
mildew and the sweaty armpits of men unaccustomed to wearing
suits. She excused herself abruptly and hurried back downstairs.
Tongues wagged in the pews, pleased to see her obvious grief at
losing her mother-in-law. She leaned her head against the bathroom divider and listened to the wooden shuffle as a hundred dragging feet slowly escorted her mother-in-law's carcass outside to the
graveyard. She marveled at the refining effect that could be delivered by a simple pine facade. She knew from memory the slick
winding path that rode up over a small hill and out of sight, then
ended at a ratty patch of unkempt field sprouting a harvest of head
stones. And that Bobby and the other pallbearers would make a big
performance about almost falling on the rain-greased ground and
end up engaged in a contest of muscles, shoveling mud back into
the grave as though their very lives depended on it. Soon she heard
the tramping of feet as the first few returned back to the church.
Before long she again heard the bathroom door squeak open, ush-
ering in the smells of syrupy perfume, fresh coffee and the excited
chatter of several female voices. Taking a breath to brace herself,
Victoria opened the cubicle door and stepped to the sink. Dropped
conversations hung on the air as quick looks were slipped from eye
to eye behind her back. Rose stood next to the door, and Victoria
quickly averted her eyes when their gaze met.

"Oh! It was you in there, Vic. Imagine that," one of the women
said. "We were just saying how nice it was to see you out again. Did
you enjoy the service?"

"Hmm," Victoria murmured as she angled her way toward the
door.

"Well, that's good. Quite an awful thing that spill you had."

The always-helpful Millie Miller rushed to gather up some
paper towel and handed it to Victoria to dry her hands.

"Thank you, Millie."

"Don't run off, Vic. Okay? I have something for you."

"For me?" Victoria asked warily, the room growing suspiciously quiet around her.

Millie nodded enthusiastically, red curls bobbing like rusty springs across her shoulders. "It's upstairs in my coat. Are you going up or should I bring it down?"

"No, no. I'll come up with you," Victoria rushed, seeing a clear route free of all the questions she felt stirring up around her.

Slipping out the door, Rose somehow attached herself along by engaging Millie in a question about the girls. Turning the landing halfway up the stairs, they were met by Doris, half encircling her older sister, who she was slowly helping down the stairs. Mrs. Spiller had been forcibly moved into the home weeks before, and the changes were obvious. Her white hair was neatly split down the center and pinned into place by two bobby pins, and she was dressed in a matching newborn-girl pink sweater-and-slacks set. The two of them were thrown off balance by the sudden encounter and almost toppled down the stairs.

"It's her, Doris! It's the gypsy!" Mrs. Spiller whispered loudly, both arms wrapped tight around her bible.

"Hush," Doris replied sternly, struggling to regain her footing. "That's enough of that now, Agnes. Remember what the doctor told you? There are no gypsies or anyone else stealing your money. It's just your mind playing tricks. It's no good anymore. It's all fuzzy now, remember?"

"No!" Mrs. Spiller hissed back. "It's her. The gypsy. I saw her take it. I did. I saw her."

"That is enough, now, Agnes. Anymore and we'll have to take you back to the home." And then, not quite able to meet Rose's glare, Doris apologized profusely for her sister's outburst.

Rose looked at Victoria and smiled. Looking down, Victoria mutely moved aside as Rose pushed past her and continued on up the stairs without acknowledging Doris's words.

Apprehensively, Victoria followed Millie upstairs to the coatroom. She waited with growing frustration as she watched her slowly extricate a handful of envelopes from her raincoat pocket.

Carefully she took an elastic off the tidy pile and began to finger through them. Millie was one of those people whose own neediness was to feel needed, and she savored the feeling of having in her possession something Victoria appeared so eager to have. She paused several times, inspecting the writing on the envelopes as if it were written in code rather than plain English, then continued flipping through them leisurely. Victoria clasped her hands together to prevent them from reaching out on their own accord and rudely snatching the envelopes out of Millie's grip.

Finally she stopped rearranging the letters and slid a large package free. "It's from Elliot," she whispered. "He just wrapped up his business here and asked me to give it to you."

Unsurprisingly, Rose appeared in the doorway and began digging through her coat for something she obviously had no interest in finding.

Victoria started to tremble. Reaching out she took the papers from Millie, but her hand fumbled.

Rose struck like a serpent.

"Whoops," she said, grabbing them up almost before they hit the floor. She pulled a shiny silver pin free from a map then handed the pile of papers back to Victoria with a wide smile.

"Rose!" Victoria cried out. "What did you do that for?"

Rose looked convincingly hurt. "There was a pin stuck in it, Vic. I just didn't want to see you get hurt." She looked at Millie for support. Millie raised her eyebrows and offered Rose a sympathetic look as Rose walked pointedly from the room. Millie had no idea what had just taken place, but she was very sure it was something big.

"Um. Anyhow, Vic," she stammered. "I've got to run. So. Um. Take care of yourself, okay?" Quickly gathering up her coat she followed Rose out into the vestibule to find out more about what she'd just missed.

Victoria nodded. "Thank you, Millie," she said absently, her mind consumed by the sealed envelope she held in her hand.

Not willing to be disturbed in this moment of truth, she slipped from the church and splashed coatless through the rain to the truck. Pressing the envelope tightly against her cheek, she closed her eyes and tried to feel her way back to Elliot's presence. She stroked the fine white paper, traced her name written in his hand. She brought the envelope to her nose, trying to find the lingering freshness of his scent. And finally, slowly, she coaxed the envelope open. Feeling inside, she pulled out a tightly folded paper and unfolded it with growing apprehension.

Dear Victoria,

It has been three months since Rose gave me your letter and, although I will respect your wishes, I find I can't bring myself to leave the valley without at least saying goodbye. Which isn't to say I agree with, or even understand, all of your reasons, but after talking for a long time with Rose, I had to concede this is probably the best arrangement for everyone now that you and Bobby have decided to work things out. But, you'll forgive me for wishing things had turned out differently between us. If you ever change your mind, take this map and pin and if luck is on our side, maybe fate will bring us together once again.

Fly free,
Elliot

~ Chapter 25 ~

The wedding had been planned, then—to the great irritation of Benny Olson—postponed to allow for the ordering of the only wedding dress in the entire country that would possibly suit his third youngest daughter. After eight weeks and a back order of several more days, the dress finally arrived and was coerced to fit by the addition of a girdle and the skillful manipulation of several seams by experienced hands.

Pews were squashed tight early and it was standing room only as people, invited or not, packed into the tiny church to witness the vows and the volume of puffiness the dress was unable to conceal. Most people were as sufficiently shocked as they could have hoped, and Pearl even offered quite loudly that if they didn't loosen the girdle soon, the girl and the baby would probably both end up killed. But the girdle stayed laced-up brutal. A pale Amy held one hand on each side of her icy satin dress to hold it in place and prevent it from riding up over her baby-ball belly and giving her secret away.

The reception had originally been planned to take place outside in the yard. But with the sky whining down a cold rain, the event had been transferred to an empty corner of Benny Olson's hay barn instead. The irony of the situation was lost on few, and Pearl was quick and loud in her efforts to make up their loss. In all other respects it was a normal Hinckly wedding as well: an overall good time had at the expense of the bride's father, who tried to mingle and mix amicably while all he could see were dollars and debt in each glass and plate of food, half-eaten, dumped or forgotten and happily replaced with new ones. Happening around the corner to find Pearl and Bud Bentley stuffing a duct tape–reinforced bag full of muffins and buns and cheese for the café, he struggled valiantly to hold his tongue for the sake of his undeserving daughter.

Mrs. Barlow was the resident cake decorator, a hobby she'd taken up when she found it not only provided some extra cash but also offered an additional lure to get people into her store. Amy and Mark's cake had turned out pretty spectacular. She had been more than a little pleased with herself, hollering and fussing and waving dimpled Jell-O arms as it was unloaded from the truck and set up five pillars high at center table. Garish sugar flowers bloomed profusely from anywhere they had even a remote chance of sticking, while achingly bright lime-green leaves attempted to smother them with the prolific abundance of English ivy.

Not quite satisfied with her masterpiece, she had circled the table, taken out a crumpled piece of paper from her purse and, after studying it for an exaggerated moment, proceeded to add six more orangey-yellow roses to the top layer. She may as well have had a picture of Benny Olson's false teeth in her hand, so complete was the inaccuracy of her replication of the lily-white-and-lavender cake in the picture Amy had asked her to reproduce. Congratulating herself liberally, she more or less centered a tiny bride and groom into the orangey-yellow roses, their smiling plastic faces stricken in stunned eternal bliss.

A receiving line had been formed, Mrs. Lyncroft taking it upon herself to call some order to the festivities. Guests caught on their way to the buffet table or presumed to be wandering aimlessly found themselves corralled and redirected down the receiving line to shake hands, nod and smile stupidly as they searched vainly for something socially acceptable to say. This last prerequisite unfortunately held neither instruction nor obstruction for Bobby, who found socially acceptable just about anything he wanted to say. Victoria, having attended only because he'd insisted, followed behind him, trying to hide her embarrassment as he told crude jokes and mortified the young bridesmaids into giving him kisses.

Against the back wall of the barn, a hay wagon stacked with bales had been reworked into a stage and from here a few random notes began to sound as the band got ready to perform. Not a band in the traditional sense of the word, Hinckly's dance music was provided by anyone who had an instrument and thought he could play. The result was an eclectic bunch, comprised of everything from banjos and violins to accordions and spoons. Peter had even brought along his dad's bagpipes, which someone, having learned from prior experience, had mercifully stolen and hidden away. Propped up against the hay wagon wheel, Billy Bassman had found a stick and a metal feed pail, which he banged at randomly between drinks.

Eventually a wedding waltz broke out. For a scandalous moment whispers ran through the crowd as Mark and Amy argued over whether or not he'd join her on the dance floor, her father already having flatly refused. Finally he relented, embarrassed but also quite thrilled as the crowd broke into relieved applause. No sooner had they sorted out their feet, however, than the music trickled to a stop. The young men were unable to play slow and the old men refused to play fast, resulting in such an infraction of timing that everyone had gotten lost. Abruptly Mrs. Lyncroft, who directed the church choir, pushed herself into place in front of them and quickly got them tied back together in a somewhat synchronized effort. Hardly catching a beat, Mark resumed whirling Amy around the dance floor. He might've danced with a broomstick for all the care he afforded her, constantly stepping on her feet as he reached out drunkenly to punch at his friends, who jabbered insults at him as he galloped by.

JJ, Bobby, Petey and a few others stood loosely just off the edge of the dance floor, leering at the girls until they'd become drunk enough to ask them to dance. Victoria, painfully tired, settled herself into a circle of nattering women, where she wouldn't be required to contribute to the conversation. Rose sauntered across to the other side of the barn, wearing an elegant black dress, new, as were the ones her daughters wore, almost swallowed up in flouncy ruffles, as they followed along behind their mother. Another rumor had been making the rounds, and Victoria had heard it several times, biting her lip and saying nothing as someone or other told her how Rose had been the unfortunate but fortunate beneficiary of a family inheritance. Since Rose had originally arrived in town on the Greyhound bus with no luggage and no past, it was an easy game to play. She simply released a rumor then sat back and watched it spawn. This latest one had already morphed into several different versions and ever-increasing sums. Victoria watched out of the corner of her eye as Rose walked toward a group of women whose circle readily parted to receive her. Rose immediately captured the conversation, and Victoria quickly looked away as eyes full of curious pity slunk her way.

Loud voices erupted behind her. Whirling around on her heel, she searched for Bobby's whereabouts. Not hard to locate, she saw him standing in the center of the room surrounded by a small crowd.

"Bullshit!" Mark slurred loudly, shoving Bobby off-balance.

Bobby teetered back to center and returned the shove. "Not bullshit, you little dumb ass. It's frickin' true."

"Bull-bloody-shit. That ain't never bloody happen."

"Bloody did too! My grandpappy even saw it."

"A whole frickin' cow?"

"Damn rights. Whole frickin' thing. Pick it up like nothing."

"Bullshit!" Mark belched. "Ain't no bloody way one man's gonna pick up a whole cow."

"Well, just think about it a minute, you peckerhead. Makes perfect sense. You lift the thing every day from the time it's born and you get stronger as it gets bigger. It's progressive. Cows ain't grow that fast. Iffin you could lift it yesterday then the next day it's only gonna be a tiny bit bigger."

"Ain't no way," Mark laughed derisively. "Ain't even bloody logical."

"Don't make no matter if it's logical. Makes sense. And 'sides, it bloody did happen. My grandpappy said so—"

"Well, your grandpappy's full of shit."

"You calling my grandpa a liar?" Bobby bellowed, shoving Mark backward and spilling both of their drinks.

"Hey, asshole! Keep your friggin' hands off. Ain't calling the old coot piss-all. I'm just saying maybe you ain't got the smarts to know when you was being shitted."

This accusation was a challenge so obvious Bobby couldn't ignore it. Victoria cringed inside as a few testing shoves were exchanged before Sam intervened and hauled Bobby off to refill his drink.

As the night wore on the crowd wore out, until all that remained were those who relished themselves either incredibly good-looking or witty or both and those who found themselves stuck listening to them. The band had dwindled down to a few drunken musicians, their cacophonous noise being enough to convince even the howling coyotes that it was time to turn their tails toward home. Victoria drifted off to the shelter of shadows, half the barn now in darkness after someone, stumbling across the extension cord, had disconnected most of the lights. An aching need to sleep numbed her consciousness until suddenly hostile shouts jerked her awake. Stepping back deeper into the darkness, she saw flailing fists and battered faces. At once she realized that Mark and Bobby were at it again. This time, from what she could decipher from the spitting, violent voices, it was because Bobby had taken several liberties, not the least of these being French-kissing the bride. A straggly knot of onlookers formed around the fighters, cheering on their favorite, while Amy, in full pout, ran to the sanctuary of her own bed inside her mother's house.

"Whoo-hee! I frenched your bride, I frenched your bride," Bobby sang as Mark circled rabidly.

The two men snarled their arms around each other tight as bulls' twisted horns and, finding they could no longer punch, resorted to trying to topple one another onto the floor instead.

Staggering crookedly around in circles, jeering and taunting into each other's bloodied face, they worked a haphazard path toward the head table. The gaudy spectacle of the wedding cake seemed to draw them in like a beacon. And sure enough, that's where it happened. They jostled first Bobby's way, then Mark's and then back over Bobby's until he suddenly lost his footing, sending them both crashing over the table and onto the floor with five stories of wedding cake schlumping down on top.

Electricity surged through Victoria. Her mind jolted, unable to comprehend what her eyes had just seen. Not the fighting or the destruction of the wedding cake, neither of which were unknown at a Hinckly wedding. What she had seen was far more shattering. Far more perverse. The image filled her mind as graphically as the scene now laying before her. No more than a flash on her retina, but she had seen it accurately and undeniably. The two of them, only a breath apart, glowering into each other's face, the one contorted, raging mask a perfect mirror image of the other. The reality of it struck like searing bright light, instantly vaporizing the layers of self-deception that had protected her for so long.

The plank floor begins to tilt beneath her. Swaying, she sits down on a bale of hay, dazed. She tries to breathe, but breath will not come to her. She is too far gone—high above the stratosphere looking down, whirling soundlessly above the Pandora's box below. She now holds within her a knowledge she cannot know. No longer can she deny the debilitating exhaustion, the ferocious nausea. They announce themselves clearly and unequivocally. And they announce themselves as the embodiment of young Mark himself.

"Ya, you ain't so bloody smart, hot shot," Bobby growls. "I frenched your bride and now you's sleeping alone."

"That so old man? Well, I more than frenched your bride. I boned her."

"Bullshit!" Bobby spits blood into Mark's face.

"Wouldn't you like to think so? What you think she was doing that night, slinking around in that green dress?"

This information catches Bobby up short, and he doubles over like he's taken a shot to the guts. Mark laughs at this apparent bull's-eye, the grin quickly falling off his face as Bobby wrestles the Enfield free from his boot and staggers back upward. A voice shouts with panic and for a moment she feels it must be her own. She watches, curiously detached, as people begin to scurry frantically about, grabbing coats and hats and sleeping children, tripping over cords and chairs and each other as they breathlessly make their way out of the barn.

"Vic! Where are you, goddam it?"

She tries to press herself into the shadows, but it is too late.

"That true? That true you been dicking this little cockroach?"

"Bobby, no. I—"

"All that shit Rose been telling me the truth, Vic? Is it? You been having a little something on the side? Huh?" He is wild-eyed now, the revolver waving dangerously as he rages on.

"Bobby, don't. We can talk—"

"Ya? What can we talk about, Vic? You having an affair? Well, got you a little news here. I been having a little affair of my own. Betcha didn't know about that, did ya?"

Victoria stares through him as she realizes the fetus in her womb places her in a full checkmate. The barn is almost empty now, nobody else daring to move.

"Ya, me and old Enfield here, we got us a little thing going. Two of us, we got us an arrangement, see? First I blow little Enfield and then little Enfield here blows me," he taunts, slowly taking the revolver's shaft in his mouth and tonguing it wetly. "That what you want to see, Vic? Huh? That what you came here to see?"

Victoria stares at him in seething silence.

"Huh?" he hollers, jamming the gun up under the folds of his neck. "That what you want to see, Vic? You want to see old Enfield here blow me? Huh? It's all up to you, sweetheart. What's it going to be?"

"No, Bobby. It's not all up to me. It's up to you. You want to blow your goddam head off, go ahead."

Bobby's mouth flies open, contorted with stunned rage.

"I will! I'll do it. That what you want? I'll do it!" he yells, shoving the gun even tighter up under his chin.

Eyes furious, Victoria holds his glare.

Slowly an embarrassed smirk begins to curl his lip as he lowers the revolver toward the floor. "Ya, who's the crazy one now, huh? You see that, Sammy? This crazy woman wants me to shoot myself."

"Vic ain't crazy, Bobby. She had me dump the powder out of those bullets after that time out at the sale."

An overwhelming exhaustion crushes the breath from her as she turns and walks from the hay shed. She is vaguely aware of a commotion behind her, and she instinctively knows it is Sam, preventing Bobby from following her. Mud oozing up over her shoes, she runs toward Bobby's truck and gets in. Fumbling under the papers on the seat, she finds the keys, starts the truck and bounces heavily through the ditch as she turns the truck around and guns it.

Time ceases to function. As if someone has edited and cut out all the space in between. One moment she is at the trailer, the next she is barreling down a back road on her way out of town. The further from the trailer she drives, the clearer the whole joke of her life becomes. She can almost see it imprinted as a stark laughing relief against the rain-drizzled sky. She feels immensely tired, weighed down heavily by the manacles with which fate has bound her. She is tired of living this paint-by-number life. She knows now she should have left long ago. When she was younger. When she still had some fight left in her to get her through each day. Now, she simply doesn't care. She has nothing. She is nothing. What a fool she'd been to think fate could ever have been a conquerable enemy. Fate, which had written her future and foretold her past. It was not a game one could win. But, although fate may have chosen the stage on which she would live her life, she herself would have the choice of where she would end it. Flooring the truck, she flies through the night as if she's already disconnected from everything physical. She drives recklessly on the seldom-used road, a short-cut up out of the valley where it joins with the highway that follows along beside the river.

The grainy yellow gaze of the headlight catches something on the road ahead. A heaving and falling motion that calls back visions of the neighbor's horse last spring, laying on its side in the ditch, thrashing dangerously to regain its feet even though its leg was so cruelly broken that white bone splintered out through the skin.

For a moment she considers driving by. But something deep inside compels her not to. She slows the truck to a stop in front of an old blanket partially submerged in a muddy puddle of water. Getting out, she approaches apprehensively. Maybe she has just imagined the movement. Given the night and her nerves, it is possible that she has. She calls out softly. There is no answer, and she almost allows herself to believe that she has stopped for nothing more than a filthy quilt discarded along the edge of a lonely road. But she knows better. She kneels down beside the puddle and whispers.

"Mrs. Spiller? Mrs. Spiller, are you okay?"

The blanket quivers slightly and she shrinks back from it.

"Who's there?"

"Vic . . . uh, um, it's Georgie, Mrs. Spiller. Georgie Stone. Can I help you?"

"Oh, thank the dear Lord," the old voice croaks. "I need my boys, Georgie. Can you get my boys? I've fallen. I've fallen and I can't get up. And the tide's coming in and it's going to wash away the Lord's Good Book. Take it for me, Georgie. Please. Take care of it for me. It's the most precious book in the whole world."

She tries to help as Mrs. Spiller struggles inside the blanket to free the Bible. The effort is considerable, too much considering how totally the old woman's strength has been absorbed by the rain and the cold night. "Please. Put it in the house for me will you, Georgie?"

Taking the grimy book, Victoria walks back to the truck. Its cover is completely defaced with mud, the binding wrenched crooked from the force of Mrs. Spiller's fall. She resists an urge to heave it into the bushes. Rage seethes up inside her until she can taste its bitter fruit. How could a fair and just keeper allow such atrocity? And how could this cicada's shell of humanity still glean to such faith when even she must know that if ever a sparrow had fallen unseen, surely it was she?

Throwing the Bible onto the seat of the truck, Victoria walks slowly back to the inert hovel of gray blanket. Her mind spins. She can't leave the old woman this way. But she has no intentions of turning back toward the valley either. She hears laughter in the pattering rain as she kneels down beside the puddle and eases the blanket back from the skeletal outline of Mrs. Spiller's face. The eyes are tight lines, squeezed shut against the pain. A lone tear slips free as thin lips, dry as chaff, part in a hoarse whisper. Victoria leans in closer.

"Please."

Leaning back on her heels, Victoria studies the puddle as the rain drives lances through the night. Moving forward, she gathers the near-weightless form into her arms and rocks it gently. The scent of pines floats over them. Pulling the blanket back up, she moves with a gentle rhythm, patting the tiny shoulder lightly. Carefully, she begins to lean forward, tenderly turning the old woman's face downward into the puddle beneath them. She easily resists the feeble struggle that pulses once, twice then ceases as one of the gnarled hands falls free then slowly begins to curl in on itself like a dying leaf. She leaves her that way, face down in the puddle: an unfortunate, merciful accident that someone else will find by the light of another day.

Angling the truck around the still form, she smashes her foot into the gas pedal and swerves wildly. Thoughts overtake her, and she is carried along in their steady stream until suddenly, instantly it seems, she is angling off the highway, gripping the wheel tightly as she bounces toward the strip of black river below. Stopping just short of the water, she twists off the ignition, settling the night back into darkness.

The interior light, which works only at random intervals, flickers on as she opens the door to get out. She pounds it back off. Leaning against the side of the truck, she pulls herself free of her shoes and clothes and throws them back inside. Blindly patting across the seat, she finds the slippery coolness of her dance dress and pulls it toward her, sending Mrs. Spiller's bible sprawling to the floor. Caressing the dress, she slips it on. It is stained now. Worn. Certainly it is not as perfect as it once had been, but somewhere in its embracing silence she can still hear the whisper of what might have been.

The night has eased slightly, clouds parting to make way for the moon. She wades thigh-deep into the rain-dimpled water. Hesitating briefly, she looks up, transfixed by the luminous glow of the moon, listening to the deep murmuring of the ancient river. Her eyes slowly sculpt the softly hanging arc, her hands tracing the bulging roundness of her abdomen. She stands like this for an eternity, quietly questioning the universe above her. More than anything else in the whole world she wishes she could just take her child and place it high above the travesty of life. Nestle it safely in the moon's gentle arm. And yet it cannot be. Too much has become suddenly, tragically clear. As lucid as the frigid water. As palpable as the sharp gravel biting into her feet. The truth can no longer be denied. Mark is Bobby's son. And now, safely hidden in her womb is the next link in fate's interminable chain: Bobby's grandchild.

Stepping further out into the stream, she falters slightly as the unexpected force of the water catches her off guard. Regaining her balance, she steps into a thin slash of moonlight and pulls her dress off over her head. Holding it tightly with one hand she watches it sink and bob as the current snatches at it greedily. Releasing it, she follows its progress downstream, the river taking it away with surprising swiftness then twirling it off to the side, where it becomes tangled in the water-logged limbs of a fallen tree.

Looking down at herself, she feels a momentary thrill of release. Black water has swallowed the bottom half of her up to her breasts. Almost gone and yet fully alive. This is what it will be like, she muses. When death comes, this is what it will be like. A seamless absence of self. A painless ceasing. Taking a deep full breath, she slips beneath the darkness and begins to swim. The river is wide, the undertow treacherous. She'd grown up hearing of their victims. And if they failed to claim her, there was the rapids and beyond them, the waterfall. She swims as strongly as she can, anxious for the deep water. Time becomes lead. She is impatient for the moment when her thoughts will enter the blackness as well.

Suddenly, her head shoots clear of the water. Gulping for air, her arms flail, struggling to keep her afloat. She is not alone here. She has felt something move. Something not of her. Something distinct and tangible and foreign. A gentle tumbling flutter. Like two butterflies somersaulting inside her womb. She starts to call out, shocked into speech by the utter fascination of it, but fishy water swells over her filling her mouth. Panicked, she reverses direction, starting back toward the shore. A silver ripple indicates the bank, and she is frightened to see how far she's swum. Floundering uselessly, her arms and legs move sluggishly against the firm resistance of the water. Twirling helplessly downstream, the currents pull her under several times and she struggles back to the surface, snatching desperately at the air.

Something smashes into her from behind, and she claws at the slimy branches of the half submerged tree. The water swirls violently against her threatening to pull her loose. Carefully she works her way toward the shore, solidness finally finding her feet. Crawling up the bank, she collapses, far too exhausted to cry. Her hands search over her stomach, pressing, urging her child to again signal its presence. She marvels over what they have just accomplished. Still unborn, and yet together they have cheated death. What bigger obstacle can fate possibly throw their way?

Rising on unsteady feet, she begins to thread her way back through the maze of underbrush. Cold begins to grip her, the night air dipping sharply. Shaking uncontrollably by the time she reaches the truck, she climbs in, turns on the heater and struggles back into her damp clothes. Staring out at the raging river, she is horrified by the vast craziness of what she's almost done.

Reaching into the darkness, she finds her purse and pulls out Elliot's map. Unfolding it across the steering wheel, she can just make out the borders of vague countries. Holding it by the top corners, she lifts it higher and loses her breath. Beaming through at her, clear as his voice, is a thin pinprick of moonlight. Grabbing the map into one hand, she swings around and pounds at the interior light as it flickers back on, erasing the telltale shaft of light. Slowly her attention is called to the mess of papers strewn across the seat and floor. Mrs. Spiller's Bible lays splayed upside-down, curious bits of paper protruding from it. Picking one up, Victoria brings it closer to the light and examines it closely. Her hand flies up to cover her mouth. Reaching down she picks up the Bible and carefully, almost reverently begins to leaf through it. She cannot believe what her eyes are seeing. There, tucked between the brittle yellow pages, are tightly folded one-hundred-dollar bills. Old Testament and New: a whole Bible full of good fortune.

A sound encroaches on the night. Stuffing Elliot's map back into her purse, she grabs up the Bible and bolts from the truck. Scrambling up the hill to the highway, she can just make out a vehicle in the distance. It's a truck. A big truck. A big semi truck full of something and on its way to somewhere. She knows she will get but one chance to do this. Walking straight out to the center of the road, she begins to wave frantically even though the truck is still too far away to see her. It keeps bearing down, its headlights just beginning to split the darkness around her. Clearly the driver hasn't seen her. Doesn't expect to see her, or anything else except for maybe the odd startled deer caught in his headlights. She begins to seriously doubt her plan but holds her ground. Suddenly an explosion of noise erupts the night, the big rig huffing and skidding and fuming itself to a stop.

"That's a mighty fine way to end up road kill, young lady!" the driver hollers out the window.

"Sorry," she says, climbing out of the ditch she's run into at the last moment. "I was afraid you wouldn't see me."

"You're afraid I wouldn't see you so you stand in the middle of the road! Not such a great strategy, I'd reckon." He chuckles kindly, relieved that a serious catastrophe has been averted. "What the heck you doing way out here this time of night anyhow?"

"Uh. My car broke down."

She waits as he checks his mirrors for her nonexistent vehicle. He nods, knowingly. An easygoing man, he is a veteran of the road and has long ago learned that one can never tell who might cross one's path, but when someone does it is usually best to not ask too many questions.

"Where you headed?" he says.

"Where you going?"

He laughs heartily. "Winachee Falls. I can take you that far, but after that you're on your own. Okay?"

"Okay. That'd be great. Thanks," she says, then crosses around in front of the headlights, which each blink once as she walks by, and crawls up into the cab. The truck bounces and shakes then slowly begins to pick up speed as he effortlessly wrestles it through several gears.

"Name's Frederick," he says, offering out a large, callused hand. "But folks call me Fred."

"Hi Fred," she says, as she shakes his warm hand. "You can call me Victoria."

About the Author

KJ Steele writes about the characters who will not otherwise leave her alone. She is fortunate to be surrounded by beautiful nature, a loving family, and good wine. She is the author of one other novel, *The Bird Box*.